W9-CUE-416

BLOOD AND DREAMS

Blood and Dreams

Leslie Waller

G. P. Putnam's Sons   New York

Copyright © 1980 by Leslie Waller
All rights reserved. This book, or parts thereof,
must not be reproduced in any form without permission.
Published simultaneously in Canada by Academic Press
Canada Limited, Toronto.

Library of Congress Cataloging in Publication Data

Waller, Leslie, date.
  Blood and dreams.

  I. Title.
PZ3.W1557Kat [PS3545.A565] 813'.54   80–15893
ISBN 0–399–12564–7

PRINTED IN THE UNITED STATES OF AMERICA

Acknowledgments

For their help with the research and planning of this novel, I am indebted to Rita Sbisa Mahen, C. Manley Le Notre, Dr. Horace Marston, Dorothy Gallagher and my editor, Phyllis E. Grann.

 *Prologue*   1878

In the hot afternoon sun of New Orleans, the tall girl with the bright hair walked quickly along Dumaine Street toward the river. Staring ahead of her, glancing neither right nor left, Kate Blood looked older than her fifteen years, more serious, more preoccupied. She had just finished her last class of the day at the Sacred Heart Convent near Bourbon, and she had only a short time before meeting her father for an early dinner.

Kate had her father's height and fair complexion. Her long hair was nowadays called strawberry blond, yellow like her father's but with a reddish glint. She had reassured the Madames of the Sacred Heart again and again that on no condition had she ever tinted it.

As she strode toward the levee—they'd renamed it Decatur Street, but nobody called it that yet—she was attracting covert attention from the Creole bloods she passed. The attention was partly for the novelty of her fair good looks in a city of ivory-skinned brunettes with eyes the color of *café brûlot*. It was covert because Kate Blood was the oldest daughter of a very powerful man.

As she neared Royal, a young man on horseback clattered around the corner heading in the direction from which she'd come. He reined in, and with no change in his dark face, tipped his tall beaver hat. Kate brushed past without acknowledging this less-than-covert salute.

She knew him, of course; of him, that is, heir to two of New Orleans' largest fortunes, Edmund Crozat. But they had never been introduced. They never would be.

Just as well, Kate thought. She had no time for conceited Creole dandies. Her father had lately decided, yesterday in fact, that he would never find a bookkeeper as honest and accurate as his own Katie-girl herself.

It hadn't occurred to Cornelius Blood that his bookkeeper had to visit each of the dozen whorehouses Neil ran in the Tenderloin, check receipts with as many madams, get reports from several dozen street pimps and steerers, check the bartenders' records and those of restaurant chefs as well as police lieutenants and sergeants on the Blood payroll. And, what was more, this bookkeeper had to spot cheats and swindlers, know to the two-bit piece how many girls turned over how many beds how often, and make certain the barmen weren't watering the liquor. Neil Blood had only two rules for what the *Mascot* would eventually call his "empire of crime": good booze and no virgins. He wanted no girl ruined under his roof.

But what of his darling Katie-girl? In such a place, with such people? It had started as just a temporary job in Neil Blood's sumptuous office above the restaurant at the corner of Basin and Customhouse. The Wicklowe, he called it, after the county he'd fled during the Famine to try his luck in the New World. But luck didn't account for such success. Tall in any crowd, he stood out in other ways as well. His quick mind and easy manner were part of it, but he had something more: an awesome self-confidence that won followers of strong loyalty in this ripe, fickle city. People liked rubbing elbows with such a winner. They flocked to his houses and thronged to the Wicklowe. Surely it was respectable enough for any daughter of his. Didn't all of the city's finest men lunch there?

His bookkeeper had gone west for his health, literally, since Neil had caught him with his hand in the till. Kate was only to help while a new man was found. But before then the columns of figures had taken on meaning for her. Talking to the runner who brought her sheafs of daily receipts, she'd convinced the lad to take her with him on his next rounds.

Even then she'd no idea what actually went on in these houses, since she'd made the rounds by day. So when she asked her father to explain, she was unprepared for his reaction.

"Where is that runner?" he shouted wildly. "I'll murder him with me own two hands!"

Neil Blood's wrath exploded a welter of frustrations all at once. Kate's poor mother had died bearing their sixth child in as many years. They'd been raised a bit haphazardly, Neil admitted, with a great burden on the oldest, Kate. Now this. And no woman to explain it. None. All the respectable females in New Orleans existed by refusing to admit the existence of places where women . . .

"Dear Jesus," Neil moaned in an ecstasy of self-pity, "why me? An honest man giving honest measure, giving the people what they want?"

"Of that I'm certain, Father," Kate reassured him. "But what is it they want? To relax a bit? Is that it?"

A sigh of relief eased her father's troubled face. "That's *all* it is."

"Doing what?"

Neil Blood had an inspiration. A tiny grain of truth might do the trick. "Does it matter, Katie-girl? Hugging a bit, cuddling? Innocent pleasures."

"The way you do with us kids?"

He paused. "Somewhat along those lines."

"And these poor men have no one to fondle?" she persisted. "So they have to pay for it?"

"Somewhat like that."

"Oh, the poor things."

An unspoken arrangement had been reached. He was off the hook. What these women actually did, Kate later learned the way most girls did, in guilty whispers from other girls. If she'd attended one of the parochial schools for the lower classes, she wouldn't have found out a thing, the girls being that ignorant. There was something to be said for an expensive education among the high and mighty.

So the temporary bookkeeper was about to become the permanent one, with a bodyguard when she made her rounds of the district. What would the Madames of the Sacred Heart say if ever they knew of it? Unthinkable? But it was an arrangement that served Neil Blood well, at least for the moment.

To his under-the-table partners he announced: "The problem's solved. I trust her, me boy, and so the bloody hell will youse."

Which they did, all of Neil Blood's partners, the respected merchants, stuffy financiers, pious politicians, the highest reaches of New Orleans society, both Creole and American. Whether they liked it or not, they would allow this fifteen-year-old girl to oversee their investments in the red-light district of their native city.

Leadership that joined with reliability and inside information was rare. One man had all these in abundance and he was not hard to approach. The charisma of winning was already part of his character. Thus men of lesser character, but more cash, felt secure in Neil Blood's hands. He took good care of them, and himself, too.

Power was gravitating to the hub where Neil Blood sat. The *Mascot* would later caricature him as a spider with a thick blond mustache sitting at the center of a vast web, but this would be much later, when he had become the Shadow Mayor and Governor. Right now, busily consolidating this power, he was lucky to be able to unload responsibility on Kate.

She had reached the corner of Dumaine and the levee, so preoccupied with her thoughts that she had no idea the Crozat boy had quietly turned his horse to follow her progress.

The week before had been Edmund Crozat's sixteenth birthday. He had accepted with a grave expression two gifts from the deepest recesses of his father's heart. One present was a framed parchment on which the family tree had been painstakingly embossed in black, red, and gold. The other was Amalia, his father's forty-five-year-old octoroon mistress.

Astride his horse now as he followed the girl with the red-blond hair at a discreet distance, Edmund frowned. The Crozat look already lay upon his young face, the foxy look of all those bankers and cotton factors whose names graced his father's side of the family tree. A rather fierce air about the eyes, Edmund remembered, which were set intimidatingly wide apart over flushed high cheekbones. He knew from his mirror that his was the pure Crozat face, tapering to a discreet mouth over a narrow chin. He hated the look.

In silhouette, he thought, grinning maliciously, it was rather like one of those Mongolfier balloons he had read about, all paper and hot air. That definition also applied to the Crozat work, which involved the costliest kind of paper, lines of credit, brokerage commissions, debentures, factoring of receivables, bolstered by costly French-Creole hot air to reassure idiot plantation owners. These worthies needed to believe they were not, in fact, at the mercy of weather and their own stupidity. But always, overnight, with a flood or a drought, the Crozat paper floated back to earth and plantation ownership changed hands. The Crozats could foreclose with a snap like a trap breaking a possum's back. It was the only thing they did quickly.

He reined in his horse. What was the point of following the blond girl when his own quadroon, Ynes, was waiting for him in her little cottage at the upper end of Rampart? She would have chilled the *bière douce*, which she fermented from pineapple and rice. The two of them would be reduced by the sweet beer to helpless giggling, like two children. What need, Edmund wondered, did he have of his father's ancient cast-off mistress?

The weight of his family seemed to press down upon him, like the heat of the afternoon sun, oppressive, all-powerful. To be a Crozat, he thought, was a heavy burden. His mother's family, the Almonaster-Nuneses, weighed just as heavily. He felt pinned down. Whatever he would have wanted to be, they would see to it that he followed their lead, not his own.

The Crozat frown darkened. He'd studied enough history to see that it was a chronicle of individuals who rose higher than the rest.

And quickly, too. One lived such a short time before yellow fever or cholera or malaria struck one down. The dismal list of Edmund's friends or cousins his age who had already died made it clear to him that one had to begin life early.

Wars did that too, he reflected gloomily. One rose rapidly to prominence, or one died. In the War Between the States there had been generals in their twenties.

Or think of Ynes, he reminded himself, an odd, malicious grin on his face. Not yet thirteen, and already the most accomplished of her profession in all of New Orleans.

Ahead of him, Edmund saw that the girl with the red-blond hair had reached the levee. There was something about her that still held his attention, a determination to her walk unusual in a woman. He continued to stare. Across the wide street from her, to the left of the French Market, where Gallatin slanted away to match the curve of the river, a group of Yankee soldiers was loading a wagon.

Edmund stared coldly at them. The main battalions had already left, ending a shameful military occupation that had lasted sixteen years. Edmund could never remember when there had not been Yankees in their blue wool sauntering the streets of his beloved New Orleans.

He jiggled the reins, and his horse moved forward at a slow walk.

Kate Blood watched a small knot of boys tormenting the soldiers. They wore the insignia of Indiana Volunteers. In full marching gear they waited under the hot sun for orders to drive the wagon away. Away, Kate thought, out of our lives forever!

To their discomfort was added the jeering boys, among whom Kate saw her youngest brother, Ned.

The barefoot boys danced in and out among the heavy-laden Yankees in their thick wool uniforms, bearded faces dripping perspiration.

"Hairy face!"

"In Indiana the women marry apes!"

"Son of a monkey!"

Because he reacted badly to the taunts, the youngest of the three soldiers was the focus of the boys' tirade. He swatted at one of them, knocking him off his feet. But the boy scrambled up and launched a kick at the soldier's shin. Cursing, the soldier brought the heavy breechloader down from his shoulder in a diagonal sweep aimed at the boy, who danced back out of range.

"Baboon!"

"Indian ape!"

At this hour, the levee was almost empty of the heavy drays and wagons that usually moved along it. Kate started across the broad street, intent on snatching Ned away. He was only eleven, going on twelve, and surely the slightest of the Bloods, thin as a rake and as short as the heavy rifle the soldier was using as a club.

"Ned!" Kate shouted.

The soldier looked up, as if this were a new taunt. The boys ringed him, jigging like the monkeys they accused of siring him. The fleetest of them was Ned, jumping in and out, his piping voice like a tin whistle.

"Can't catch me!" he screamed. "Ape! Ape!"

Then he stumbled and fell. The soldier lifted his heavy weapon high in the air. His arms grew taut with effort. He would pulverize this jeering baby. He would pulp his nasty little brain.

"Ned!"

All the levee froze in Kate's eyes. Ned lay stunned. The rifle butt was moving down.

From behind her a clatter of hooves rang across the wide street.

Edmund Crozat dug spurless heels into the bay flanks of his horse. He flashed across the levee, tall hat toppling into the dust. Hearing the noise, the soldier looked up in time to find the heavy gelding on top of him, riding him down.

He fell sideways in a clatter of tin cups and unsheathed bayonet. Edmund reined in the horse, wheeled, and dipping low over the saddle, reached down to grab at the belt around Ned's skinny middle. He lifted the child from the cobblestones and dashed back across the levee to where Kate stood.

"Yours, mamselle?" he asked, his face bright with exertion. She stared at him in silence, aware of every line of his handsome face.

He let the boy drop, wheeled again, and leaned over to retrieve his tall beaver hat. Carefully he brushed it clean and restored its nap with a few deft strokes of his cuff. Then he tilted the hat to Kate and disappeared along Dumaine, heading in the direction of Rampart.

Across the street the soldier Edmund had ridden down was batting at himself as he got aboard the wagon, sending up puffs of dust. He seemed to have forgotten the ring of taunting boys, most of whom had disappeared. Without a backward look at the one whose head he had nearly pulped, he sat down in the wagon, and in a moment it rolled away.

The levee was deserted. Ned scrambled to his feet. "Katie!" he piped. "Did you see? Didja?"

But she was turned away from him, gazing up Dumaine at a horse and a rider she could never follow.

Part One

1888

1

The part of Louisiana that stretched east from the Texas border to the Red River's meandering stream was partly open land, grilling in the hot spring sun, and partly cultivated spreads of cotton, the plants still low, bolls not yet developed. Black sharecroppers bent over double between the rows, chopping weeds. It would be months before the plants were high enough to flourish on their own. It would be August before the pressure of cotton growing within the bolls would open them. Almost overnight, the field would turn white.

The two men in the buckboard wagon paid little attention to the landscape. They had spent a frustrating week along the Texas line beneath Shreveport. Now they were heading east toward Winn Parish to investigate a small lake in the hills above the Red River that, strangely, contained not fresh water but salt.

Anomalies like that interested both men. The older of the two, in fact, called himself a geologist, a rather new profession for that age. He was a squat man in his mid-thirties, with a hammered-down look, as if the merciless sun had pounded on his head, giving him a bull neck and immense shoulders.

The other was in his mid-twenties, slim, dark, taller than the other and fully a head taller than he had been ten years before on his fateful sixteenth birthday. A soft white panama with rolled brim protected his ivory complexion from the glaring sun. In the shadow of the brim, wide-set dark eyes over high cheekbones stared straight ahead along the nar-

19

row ruts. Edmund Crozat hated these field trips, far from the comforts and diversions of his native New Orleans, but it was necessary that Rynders understand precisely the mission for which he had been hired.

In the back of the buckboard, under a concealing tarpaulin, lay the tools of Clem Rynders' trade: augers, pipe-leg tripods for lifting and dropping ram drills, sticks of dynamite, picks, spades, boxes of fulminate detonator caps cushioned in beds of sawdust and straw.

For some years Edmund had bought such equipment on his own, under assumed names, for his solitary forays into the backwoods areas of the state. His father, who of course had to be told, had at first been appalled, until Edmund made him understand that there might be much money in oil lands discovered, bought, and controlled by Crozats.

In such a fashion, Edmund had postponed from his eighteenth to his twenty-first birthday the inevitable day when he would have to don banker's drab and march each morning to the family offices in the square it owned between Exchange and Chartres streets. When that day finally arrived, he had still not emancipated himself.

That was how he thought of it. Oil was his dream, the fame and fortune of finding it and of bringing his native state in one stroke from eighteenth-century agrarianism to what Edmund conceived to be the bustling industry of the coming twentieth. But this dream, which thrived on its own impossibility, was sham. Fame, yes. The gratitude of his fellow Louisianans, why not? But fortune! In his own name! The true dream was of emancipation, finally, from the deadweight of deadly family tradition.

His sister, Olivia, sometimes pitied him. "It's a curse to be born into this family with too much insight," she had once said. "To see the Crozats clearly is to yearn for early death."

"Early emancipation," Edmund had growled. He was still enough of a good Catholic to worry over Olivia's hint of suicide. All that French symbolist poetry she read, Mallarmé and the like.

Now, jouncing along in the buckboard, he yearned for the quiet of his apartment in New Orleans. This would be his last field trip. From now on, the secret search would be in Rynders' hands.

By sundown they had crossed the Red near St. Maurice. In growing darkness Edmund consulted the hand-drawn map he had brought with him.

"We have a poor choice," he said at last. "We can camp tonight on the banks of Saline Lake. Or we can push on for Winnfield, where there may well be a hotel with a drinking annex. In the morning, we can return to the lake."

"Whatever you say, Mr. Crozat."

"I say we sleep in beds tonight, like human beings."

Edmund rattled the reins against the horse's back, and the beast started forward with some reluctance. Wagon wheels slipped in and out of ruts, jouncing the two men, who rode in silence for a while.

"You know . . ." Rynders began at last. He paused. "You know, meaning no offense, but it's a strange thing to see a gentleman of your background on a buckboard. That is," he hurried on apologetically, "when you could be back in your own place in N'Awlins. I did admire that place of yours the time you had me up there." He paused again, even more diffidently. "Why would a man want to leave it?"

"All the comforts," Edmund agreed in his low-pitched voice. It had a strange, crackling quality about it, as if each word were produced under some inner pressure that had nothing to do with the air passing through his larynx.

"All the conveniences," he went on. "A charming place, the Pontalba Apartments. The old redheaded baroness was a cousin of my mother's. Micaela Almonaster de Pontalba, she was called, a prime example of business genius misplaced in the head of a woman."

The wagon stuttered through a dried-out creek crossing, making conversation impossible. Then Edmund said, "She made a deal with the city that still inspires my envy. A tax exemption on all her property if she cleared out her old houses around the Place d'Armes and put up the two apartment buildings. In return, she named it Jackson Square and commissioned that horrible equestrian statue."

He was silent for a moment. "I leave such comfortable surroundings because of you, Rynders. You are new to this business. I have been doing it by myself, alone. Now I want professional assistance and I want it carried on with the same secrecy and zeal that I myself give it."

The squat man shook his head. "It's a dream, you know."

"You are quite wrong," Edmund assured him coldly.

"Oh, I don't mean the oil. It's there. We've seen enough traces floating on top of creeks. I mean the usefulness of it, Mr. Crozat. No offense, but why is a gentleman of your background spending so much time and money on something of so little demand?"

"You think so."

"If it was gold," the geologist went on, "or iron ore or copper or tin or a dozen other valuable resources. But petroleum?"

"No real demand, you say."

"I grant you kerosene. I'm old enough to have lived through that revolution. Candles and whale oil have surely given way to King Kerosene. But with your family holdings in cotton and sugar and rice, what do you want with oil? It's a messy business."

"There I agree."

"If we find it," Rynders reminded him, "it ain't going to be that clean paraffin-base stuff that Drake drilled up near Titusville, in Pennsylvania. I was there, you know, working for that miserable bastard Rockefeller. No, around here it'd more likely be the asphalt-base stuff they have over Texas way. No offense, Mr. Crozat, but what does a Creole gentleman want mucking around in that sort of swill?"

For a long time Edmund had let the horse wander along the rut at its own speed. Now the small town of Winnfield could be seen in the dusk, at first only its church steeple, rising above the purple haze, then a few buildings. A light came on in a faraway window. Edmund slapped the reins hard.

"Giddap!" He grinned lopsidedly. "Rynders, when you visited my apartment, I believe you were introduced to my sister?"

"I do recall the lady."

"You sound a bit hesitant. Olivia is not what one would call forthcoming. She's a quiet girl but a ferocious reader and correspondent. I have her to thank for what will someday replace this dawdling old horse."

"Beg pardon?"

"The horse, man!" Edmund repeated impatiently. "It was Olivia who ran across Etienne Lenoir's work in France. She is an omnivorous reader of the journals. Lenoir has improved Barnett's compression engine and quieted its noise."

"Some form of steam, is it?"

"No, it burns coal gas and air. It explodes them. The power produced is tremendous. In Darmstadt, Otto Daimler has produced a four-cycle version that can burn almost anything, Rynders, even kerosene. Even naphtha."

"To what purpose?"

"Three years ago, in Mannheim, Benz linked such an engine to a vehicle. I have seen no drawings, but it is described as having two rear wheels harnessed to the engine. One front wheel is used for steering."

Rynders' broad face wrinkled in a frown of distaste. "There have been many such novelties. A sort of vehicle has been linked to a small steam engine."

Edmund nodded gravely. "Using kerosene as fuel."

The geologist was silent for a moment. "I'm beginning to get your drift, Mr. Crozat. But look at it from my point of view, meaning no offense. You've spent years of your own time and who knows how much money on finding oil in Louisiana. Just to propel these little vehicles?"

"And more."

The lights of Winnfield were closer now. The sky overhead had darkened. With the coming of night, the air around them became cooler, more soothing. Both men were silent, enjoying the relief of being, for the first time today, almost chilled.

"Much more, Rynders," Edmund said at last, rousing himself and cracking the reins harder. "You're a scientist. Does the name Lilienthal mean anything to you? A German. Or Octave Chanute, a Frenchman now living in America?"

"Can't say they do."

Edmund frowned in the darkness. "Well, perhaps science is better for being self-contained. You wear the blinders of the geologist and you see only geology. What do experiments with gliders have to do with geology? But I am no scientist, Rynders. So I wear no blinders."

"I must say you keep well-informed."

"My sister produces a great fountain of information that one will never find in one's newspapers, and a flow of names that may one day be famous. As mine, perhaps," he added softly, almost to himself.

"The Crozat name," Rynders picked up, "is already famous."

"For money-lending," Edmund responded. "You know how dearly the world loves any man who uses money to make money. What was it you called Rockefeller? A miserable bastard?" He laughed. "How many Crozats have been called that, and worse, behind their backs?"

The geologist was silent, and Edmund drew his own conclusions from the lack of protest. What else could one feel for the family that stole land by deft manipulation of bits of paper? That profited from the blows of weather, or the unrest of laborers.

"What else does Miss Crozat have to report?"

Edmund shrugged. "I pick and choose among her information. For instance, she is in correspondence with a certain Monsieur Debussy and one Signore D'Annunzio. She tells me they, too, will be great names one day. But their connection with oil is remote."

"She must write several languages."

"All the civilized ones. And she is studying Russian at the moment."

As they rattled into Winnfield, the night had grown quite cool. The dirt streets of the town were deserted, its few stores shuttered. Down the street a two-story frame house bore a sign that spelled out in peeling letters "Hotel, Stables, Dinner."

The two men entered the lobby and found it as deserted as the streets outside. Edmund pounded on a desk bell. After a long wait a frail old black man in dark gray suit, vest, and white shirt appeared from somewhere in the back.

"Dinner's over, gentlemen," he began apologetically. "Cold sandwiches?"

"And rooms?"

He picked two keys off the rack behind him, seemingly at random. "Wash-up is back there," he said, pointing to the corridor from which he'd appeared. "Cold water only," he added. When he saw that Edmund had made no effort to pick up the keys, he went on in the same sorrowful tone, "This is Winnfield's onliest *ho*tel, gentlemen."

Edmund managed to remove the frown. "Not too bustling a place," he suggested. "The streets are quite empty."

"That'll be the Reverend Leathers, gentlemen. They's a box social over to the Reformed Baptist Church, and ain' nobody in town don't go to hear Luke Leathers."

"Your minister?"

"White folks' minister," the hotel man explained. "His brother Mike likely'll say a few words tonight, too. Mike Leathers is their representative down at Baton Rouge."

It had been almost a decade since the capital had been moved there from New Orleans, and more than two decades since the blacks had been freed, but Edmund knew enough not to repeat his earlier, ingenuous question. Mike Leathers would be the whites' representative. Whatever laws promised, full suffrage, no Negroes voted in Louisiana except for a few in his home town. The laws gave and the laws took away. Suffrage was neatly hedged by conditions, few of which any black could fulfill.

Later, not exactly refreshed, but certainly filled by fresh-ham sandwiches on thick slabs of bread, cold red beans and rice optional, Edmund and Rynders wandered out into the street. The number of buggies and wagons tied up in the distance gave them a fair clue to the whereabouts of the Baptist Church.

". . . and Winn Parish is no newcomer in the battle to protect the rights of the laboring man," a strong voice inside proclaimed.

The two men paused outside the ramshackle frame church. It was its steeple they had seen from the distance. ". . . me remind you how Winn Parish fought long and hard not to secede from the Union when all about us hotheads counselled . . ."

Edmund found the voice pleasant, but hardly pious in content. Perhaps the politician brother, not the clergyman?

". . . some years back, when the farmer's union was formed, Winn Parish welcomed this plan to free us from the yoke of sharecropping and the crop-lien system, under which you didn't dare die, no sir, 'cause you owed the company store too much."

Bitter laughter sounded inside the church, and a whooping kind of catcall, directed not at the speaker but at what he was attacking.

". . . Mr. Gompers brought in his Knights of Labor a few years back and started to get the sugarcane workers together, Winn Parish was solidly behind them, too."

"Not too close behind!" some wit called out, to general laughter.

Rynders turned to Edmund. "What's that supposed to mean?"

Edmund put his finger to his lips. His reluctant role in the family business was central enough that he knew every intimate detail of the great sugar-strike massacre of 1886, but he wasn't about to whisper it to this half-literate geologist.

The Crozats, as usual, had profited handsomely from this new anguish. The crop of 1886 was a bumper one. The Knights had called their strike at a strategic moment. None of the plantation owners would negotiate with them, however, preferring to wait till dissension broke out among the strikers, since the Knights were organizing both whites and blacks indiscriminately. Then, in November, an overnight frost showed the planters that they could lose the whole crop. They quickly imported killers from every part of the state. On November 22 they launched an all-night massacre of black cane workers. By morning the strike was broken.

But too late for some planters. They had waited too long either to talk or to kill. Once again Crozat paper smothered them in foreclosures, and once again ownership of valuable delta land changed hands overnight.

". . . using the color of your skin to divide us and pick us off. But I ask you, you owe your whole harvest check to the company store, does it matter a hoot whether you're white or black?"

The audience seemed reluctant to respond to the rhetorical question. Edmund gestured to the church door.

"It sure ain't my idea of an evening out," Rynders complained.

"But it's the only show in town."

Edmund led the way inside the packed church. The man standing on an overturned bushel basket in front of the regular pulpit didn't really need the extra height to be head and shoulders above the congregation.

Lanky and sun-red in face and neck, he had the rawboned country look of the typical "Kaintock." Edmund had been raised to disdain these gauche, loud-talking Americans who had invaded New Orleans earlier in the century, keelboatmen, runaway criminals, hard-drinking, murderous, boastful, as lacking in culture as Barbary apes, whose idea of entertainment was to get puking drunk, knife some luckless whore, and lope out into the night howling, "I'm a ding-dong whelp of an alligator and a she-wolf!"

". . . what I'm hoping to do at the legislature, with the help of all you good folks who have sent me there to be your voice and your right arm."

"What's yer left arm doin', Mike?" someone called out.

"Pushin' us inta th'arms of the niggers," someone else hooted.

He raised his hands and finally got silence. "None of you here tonight," he told them, "will ever get ahead of the game the planter lets you play with his cottonfields. Not till you see that it's the same for black as white. Not till you stop hatin' the nigger just because the company wants you to."

In the confused silence that followed, Edmund raised his voice. "Are you saying the company tells them whom to hate? That's insane!"

Everyone turned to look at the newcomer. Mike Leathers peered across the church at Edmund. "I can't say I rightly recognize you, Mr. . . ."

"Nemo," Edmund spoke. "Captain Nemo."

"Captain," the politician said, giving it an ironic sound, "I don't recollect seeing you around these parts before, but you've asked a fair question."

"And I'm answering it," another man interrupted. He uncoiled a body as lanky as Mike Leathers', with the same rawboned look. He mounted to the pulpit and grasped the lectern with both hands, as if handling a shotgun much used. Edmund decided this would be the hellfire preacher, brother Luke.

"It is not given to man to look into the hearts of other men," the minister began in a flat, no-nonsense voice. "One man can look into one heart, his own. That's the limit the good Lord deals us, friends, like a hand of poker. Unless you *cheat*," he suddenly thundered, "unless you *lie* and *steal*—you cannot know the other's heart or hand. That is *God's way*!" he shouted.

Then he paused for an intake of air, filling his lungs as if to bellow forth again. But when he spoke, it was softly, almost a cooing voice, that nevertheless carried across the entire church. "Even so," he mused aloud, "so many of us don't want to know what's in our hearts because we're afraid to find out what's there. . . ."

Edmund stepped back out the door of the church, with Rynders following. They stood for a moment in the darkened street.

"For a man who's traveling incognito," the geologist began, "meaning no offense, but you sure got the center of attention in there."

Edmund started to say something, then shook his head impatiently and led the way back to the hotel. "We have to get an early start in the morning," he said as they went upstairs to their rooms. He paused at his door. "Rynders, I don't make many mistakes, but you just saw one. I'm returning to New Orleans in a few days. You'll be on your own. I'm asking you a rather peculiar question. Will you be more discreet than I was tonight?"

"I sure as hell will, Mr. Crozat. I don't see the inside of a church from one end of the year to the other."

"I don't mean that. I meant mixing in local affairs. But the stupidity of these backwoods reformers is hard to suffer in silence. The idea that they can cleanse their hearts and love their black brethren. It's . . . it's . . . ridiculous."

"Well, no offense, but I'm an Ohio man originally, and we sort of take a little calmer view of the niggers."

"Do you?" Edmund surveyed him coldly. "Do you have an accurate notion of how I view them, for example?"

"Well . . ." The geologist was silent for a moment. "I . . . uh . . . maybe I'd better back off a mite on that one."

"Maybe you'd better," Edmund agreed crisply. "Good night, Rynders. We'll meet downstairs at daybreak."

He let himself into his room and locked the door behind him. Then, with a sigh, he pulled off the wide-brimmed panama and sent it sailing onto the bed. Perhaps this whole business was a mistake, he thought.

Hiring Rynders, who seemed to have the perspicacity of a brick wall. Spending his time in the field, searching for something that might never amount to more than mineral oil to blow the bowels of America clean.

Edmund lay down on the bed. His long, thin fingers softly stroked the luxurious fabric of the white hat beside him. To be back on Rampart in Ynes' little cottage. To be in the Crozat box at the opera house, hearing Lilli Lehmann sing the *"Casta diva"* from *Norma*. To dine afterward, near midnight, at the Wicklowe with Jed Benjamin and Ned Blood, listening to the gossip of the day. To sit quietly in his apartment, reading the latest journals Olivia had marked for him, sip an iced absinthe and plan his plans, seeing farther ahead than anyone, to . . .

To defeat? To sinking back into the safe fabric of family, his share of foreclosures, his added brokerage percentage? Great work, *mon fils*, his father would say.

Edmund jumped off the bed and went to the window. He gazed out at the quiet town, looking along the main street to where buckboards were hitched and the Leathers brothers were giving the faithful their own populist view of heaven on earth.

No, by God, he would not fail. He had devoted himself to this above all else. There was a streak of steel that ran through the Crozats. With this blade he would slash his way, not to defeat, but to victory.

2

In the pleasantly crowded graveyard behind St. Roch's chapel, shamrocks grew.

Kate Blood had never actually seen them, but a friend from her schooldays at Sacred Heart—one of the few schoolmates who still "saw" Kate socially—had told her of the bright green clover and hinted that the number of four-leaved ones was unusually high.

Kate felt like a fool. Normally she visited St. Mary's church, next to the Ursuline convent. Mass she attended on Sundays with her father and the rest of the family at St. Patrick's, not far from their old neighborhood in the Irish Channel, where they'd grown up in near-poverty before Neil Blood had become rich enough to move away.

But this was a special novena Kate was making, a secret from any of her family. Her sins had finally moved her to it.

Her confessions in her teens had a kind of second-party quality. Kate's sins had mainly to do with being witness to the sins of those in the red-light district. But over the years, as she passed Edmund Crozat in the streets, her thoughts began to have a sinful quality of their own.

Everything about him attracted her. She adored his appearance. She admired his growing reputation. She overlooked the name he had for womanizing and the occasional duels it was said he fought. Eventually—she couldn't remember exactly when this torment had begun, but it was probably when she came late into her womanhood at seventeen years of age—it became clear to her that she lusted after Edmund Crozat. That was the only word for it, and it was a cardinal sin.

Avoidance of this sin became increasingly difficult. For one thing, Edmund Crozat remained a bachelor. For another, now that young Ned Blood was a reporter for one of the scandalous weekly newspapers around town, he and Crozat had become friends. They hobnobbed with the impresario who brought most of the city's cultural events to town, the celebrated Jed Benjamin, son of Jefferson Davis' right-hand man during the war, Judah Benjamin.

With the unhappy result that, visiting Ned at home one lazy afternoon, Edmund Crozat had finally been introduced to Kate Blood . . . and nothing happened.

This had been a year ago, when Kate was twenty-four. She found it impossible to believe that a fine, sensitive, brilliant man like Edmund Crozat could fail to sense what she felt for him. But couldn't it have been the other way around? Hadn't she perhaps bared her heart in small gestures or incautious words and turned him against her? To be ignored was bad, but could be cured in time. To be found out and spurned—that was a mortal blow.

And so, the novena. For eight Fridays Kate had visited other churches, reciting the prescribed prayers. Today was Good Friday and she had traveled for the last of the novena out to Prieur and Music Street, on foot. She particularly didn't want the Bloods' groom to take her there. This novena was between her and St. Roch and no one else. And now, as she sat in the chapel and looked around her, Kate Blood suspected she was a fool indeed.

The church was filled with nothing but women, most of them her age. Spinsters, Kate thought, praying to the popular saint for relief from such a fate, be the man ugly, lame, dull, vicious, or dim of brain. Any mate was better than none.

Kneeling, her head bowed against her clasped hands, she finished the long prayer. O St. Roch, powerful intercessor before the throne of Almighty God, help me to gain my special request.

She took a long breath. On this final day of thy most solemn novena, she prayed, I humbly beg for the love of Edmund, that he may be united with me in holy matrimony. Please hear my prayer and plead my cause. I ask it in thy name and in the name of the Holy Family, Jesus, Mary, and Joseph.

"Amen," she said aloud, crossing herself.

She left the pew, genuflected, and walked down the aisle of the narrow chapel with its tall, thin windows, arrows pointing heavenward.

A new sin for confession, Kate told herself. To the sin of lust, add the sin of pride. Kate Blood wants one certain mate and no other. And that, she added, dipping her finger into the holy-water font and crossing herself again, is why she is such a great fool.

She stared back down the narrow aisle. The sin of pride indeed, she told herself. There were men she could marry. That wasn't the problem. Timmy Larkin, the alderman's son, had been proposing for three years now. Two senators had fought a duel over her, the rivalry was so intense. There was that planter from down in Placquemines Parish who had a fortune in sugar and rice. She lacked no escorts for the opera. The trouble was—the trouble had always been—that she could see none of them, because blinding her with its brilliance was the image of Edmund Crozat.

She seemed always to picture him as he'd appeared ten years ago, dashing across the levee to ride the Yankee down and save Ned. It wasn't fair to the rest of her suitors, honest men and not hard to look at. But they didn't have Edmund's dark, piercing eyes, set so wide they seemed to see beyond a girl into some deep desolate place. Or his fine tapering hands that would stroke a girl and . . .

She knew enough about herself to understand that without the dream of having Edmund Crozat, even when she was much younger, she could never have done the things her father asked her to do. Neil Blood was a taker. If you offered, it was accepted at once. And soon your whole life was mired down in the sordid details of his business. She had remained untouched only by holding onto her dream that Edmund Crozat would come one day on his horse and . . .

Kate shook her head. She was worse than a fool. She was half-sick in her mind over the man, spurning eligible suitors in order to pray for what she couldn't have, like an ignorant farmgirl who believed in every silly superstition there was.

What had the convent done except educate her far above her station in life, making her reach for the unattainable? It had been a wicked idea of her father's, using his influence to make the Madames accept her as a day student. His motives might have been good, but the end result was the mischief from which she now suffered, the humiliating love for a man she could never have. She turned and left the chapel.

Greenery was still spare in the graveyard, thin springtime plots running between the raised tombs that, as in all the city's cemeteries, were built well above the ground.

Kate looked this way and that. Shamrocks? Yes, over there, in abundance. She dropped suddenly to her knees, as if in church again. St. Roch, help me now. Superstitions be damned.

She needed an omen, an augury for good or for bad. There!

No. Three leaves, not four. She inched forward, her fingers brushing tiny plants this way and that. Her reddish-blond hair glistened in the pale April sunlight under the white lace mantilla she wore.

There! No. No luck. Her cheeks were burning. Her heart seemed to knock against her ribs. One of the clovers *had* to have four leaves. But none did.

Dear God, what a fool.

She jumped to her feet and ran from the graveyard, then slowed to a walk as she returned to the Old Quarter. The pounding of her heart eased to a more normal tempo. She could feel the heat leave her cheeks.

This was the torment of the damned, surely enough, but she knew it was also laughable. A twenty-five-year-old virgin who had daily intercourse with the lewdest of God's creatures? Who called world-renowned madams like Josie Arlington by their first names. Who, if she dropped her reticule by accident, could count on a dozen of the town's most debauched pimps to rush forward and return it to her. Who knew the technical name of every trick and circus turn the girls performed, singly or in twos and threes. Who understood the private vice of every politician, financier, planter, or captain of industry, and how much it cost to have his particular itch scratched.

Her pace quickened as she neared the border of the old town at Rampart and Esplanade. Ahead of her, moving with the ponderous unsteady gait of an elephant, Senator Beaudoin approached, tiny eyes in their netted pouches of fat swimming this way and that. Countess Willie V. Piazza charged the senator a hundred dollars, in advance, for dressing him in women's clothes—specially made for his immense girth—while three naked young men whipped him. The senator's eyes, catching sight of Kate, disappeared in a smile. He tipped his tall hat gravely as she passed.

Behind the senator, hidden by his pachydermal haunches, strolled yet another of Kate's wide circle of acquaintances, Alexander Badger, not a frequenter of the bordellos, but one of Neil Blood's covert partners.

His small, thin body, with its odd little potbelly, came to a quick stop as Badger lifted his bowler hat. "The fair Mamselle Blood," he cried. "Your servant, mum."

Kate smiled. She liked Badger and his quaint English accent. He had come to New Orleans to handle the extensive affairs of one of the great British cotton mills which depended on the city as a major source of raw material.

"You're looking very pleased this afternoon," she responded.

"That I am. Daisy is expected on the next clipper from Liverpool."

Kate's mind clicked back into her memory, which was even more prodigious than her father's celebrated head for names and faces. "Will this be your daughter's first visit here, Mr. Badger?"

The man positively beamed. "This will be her eighteenth summer," he said. "I'm hoping to have her with me until she returns to England in the fall."

"Shall I have the pleasure of meeting her?"

"More than that, if I may prevail upon your good offices." The Englishman paused, as if trying to phrase his request with the greatest diplomacy.

As North American representative for Fiddoch, Larned & Co., Ptly. Ltd., Kate knew, he had served his firm well. Apart from this faithful service, however, Alexander Badger had done himself an even greater one.

Using Neil Blood as his front, he had invested his small fortune in cotton futures, to be rewarded by a large fortune. It was not, perhaps, entirely ethical. Fiddoch, Larned's man, by what and when he bought, played a major role in controlling the cotton market. So his guesses at the market's future were quite in the nature of self-fulfilling prophecies. But Kate accepted this as the nature of all speculation, whether in cotton, sugar, stocks, or bonds. The insiders controlled the show. The outsiders paid dearly for being allowed to watch.

"You know in what great esteem I hold you, young lady," Badger was saying, by way of prologue, "so much so that I should wish for no more gentle and knowledgeable a companion for my Daisy than you. But she is an innocent child when it comes to the wild ways of these colonial parts."

Kate was used to receiving the kind of request Badger was about to make. Befriend my daughter (wife, cousin, aunt) and introduce her to the upper life of this insane city, but for God's sake, never share with her your intimate knowledge of the crimson underside.

"Ah, Mr. Badger," Kate said in her kindest tone, "you forget we New Orleanians were never a colony of your mother country. Not even," she added in a harder voice, "we Irish."

Badger had the grace to blush, no easy matter for a cotton trader. "Why of course," he admitted. "It is to France and Spain you owe your colonial allegiance."

"Not we Irish."

The Englishman made a fussy gesture with both hands, as if brushing away a cloud of gnats. "Quite so. Quite so. Now, as to Daisy."

Kate produced a clear-eyed smile. "I shall be happy to introduce her to the finer circles of our community," she promised. "Those where I am welcome, that is."

"And whose door is not flung wide to the fair Kate?" Badger countered, trying for a tone of flattery.

"Why, those of families who do no business with my father," she explained in an innocent tone. "There we Bloods are unwelcome, Mr. Badger. The doors remain closed. And locked."

The conversation dawdled as Badger remade his point several times. Kate's thoughts strayed. Edmund Crozat had visited her brother in Neil Blood's house, but Kate Blood would never be welcome in the Crozat home on Royal. Nor at Crozat's bachelor quarters in the Pontalba Apartments. His sister, who was Kate's age, and like her a Sacred Heart graduate, would see her no more. That could be borne. But for Edmund to remain so coolly aloof from Kate's life, that was unbearable.

She could feel her cheeks begin to burn again. He was like a fever in her blood. Edmund Crozat was her disease.

"I beg pardon?" Badger asked abruptly.

"Yes?"

"You mentioned a disease?"

Kate frowned. Had she spoken her thoughts? Was she that mad with the infection? "Surely not," she said a bit shakily. "The new drains and levees, they tell me, have made New Orleans quite a safe city at last."

Badger nodded. "Except for these damnable—excuse my words, mamselle—mosquitoes."

Kate laughed. "But we won't be plagued with them for a while yet. This is only April."

"Ah, but the Liverpool clipper is due on the first of May."

"With your darling Daisy. I shall have to provide you with some of our finest netting, sir, suitably decorated with crocheting. My sister Agnes, who is finishing her novitiate with the Carmelite sisters, is quite adept at such work."

"And how is the rest of your illustrious family?"

"Brother James is now Father James Aloysius Blood, S.J. He leaves the Jesuits at Baltimore in June and is to take up scholastic duties at Ignatius Loyola here in New Orleans."

"A plum."

"Yes, quite," Kate agreed, neglecting to add that it had taken her father a year of conniving with Cardinal Contreras to get this assignment for his oldest son. "And Patrick has joined the force, just this week," she went on smoothly. "He's to report directly to the new chief of police, David Hennessy."

"And your sister Mary?"

"Expecting again." Kate failed to elaborate on the terse report. There had never been a contest between herself and Mary for either looks or brains. Mary knew she was plain and a bit slow when she married Alderman Abner N. Hinckley. She also knew that in the undeclared war between sisters, she now had her own weapons—her children.

"And Ned," Badger persisted. "You fail to speak of him."

"He advertises himself," Kate responded curtly.

"And amusingly, too. Where does he get all his inside information? And write it up so entertainingly. I read all his articles and never know whether to laugh or cry at some of the villainy he uncovers."

Kate nodded but said nothing. All roads led her heart back to Crozat, she thought.

Surely Ned knew how she felt about his friend? Surely he was failing sadly in brotherly feeling not to make new occasions for her to meet Crozat? What were brothers for? She would have to prod Ned, and soon, or he'd do nothing further.

"May I ask you, sir, the time?"

Badger assumed a look of importance as he delved inside his coat to probe among the vest pockets that hid his potbelly. At length he brought forth a large, heavy gold repeater watch, carefully flipped open its lid, and consulted the dial.

"I make it nearly five o'clock, lacking a minute."

"Then I must run." She curtsied. "Please let me know the moment Daisy graces our shores." She dashed away as Badger once again lifted his bowler to her.

At this hour, the affairs of Cornelius Blood slowed, allowing him a brief pause between matters of the sunlit hours and those of the night. He would be relaxing in his office above the Wicklowe with a cool glass of beer and one of the short, thin panatelas made for him in Havana. His door would be closed to the entire world, save Kate, who was hurrying south along Rampart. To her right were the small, tasteful cottages in which the city's finest quadroon mistresses lived. She was passing the corner of Barracks Street when she saw the rider in the distance.

Kate recognized him at once, although he was still more than five squares away, near the old Congo Square at Orleans Street, where the black people still did their voodoo dances to the pounding of African drums and the beating of sticks. They called it Beauregard Square now, but the dances continued, as they had for centuries.

He looked tired, even at this distance. His horse moved listlessly toward her. His beautiful white panama hat with the rolled brim looked stained and dusty. As he drew closer, Kate stopped on the banquette, smiling faintly. Crozat reined his horse to a halt in the street and swept his hat from his head. "Good evening, mamselle," he said in that strangely taut, deep voice of his that made the skin across her shoulders prickle.

"Good evening, m'sieur. You have had a long ride?"

He nodded wearily and seemed about to explain. Then his lips pressed shut on the words. They watched each other, almost like conspirators. We both have a secret, Kate guessed.

"We don't see you at our home lately," she ventured.

"I've been out of town."

"Business?"

"One might say that." He stopped, refusing again to explain.

How to break through the icy wall between them? Kate wondered. How to reach out to him without seeming . . . ?

"Then you are in grave need of refreshment," she told him.

His glance raised past her to the line of cottages on the rampart. Then he looked back at her. "One might also say that." He smiled sardonically.

"At this hour, the Wicklowe is a quiet place."

He failed to respond, and instantly Kate's cheeks grew fiery. He was on his way to his mistress, of course. The celebrated Ynes Fleurigant, in her early twenties and already reigning queen of the quadroon community.

"Perhaps another time," Crozat was saying, "Ned and I shall . . ."

His voice seemed to fade. He was being the Creole gentleman, turning her aside in as graceful a manner as possible after she had charged at him like a mare in heat. Saluting her again as he replaced his hat, he trotted off, leaving Kate standing like a pillar of crude lust, burning for the world to see.

She strode toward the far end of the old town, but of course she had to pause at Customhouse, before turning toward Basin, pause, and glance back.

And there he was, still astride his horse, the way she saw him always, in real life and in her dreams, waiting like a Creole gentleman for her to leave Rampart Street, so as not to offend her by dismounting before Ynes Fleurigant's steps.

Kate left Rampart Street and Crozat, pushing past strangers and acquaintances alike in a desperate hurry to find a haven at her father's office.

She was no match for the exquisite manners of these Creoles, she lectured herself, face still burning. They had the innate ability to make a person feel clumsy and rural, like some great clodhopping backwoods lass, not by saying a word, just by the way they comported themselves.

The gall of the man! Waiting for her to clear Rampart Street and leave him with his mistress. The bloody nerve of the Creoles.

She pushed wildly through the Wicklowe's swinging teak doors, set with diamond-cut panes of lead crystal, and started up the private stairs to her father's sanctorum. How she hated Crozat! How she loved him! Was there no way to purge him from her blood?

She had survived every other plague and fever that New Orleans visited on her. But how could she survive Crozat?

3

"They tell me," the sketcher said, putting down his sharp-pointed pencil for a moment and turning from the nude models to look at Ned Blood, "that your brother Patrick has joined the police. A bit awkward, eh?"

Ned inhaled on his cigarette. When he felt the cough begin, he covered it with a laugh. He'd let his education lag too long, he realized. To be twenty and just learning to inhale was altogether too retarded.

"Why awkward?" he asked. "Because his youngest brother sits around whorehouses watching sketchers? Or because his father owns most of the better houses in town?"

He glanced around the brothel—one of Harriet Macklin's houses, with a rather unsavory name for a high disease rate—and let his gaze settle on the two naked girls posing for Archer. The sketcher was an old hand at portraying scenes that his newspaper could engrave and publish without being so obscene as to cause righteous wrath among the respectable establishment, nor so puritanically dull as to glaze readers' eyes.

He had posed the petite brunette astride the lanky redhead, who was down on all fours, shaking her head sideways like a vexed mare. Archer penciled in camisole shifts to cover the women's bodies. The touches were all discreet, Ned decided, and the pose was good clean tomboy fun, wasn't it? The petite brunette brandished a small whip, but only in the air. As an illustration for the article Ned had written, Archer's drawing would be an elegant compromise between journalism and advertising.

Like most of the newspapers in this town, Ned added silently. He was under no illusion that his job with the *Weekly Almanac* was true journalism of the kind they practiced in less corrupt cities. The *Weekly Almanac* had its share of stories designed to seem like scandalous exposés. But it also carried the madams' advertising, both as commercial announcements and as items in what purported to be newsy columns of gossip.

Archer's sly portrait of the dark-haired mistress whipping her ungainly mare would illustrate a cautionary tale about the dangers of patronizing any but the "best" houses and eating places. The terrors of venereal diseases, alcohol, and drugs, but also of physical abuse by whores and their male consorts in the cheaper bagnios, were dwelt upon at some length and in the kind of cold, cutting prose that Ned felt happiest writing.

Oh, he was indignant. He was never any less than indignant. But his aim was not to tell of that rising anger. Rather it was to make his readers feel angry on their own, just on the merits of the reporting.

Ned had spent a long time reaching the Northern muckraking writers like Lincoln Steffens and the revealing biographies of Ida Tarbell. He was as dedicated and as indignant as any of them, but he had his own methods. As he watched Archer sketching, he remembered that the muckrakers were outsiders, peering into the hidden heart of hypocrisy. He, youngest son of the man who really ran New Orleans, was a privileged insider.

Which made his job that much harder.

"Bring down the whip a little," the sketcher muttered.

The small brunette, happy at being able to relax her upraised arm, laid the cutting loop of the quirt across the bare back of her mount. "No," Archer corrected her at once, "the leather can't touch her."

"Who's this meant for, Archer?" the redheaded steed asked. "Some kind of mollycoddle Baptists?"

"Shut up and eat your oats."

Ned smiled a bit crookedly, the way his friend Edmund Crozat did. He admired Edmund a great deal, because the Creole was doing what Ned Blood didn't seem able to accomplish: cutting himself free of his family.

The main control Edmund's father had over his son was the crushing weight of the Crozat and Almonaster-Nunes fortunes. What Neil Blood used to keep his brood in line was his position in their native city, his intimate knowledge of the invisible threads that tied that power to others, and them to him. Blood was more than the boss of New Orleans, he was its chief interpreter, the man with a very rare map of its inner workings, its secret conduits, its closeted skeletons.

To that child of Neil Blood who had devoted himself to journalism, the riches of information his father controlled were tantalizing, beyond the realm of desire, well into the pain of torment. Ned lived near the center of the very knowledge he most wanted to ferret out and publish. He could almost touch it. Yet he could not touch it.

In the agony of his frustration, it had not yet occurred to him that someday, to fullfil his dream, he would have to kill his father. That the ultimate truth of this deceptively sleepy town on the Mississippi, if put into print, would bring Neil Blood down to defeat and death.

No thoughts of parricide filled Ned's head now as he watched the models scratch themselves impatiently. The mosquitoes made nude modeling a high-risk profession. "Archer," he murmured then, hoping that his words didn't reach the models' ears, "you're making them too wholesome."

The sketcher frowned. With a small roll of gum eraser he removed the happy-go-lucky smile on the jockey and replaced it with a more lascivious grin. "Degenerate enough, Neddie?"

"After all, the article's about the dangers of cheap dens."

Archer smiled serenely. "A cheap den is one which does not advertise in the *Weekly Almanac*. Correct?"

"Correct."

Ned took another puff of his cigarette. This time he managed to inhale most of it without coughing. Journalism, New Orleans style, was a high-risk profession, too, he mused. You walked a thin line, tickling your reader's prurient tastes to get him to read a bit of the truth about the world he lived in.

Ned felt certain, based on his readings of Steffens and of Sam Clemens' novel, *The Gilded Age*, about corruption in our nation's capital, that a steady drumfire of revelations, of exposés, of private scandal aired publicly, would soon result in revolt at the polls. There would arise candidates of principle. Voting for such new men would no longer be a waste of a ballot and a mockery of the democratic process. Votes would then count for something.

He, Ned Blood, would handle this revolutionary process of education for the voters of New Orleans and, in fact, of Louisiana. No matter what life seemed like—dank hypocrisy everywhere—people were innately good. Know the truth, he repeated to himself, and it shall make you free. Without warning, that slightly lopsided smile of Edmund Crozat's reappeared on Ned's lips.

Know the truth but honor thy father, Ned told himself sourly. He made a disgusted face, ground out the cigarette underfoot, and moved around Archer to stroke the petite brunette's rear end. "You poor girls might as well have a bit of fun while we're tormenting you."

"Why, Mr. Blood." She grinned and moved her buttocks slowly under the stroking. "If you could manage to keep the mosquitoes off my derriere as well."

"Stop wriggling," the sketcher snapped.

"And mine, too," the redhead chimed in. "It's little enough to ask."

Ned patted her behind. "Nice horsie."

"Ned, you're slowing me down," Archer complained. "If you have other plans for the ladies, hold off till I'm finished here."

"What plans would I have for such jades of low repute?"

"Shit to that," the tiny brunette cried out. "You won't find a cleaner girl anywhere on Basin."

"Little Casino," the redhead muttered.

The dark-haired woman brought the whip down hard on the other's back. "Damned lie. I never had Little Casino, and you know it. Whereas"—she turned on Ned—"you'd better wash the hand that patted her ass, Neddie. If you don't want it dropping off one of these days."

The redhead jumped to her feet, toppling the smaller woman. "Take that back!"

The naked women grappled and began rolling over each other on the floor. Archer quickly flipped to a fresh piece of sketching paper and began a new drawing. Ned reached inside the cluster of flailing arms and picked up the petite brunette, lifting her bodily and putting her down in a dusty velours armchair a few feet away. "You're too sensitive," he chided.

Her breath was sobbing in and out in spurts of anger. "We have our pride," she managed to tell him. "We do all the circuses and shows you gentlemen ask for. Right, Flo?" she asked the redhead. "How many times I went down on Flo for the pleasure of some gentleman. How many times Flo took on Old Cabouchon's donkey with that prick like a baseball bat. For some gentleman's pleasure." Her breath grew calmer. "We do what you pay for," she told Ned. "We don't have much pride. But some."

The redhead sat cross-legged on the floor, nodding her head. "Miss Harriet may run a less expensive place than most," she said, "but what we do here is just what they do at Lulu White's Mahogany Hall, or Willie V. Piazza's joints. Only, we don't get too many senators and presidents of railroads down here. But it ain't no crib joint. Most of the girls are clean."

"Most," the brunette agreed.

Ned picked up the quirt and slapped its leather loop against the palm of his hand. "Ladies, you have made your point," he said then. "In fact," he went on, turning to the sketcher, "I think they have made *the* point itself."

Archer was finishing a quick scrawl of the two naked women rolling over the floor. He looked up, not having heard Ned's words. "What?"

"The whole point is male demand, female supply." Ned paused.

"What the hell are you raving about, Neddie?"

"Men require certain services. Women provide them. But men make the profit on what women do. You think Miss Harriet gets to keep the profit from her joints?"

He turned to the small brunette. "You have eyes. You know Hattie is owned by Senator Bechemere and the Matrangas and the former chief of police and one or two cotton brokers. They put up the money for all this . . ." He indicated the great mirrors, the sconces, a gold-inlaid Pleyel pianoforte covered by an ornate shawl with bugle-beaded fringes. "And Miss Harriet just never can pay it all off. She keeps a little, same as you do. But Bechemere and his consortium of investors get the lion's share."

Archer was sketching again, this time a quick drawing of Ned Blood, arm upraised, mouth open, eyes blazing. "It's ingenious," Ned was saying. "It's diabolical. Men profit on the swinish tastes of men. And they always have the women to blame in case someone wants to point a finger, eh?"

He laughed softly. "Why do you girls put up with it?" he demanded. He knew Archer's pencil was flying across the paper, but he ignored it. He felt swept up by the same feeling he had found in the Russian novels he read, the sure knowledge that truth resided in the depths of society, not the heights.

He stared boldly around him. All masks were down here. All shams lay bare. At this bedrock level, hypocrisy could find no foothold. Here was truth.

"I know you have to live," he told the two whores. "I know this isn't a hard way to make a living. Miss Harriet takes care of you the way she'd take care of a horse that pulled her trap."

He took a shaky breath. "But you can earn a living other ways. Ways where you don't let them shove your noses so deep in shit."

The women stared mournfully at him for a long time. In the silence, the sketcher's pencil scratched busily for a while. Then it, too, stopped. Archer put down his paper pad. He clapped his hands together three times. "Bravo," he said in a hollow voice.

"Yeah, bravo." Both women clapped loudly. The sound echoed emptily through the bordello, deserted at this early hour.

Ned relaxed. People were really impossible, weren't they? He knew
better: you couldn't sway them with indignation. You had to remain
cool and deadly, working your rapier thrusts in the dark, so that they
hardly knew you had touched them till they began to bleed.

One day he, Ned Blood, would put this whole hypocritical farce
together, all of its threads tied tightly, names named, dollar amounts
totaled, political protectors identified, respectable investors singled out
for the whoremongers they were, all those planters, brokers, bankers
with their secret investments in the District. Everything.

As Ned Blood rose to the heights of Steffens and Tarbell, no name
would be missing. Certainly not the key name of Cornelius Blood. His
would lead all the rest.

"Hold it!" Archer cried out. "That glare in your eye!" His pencil
scratched furiously. "My God, you look like a bloody maniac, Neddie,
my boy."

4

At the corner of Bourbon and Toulouse, in the heart of the Old Quarter a few squares from the river, stood the ornate four stories of the French Opera House with its tall, narrow windows and leaded panes. Gaslight lanterns jutted forward on wrought-iron sconces. Four thick square pillars stood at its entrance, papered with playbills. Past it ran the new car tracks, set in oversized oblongs of stone used to pave the street.

The building curved at one corner. High on the third floor, this curve produced a sumptuous office for Jed Benjamin, who could gaze down at the patrons arriving on an opening night before hastening to the lobby to greet them by name.

By 1888 the house was set determinedly in its old-fashioned, Creole-French way, parquet ground floor covered with upholstered armchairs. Some box stalls, shaped like bathtubs, were therefore called *baignoires*. Along the immense spread of the horseshoe, with its fifty-two stalls, twenty larger ones were protected by grilles. Creole families in formal mourning could still attend a concert or opera without being the object of intense whispering. (*"Mon dieu*, and *pauvre* Mignon scarcely in her grave!"*) Above the horseshoe rose two more rings of stalls and seats, until the steep top balcony, the *poulailler*, or chicken-coop, with its plain benches, was reached.

Benjamin used to pace the inner corridors of the theater as if he owned it, but he merely leased office space there. Of all New Orleans' impresarios, however, he brought more attractions to the French Opera House. He adored the place.

When he sat, as now, at the ornate mahogany desk with its brass fittings in the high third-floor office, his back to the curved corner, and looked at the soft, dark features of Olivia Crozat, his heart swelled with pride at his privileged position in this bustling metropolis. True, Benjamin was an old New Orleans name, covered with glory by his father in the War Between the States. But when all was said and done, it was a Jewish name.

". . . not Patti again," Olivia moaned.

"And why not?" Jed responded. "She was discovered right here in 1861 by Boudousquie himself. She has been a pillar of this house for two decades."

"But her voice . . ." Olivia let the thought trail off. Although she resembled her brother, in having the wide-set Crozat eyes and pointed chin, she had none of Edmund's snap or thrust. She preferred not to be forthcoming, except with old friends like Benjamin, and even then she preferred to express herself indirectly, without Edmund's arrogant sureness.

"Her voice carries a price tag of five thousand dollars a performance," Jed reported. "But remember, Olivia, this is her farewell performance in her native city. It will be a moment of such intense emotionalism that if I charge the unheard-of price of ten dollars a ticket I will still sell out the morning of the announcement."

"Absolutely final farewell performance?" Olivia murmured dubiously.

"Kitty-catty," Benjamin responded.

"And she was not born here," Olivia went on surely, "but in Madrid, of Italian parents. Nevertheless . . ." Again she let the thought die away.

"What a lot of odd things hide inside that pretty head of yours."

"It's one of those odd things of which I came to speak," Olivia reminded him. She put a rolled paper, tied with a ribbon, on the desk. "Through friends, Yancey Morgan has put a song on paper."

"Sweet child, why?"

"Yancey neither reads nor writes music. But he composes it. I think his work deserves the written form."

"But it's only ragtime, Olivia."

The dark-haired young woman paused for a moment. "I have heard Yancey play it on the piano."

Benjamin looked shocked. "Not at his place of work."

"At Edmund's apartment in the Pontalba. I've had a Pleyel shipped over from Paris, the medium-sized grand. And we have our Sunday afternoon . . . ah, musicales."

"You and Edmund?"

"Impossible. The idea of him sitting through an afternoon of music . . ." She smiled. "But he is partial to ragtime and that other music Yancey Morgan plays. The music to which there are words."

The impresario nodded. "They call it the blues. Quite emotional at times." He picked up the roll of paper and slid the ribbon off. For a while he stared at the written staffs of music. Then he hummed softly. "This is that slow rag he does," he said at last. "A very sweet melody, really."

He looked up from the music. "Olivia," he said at last, "it's my duty as your friend, as Edmund's friend, to tell you that no one will thank you for taking an interest in nigger music. Instead, they will whisper behind your back. You do understand that this is the music of the . . ." He cut off his words and cleared his throat.

Jed Benjamin's high, freckled forehead was damp. His carrot-colored hair was receding at a pace much too rapid for his thirty years. He pulled a lace-trimmed handkerchief from the breast pocket of his dark blue velours jacket and dabbed at his forehead.

"Let me put it this way, Olivia. This is the music of the lowest classes, of the lowest places in which they disport themselves. I know you are a modern lady who likes to speak plainly. That is plain enough, is it not?"

"And is the music infected by its origins?"

The impresario laughed sardonically. "Many believe so. The propulsive rhythms. The . . . ah, unconventional syncopation."

"You are becoming positively anatomical, dear Jed."

Benjamin's face went red. "You are a tease, mamselle," he said at last. "It gives you pleasure to discomfort me."

"You do all that to yourself, I assure you." Her wide-set eyes flashed down to the roll of music. "Can you help me with Yancey's composition? I know you have friends among the music publishers."

"Yes, I do."

"Jed, do they never weary of reprinting the tired songs of Europe?" she asked, suddenly moving past her normal tone of diffidence. "Are none of them interested in the American music we have here in New Orleans?"

"If I were to put it to them that way. But there would be little profit in this for Yancey. They would pay him ten dollars and own the song forever. Yancey gets a tip that size just for playing what one of Lulu's Mahogany Hall customers ask hi . . ." The words stopped in Jed's throat.

Olivia smiled sweetly. "You will choke someday on that imitation you do of a Creole gentleman."

Once again Benjamin's face darkened. "Imitation?"

"You are not one of us," Olivia told him flatly. "And thank God for it, Jed. The world would be a dark, cruel, dour, and anguished place if all the men were Creole gentlemen."

"Oh." He relaxed. "Then it's a compliment, is it?"

"You Jews are quick to offense."

"Yes, very."

She nodded. "Do you fight many duels over it?"

Benjamin sighed unhappily. "A few."

"As many as Edmund?"

He failed to respond. Instead he smoothed the music out flat and put a heavy inkwell on it to remove the curl. "I'll send this to Stark, in St. Louis. Or Joe Stern in New York." Behind his desk an ebony grandfather clock whirred and struck six times. "You'll have to excuse me, Olivia."

She got to her feet before he could come around the desk to assist her. "Off to the Wicklowe?" she asked.

"As a matter of fact, yes." He paused. "It's really quite a proper place, you know. Ladies of your background have been known to dine there with their husbands."

"But a maiden lady would not do so with her escort," Olivia suggested as they walked to the door of the office.

"It's not the Wicklowe itself, you understand."

"I quite understand. It's the owner's other interests, elsewhere on Basin Street." She laughed at the look on the impresario's face. "You can drop the imitation with me, Jed. I have a clear idea of what gentlemen do with their evenings."

"One has to keep one's ear to the ground in my business."

"That far down to the ground?" she teased. They were descending in half-light one of the twin staircases. "I understand you make the rounds with Ned Blood, helping him with his journalistic reportage. Jed and Ned . . . and Ed," she added on a slight upward shriek of laughter.

"What's funny?"

"No one on the face of the earth has ever called my brother Ed."

They were standing outside on the banquette, but under the overhang of the theater's portico, which extended to the street curb itself. "He isn't that often with us," the impresario assured her. "Edmund is a dedicated man these days. We see less and less of him."

"He's always been dedicated. The intensity is frightening."

"To what end?" Benjamin asked. "He tells us nothing."

"Then neither can I," the young woman assured him. "It's Edmund's dream." She took Benjamin's arm. "Let's walk a way together. I shall leave you at the corner of Customhouse."

"You won't accompany me to the Wicklowe?" They were strolling slowly south along Bourbon Street. He seemed relieved that they would soon part. Olivia caught the note in his voice.

"But a moment ago, upstairs, you were calling it quite a proper place." At Customhouse she turned them west in the direction of Basin Street, where the Wicklowe stood. "Lead on."

"Olivia, you're teasing again."

"Lead on, I say."

"Our presence there together could be misconstrued . . ."

Her dark eyes flashed sideways at him. "With what result? That my name would be sullied?" When he failed to answer, she added, "Or that you would incur the wrath of Jean-Paul Crozat, the little emperor himself, who oversees the life of his only daughter like a jailer a convict?"

Benjamin shook his head. "You lead a very free and active life, my dear."

"Only thanks to Edmund. At home they do everything but lock the door of my room. Only in Edmund's apartment am I free."

"It's quite proper to protect a Creole daughter that strictly. You should be pleased that they let you blossom a bit under Edmund's aegis."

They had reached Burgundy Street. The Wicklowe was only two squares farther. "How can they stop me?" Olivia asked in a dark tone of voice, more to herself than aloud. "The age of the imprisoned virgin is ending all over the United States. It is only here, under our wretched Napoleonic code, that female children lead such degraded lives. Yes, I'm lucky to have Edmund. But why must a man always be my protector?"

"That's the French way." Jed Benjamin stopped short at the corner of Rampart. "We must take our leave now, mamselle."

"But there is the Wicklowe, only a square away." Olivia's eyes narrowed slightly as she stared at a diamond-pane leaded window on the floor above the ornate entrance to the restaurant. "That girl! It's Kate Blood."

The impresario glanced at the window. "I believe it is, although I've never been introduced. Quite a handsome young lady."

"Handsome? She's beautiful!" Olivia snapped. "As a girl at the convent, she was only pretty. But there's something about her now. Don't stare, Jed. She'll notice us."

"Not likely. She seems rapt in her own thoughts."

"Has she ever considered a career on the stage?" Olivia wondered. "Her kind of face is . . . more intense than life. It projects emotion. Those green eyes. Those hollows under the cheekbones. That vulnerable mouth. And the skin, Jed, that peaches-and-cream skin. She's larger than life, more keyed-up. Even a square away, you know what she's thinking."

"And what is that?"

"Why . . ." Olivia faltered for a moment.

"Pray continue," Jed urged her.

She sighed. "The message is one of misery. I have rarely seen such unhappiness and such beauty in the same face."

The impresario stared boldly at Kate from a distance. "Seems fine to me."

"Fool."

"She has everything you pine for," Jed told Olivia. "Perhaps her family is not as well-to-do as the Crozats. What family is? But she is her father's right arm, they tell me. She has the freedom you prize so heavily. She comes and goes, her own mistress, and second-in-command of an enterprise of tremendous scope. Unhappy? Kate?"

Olivia's dark head bobbed twice in a solemn nod. "Unhappy," she said in a low voice. "Kate."

5

There was often, Ned Blood told himself, a mysterious thread of lucky fate that seemed to bind his affairs together. The night before, lounging in the back of Lola Montgomery's Pussywillow Club, talking to another reporter who had a piece of a big story that seemed to lead nowhere, Ned had made a great decision.

"The big truths," he had told the other fellow, "are not lying around on whorehouse floors waiting to be stumbled over."

This was a radical departure from his usual Dostoyevskian notion that only in the dregs of society were pearls of truth to be found. But he was tired of poking in dirty corners for salacious gossip about pimps, whoremongers, gamblers, and the like. He was after bigger game. The place to begin such a hunt was the state capital, Baton Rouge.

That was the mysterious thread of fate at work. Having decided to go north to the capital, he journeyed across the river to Gretna and learned that the fast paddlewheeler the *Rogue Queen* left New Orleans on the first and fifteenth of the month. And today was the fifteenth.

The steamer was of the older, wood-burning type, with a rear paddlewheel, a plain riverboat dedicated to freight, not passengers. But it had two comfortable cabins. "Both've 'em'r booked," the captain told Ned.

"How about deck passage, then?"

"Sleep under the stars? S'up to you, boy."

"Who's got the cabins?"

"A Mr. Alexander Badger and a Miss Daisy Badger. Limeys, both of 'em."

"Deck passage, then," Ned paid the captain in advance and went home to pack a bag.

Out of sight of the Gretna docks, he suddenly leaped up and danced a wild jig step. What Ned had always looked for was something bigger than New Orleans, continental, transatlantic, even cosmic. And surely Mr. Badger, who said he was a simple mill representative from England, would be a key figure in such international intrigues. Grinning with anticipation, Ned hurried back to New Orleans to pack for what promised to be the story of a lifetime.

In her father's judgment, Daisy had developed into a rather plain girl in the year since he'd seen her. She seemed to tower over her short, skinny father. Even his little potbelly failed to give him the proper presence beside her. Why, she was as tall as Kate Blood, he reflected, as they boarded the *Rogue Queen*, five inches over five feet, far too tall for anyone of the feminine persuasion. And so inexperienced it hurt to look at her.

Daughter or no, attractive or not, Badger had business upriver this time of year. July was hot as Hades, of course, but cotton bolls would be filling and planters would be able to make forecasts. On behalf of Fiddoch, Larned, Badger needed to know whether this year's rumors of a bumper crop were justified. On behalf of his own speculations in cotton futures, which had already made him almost a millionaire in American dollars, Badger needed to judge for himself whether the big crop would produce a healthy plethora or a glut.

It was a time of consolidation among the planters, Badger knew. He himself had watched the situation change dramatically in recent years. It was true that some yeoman farmers remained in the market, in places like Winn Parish, working their own land. But most cotton was now produced on large plantations by sharecroppers or convict labor.

In a growing number of places, ownership was absentee. Often the owner knew nothing of cotton and cared less. He had come by his plantation—as the Crozats had, for instance—by foreclosure. There was no longer any connection between the man who owned the land and the crop he raised and sold.

Badger was aware that anyone with access to a telegraph in Shreveport or Baton Rouge could know overnight what cotton was selling for in Liverpool. And for a while, some of the big planters had grown quite independent, or as it was put in their quaint patois, "uppity," but the depression of 1873 had brought them smartly about. Cotton had dropped below five cents a pound for a while. It was a learning experi-

ence, Badger remembered. It efficiently removed much of the uppiti-
ness.

The *Rogue Queen* had pushed north against the Mississippi's lazy
southward surge and stopped overnight at Baton Rouge, where Daisy
retired early while her father set out for an evening on the town. Here in
the capital, his job was to gather information and he made use of his
famous empty leg as he engaged in a series of talks at the local bars.

The town seethed with talk of tariffs, shipping-fee regulations, and
the like. Quite an exciting place to be, at times like these, Badger
decided at midnight as he entered the gaslit lobby of the sumptuous
Palace Hotel. In the hotel's lounge he could count on meeting those few
legislators with whom he had not already talked during this long and
useful night.

Instead, inertia overcame him. Abruptly he sank with a "whoof!" into
the dusty red velours center of a lobby armchair, finished in elegantly
carved walnut. The slight young man who had been following him most
of the evening and staying in the background, but not out of earshot,
greeted him with all the air of a new arrival.

"What, you here?" Ned Blood demanded. He stuck out his hand.

Badger immediately sat up straight in the upholstered chair. "Neddie! What sort of scandal are you tracking down?"

"Truly, none," Ned assured him. "And you?"

"Keeping the old ear to the ground." Badger struggled for a moment
to hoist his skinny frame out of the grasp of the upholstery. "Let me buy
you a drink, dear boy," he said, leading the way to the bar.

Whatever Badger's game actually was, Ned learned some time later,
the cagey Englishman wasn't about to disclose any of it over a casual
drink or two. Ned realized what a fortunate position he was in, however,
as the son of Badger's undercover business partner. Everyone's undercover partner, when it came to that.

How many other reporters in New Orleans carried that kind of key in
their pocket? But then, Ned told himself as he strolled back to the
Rogue Queen at three A.M., how many of these gossipmongers have
aspirations to follow in the footsteps of Lincoln Steffens?

He had left Badger in the hands of some sleepy-seeming Cajuns who
were proposing a poker game. Warning them to make certain Badger
got back to the docks by sunup, Ned wandered off. He now realized the
Badger story would take a great deal more work to develop. For one
thing, you could pump him for hours without getting more than a drop
or two of useful information. For another, he was a wily old cuss, full of
tricks. He'd invited Ned to continue with him aboard the *Rogue Queen*,
which would move upriver in the morning for Shreveport. Badger was to

be the guest of the overseer of Whiteacres, one of the big upstate Crozat plantations.

The Englishman had been the soul of hospitality. Fishing a key from his pocket as the Cajuns began shuffling cards, he thrust it on Ned. "Mine's the port cabin, Neddie. As I'm not sleeping, you use it."

Walking up the plank to the steamer's deck, Ned realized he had no idea which side was port, nor was there anyone in sight who could help him. Carefully he slipped the key into the brassbound lock of the mahogany door and slowly eased it open.

He quickly stripped of his boots and clothes and got in under the draped mosquito netting. A moment later, he felt a warm body beside him.

"Um?" someone asked.

"Good Lord! I beg your pardon, miss."

A long, soft arm glided across his chest. Fingers felt his nipples, then patted him comfortingly. "S'all right," a sleepy voice assured him. "Just don't wake Father."

The next day the *Rogue Queen* steamed past the town of Incline and headed west through rapids and around shoal bends, pushing firmly up the Red River toward Shreveport. Before it docked there, however, it paused briefly at St. Maurice Landing around noon.

Ned, who had gotten out of Daisy Badger's starboard bedroom before dawn, now presented himself to her father. "Can I help you with your baggage, sir?"

"I'm all right," Badger informed him. "But knock on my daughter's cabin and make sure she's ready."

"Miss Badger," Ned called, rapping politely on the mahogany door he had so easily entered last night.

She opened it slowly. "I beg your pardon?"

It was Ned's first view of her in daylight. Taller than he by an inch, she looked rather too slender, although his own memory contradicted this. "This is Ned Blood," her father said, carefully smoothing down his hair.

"Father, your collar." The girl began tugging Badger's collar and tie into some semblance of order. "How do you do, Mr. Blood?" she added so coolly that if Ned had been so inclined he could have taken it as a snub.

The three of them moved slowly down the gangplank to shore, where stood a tall young man wearing a wide planter's hat. He gestured lazily to the arrivals, and when he swept off his hat, released a great head of wavy black hair.

"Ringrose Waddell, at your service," the dark young man cried out.

His long face was handsome in a loose way, but Badger had always felt Waddell's eyes were set too close for comfort. There was also a certain insolence in his manner that Badger found disturbing.

When a Creole was insolent, one knew it immediately, as one did back home in England. But Waddell was slyer, in the new style of young men today, a kind of reverse politeness.

"The estimable Mr. Badger, sir," he called out, sweeping his white hat in a broad salute. "And this must be the indescribable Miss Badger?"

Fiddoch, Larned's man frowned slightly. "Daisy, Mr. Waddell. And this is my friend Ned Blood."

Badger shifted uneasily from foot to foot. He rarely felt at home among the grave Creoles of New Orleans, so he welcomed these upriver trips because he would find himself among "his own kind," meaning people with English or Scottish surnames.

The trouble was that few of them had come to America that recently. Grandfathers had settled in savage outposts like Kentucky and Tennessee and Arkansas. The English idea had suffered a grandiose expansion that always made Badger as uneasy as did the locked-in darkness of the Creoles.

A black man drove a buckboard with their luggage off along a dirt road. Waddell escorted them to a snappy-looking two-horse phaeton, its varnished cloth top glinting in the sunlight. "We'll be making far better time than Uncle Cudgo," Waddell announced.

There followed perhaps the wildest ride Badger had taken in this land of demon horsemen, murderously swift drivers of buggies, and pilots of boats intent on scraping each other's paint in tight turns. The buggy jounced, leaped, sideslipped, hammered, and swerved as Waddell, whipping the two horses into a foam, rattled insanely past the aging Negro on his one-horse buckboard. Now and then the lunatic Waddell would turn and peer through the small oval isinglass window bound into the rear of the phaeton's cloth top, nodding energetically to his rear passengers as if to say: "Don't worry, we'll get you there in time," although Badger could not remember having asked for speed.

Arriving at Whiteacres, Badger and Ned got down in the gravel driveway and began slapping their clothes, sending up clouds of dust. "Damned impertinent booby," Badger muttered, for Ned's hearing alone.

"Beg your pardon, sir?" Ned asked.

"That ride."

"Fun, wasn't it?"

Daisy, who seemed as unaffected by the ride as Ned, alighted with Waddell's help. He held her hand too long as he showed her the facade of Whiteacres.

" 'Tisn't much, mamselle," he drawled, "but we call it home."

"You and Mrs. Waddell?" Daisy asked. Her voice, Badger was pleased to note, had a quality of diction and tone that cut through Waddell's lazy drawl like a rapier point through a pig bladder.

"Lord a'mercy, Miss Daisy." Waddell managed to look embarrassed and lecherous in the same moment, "the only Mrs. Waddell I know is my saintly ma, back home in S'n Louie."

Badger gazed at Whiteacres. Two and a half stories high, the mansion had a Grecian facade of two-story columns, fluted in wood.

It was a roomy-enough place, and Badger felt beholden to the Crozats for offering Whiteacres' hospitality for as long as he stayed in Winn Parish, but he did hope his stay would be mercifully short. He had been lending half an ear to the infuriating Waddell, who was going on at some length to Daisy about the provenance of the place.

". . . built by slaves inside and out. Took 'em nine years, starting about 1840. An Englishman's idea of what a country house ought to be. . . ."

"English, you say?" asked Badger.

"A Mr. John Duffy he was, sir."

"Irish." Badger's mouth opened and shut like a trap. He turned away, but was unable to stop from hearing Waddell's epilogue.

"A great one for booze, so they say. Mistreated his slaves something fierce, and so did his son. And they tell me his granddaughter does well with the whip down in New Orleans. Name of Carolina."

Badger turned back to the young man. "She's not in the cotton business, I take it?"

"No, sir." Waddell's eyes swam sideways in a half-lewd, half-sheepish movement toward Daisy. She's in the . . . er, um, entertainment business, so they tell me, sir. I understand Carolina has a house on—"

"That'll be quite enough," Badger cut in. "We've had one devil of a trip in that phaeton of yours. I'll ask you to show us our rooms, if you please, sir."

Dressing for dinner, Ned hoped to have a private moment with Daisy, but when he knocked at her door, she firmly shut it in his face. He walked slowly down the curving stairway to the ground floor. A faint coolness came in through tall open windows that reached the floor. Candles flickered in hurricane glass holders. Ned decided that none of this grace could come from an oaf like Waddell. It was probably the Negro butler and cook who understood such amenities. He could hear other guests descending the stairs.

Ned was familiar with back-country hospitality. Any evening meal might be joined by arriving travelers. For what other reason would such a countrified person as Representative Leathers be invited to this place, and what was one to say about his companion?

Ned knew Mike Leathers by name only, having heard it cursed often enough. Other legislators referred to him as Nigger Mike. Not that there was black blood in his ancestry, or perhaps, Ned added with silent caution, no more than was usual in this corner of the world. It was his blind indifference to race that singled Leathers out as a nigger-lover.

His ancestry was what passed for respectable in these parts, a preacher brother and a lawyer father, Christy Leathers. From offices on Lafayette Square, near the old *cabildo* in New Orleans, Christy also did a sizable insurance business. Ned had met the man a few times at the Wicklowe, where Neil Blood had introduced him as "the man who keeps those upstate turd-kickers in hand." A fixer, evidently, shuttling north from Catholic New Orleans to make deals with Protestant legislators from upstate farm areas.

By all accounts, however, his own son Mike was not one of the lawmakers over whom Christy Leathers had control. The two disagreed on almost everything. And surely the father would violently object to a young legislator, albeit a bachelor, escorting this child of nature he had brought with him tonight to dine in this elegant room at the Crozats' expense.

Luanne Grimes was the name under which her gentleman friend had introduced her. She was a tiny thing, with enormous black eyes and long lashes, top and bottom, that looked like ravens' wings.

Of course, Ned added to himself, one saw the eyes only at second glance. At first one's attention was riveted on her immense, upthrusting breasts, their great nipples pushing against the dainty fabric of her dress.

". . . over to the salty lake, they tell me," Luanne was telling Waddell, who bent toward her until his rather wolfish nose might have buried itself between those glorious globes. "I don't pay it no mind at all. Mike, Mr. Leathers here, does the worryin' of it for me, so he does."

Ned's glance went to Leathers, who was deep in a discussion with Daisy of the crop-lien system under which yeoman farmers who owned their own land had to mortgage it in advance to companies—like her father's, Fiddoch, Larned, although Leathers hadn't mentioned it.

Against a drawing account at a company store, the farmer bought his staples, hardware, and the like. Inevitably he ended each year turning over his crop to the company and still owing money.

"Which puts him in the same fix as the sharecropper," Leathers told Badger's daughter.

"You don't want to pay too much mind to Nigger Mike, Miss Daisy," Waddell said then. "He's a good old boy, but he surely does have strange ideas."

"I'm not alone, Ringo." Leathers' rawboned face, burned red by the sun, craned forward a bit to see past Daisy. "Soon there will be political parties taking these issues direct to the ballot box."

"That's okay with me," Waddell drawled. "Just so long's the niggers don't vote." He paused, and his normally loose glance—which seemed to imply that he was either immensely bored by the conversation or had his hand under the table fondling Daisy or Luanne—seemed to sharpen. "Luanne says when her paw died she got that five-hundred-acre tract back near the salty lake. It's nothing but hardscrabble and snakes, and worthless as a fiddler's bitch, but for charity's sake I might be persuaded to take it off your hands."

"You just might"—Leathers smiled—"if it was for sale. But it ain't."

"That a fact? I heard you maybe got cousin trouble," Waddell mused aloud.

"People do talk."

"So it maybe ain't Luanne's land to sell?"

"Set your pea brain to rest on that one, Ringo," Leathers assured him. "She owns it."

"Shall the gentlemen adjourn," Badger suggested, "to the library?"

The younger men looked at him as if he had two heads. Then slowly Waddell got the drift. "Guess so," he said graciously, getting to his feet. "Will you ladies excuse us?"

He led the way to the liquor cabinet in the next room. For a moment he stood in moody contemplation of the cut-glass decanters there. "This here," he announced at last, touching the left-hand container, "is good Monongahela rye we get regular, by the keg. Cuts like a diamond. That there pizen is five-year corn whiskey they make over in Shreveport. And this dark paint is Tennessee sour mash, sweet as pure love." He paused judiciously and slowly tapped the colorless liquid in the right-hand decanter. "This here snake-killer's a cane whiskey the darkies make. They call it jake leg, on account if it don't turn you stone blind, it gives you the staggers. Sort of like a rum, I'd say. And it's my personal preference."

He poured four fingers of the water-clear liquid into a tumbler. "Your pleasure, Mr. Badger, sir?"

Things got confused after that, at least from Ned's viewpoint. He remembered Mike Leathers and Ringo Waddell carrying Badger up the stairs and tucking him away for the night, an early victim of the jake leg.

After a while, only Ned and Mike were in the room. Ned had no idea where the rest had gone, but it didn't seem that important at the moment. "F'y'held a gun t'm'head," Mike Leathers stated somewhat hazily, "I would be forced t'vote fer that there Tennessee sour mash, so I would. But don't tell nobody, you hear?"

Ned nodded slowly and very sagely. Affair of state. Louisiana legislator couldn't confess yearning for Tennessee whiskey. "Y'know," he told Leathers, "I have met your paw downstate."

"Figured as much. You'n me," Mike said, "we got some powerful hornswogglers for paws, ain't we, now?"

"That is a fact."

"Great, primeval deceivers and betrayers of the voting masses."

Ned laughed. "Primeval. Someday we might just sink the two of 'em."

"Might and will. The tide is turnin', Ned Blood."

"I'd love to believe," Ned assured him solemnly. "I would love to believe. Love to."

"In what?"

"That you are actually a real person. That you can drum up support from others in the legislature." Ned took a long, soothing breath. "That you won't be shot down by some of the planters' hired killers. Or voted down by your own consich . . ." He stopped. "Constitch . . ." He stopped again.

". . . uents," Mike finished.

"Or whatever malign fate lies in store for you," Ned said with sudden clarity, lurching up out of his chair and standing erect. "Maybe you'n I ought to talk some more. Sober."

Leathers got to his feet. "I better round up Luanne. It's a long ride back to Winnfield."

"Y'r not staying th' night?" Ned belched softly and couldn't stand the taste.

"Well, they's only one bedroom free. And I figure the only thing a girl like Luanne has is her reputation. Am I right?"

Ned nodded slowly. "That and those two lovely . . ."

"Well, yes, there's them." Mike Leathers clapped him on the arm. "You come see me. And nary a word to our paws."

Ned stumbled up the long curving flight of stairs and wondered which room was his. With any luck, he might find himself once again in Daisy's bed by mistake.

Grinning, he listened at one door to the long, slow, powerful snores of the man from Fiddoch, Larned. Too bad he was so closemouthed by day, Ned thought. But there was still a lot to be learned from trailing him around. This trip had by no means been a waste of time. The next room would be Daisy's. Ned eased open the door.

"Ringo?" Daisy whispered.

"Aw . . . shit."

6

The pleasant little cottage on Rampart Street was cool on this hot July afternoon. Although its windows stood open, they were shaded by louvered shutters that blocked the sun but let in the breeze. Inside Ynes Fleurigant's bedroom, so large it took up half the house, breezes came from three directions, a masterpiece of planning.

But Edmund Crozat had not left their comfort to the planning of some long-dead architect. Among the various artisans of New Orleans, Edmund had commissioned two devices from plans mailed him from England. One was a contraption called an electromotive engine, with windings of copper wire that whirled a thin metal-bladed fan. Its source of energy was a battery of eight glass jars under the bed containing a liquid in which copper and zinc posts were bathed. It produced an essence called electricity, which ran by wire to the fan.

But the bed rarely needed cooling these days, Ynes reflected. She had been waiting for Edmund for some time now. Of late, he was usually late. The late Sieur de Crozat, she thought. Without help from the electrical engine, their love was cooling off on its own.

On the long wall of the bedroom, between two of the louvered windows, Edmund had last year caused a gigantic mirror to be hung. It had come, Ynes knew, from one of the sporting houses in town which had partially burned down. Men just naturally got rowdy and careless with matches in such places.

She stared at herself in the mirror now, seeing her pale body, clothed in the thinnest of coffee-colored *peau de soie*, which through its diaphanous folds displayed her much lighter skin, cream seen through brown, the whole framed by the large ornate bed and, finally, by the intricately carved gold-leaf contortions of the mirror's cornice.

It was a frieze of cupids and arrows, but in the time she had spent over the past year or so waiting for Edmund, Ynes had had ample opportunity to know that never once had the carver repeated himself. Each cupid was different. The whole must have cost Edmund quite a bit of money.

Not cheap, the Crozats. Poor old Amalia Rassac, now half-blind and in her fifties, had been pensioned off as mistress to Edmund's father with a quite handsome monthly stipend. And Edmund, who had come into money of his own at twenty-five, left by his paternal grandfather, never hesitated to spend whatever she asked of him for the cottage, her dresses, their meals here, and even something for her to put away for her old age.

What more could a quadroon ask? Ynes wanted to know as she lay there waiting. It wasn't as if marriage had ever been in the cards. In a long history of Creole-quadroon relationships, some of which lasted longer than most marriages, not once was there a thought of the man marrying his quadroon.

She shrugged, and her beautifully formed breasts swung sideways within the coffee-colored *peau de soie*. She stared at her face under the intricate dark curls she spent so much time on. No doubt about it, she was the prettiest of the quadroons.

Her pale gray eyes were startling enough, but she had learned how to make them even more memorable by faintly darkening her lashes and brows. Her nose—really her best asset—had the aquiline quality that any Creole would covet. Ynes' mother had the same nose, narrow, with thin oval nostrils that flared when she was angry. Her mother had explained that this was because their ancestors had come from the deserts of Araby.

However she came by it, Ynes had her beauty and little else these days. Edmund had grown preoccupied with business.

It was not another woman. Ynes had her ways of knowing this. It truly was business, and it took him away from her as surely as if it were indeed another love.

She watched her face, relaxing the faint moue of discontent she saw there. No lines, girl. If it wasn't a woman, then it didn't matter. Edmund would be hers for the rest of his life, body and soul. It often happened so. A man already married to business remained faithful to his quadroon until death.

This was even more true when they had children. She and Edmund had somehow avoided that, but it was inevitable, was it not? And Edmund would be as generous with the children as with her, perhaps leaving bequests in their name on his death, or surely sending them to fine schools back east or in France.

She and Edmund had been children themselves when first they met. It was only natural that at some point there should be a slight cooling down of their ardor.

But coming together at such a young age had a mystic significance of its own, Ynes believed. They had together taught each other all the mysteries of sex, the intimate sharing of each other's bodies, slowly, deeply, in ways that perhaps no one else had ever before enjoyed.

She smiled at her own naiveté. Surely she and Edmund had invented nothing new. But in the process of discovering everything that could be enjoyed, they had joined souls. Yes, clearly, that was it. Their souls were one. Edmund could journey to the ends of the earth on his secret searches, but his soul could never for a moment leave her bedside.

Ynes watched herself in the mirror. She began to fondle her breasts through the diaphanous fabric. The faint friction aroused her.

She heard a key in the outer lock. A moment later, Edmund's boots cracked across the parlor floor. He opened the bedroom door slowly and watched her continue to caress herself.

"*Charmant,*" he murmured.

"As you desire me, *mon brave.*"

He took a step into the room and closed the door behind him. Then he opened a small cupboard and removed a glass tumbler and a bottle with a bright green liquid in it. From a pitcher he poured water into the tumbler. Then he let a trickle of the green fluid flow into the water. A milky cloud spread through the tumbler, and a sharp, powerful odor of anise filled the bedroom.

Ynes watched without speaking. Her lover stood before a tall wicker armchair and held the glass of milky liquid against the faint glow of afternoon sunlight. "There you are, my friend," he said in a low voice almost not meant for her.

"There is ice in the kitchen," Ynes told him.

He shook his head. "Later. For the second drink." He sipped the cloudy fluid. "If there is one."

"But you may have as many as you wish."

"Normally, yes. But this evening my esteemed parents . . ." He paused and sipped again. The tumbler was now half-empty. "My esteemed parents are paying a formal visit to my apartment."

Ynes suppressed her sudden feeling of anger. He came less and less often, and when he did, he had to hurry away. Nevertheless she slid gracefully off the bed, removed his jacket, and loosened the cravat around his ruffled white shirtfront. Then she knelt and unfastened his embroidered suspender braces while he finished his drink and removed his shirt. He sank back into a wicker chair and she pulled off his boots, then his trousers, and finally the underbreeches that came to his knees. Slowly she caressed the calves of his legs, and then his thighs.

"You are terribly tense."

"Just the new mount. He's not used to me. I have to keep showing him who is master and who is horse."

The strangest thought lodged in Ynes' brain. I am his mount, she told herself, and he knows it. And *he* knows *I* know it. He is thinking the same thing even as I think it. We are one. We will always be one.

"Your filly is in sore need of riding," she murmured.

His eyelids flickered. So he *had* been thinking the same thing. But instead of admitting it—these Creoles admitted nothing—he closed his eyes and sank back farther in the chair. "It's been a long day," he said. "You ride me."

Without further comment she stood up and let the *peau de soie* slide from her shoulders to a rich puddle of folds on the floor. Naked, she opened his eyes by lightly touching each lid. He stared up at her breasts, then slowly down to her navel and the thick puff of dark curly hair beneath it.

She leaned forward to bury his face between her breasts, moving slowly, with a light touch. He had cupped his hands around her buttocks. Now she put a knee to either side of him and squatted on his lap, facing him. He could feel the crinkly pubic hairs caress his penis as she moved slowly forward and back. He groaned softly. Their glances were locked, but at the groin they were rubbing against each other now. She could feel his penis spring to life and begin to probe for an opening.

She drew back out of range. He frowned. She moved forward and began the teasing again. Once more he tried to enter her, and again she withdrew. "You are a true little devil," he muttered in that crackling voice of his.

She stood up and moved to the bed. *"Fais dodo,"* she ordered, sitting on the edge of the mattress.

Moving in an almost hypnotic trance, he sank forward to his knees on the floor and began kissing the crisp mound of dark, curly hair.

He reached the Pontalba Apartments with half an hour to spare before the arrival of Maman and Papa. The problem was not to have everything in readiness. Edmund's butler would have seen to that, and in any event, Olivia had arrived, making sure there were flowers and chipping ice by hand for the Sazeracs their father required.

No, the problem was Papa. Now that Edmund was in a modest way independent of the main lode of Crozat millions, Papa had become querulous.

No Creole son, not even one who longed for freedom as Edmund did, would lightly turn his back on the full weight of his inheritance when Papa shuffled off this mortal coil and retired to the great counting house in the sky, as Olivia sometimes called it. But the control was less total. The full murderous weight no longer pressed Edmund's nose into the earth. His grandfather's modest bequest was enough to shake Papa's confidence. So he had become a nag.

Edmund's apartment occupied a floor-through at one end of the long Pontalba building, the northern one that faced its sister across Jackson Square, with Old Hickory astride a rearing horse, tipping his hat in tribute to the scene of his finest hour, the defense of New Orleans against the British in 1814.

With three exposures fronting on the river, and the help of a larger version of the electromotive machine, Edmund's four-room apartment was cool enough, even though it occupied the second floor of the Pontabla and had no sunshade gallery to protect it, as the ground floor did. His parlor stretched almost fifty feet, and half as wide, with Olivia's "musicale" corner taking up one end, an ebony Pleyel pianoforte, some music stands, potted palms, slim bentwood chairs, and a deep russet violoncello negligently tilted against the wall.

As Edmund let himself into the apartment and surveyed it, he realized that more than the music corner was Olivia's. In fact, bit by bit she had turned it from the rather Spartan quarters he had first installed into a charming retreat, with good rosewood tables, walnut chairs with cane seats, an *escritoire* of intricate burl that opened into a whiskey chest, and, everywhere today, flowers. The effect was still masculine enough, Edmund knew, but hardly the look he would have chosen for himself, in which the only decoration would have been newspapers and magazines scattered about the room where he dropped them.

At the doorway of the parlor, where the entry foyer led into it, stood a small table on which sat an unusual instrument, the first telephone to be installed in the Crescent City. Edmund had few fellow subscribers to this unusual—and in most people's view, unnecessary—service. But it gave him pleasure to look at it, or to lend it to Jed Benjamin on occasion, when the impresario had to call a prospective patron. One day, Edmund knew, like the electromotive fan and the cylindrical Edison phonograph in the music corner, these inventions would be worth having.

Olivia came up behind him as he stood there, and pecked his cheek under his ear. He flinched, startled. "You move too softly," he complained.

"All Creole belles move on gossamer."

He turned to her. The effect was like staring into a reducing mirror, his own face gazing up at him in smaller form, framed in dark hair parted in the middle and pulled firmly down over her ears before waving back into a chignon.

"Et Papa . . . Maman?"

"Tôt ou tard." She moved past him into the parlor and did a small dance figure, arms out, ending in a turn that wrapped her arms around her while her feet took the first position. "I gave Thomas the evening off. You don't mind?"

"But who will serve?"

"Trust me, Edmund. In Papa's frame of mind, you do not want to remind him that you squander your patrimony on butlers and such."

"Grandpa-trimony," Edmund corrected her with a lopsided smile. "If I wait for my patrimony, I wait another quarter of a century, Livy. Crozat *père* is a healthy man in his middle years."

"Unlike *pauvre* Amalia. Early senility. How Papa must have used her. *Un veritable animal, hein?"*

Edmund produced the Crozat frown. "Loose talk."

She danced off across the parquet floor, making shooing motions with her slender arms. "I trust," she added in the middle of an entrechat, "that you use Ynes more kindly?"

"You are a goose, Livy. You must never—" He stopped, hearing the peal of his front doorbell. Whatever behavior he was proscribing, Olivia would never know. The two of them went to the door and threw it open.

"Bienvenue!"

"Allors," Papa Crozat said, advancing into the room and pompously shaking Edmund's hand.

This was not his first visit to the Pontalba rooms, but the first since they had been fully furnished. He took a small turn on tiny feet enclosed in patent-leather boots, and escorted forward into the foyer the former Ana Almonaster-Nunes, his bride of almost thirty years, with a pedigree only slightly shorter than his own.

He presented his wife to her son and daughter as if all three were strangers, all the while preening his Napoleon III mustache, which, like his thick head of hair, was as resolutely black as discreet coloring could make it.

Ana Crozat curtsied, although there was a faintly ironic look in her eye which both her children recognized, a look that said "how stuffy these French can be." She was more of their generation than her husband's, having been just short of her sixteenth birthday when she delivered Edmund to the world.

The birth had been greeted with almost as much reverence as one in

Bethlehem nineteen centuries before. To have bound the Crozat fortunes to those of the Almonaster-Nunes was an event most Creole families considered global in impact.

There had been a Crozat at the founding of New Orleans, or shortly thereafter, who had received from Louis XIV a royal franchise in 1712 to operate Louisiana as a commercial enterprise. This he did by selling slaves and combing France's jails and bordellos for likely white emigrants, kidnapping the unwilling ones when necessary. It was not until 1769, when Carlos III of Spain sent General Don Alexander O'Reilly and twenty-four warships to take possession of the city, that the first Almonaster-Nunes arrived, to become a *regidor* of the *cabildo* who held the title of *alcalde*.

With O'Reilly's approval, he also headed the secret group of assassins known as the Santa Hermandad. This saintly brotherhood of night riders murdered Jews, Protestants, heretics, and other undesirables, confiscating their property for the greater glory of Spain, or in this case, Almonaster-Nunes himself. The blood money bought ships. Over the next century, despite the depredations of Laffite and other corsairs, half a hundred Almonaster-Nunes hulls plied the Caribbean and the Atlantic crossing, carrying cotton, coffee, sugar, and tobacco to the Old World and returning gunwale-deep with slaves.

The last of this freebooting line was a dainty lady in her early forties, with dark eyes and an ever-present mantilla of the finest handmade lace. She had dozens, airy *punto in aria* designs from Venice, braided Honiton from England, diamond-meshed Alençon and Valenciennes from France, and the fine crochet of Ireland. On her marriage, she had surrendered her entire family inheritance to her husband, as was the custom. It was from her household allowance that she saved to buy these expensive bits of fanciful design, her only true possessions.

"Please," Edmund said, turning sideways and executing a kind of commedia dell'arte bow and flourish as he indicated his parlor. "Maman, *un petit café?*"

She ducked her head in a birdlike gesture of assent, her glance still ironic. *"Pourquoi pas?"*

"I shall make it," Olivia said, heading for the kitchen.

Opening his *escritoire*, Edmund surveyed the supply of liquors there and noted that Olivia had filled the cork ice chest, tin-lined, with chips from a larger piece. "The usual?" he asked his father.

"There is nothing usual about a well-made Sazerac."

The elder Crozat had a precise, didactic manner of speech, as if reading his lines from a book of great universal authority. Edmund nodded gravely and put ice into two short, heavy crystal tumblers. In two others he poured bourbon and vermouth over sugar lumps and added a dash or two of bitters. He put ice in these glasses, then turned back to the now-chilled tumblers, from which he removed the ice. He swirled two fat drops of absinthe in each until the liquor coated the inside of the chilled glasses. The odor of anise arose. At last he poured in the cold contents of the other pair of tumblers and twisted a zest of lemon peel over each.

Face still grave—the ironic gravity of his mother, perhaps—he presented one tumbler to his father. "Your good health, sir."

Crozat *père* sampled the Sazerac daintily, like a cat testing cream. Then he gave a curt nod. "Adequate," he announced, and began serious sipping of his drink.

Olivia returned with a tray on which a small pewter pot and two demitasse cups sat, already filled with dark coffee, gently steaming. Edmund knew they also held an ounce of brandy each. It was Mother's private weakness, as it was of many another Creole lady. It could be produced discreetly, without the dramatic addition of cinnamon, cloves, orange, and flames that accompanied the true *café brûlot*. And it had the same amount of brandy in it. So, after all, why not?

His father settled back in one corner of an upholstered love seat. He frowned first at his drink, then at its maker. "Is this the full extent of your domestic capabilities?" he demanded then.

Edmund shrugged. "I get along, sir, like any other bachelor."

"Precisely," his father told him. "You scrape along, a notch above the beasts of the field. If we were not generous enough to allow Olivia to oversee your arrangements here, you would be camping in squalor, my boy. Of that you may be certain."

Edmund produced a beautiful replica of his mother's smile. He was interested to hear the way his father justified allowing poor Olivia a tiny crumb of freedom. And he was not about to spoil it for her.

"As you say, sir."

"What I say," Crozat *père* announced, charging the air suddenly with ominous vibrations, "what *I* say is that a man of twenty-six should have been married for several years now. That . . . is what I say."

"But surely it is never too late to marry."

His father cocked his head and rolled one end of his mustache between his thumb and first finger. He sipped his Sazerac with the air of a judge at a contest; the verdict was still not in.

"It is never too early to begin the process," he stated at last. "A Crozat cannot simply run off to Gretna Green like a Protestant Kaintock and marry before a civil official. A Crozat marriage can, and should, take months, even years, before it reaches finality. Do I make myself clear?"

Edmund nodded. The marriage of his father to the Spanish-Portuguese heiress had begun in negotiations when the girl was twelve years of age. Banns had been posted when she was thirteen. Instead of the usual three weeks, the families let a stately year go by before staging one of the largest weddings St. Louis cathedral had ever held. Married at fourteen, pregnant at fifteen, and delivered of Edmund before sixteen. The mills of the Creoles ground slowly, but exceedingly fine.

"You are saying, sir," Edmund interpreted, "that I should begin now to search for a bride?"

"I am saying nothing of the sort." Crozat *père*'s mustache bristled. "Your mother and I have begun that search. In due time you will be informed of its outcome."

Something red and violent flashed behind Edmund's eyes. He tried to calm himself by sipping his drink, but the sweet liquid only seemed to inflame him.

"*You* will inform *me*?" he demanded.

"As is the custom."

Edmund took a deep breath and found that he was trembling. He glanced across at Olivia, who instantly took her cue. "That is the old custom," she piped up at once. "It certainly had its reasons in former days. But we live in very different times now, Papa."

Her father turned coldly to her. "You are forbidden to speak," he said in a dry voice. Then, to his son: "One expects to hear nonsense from an unmarried woman—who is moreover almost beyond the age of matrimony—but you are a man. You understand the need for these traditions."

Edmund had control of himself again. Like a canny duelist, he decided to pink his father from a different angle. "Olivia is twenty-four, *mon père*. She does not lack for suitors. Only the oth—"

"Enough!" Crozat thundered. He rose slowly to his full five-three height. "I know of these unsuitable suitors. Musicians. Poets. Artists. Rabble! Flies buzzing carrion! You, too, are forbidden to speak."

He began pacing the floor. "One child tells me the old ways are passé. The other resists them in his subtle way, which he believes I do not notice." He turned to his wife. "Is this how one talks to one's father?"

Her smile was a thing of pure beauty, "M'sieur Crozat," she informed him, "you have forbidden them both to speak. The floor is entirely yours."

He stared at her, almost getting the irony, then dismissing the idea that his wife would have the intelligence for it. He turned on Edmund. "Be advised, sir," he told his son, "you shall be married within the year, and to the girl of my choosing. That is the final word on the subject."

Edmund glanced past his father to Olivia. He was tired of this petty little tyrant staging his scenes. This was his apartment. With a clear, cold mind he was now about to open a rift that might well become a chasm. This little man had to be taught a lesson. He was a guest here, not a visiting potentate.

"Actually," Edmund said in his low, tense voice, "I had always thought I would marry Olivia."

"*Quoi?*"

"Who else would be worthy of a Crozat?"

His father stared in horror at him, lips working over a series of rejoinders, then dismissing them. He moved to his wife and clutched her arm. "Come. We are not welcome here."

But she resisted the suggestion. "You never could take a joke, Jean-Paul. Edmund has always had a playful sense of humor, as you know."

Crozat *père* frowned first at the lace top of her head, then at his son. "I am not so senile that I cannot recognize insolence when I hear it. Insolence and worse. Scandal."

Before Edmund could respond, Olivia moved between him and his father. "You have been working Edmund very hard, Papa. He never complains, but I can see the signs."

"Work! He steals time from my office for his wild-goose chases. This madness, too, will stop. I have been entirely too liberal. There will be no more of these fruitless adventures. You can tell your brother his search for the *feux-folle* has ended. Forever."

Edmund could feel his right arm trembling with the powerful urge to strike his father across the face. Once, twice. Olivia darted to his side and took the arm in both of hers, smoothing it gently. "You cannot ask him that, Papa."

"Goddammit!" Edmund roared.

He flung his arm clear as if flailing at an insect. "I am standing right here. Me, *moi-même*. Do not address me in the third person, any of you! Take your wives, m'sieur. Take your threats. Remove them from *my* apartment. If you cannot accept my hospitality without insulting it, then you were quite right. You are not welcome here."

A silence settled over all four of them, so similar in appearance, only Edmund a head taller than the rest. He had turned haughtily away and was staring out the window at the river. A keelboat worked its way upstream, tacking from shore to shore against the current. He poured straight absinthe into his glass.

The first to speak was his mother. "Olivia," she said, "will you be good enough to prepare for me another of your very fine coffees?"

"*Oui*, Maman."

"I, for one, am not leaving this place," Ana Almonaster-Nunes Crozat flatly told them. "It is like watching two rams in the season of rut, you two. No one leaves until you have discussed everything calmly, like gentlemen."

Edmund turned back to her. She was watching her husband closely. "Sit down, Jean-Paul," she said then. He hesitated. "Sit down," she repeated. Slowly, he did.

"Edmund," she ordered. "Make another Sazerac for him."

7

The late lunchers at the Wicklowe, having dined in splendor, were sleepily returning to offices where, behind drawn shades, afternoon naps would help settle the five- and six-course meals of which they had partaken, washed down by wine, beer, and spirits.

Most of them would be safely snoozing in their banks, brokerages, and executive offices by three o'clock. Kate Blood usually waited until the last of these somnolent waddlers had cleared the premises before arriving at the Wicklowe to pick up her bodyguard-assistant named Billy O'Hare, a young fellow her father thought could handle himself well enough to accompany Kate on her rounds of the District.

Billy was a wiry lad about Ned's age, twenty or twenty-one, with something of Ned's look about him, quick and slight, but slow to speak. He carried a neat nine-inch cosh in one pocket, weighted with half a pound of lead shot, and he knew exactly where to aim it, in that sensitive area between a man's ear and neck where it produces little in the way of a bruise, but a great amount of sudden sleep.

Billy O'Hare jiggled the reins on the two-wheeled cart Kate preferred to use on her rounds. Hardly more substantial than the sulky used in racing, it was just big enough for the two of them and easy to guide through the narrow streets and traffic jams along Basin Street. Her father would have preferred a four-wheel buggy with leather quarter-top and, perhaps, side curtains as well, behind which his daughter could enjoy her privacy.

To Kate, the silliness of the idea was self-evident. Either you didn't let your daughter in on your business or you did. And once you did, in as thoroughgoing a manner as had Cornelius Blood, there were no longer any questions of privacy, were there?

Kate climbed up beside Billy. "Start at the House of Blue Lights," she told him. "I hear the head barman, Doheny, has been watering the rum with sugar water. Have you heard the same thing?"

"Yes, miss." O'Hare slapped the reins, and the cart jolted forward. Billy's accent was so thick that the words came out "Yuss, muss," but by now Kate was quite used to any of the ways in which her fellow New Orleanians spoke the common tongue.

"He expects me an hour from now," Kate mused as the cart rattled along the rutted cobbles. "And if I know Doheny, he just woke up. So we'll drop in on him while the sugar water's running free."

"Doheny won't enjoy that at all." O'Hare let out a thin hiss that was supposed to signal laughter. He was slight enough in build so that the sap in his pocket caused him to sit off-center as he drove the trap.

Kate sat back and surveyed the District. Slowly, it was coming awake. Most of its denizens and workers hadn't gotten to sleep until dawn. Only important owners like Neil Blood regulated their waking and sleeping patterns to match those of the respectable investors for whom they fronted. The sign of a truly successful owner was that he kept bankers' and brokers' hours.

"Dainty ribbons," a street vendor called.

"Dainty bows.

"Dainty fingers;

"Dainty toes."

By half-past four Kate and O'Hare had finished their rounds and were returning down Basin to the Wicklowe. "Did you believe Doheny, miss?" the young man asked.

"That it was flavoring?" Kate laughed. "Did you ever hear any sailor call for sweet rum? If a man wants it sweet, he takes it as punch, I'd say."

O'Hare nodded thoughtfully. "You shoulda let me whack him one."

Kate shook her head. "Doheny's a head and a half taller than you, Bill. He knows I'm onto him. If he knows he's being watched, that's nine-tenths of the battle."

Billy frowned and thought for a long time. "It's easy to see where Mr. Neil's brains have been mostly inherited, miss," he said in a suddenly reverential tone. "Me, I'm for whackin' sense into 'em. But your way's smarter, so it is."

"Till Doheny starts watering the booze again." In the distance, Kate caught a glimpse of Edmund Crozat, on foot, moving in her direction. "Slow us to a walk, Billy."

A few moments later the trap met Crozat at the corner of Conti. With a gesture, Kate ordered its progress halted. Gazing down on Edmund Crozat was a novelty for her. She smiled. "I almost failed to recognize you, sir, without your horse."

Crozat doffed his hat. "That's a fast little cart you have, Miss Blood. I shouldn't think Basin is the right course for speed, however."

Kate made as if to step down, forcing Edmund to help her descend onto the cobbles. His fingers on her arm were hard, but a peculiar tremor made her wonder if he were shaking, or she. It seemed to come from outside them, a faraway rumble as of heat lightning. "Take the rig back, Billy," Kate called. O'Hare snapped the reins and rattled off.

"It's not speed I'm after, Mr. Crozat," she said then, as if nothing had happened. "It's maneuverability."

Edmund nodded solemnly. "Quite so. On your appointed rounds, maneuverability must be a major consideration."

Kate frowned. "Is that meant unkindly?"

Edmund's dark eyes opened wide. "In no manner, dear Miss Blood. Just that your mission is one of . . . ah, delicacy and responsibility, is it not?"

"It is."

She glanced up at his impassive ivory-skinned face with its Creole tinge across the cheekbones. A faint aroma of anise surrounded him, not unpleasantly. "I had no idea you took such notice of my comings and goings, sir."

"I would hardly be a faithful son of New Orleans if I did not note the progress of one of her most attractive daughters."

The afternoon sun heated her face. Kate stepped onto the banquette and stood in the welcome shadow, as did Edmund. "I suppose," she said then, "that my work must occasion a certain amount of attention. And talk."

"It is part of the routine of the Quarter. Few have any comment to make."

"And if they did?"

Edmund's extraordinary eyes burned softly. "And if they did?" he echoed.

"What then would they say of me?" Kate finished.

"I have no idea, Miss Blood, what the common tongue says of you."

"Then you yourself."

He gestured uneasily. His long fingers groped the air shakily. "I do not presume to judge."

"What, never? Have you never discussed me with your sister, who was for so many years my classmate at the convent?"

"We may have." He was trying for a light tone and finding it hard to come by. He stood with his back to a rose-brick wall. Now he leaned against it, as if for support.

"You must understand that New Orleans is a very provincial town, Miss Blood. You and I have, in a sense, grown up together in this quarter or another nearby. We have passed each other a hundred times a year on these streets. We have seen each other grow from childhood to maturity, much as if we were distant members of the same family." He paused. His eyes looked blank now.

"And yet," he went on almost reluctantly, "what do we know of each other, or of the hundreds more whom we greet as we pass by? We are more than acquaintances, less than friends. For me to comment on your rounds, your work, is presumptuous in the extreme."

"Unless I ask for it."

"Ah. As to that . . ." He stopped, frowning. "It occurs to me that you are a very catlike opponent, Miss Blood. I feel as if I am in court and you are the prosecuting attorney."

Kate managed as big a smile as she could. "Surely we are acquaintances on the way to becoming friends. I harbor no thoughts of you but friendly ones."

"You remove a great load from my heart, Miss Blood."

"But friends are frank with friends. It may be good practice for you to be frank with me. What *do* they say of my working for my father?"

"One cannot choose one's family," he blurted out.

They stared at each other, impaled on the sharp tone in which Edmund had voiced his thought. "I speak of my own life," he hurried on. "I feel the burden of family only too keenly. It is not in me to find fault with someone else who is caught in the same toils of family duty."

Kate watched him for a long moment. They had never before spoken to each other as they had in the last minutes. On no account must she let the intimate note die away. She had never heard him speak of his family before. He had apparently been drinking absinthe—but he clearly was not drunk.

"In Chicago and New York," she began then, "I am told that women my age do office work for weekly salaries. Suppose I were not the daughter of Cornelius Blood, but performed my duties in return for a salary from him. What would you say of me then?"

He laughed helplessly, letting his hands fall to his sides. "I *am* on trial, am I not? And no one has read me the charge."

"No, it's I who am curious," Kate explained, "to know what people think of me."

"And it is my misfortune to happen along at such a moment, is that it?"

She nodded. "Precisely."

He sighed unsteadily. His expression grew more serious. "I question the whole idea of giving a young girl a convent education and then sending her out among the lowest swine on earth."

"Oh."

"Yes."

"I did ask for that," Kate murmured.

"I hold very conventional opinions, Miss Blood. I believe in shielding women from this kind of filth. I believe that unless we do so, we forfeit any right to hope for progress. Women are the begetters and educators of the next generation. If they cannot be shielded from the horrors of today, what kind of tomorrow can we hope for?"

Kate nodded slowly. His viewpoint, which she had heard before, managed to put the best possible face on what was otherwise sheer male hypocrisy. The problem of replying was complicated by the fact that where something has been made too much of a mystery, people will naturally try to fathom it. Many women had.

What went on in the lounges and cribs of the District—perhaps not in the technical detail Kate knew it—was not unknown to respectable women. Thus hypocrisy answered hypocrisy. Hadn't Kate herself had much of it explained in behind-the-hand gossip at the Convent of the Sacred Heart?

"Your opinion does you credit," she said at last. "But shielding women from reality only . . ." She paused and gestured helplessly. "It is a matter of barriers," she said then. "Of barriers to the flow of communication between husband and wife."

He grinned crookedly. "And is either of us such an authority on married life, Miss Blood?"

"You touch me there," she responded, like a duelist being pinked. "But I think you and I are rather better observers than most people. And we have observed a few marriages in our time, have we not?"

He eyed her speculatively. Kate assumed he was wondering just how much she knew of his past reputation as a famous cuckolder of husbands and a much-sought-out opponent in duels of honor.

"A very American view of marriage," Edmund said at last, giving the nationality a peculiar stress. "I have heard of such marriages in the East and North. A sort of love partnership. But I need hardly remind you that here we live in a different world."

Kate sighed. "We do indeed."

"Perhaps a world whose time is passing," he went on quietly. "But surely not in our time, Miss Blood. And until it does, there is no room in the conventional New Orleans marriage for such luxuries as . . . ah, communication."

She gave him a startled look, and he had the good grace to produce a self-deprecating smile. Only a flash of it, Kate noted. "Yes," she said finally, "it is the American idea of marriage. And the last I heard, this city of ours was still part of America."

He threw his head back and laughed. "You are a truly formidable prosecutor!"

Several passersby stopped to find out what was so amusing. Edmund grimaced at them. "Rather an intimate conversation for such a public place," he muttered. "I'm afraid I lost myself just then in admiration of your . . . ah, spunk." He considered the word. "Spunk. Yes. There is something in a Creole upbringing that breeds the spunk out of our demure little brunettes."

"I seem to remember Olivia had a mind of her own."

But he wasn't listening to her. "Someday we may indeed join the United States again, but I won't welcome it."

"Why should you?" she countered. "Right now men have everything to their complete satisfaction. Little wifey at home, minding the children, gay female companions to roister with in the District, and a mistress tucked away on Ramp—" She stopped herself.

His face had gone absolutely dead. She looked down and watched the way his fingers, clamped on the broad brim of his panama hat, were crushing the woven straw. Then she looked up into his eyes. A flame kindled behind them, but only for an instant. Then it died and his face went gray again, as if with fatigue.

"As you say." He took a step back from her and stood in the sunlight, eyes narrowing against the glare. He looked almost ill, Kate thought.

"I'm sorry."

"Don't apologize," he told her. "You're an unusual young woman, Miss Blood. Through an accident of fate, you have access to more of the truth of life than any of us need. It has made you . . ." He paused.

"Too talkative," Kate suggested.

He smiled charmingly. "Too incisive," he amended. "And much too wise."

He lifted the white straw a bit unsteadily, dipped it to her, placed it on his head, and walked off along Basin in the opposite direction from the Wicklowe.

8

It was Cornelius Blood's "easy" time, between five and six in the afternoon, when no one but Kate could interrupt him. This privacy was enforced by a crusher of grandiose proportions, one Luca Sgroi, an emigrant from Palermo with a glandular condition that made him even taller than his boss. Luca stood six and a half feet in height, very little of it fat. He was not, however, fast on his feet, and Ned Blood was.

Always had been. On this September afternoon he gave the Sicilian giant a big grin, sidestepped deftly, and got inside his father's office, where, presented with this fait accompli, his own six-foot-tall father wearily waved Luca off and turned to his youngest son with a look of ineffable wariness.

"What now?" he growled.

Ned sat down in one of the immense captain's chairs upholstered in morocco leather and studded with nailheads said to be gold. "Just a family chat," he said, holding up his hands on either side as if to show he carried no concealed weapon.

"Though it pains me to say so," Neil Blood announced, "of me own flesh and blood, you are a royal pain in the behind. Stop playing games with Luca and get the hell out of here."

"Is this the celebrated Blood hospitality?" Ned countered. "The Unofficial Greeter of New Orleans? The Shadow Mayor of the Crescent City? The Éminence Grise of our fair metropolis?"

"Ah, shut yer gob," Blood said in a disgusted tone.

76

"Ever since I was a little kid, your slogan was always, 'when you talk to me, shut up.' The only one who'd listen to me was Katie."

"Another cross," Neil agreed moodily, "for that fair lass to bear. What *is* it, Neddie? And make it sudden."

Ned sat forward. "Now, you know our deal, Da. I don't write about your business, just everybody else's. But there's a rumor the city's expecting royalty."

Neil Blood sat back in his own captain's chair and stroked his bushy blond mustache. Royalty itself was no novelty either for the city or for him. Whoever visited New Orleans, be he U.S. senator, crown prince, or heavyweight champion, was taken for his first call to the Wicklowe and only later to one of Neil's better houses and classier girls.

"There's always rumors," he said in a negligent tone.

"But they're what I live on, Da. Once I get it backed up with facts, a rumor makes nice green simoleons for yours truly."

Blood winced. He had no use for the new way of talking, most of which his youngest son either invented or picked up before anyone else. And as for making your living off words, what kind of nonsense was that?

When he'd fled the Famine in '51, a skinny lad of fifteen, Neil's first job in New Orleans had been loading and unloading bales at the docks. They had slaves to do it, but slaves cost more to feed and maintain than Irishmen. For busting your gut from sunup to dusk, helping heave four-teen-hundred-pound bales, Paddy got a dollar a day. It was his lookout whether he could stay alive on that. He was no man's property, thank you. He was a free man.

But Neil Blood had the brains to see that a brothel runner got two dollars a day for light, fast work, steering customers, carrying messages, watching out for any police who hadn't been paid off and were looking to be greased. You met a better class of people, and pretty soon, as your muscles toughened, you graduated to bouncer. Then, with a partner, you opened a barrelhouse. The rest was easy for a lad with his eye on the main chance.

He had always had that, even back in starving County Wicklowe. It is sometimes thus: a man outsized in body has the gift of unusual intelli-gance as well. Neil had only to see the bubbling stew-pot that was New Orleans to know that a man with the gift of gab and a clear insight into what moved other men could make himself rich. In this greedy scramble of a city, he would also have to make others rich in order to better himself. For such a large man, that was small dues to pay.

But along the way, you really worked, not this silly scribbling Ned did, scrounging around for rumors. Neil knew, for example, that at least three royal travelers were due in the next few days, singly, with hush-

hush retinues. The least of them was Plon Plon, the impotent Prince Napoleon, hardly a claim to much royal sucession there. The two important boys were a lad named Nicholas, whom they called the Czarevich, crown prince of Russia. And the other was a certain Mr. Windham of London, one name under which the Prince of Wales sometimes traveled.

"Tell me a little more about the rumor," he asked his son.

"Big," Ned responded. "Will soon be king or emperor or something grand."

Neil Blood nodded noncommittally. Probably Edward Saxe-Coburg Windsor himself, who'd been waiting a hell of a while for the old queen to die. "No," he lied to Ned, "nothing like that coming down the pike in the near future."

"Da," Ned said. "You're a hard man to bargain with."

"I have nothing to tell you, Neddie."

"What if I told you Alderman Larkin has been euchred out of his eight-percent ownership in Willie Piazza's house? And the Matranga boys have replaced him."

Blood leaned forward. "The Black Handers bought out Larkin, did they?"

"Forced out."

"Who knows this, Neddie?"

"Larkin. Tony Matranga. And me."

The master of the Wicklowe sat back with a grunt. "Okay. It's the Prince of Wales himself, due here on the packet from Southampton tomorrow evening. Traveling under the name Windham."

Ned grinned and leaned forward to shake his father's hand. "I knew you had a price, you devil."

Neil waved off the handshake. "Now be off with you."

Ned got to his feet, smiling faintly. "I wonder . . ." he said then. He watched his father reject, then take up the bait.

"Wonder what?"

"What information I would need to trade you for the secret of the new reform government."

Neil Blood's pale blue eyes stared up at his youngest son. "What in hell's name does that mean?"

"You and a few of your higher-placed cronies are going to topple the corrupt ring that's run New Orleans—meaning you and your cronies—and replace it with a reform group as pure as refined sugar. And the voters are going to believe it, too."

His father sat silent for a moment. "Ned," he said then in a heavy voice, "sit down. There is one problem we have to get together on."

"Yes?"

"Katie."

Ned sat down. "What's the matter, Da?"

"She ain't herself, not by a mile she ain't. She's gone all moody and tearful. It's been going on a year or more, but lately it's getting worse."

Ned Blood thought for a while. "I've seen it," he agreed then. "So has Jimmy."

"Father James the scholastic," Neil Blood retorted, "is the last person I'd go to for this kind of advice. Jebbies only have one answer. Of all me kids, Neddie, though you're a loafer and a blatherskite, you've got an idea of the world and what makes it go round. And so does Katie. And I know youse two are close. So I'm appealing to you, son."

The journalist made the same empty-hands gesture with which he'd greeted his father. "I can only guess. And you won't like it."

"I don't have to like it. Cough it up."

"Love."

Both men sat there contemplating the word for a long time. It seemed to reverberate in the walnut-paneled room, then sink without a trace into the thick Persian carpet. Outside, a small dray clattered by on Basin Street.

"Fix yer pots," the tinker cried.

"Fix yer pans.

"Fix 'em wid

"Me own two han's."

The older man was the first to stir. "If it's Larkin's pup, Timmy, you can ease your mind. Kate has never loved the man."

"No, someone else."

"That planter from Placquemines? What's the impediment, then? I don't mind having a planter in the family."

"We're not talking about what you want, Da. We're talking about what Katie wants and can't have."

"The hell you say. She can have any man she fancies."

Ned paused to reconsider. "You're talking about it like a business deal. I'm talking about what they call passion."

His father's eyes narrowed. "It's hurting her, is it? Who's the man?"

"Did she ever tell you about the time a Yankee soldier nearly killed me?" Ned asked.

"Better luck to the Yank next time," Neil Blood growled. "I'm asking who is the man that's hurting Katie."

"It's the fellow who saved me."

"His name?"

"Pa, there's nothing between them. Nothing on his side at all. It's in

Katie's heart. She's never spoken of it straight out. But the one time I saw them together, I knew. And then, just the other day, she kind of hinted that she thought I might sort of bring him around some evening. And another thing, she doesn't know I followed her because I was worried what she was up to. It was a novena she made. To St. Roch," he added significantly.

"Who's the man?"

"I said you wouldn't like it."

"Who?"

"Edmund Crozat."

Neil Blood rose halfway out of his chair, pale eyes bulging. "That puffed-up dandy? That . . ." He paused. "And he's a crony of yours," he added as a final insult.

"You haven't any idea of Edmund Crozat," Ned told him. "Nobody does."

"That sassy quadroon of his has the answers."

"Pa, it's not what anybody thinks of him except Katie. And she loves him."

Blood collapsed in his chair. "That's the lay of it, is it?" he muttered. "Novenas, is it? St. Roch." His face looked stricken, and suddenly, without warning, he buried it in his arms, folded forward on his desk top. A faint mewing sound came from somewhere beneath his mass of blond curly hair.

Ned bent forward. "Da?"

"She's ruined," Neil moaned indistinctly. "I have ruined the poor dear girl with my greed."

"Da?"

"I forced her into this when she was too young to understand it. For my greed, Neddie, because I could trust her and I needed someone I could trust."

"Da . . ."

"I forced her into the dirt, Neddie. To squander her tender years in the service of greed and lewdness and . . ." His voice gave out as he began sobbing.

Ned watched for a moment, then sat back and waited. When the sobbing had run its course, he saw his father's head lift very slightly. One startling blue eye, rimmed now in red, regarded him tentatively.

"Very good, Da," the journalist told him. "You do that crying thing very well."

Neil Blood threw himself back in his chair and sluiced the tears from his face as if they were sweat. "Heartless, scandalmongering pipsqueak." He took an immense red bandanna from his desk drawer and sponged his face and hands dry. "Them's real tears. More'n you'd ever shed."

Ned nodded. "A father's tears," he agreed. "Necessary detail. Now, about Katie, you agree Crozat is out of the question?"

"As a husband? Of course."

"Then we'll have to come up with someone else." A long silence followed. "Unless Crozat could be a possibility after all?"

"Never."

"He's quite a fellow, Da. He dreams big. Like you."

"Never." But the word was said almost absentmindedly, as if Neil Blood's thoughts had moved on.

His gaze shifted from his son to a framed photograph on his desk of John L. Sullivan, the Boston Strong Boy, clad in trunks, a view taken in 1882 when he won the world bare-knuckle championship in nearby Mississippi City from Paddy Ryan in nine rounds. In a strong, thick script, the photograph was inscribed: "To me finest Fenian friend, Neil."

The Shadow Mayor of New Orleans seemed to be staring through the picture at the middle distance beyond. "I know Katie," he said then. "She looks soft and pretty, but underneath, when she sets her mind on something . . ." He failed to finish the thought.

Ned got to his feet. "You're putting the brain to work, Da. Let me know when I can help." He started for the door, but stopped with his hand on the knob. "Oh, and by the way, that was as neat a way of not telling me about the reform government as I've ever seen."

He left, intending to give the door a firm slam behind him, but stopped when he saw who Luca Sgroi was holding at bay.

"Ned, my boy," Christy Leathers called. "This Cerebrus has me by the throat."

The journalist grinned at Leathers, a tall, lanky man who was never seen in sunlight, to anyone's knowledge, but who nevertheless maintained a turkey-red face and neck to go with the country galluses and boots he affected. Ned knew him as the man one had to see in order to buy the required number of legislative votes at Baton Rouge.

"If you want to see my father, he's officially not in."

"Tell this anthropoid I am your father's friend."

"I met Mike upstate the other day."

"Ned, that's nice, but this ape . . ."

Ned shrugged. "*Luca, per favore, lascia.*"

The big Sicilian grunted something and let go of Christy Leathers' scrawny neck, but kept a grip on his right arm. "I do admire your way with foreign lingo," Leathers said, "but what do you have to tell him so's I get some blood flowing in my right arm?"

Neil Blood came to the open door of his office. "Luca," he called. The big man let Leathers go and retired rather huffily to his post near the outer door with a kind of "let-them-make-up-their-minds" air of grievance.

Leathers flexed his right arm a few times and massaged his neck. "Well, nice seeing you, Ned," he said, pushing past him and taking Neil Blood with him into the inner office. The door slammed shut.

They went to the window and looked out on Basin Street. The same height, it would have taken two dried-out, sun-cured Christy Leatherses to make one sleekly plump Neil Blood. But their arms were around each other's shoulders as they watched Ned saunter out into the street.

"Let that boy of yours get well out of earshot," Leathers said. "He must be as big a thorn in your side as Mike is in mine." The two men waited.

"Gone," Leathers said. "Now, look here, Neil, you've got to do something about that damned fat Duffy woman."

"Bricktop?"

"I am referring to a Carolina Duffy, a fat nasty madam who happens to come from my home parish, up Winn way. But that's not my connection with the case." The skinny man turned and sat on the corner of Blood's substantial desk. "It's Representative Jack Bunch, from Caddo Parish, near Shreveport."

Blood frowned. "Heard he had an accident."

"That's one way of putting it. You know, Neil, there is nothing like a Protestant sinner. Take it from me, who counts himself one. You Catholics can spit it all out at confession, but we Protestants . . ." He paused and gestured peculiarly, as if trying to wash his gnarled hands and not succeeding.

"Something between Bunch and Carolina Duffy?"

"A little matter of assault and battery with homicidal intent."

"Come, now. I know her specialty's the whip, but . . ."

"Comes from a whipping family," Leathers told him. "Some very ugly stories about her paw and grampaw torturing slaves. And she's got their taste in fun, let me tell you."

"Apparently your friend Bunch shares her taste."

"That's why he can't sue her, because it all happened at her place. I mean, Bunch whipped one girl awhile, then wanted another. Carolina Duffy asked to see the color of his cash, and he confessed he was stony."

"Bad judgment."

"She took the whip away, and by the time that fat girl was finished, Jack Bunch was in shreds, Neil. His back is a mass of raw flesh. She's flayed his chest. And a little more," Leathers added somberly.

"Went for the family jewels, did she?"

"Is that one of her tricks?"

"Some of her customers like it." Neil turned back from the window and stared at the stringy politician. "I don't mind telling you, the things people want done to them is beyond understanding." He pulled at his mustache. "What do you want? She is not one of my madams, you know."

"I want her out of the District. What Jack Bunch wants is her big bloated carcass dead on a platter."

"Going to take matters in his own hands?"

"Jack?" Leathers asked incredulously. "He ain't going nowhere for six months, my friend. It'll take that long for him to recover, if blood poisoning don't set in."

Neil nodded. "Okay, she loses her house. But it's a specialty house, Christy. They get a lot of calls for her kind of service. I'd have to buck a lot of opposition around here. And what's in it for Neil Blood?"

The skinny lawyer made a wry face. "Neil, I've told you before, you New Orleanians don't pay enough attention to the boys upstate. Jack Bunch, at this moment, is a piece of raw meat. But when he's back on his feet, he's chairman of the legislature's taxation committee. That makes him a big man in Baton Rouge, and even bigger in Louisiana."

"But couldn't pay his whorehouse bill?"

Christy Leathers shook his head. "Married his money. He ain't much to look at, is Jack, but somehow he got hitched to one of the Clapp sisters in Shreveport."

Blood tried to hide his smile. "Clapp sisters? And they ain't working for me?"

The lawyer responded with a wide, toothy grin. "Don't make no nevermind about names. Eulalia Clapp brought about two hundred thousand iron men to that marriage, Neil. Under American rules, not this Napoleonic code of yours. When her paw dies, they's a nation more cash waitin' for Jack Bunch's wife. And she watches every copper of it real close."

"Married rich." Neil shook his head heavily. "That means his little upset with Carolina Duffy ain't supposed to get back to Miz Eulalia, I gather."

"You gather right." Christy Leathers' voice grew excited. "Neil, with a man like Jack in your corner, you downstate Catholics got a true friend in Baton Rouge."

Blood nodded. "Fair enough. Duffy's finished. It may take a while, even six months, but she's finished in the District."

Leathers considered this for a moment. "You mean, conniving rattlesnake," he said then. "If Jack lives, Duffy goes. Otherwise, you ain't stirrin' a finger. Old Mr. Wait-and-See."

"But it gives you the right message to bring to Bunch. And keeps him friendly."

The smile on Leathers' face was grudging. "I thought *I* was the political brain around here." He got up off the desk corner. "Can you get me out of here past that dago watchdog of yours?"

"Luca? You're looking at the future there, Christy."

"I don't get your meaning."

"The Sicilians are flocking into New Orleans. They have their little ways, you know. Luca's got a cousin name of Matranga. I hire Luca, and Tony Matranga's my friend."

"Them dagos ain't nobody's friends, not even each other's."

"They said the same thing about you upstate Protestants. Remember how you hated us mackerel-snappers down here?"

"They still hate you, Neil. The only reason they tolerate New Orleans is because they need it to sell their crops."

Neil Blood escorted his guest to the door. "That, and your fine missionary work, Christy. Never let it be said that you won't go down in history for it."

Leathers grinned almost shyly. "It's been rewarding work," he admitted.

"That's the only kind of work I'm interested in," the master of the Wicklowe told him. "What's it all about, if not rewards?"

9

"My Dear Katharine," the letter began. "You must forgive the informality with which I address an old schoolmate after all these years . . ."

The handwriting was small, neatly formed, and simple in design, not at all the rather ornate forward-slant Spencerian script Kate Blood had learned from the Madames of the Sacred Heart. The paper was vellum, thick and rich as parchment, decorated with a small family seal.

Kate sat in the office next to her father's above the Wicklowe. The letter had arrived this morning, Monday, September 17, 1888, and this was the sixth time she had read it through.

". . . but the fact that I have not kept up with you since our convent days has become a source of shame to me. What must you think of one who, like you, learned the social graces with such tender thoroughness from our dear Madames."

As it had done all day, this phrase seemed to squeeze at Kate's heart. She continued reading. "This came home to me with belated force when I invited your clever brother, Ned, to attend a musical afternoon this coming Sunday, September 23. I was struck by the thought—long overdue—that we might enjoy the pleasure of your company, too, if Ned could but escort you. With that in mind, I implore you to be forgiving enough to accompany Ned to Apartment G, Upper Pontalba, at four in the afternoon. We tend to wear what we have worn to Mass that morning. I believe this touch of informality helps us enjoy the music and each other's company more readily. With the hope that old acquaintance be not forgot, Livy Crozat."

Kate put down the letter, folded it, tucked it into its vellum envelope, and hid it under the desk-top blotter. Ned's work, she told herself. Olivia Crozat had never been a friend at the convent. None of the Creoles had given any sign that Kate Blood existed on the face of the earth. Well, perhaps Olivia hadn't been as cruel as the rest. But clearly Ned had put her up to the invitation.

"Old acquaintance be not forgot." Kate was struck by a sudden thought. Could Edmund have . . . ?

Impossible. It was insane to think he had suggested that his sister invite her.

"Your clever brother, Ned."

Clever to guess how I feel, Kate thought. Cleverer of Olivia to strike that carefully informal note, suggesting what to wear, signing it "Livy."

"Dear Katharine."

They'd never been "Kate" and "Livy." Nor were they now.

"Our musical afternoon."

"Our" was she and Edmund. His apartment. Ned had never mentioned this music before. Music was beyond Kate. She'd never know what to say about it.

And, dear God, only six days to get ready!

She had wanted to arrive at five minutes after four, but Ned talked her out of it. "No Creole worthy of the name ever came any earlier than one hour late," he explained. "You and I will sashay in about five-fifteen, Katie, because we Irish just don't give a damn."

But what with one thing and another—hooks that wouldn't stay hooked and a crisis over which pair of high button shoes was properly "informal"—they arrived at five-thirty in the middle of something quite unusual.

To begin with, while the guests were white, the musicians were all black. And while the guests wore precisely what Olivia had forecast they would wear, the musicians seemed dressed, either for a funeral or a wedding, in tails and white tie, "quite like the waiters at the Wicklowe," Ned whispered.

The two Bloods sat quietly on small cane-bottomed chairs at the rear of the parlor. Only Olivia had seen them enter, ushered in by Thomas, the butler. And only Olivia had sent a small friendly wave in their direction. The rest of the guests seemed transfixed by what they were hearing.

It was not that new to Kate. She had heard Yancey Morgan play the piano often, never in the parlor at Mahogany Hall, of course, but in a discreet side room Miss Lulu had opened. As she listened, however, Kate realized that this was not Yancey's usual jaunty ragtime. It was slower, and the black man behind him, who was playing on a marching drum, accented the beat by a light but penetrating rataplan that kept the snare on the underside of the drum buzzing briskly.

Kate caught sight of Edmund, sitting to one side, head tilted on his fingers, elbow resting on the arm of his chair. He looked absolutely engrossed in the music. It was hardly possible he had seen her enter. Then she saw that his eyes were neither on the musicians nor the guests. He was looking past them through the rear windows to the bend of the Mississippi, which headed out through the delta to the sea. Kate noticed that he sipped a milky drink from time to time.

The way she imagined his thoughts made her suddenly sick at heart. It was the essence of sadness, his sorrow as well as hers, to want something one cannot have. The music began to filter through her thoughts now, its slow, driving beat replacing her own pulse with its force.

The small Negro holding a silver cornet jammed a conical tin mute in the bell of his instrument. He had been pointed out in the street once to Kate as a barber named Buddy Bolden. She remembered being told that he had a tone people said could carry all the way across Lake Pontchartrain. When he began to play, Kate could see Edmund wandering, alone, in some desolate land. The muted cornet notes began to bounce sideways and jostle each other. Bolden was lagging behind or leaping ahead of the music, the thin, pure sound like silver darts spraying in every direction. Then he tilted the instrument higher and his tones became long and mournful again. Kate had the feeling that she would burst into tears.

At last the music ended. After a moment, everyone applauded politely except for a redheaded man with a high, freckled forehead, who pounded his hands together long after everyone else had finished. "Bravo!" he said. "First-rate!"

While Bolden mopped his face with a white handkerchief, the butler rolled a teak-and-brass cart into the parlor, on which stood a bowl of punch afloat with orange slices.

"A brief intermission," Olivia cried, getting to her feet. "And Edmund's Sazerac punch." She made a beeline for Kate and her brother.

"My dear." She took both Kate's hands and they stood there staring at each other, the tall blonde and the petite brunette. "It has been too long," Olivia said at last.

"So kind of you to invite me," Kate responded. She had practiced the remark for several days now, and also the one to follow it up. "What a lovely place this is . . ." And, improvising as easily as the musicians, she added, ". . . and what a delightful surprise to hear such music."

"You liked it? I'm glad. It's not generally accepted today, I'm afraid."

"But it's not ragtime."

Olivia gestured to the man who had applauded longer than the rest. "Jed, come and meet Ned's charming sister. What do you call the piece they just finished?"

"It's a blues," the impresario said. He stopped before Kate, took her hand, and bent his head over it. "Jed Benjamin, your servant. How a rascal like Ned has kept such a lovely sister hidden this long is quite the mystery of the hour."

Kate curtsied. "He speaks often of you."

"Don't believe a word of it." He turned to gaze at the guests. "Well, it's not exactly New Orleans, is it? No crusty Creole dowagers. Olivia, you will never cram this music down the respectable throats of the *beau monde*."

"Then it can't be very *beau*." Olivia turned back to Kate. "Yancey Morgan has written down some of his things, and Jed has arranged for them to be published. And I"—she turned back to the impresario—"have already sent a manuscript to M'sieur Debussy."

Ned chuckled. "You delight in introducing one unknown to another."

"M'sieur Debussy unknown? Four years ago he won the Prix de Rome. He is perhaps too much under the influence of Massenet, but this will pass."

"And under whose influence are today's musicians?" Ned teased her.

"None, I believe. They are true originals." Olivia turned to Kate again. "This is our original music, only ours. I feel very strongly that we must help it find its way."

"Does Debussy agree?" Ned continued in the same vein.

But Kate saw her hostess's glance shift to the other guests, clustered around the punch wagon. They were drinking in groups of three or four, but their eyes were on Kate and their voices could not be heard.

Kate stood taller. So she was an object of talk. Look at the tongues wag.

"My, my," her hostess said. "We seem to have the makings of . . ." She took Kate by the hand. "It's time you met your host," she said firmly, and plunged directly through the groups of gossiping guests, leading Kate to Edmund Crozat.

The two women stopped before the seated man. "But you two have already met," Olivia said then. "Edmund?"

He had not moved, nor had his glance left the window and the river beyond. He looked up now and got to his feet. "Good afternoon, mamselle." He took her hand.

Kiss it, Kate implored silently. Jed Benjamin kissed it. Why not you? But he shook it once and let it go. "Did the music move you?" she asked him.

Edmund seemed to make an effort to refocus his attention. "The music," he said in his low voice. "Yes, it is moving in its strange way. It makes pictures in the mind."

"Faraway places. Forlorn places." Kate watched his face register her words.

He frowned. She wanted to smooth her finger over the crease between his thick eyebrows. He looked older and too serious when he frowned. He sipped his anise-smelling drink. "Man is the only animal capable of desolation. And very few of us have the strength to follow our dreams."

"Dear me, Edmund," his sister said. "You sound so fierce."

His laugh crackled. "Don't be afraid, Livy. Most of us just enjoy ourselves."

"Thomas is running out of ice. Excuse me."

She left the two of them alone in the far corner of the room by the windows. The gossiping seemed to have stopped, or perhaps it was being more expertly concealed. And Edmund had stopped frowning at last, which brought him back to his own age.

"It was so kind of your sister to invite me," Kate began again, falling back on tested material. "I had no idea such charming apartments existed in our dusty, muddy city."

"Livy's fixed it up," he said uninterestedly.

Not forthcoming, she noted. She would have to take up the slack, but not as boldly as the other times, when she had made such an effort to draw him out. "Ned tells me . . ." She stopped.

"Nothing good about me, I'll wager."

"Quite the contrary. He thinks you're one of New Orleans' coming leaders. He says you're very deep, not like the others."

"Mere journalism."

"No, I think I know what he means. It cannot have escaped you," she suggested, "that this is a poor version of what our city was meant to be. We had greatness, and now we have graft. We had pioneers, and now we have corruptors. We had dreams, and now we have hangovers."

Shut up, Kate, she told herself in the abrupt silence. Your host must do some talking of his own.

Edmund grinned lopsidedly, a touch of malice in his look. He held up his nearly empty drink. "Ned does a thorough job of exposing some of them. Without, shall we say, breaking the bonds of filial loyalty."

Kate blinked. "Meaning my father?"

Edmund made a small exquisite gesture with his hand. It hardly moved, but it conveyed a pure "you have said it, not I" message.

Kate felt anger rising in her. She had a temper, like the rest of the Bloods, but she was supposed to be the practical one, wasn't she? She took a slow, steadying breath.

"My father is a very complicated man, Mr. Crozat. He has done reprehensible things. He has done good things, too. The world hears only of the one and not the other."

"Brava," he said. "And he has raised some very loyal children along the way," he added. "Which is more than I can say about my own . . ." He stopped himself.

"How odd," he said then. "When last we spoke, on the street, it was of marriage. Now, children. These are not proper topics for young single persons to discuss." He smiled. "Yet we seem unable to avoid them. I find this, ah . . . remarkable." He gestured with his empty glass. "More punch, Miss Kate?"

"Not for me. Please help yourself."

"It never occurred to me that you were a teetotaler."

"Can we be frank, Mr. Crozat? I don't think anything about me has ever occurred to you. But for me, the situation is different."

"I don't follow you."

"You haven't forgotten the day you saved Ned's life? You have never been entirely out of my thoughts since then."

Blind man, she thought, I am telling you something as best I can.

"There was nothing special about that," said Edmund. "As it turned out, the boy was well worth saving. I'm glad of that, but I apologize for stumbling into your thoughts since then."

You don't see it, Kate thought, when it's standing right in front of you. She wanted to take his long, thin hands and pull his arms around her. She wanted to kiss that small, careful mouth with the upper curve like an archer's bow. She wanted to feel his body against her, his hard muscles against her soft . . .

"Did I say something wrong?" Edmund asked.

Kate shook her head. Dear God, no, she thought, not a word. She managed a smile. "Ned was right, Mr. Crozat. You're deeper than one could imagine. Are you one of those men who are not afraid to dream?"

He stood silent for a moment. "What," he asked abruptly, "is your dream?"

"But I asked you first."

"A debate, is it?" He grinned crookedly and finished the last of his absinthe. "My dream . . ." He thought for a moment. "It may be far away, in one of those desolate places the music spoke about. I have no idea, except that, being mine, it remains mine."

"A secret?" Kate asked. "And so is mine. Except one clue: it is not in a far-off place. It is very close at hand."

"Am I permitted a guess?"

"Only if I am allowed one first."

"What a pity you never took up the law, Miss Blood. And what a pity I can't hire you as my attorney." He grinned disarmingly at her. "Guess away."

"Your dream." Kate thought for a moment. "It's a lonely dream, is it not?"

Edmund gestured with the palm of his hand, as if to say: This is your performance, not mine.

"Very well, then," Kate continued, "lonely because you can only achieve it alone. And it's far bigger than most people could conceive. And yet . . ." She stopped and stared into his dark eyes. "And yet there's a contradiction to it."

"Is there?" She saw that for the first time she had riveted his attention.

"Yes. The dream is immense, but it's all to achieve something very small and easy. It's a dream in which a man struggles to lift a mountain, so that he can drop it on a mouse."

"But if there is no other way to kill the mouse?" Edmund tried to keep his voice light in tone, but Kate could hear the effort behind his doing it.

"Then you *will* lift the mountain."

He nodded. "That I will, Miss Blood. You can bank on it."

He was staring shamelessly into her eyes now. "This gift of yours. It cannot be something the Madames of the Sacred Heart taught, or Olivia would also have it. But I'm wrong, of course." His glance grew more penetrating. "There's nothing sacred about your gift. It's witchcraft."

Kate nodded solemnly. "Quite so."

"Voodoo?"

"Stronger. It's the magic of the Celtic druids."

"Seventh daughter of a seventh daughter," he murmured. "I have never known a real witch before, especially not one with sunlight caught in her hair."

Kate could feel the blood well up hotly in her cheeks. "I don't want you to think," she said at last, "that I can read everyone's dreams."

"No?"

"I did tell you, did I not, that you have never been far from my thoughts." Her heart was pounding so that he must be able to hear it.

"Is that the reason?" he demanded. "Have you been eavesdropping on my dreams all these years?"

He asked with such pretended ferocity that for a moment Kate was afraid she had offended him. She had begun to breathe faster now, and there was a quaver in her voice that he could surely notice.

"There has only been the one dream," she said shakily.

"True." He took her hand.

Kate could feel the contact of his fingers like the crackling shock of a comb through dry hair. The impulse seemed to travel from his fingers through hers, along her hand and arm to her heart.

"Miss Kate," he said in his low, crackling voice, "you—"

"Mr. Crozat, suh?" The butler was standing there. "They's a peculiar gem'un outside sayin' he has t'see you, suh."

"Peculiar?" Edmund stared past him over the heads of the guests. In the door of the parlor, looking out-of-place and acutely aware of it, stood a squat, powerful man with a bull neck and broad shoulders. His coat was flecked with rusty spatters, as if he had driven through mud at breakneck speed to get here.

"Rynders," Edmund muttered. He seemed to slash a swath through his guests as he moved directly to the newcomer. Across the room Kate saw the man turn aside and whisper something in Edmund's ear.

He reacted wildly, stepping back and clapping Rynders hard on both shoulders. Kate blinked to keep back the tears. He and she had been approaching each other at last. They had been closing the gap, and suddenly . . .

She blinked again. When she looked at the doorway, both men had disappeared.

10

The Red Pole Tavern was not one of the prime hostelries of Baton Rouge, a city of lavishly appointed hotels and eating places, as befits a capital city with a large transient population of men. The Pole stood near the river landing. It was a rough place for rough customers, most of them off the keelboats and steamers.

But it was a handy spot for keeping out of sight, as a number of legislators and lobbyists had discovered. The tavern had a few private rooms where men could get together without the world knowing of it. Moreover, upstairs at the Pole, the bedrooms were small and equally private.

In one of them lay Representative Jack Bunch of Caddo Parish. There were few positions in which he could rest without exacerbating the pain of his whip cuts. Drugged with opium, however, he made the best of the parade of visitors who paid their respects.

"I am horrified beyond speech," Mike Leathers said, standing by his bedside. "I learned of it from my paw just this evening, Jack."

"He see Blood yet?"

"I believe so." Mike patted his fellow representative's shoulder. "Don't you do no talking, Jack. Just save your strength. The doc's coming back in an hour with some more of them pills."

He sat down on the only chair in the room. "I swear to God, Jack, that was one hell of an accident. I saw one of them threshing combines once, you know. I remember asking myself at the time, Lordy, what if a fella tripped into one of them things? Wouldn't he come out a bleeding mess?"

Mike crossed his legs and prepared for a long chat, one-sided as country talk so often is. He had no special love for Jack Bunch, who was always on the opposite side of anything Nigger Mike proposed in the legislature. But the man was in pain. It was his Christian duty, as Mike saw it, to visit the sick and do what little he could to help. Besides, you never knew. Old Jack might be grateful for it later on.

"What I never did find out from Paw," Mike went on chattily, "is how they come to have a McCormick thresher down in New Orleans. Mentioned something about an exhibition, was it?"

He recrossed his legs. "Puts me in mind of the time Brother Luke and me was boys, out trapping muskrats once. Luke never told me where he'd laid them traps, you know, and sure as shootin', I done stepped in one. What an almighty mess . . ."

He spun out the words with the practiced ease of a born talker. "I do hope they have sent word to Mrs. Bunch?" He saw the injured man shake his head violently from side to side. "No? Well, if that don't beat the bugs to bitin'. Just nod, Jack, and I'll make sure your dear wife Miz Eulalia gets the word right away."

Again the almost frantic negative headshake. "No? Well, I s'pect you know what you're doin', Jack. Usually do, except around threshing machines." He stopped to chuckle a bit.

"I'll be riding back home to Winnfield tomorrow morning. Gotta get out there and shake a few hands. You know how it is, Jack. The voters don't see you, they forget you. What they never remember is that you gotta be down here on their behalf. Isn't that a fact?"

He sighed and recrossed his legs again. "And I got my law practice to look after. You could put it in your eye and never blink. Hell, I don't hardly collect a dime. Mostly bags of grain or jugs of homemade. Whatever they can afford."

He watched the injured man. "You comfortable, Jack? You want me to fix that pillow? No? Got a case coming up that ought to cost somebody but won't. Inheritance. Client's paw left her some land, but her cousins, seein' how she's a minor—just sixteen—say the land belongs to next of kin. Them. Trouble is, nobody can pay even a sack of meal. Luanne's dead broke, and so's her cousins. It's a charity case is what. I guess you had your share of them, huh, Jack? But, what the hell. Luanne Grimes is good company."

Jack Bunch's battered head nodded slowly in agreement. "Oh, you know Luanne?" Mike asked. "Nice girl. Clean. Willing. And the goldurndest pair of teats a man ever pulled on. I am gonna do my level best to see she keeps that land. What's that?"

The injured man had croaked something. "Sale," he managed to get out.

"Jack, rest yourself, boy. Save your strength."

"Notarized a deed of sale," Bunch muttered.

"Huh? For Luanne?"

Bunch nodded. "Sold five hundred acres."

"Up in your Shreveport office?" Mike demanded. The injured man nodded again. "Who to, Jack?"

"Fella named Rynders. Some company."

"Can you remember the company's name, Jack?" Mike was on his feet now, standing over the man in the bed, who shook his head. "You must remember," Leathers persisted.

"Long name."

"But, Jack, you don't see what that fool girl has done. First, a minor can't sell nothing. Second, her title ain't clear. Third, if I told her once, I told her a thousand times to let me handle everything." Leathers turned away. "Damnation!"

The injured man made a sympathetic noise, and Leathers turned back to him. "She ain't got nothing in the world but the dress to cover her titties, Jack. That acreage was her ace in the hole. I don't have to tell you what life is like for an orphan girl. That land was supposed to grubstake her to a chance at a respectable life." He frowned. "What'd she get for it?"

"Dollar'n acre."

"Judas Iscariot!" Mike cursed. "I had that Ringo Waddell all primed and hankering for it. I coulda hunched him up to twice the price. A thousand dollars to a girl like Luanne is a fortune, Jack."

"Five hundred ain't tin."

"Save your voice, Jack." Mike began pacing the small room. "When that company finds out she had no right to sell, she'll be in a peck of misfortune, so she will. Fraud. Misrepresentation. Bless my soul, I am grateful for your information, Jack. But I'm damned if I know what to do about it."

"Deed," the injured man croaked.

"Save your voice, son," Leathers repeated, not listening. "First thing, I gotta find out where the deed's been registered. No, it's too soon for that. Maybe not. Maybe he registered it right here in town. Or Shreveport?"

"Maybe," Bunch agreed.

Mike Leathers held up his hand. "I want you to save yourself, Jack.

This is my problem. I didn't come here to get you messed up in it. I want you to stay calm and relaxed and just concentrate on getting well. Five hundred dollars. Lordy, Lordy, Lordy. What *am* I going t'do?"

The man on the bed opened his mouth painfully. "Marry her?"

11

The cab rattled through the streets of the Old Quarter, the horse's hooves and iron-rimmed wheels clattering over the uneven paving stones. Kate Blood sat in one corner, staring blankly out at the street. Ned sat in the opposite corner and watched her. Neither had spoken since they'd left the Pontalba musicale shortly after their host had disappeared.

They were to pick up their father at seven at the Wicklowe. Then they were due at Mary's house on Esplanade, where young families who could afford it were building new homes. Mary was really the only young one, since her husband, Alderman Hinckley, was at least a dozen years older.

He had moved cannily, had Abner. Ned knew him to be one of the city leaders involved in the reform movement, which bore the official name of Young Men's Democratic Organization. Abner Hinckley had managed to keep his nose cleaner than most of his associates, which, to Ned, merely meant that he hadn't yet been caught.

His maneuvering prior to marrying the second daughter of Neil Blood had been an education to watch, even though Ned's own sisters were involved. Abner had, of course, set his hat on Kate. But like her other suitors, Abner somehow fell short in her eyes. Ned now understood why.

So the resourceful Hinckley had instantly switched to Mary, and within six months the banns had been published. There was the small

97

detail of the alderman being a Methodist, but he proved more than willing to convert, take instruction, and participate with practiced ease in the marriage Mass at St. Patrick's.

Certainly the deluge of children that followed would have pleased, Ned felt, even the pope in Rome, two girls and Mary already in her fifth month with their third child. Abner's conversion to the Roman rites did him no harm at all in New Orleans, where most of his constituents and clients were of that faith.

"It'll be interesting," Ned ventured aloud, "to see what Pa and Abner have to say to each other at dinner. I think a deal's been made on this reform business."

Kate said nothing, still staring at the passing houses. "And, of course, Mary is going to be unbearable in her condition," Ned added. "How she does flaunt that belly."

Either Kate hadn't heard, or didn't care to reply. "And I've invited Edmund Crozat to join us," he added with brotherly malice.

She whirled on him, eyes wide, then saw the grin on his face. "Devil," she murmured. Then: "What do you suppose was so important that our proper Creole host deserted a room full of guests without so much as a fare-thee-well?"

"Do we care a tinker's dam about the guests?" Ned asked, still teasing. "He deserted *you* in the midst of what looked like a very personal tête-à-tête."

"It might have been." Kate sighed. "It was heading that way. I was doing most of the work."

"But Kate Blood is never at a loss for words."

"He . . ." Her cheekbones colored. "That man tongue-ties me, Neddie. It's as if I'm bewitched."

"You seemed to be chatting away at a great rate. Jed Benjamin remarked that he'd never seen Edmund spend more than half a minute with any woman. Except Olivia, of course."

And one other, Ned added silently. He watched his sister's distress for a moment. Then: "Give it up, Katie. Crozat is never going to marry. Unless it's one of those signed-on-the-dotted-line Creole contracts to some dried-up daughter of the idle rich."

Kate sat back, withdrawing into her corner of the cab as it rattled up Customhouse. The September sun was dying.

At the corner of Dauphine Street the hunched-over figure of a lamplighter straightened as he raised his head to light the gas lamp. The Welsbach mantles glowed brightly and in their pool of light the face of the old man looked young for an instant, lines erased, before he dropped his head and shuffled off to the next streetlamp.

Ned continued watching his sister. She was the smartest of them all, he thought, and she knew he was right. Edmund was a born bachelor, traveling as alone as a man could who bore such a weight of a family. Ned glanced up as they reached the Wicklowe. "Da's outside already. We're five minutes late. Lord help us."

The cab halted at the corner of Basin, and Neil Blood climbed aboard. He patted Kate's knee as he climbed past her to sit squarely between them. "Snap it up, driver. An extra six bits if you break the speed record."

"You bet, Mr. Blood!" He snapped the reins hard and the cab jolted off along Basin Street, heading north.

"Must've been a bang-up soirée," their father told Ned and Kate. "Couldn't tear yourselves away on time. Never mind." He patted Kate's knee again. "How was it?"

Her face was perfectly composed as she turned to him. The cab moved past lighted lamps and shadows. "Olivia was a perfect hostess. We did enjoy ourselves."

"That's just fine." Neil eyed his son but said nothing.

Then, for the third time, he patted Kate. His voice lowered to exclude the driver, who, in any event, was flogging the horse so savagely that it was doubtful he could hear anything.

"Katie," her father began, "I want to tell you this before I tell the rest at dinner. I'm only telling them the first part of it anyway, which is . . ." He drew a breath. "You're fired, dear girl."

"Da!"

"I been thinking long and hard, Katie. You're the best bookkeeper I'll ever have, but it was dead wrong for me to make you do it. Do you understand what I'm driving at?"

"Wrong?"

"You deserve a chance to rise above it, Katie-girl. And you never will whilst I have you chained to this kind of life. I'm putting a stop to it as of tonight."

Kate stared into her father's eyes, first bright in the lamplight, then shadowed. "Who would you get? O'Hare?"

He nodded. "You trained him good, Katie. I want you to have the life for which the Madames educated you. God knows I've got the lucre for it. And you never will, 'less'n you're free once and for all of Basin Street."

"You're a great one for surprises, Da," Ned said trying to read Katie's face.

"Yes, well, the second surprise is between Katie and me. It grieves me mightily to have to tell her in front of a snoop like you. Katie . . ."

"Yes, Da."

"I want what you want, dear girl. And I believe the both of us wants you married."

She sank back into the corner of the cab and turned away so that neither could see her. "Don't tell me I'm out of line," her father persisted. "It's what we both want."

"I don't get it," Ned complained.

"Then shut up."

"Are you giving her a license or an ultimatum?"

Neil turned on his youngest son. "How would you like to have to walk to Mary's house from here?"

"Da, you have no idea how it sounds," Ned spoke up boldly. "It's like you're telling her: Okay, Katie, get married fast because you don't have a job anymore."

Neil Blood had the good grace to look aghast. He turned to Kate. "Is that how it sounded? I meant it the other way."

Face still turned away, she managed to pat him on the knee. "It's all right, Da." Her voice sounded small. "It's just . . ." She seemed to pull herself together, straighten her body, and turn to face them. In the alternating light and dark, Ned thought, her eyes looked desperate.

"It's only that a lot of things have happened to me today," Katie told her father. "I saw how my presence affected others. Not straitlaced old biddies, modern young people. So perhaps taking me out of Basin Street has . . . has come too late, Da. In any case, what would I do with my days? As for the other . . ." Her voice broke.

She sniffed and sat even straighter in the cab seat. "As for marrying, the man I want lives on another planet from me. It has nothing to do with Basin Street. He has his own world. It's a world of one person, Da. Nobody else is in it, least of all me."

As if to match her, stiff back for stiff back, Neil Blood drew himself up and stared down at her. "If it's the man I've heard mentioned, he isn't worth it. A wastrel. A dandified bit of milkweed fluff. And he's as prodigious a philanderer as the Frogs ever produced. You could never be hap—"

"Do you think I haven't thought about that?" Kate cut in.

"You should."

"All of them have their women. What man?" she demanded, looking from one to the other of them, "in this town doesn't? Bought and paid for."

When neither her father nor her brother responded, Kate sat back again. "That's the way men like it," she mused aloud. "True friendship, that's between men. You don't buy it. You earn it. But when you want a little good, dirty fun, then you buy it. Next morning you tip your hat and walk away. Oh, yes, we mustn't forget children. You can't pass on your name to another generation without getting involved with a woman. But from what I've seen of marriage *or* Basin Street, it's all cash and carry."

The cab clattered wildly down Esplanade. None of the three Bloods seemed to have anything more to say.

It was Ned who finally broke the silence. "Well, Da. I don't hear either one of us trying to contradict her."

12

At seven-thirty Monday morning, September 24, two men left the small office on Carondelet Street, south of the Old Quarter, and walked to the French Market, fronting on the old levee between what was now Decatur Street and the river.

Edmund seemed to move as if on strings, slightly off the ground, his lithe body advancing in great strides while Clem Rynders hobbled along more slowly. He had not been to sleep for nearly three days, except for a few hours aboard the fast packet from Baton Rouge.

Silently the geologist accepted a French Market *beignet*, almost too hot to touch, from its deep-fry vat. Powdered with sugar, the square doughnutlike pastry came wrapped in a bit of paper. He gingerly nibbled at it while Edmund ordered two cups of coffee with hot milk and passed one to Rynders. The dry-crisp odor of chicory and coffee hovered in the humid air.

Later, back in the small office on Carondelet Street—the translucent glass door bore the name Great Southern Development Corporation— Edmund pushed aside dozens of large-scale maps in order to clear his desk. He set in the cleared area three stoppered vials of greenish-black liquid, heavily viscous.

"This one labeled 'Grimes' you took from the main source?" he asked. "Bought from this Luanne Grimes?"

Rynders nodded without speaking. His eyes were half-closed, despite the powerful injection of French Market coffee. "And this from five miles to the south? And this another five miles farther?"

"It's all in my notes, Mr. Crozat."

Edmund put the vials aside and shuffled through a pile of deeds, thick wads of pages closely inscribed in painstaking penmanship. "This Grimes deed is the key, then?" he murmured. "But these others—there are six more—you secured in order to protect the main area."

"Seven, eight with Grimes. And it's not for protection. The underground deposits extend well into all of them."

"But it's unheard of. A field of four thousand acres?"

Rynders nodded tiredly. Edmund sat back in his oak office chair, making its springs creak, and put his boots up on the desk. The office was plain, virtually anonymous. He came here infrequently, but he kept the place because he needed an address for Great Southern's bank account, now vastly depleted by Rynders' purchases.

"You've done well," Edmund said at last. "You have done remarkably well. Not merely in locating the deposits. But in moving quickly to buy the lands. And at low prices. There's only one thing." He paused.

Rynders' fatigued eyes twitched. He managed to raise his lids. "No offense, but there's no mistake about the oil, Mr. Crozat. It's damned well there. The same asphalt-based stuff they have in Texas."

"No, not that." Edmund's dark eyes flashed sideways at him. "All these sudden purchases. People will suspect something. We have to have a good answer. What reason did you give?"

"I said Great Southern was interested in making cottonfields out of junk land. Irrigation, that sort of thing."

"Good. When we start moving in our drilling rigs, we can tell them we're looking for water." Edmund smiled crookedly. "The only use I have for water," he said, opening a drawer of his desk, "is to dilute this." He brought out a small, thin-necked bottle of green liqueur. "May I offer you some? This is a celebration for both of us."

Rynders squinted at the absinthe. "Not this early," he grunted. "And not without ice. Meaning no offense."

Edmund nodded knowingly. "I regret having to dilute it at all," he said then. "But the damned stuff is bitter as sin, is it not?"

The geologist made a face. "To tell you the truth, Mr. Crozat . . ." He paused. "You go right ahead."

Edmund mixed water with the green liquid and produced swirls of cloudy white. He watched the mists coalesce into a solid, impenetrable fluid. The odor of anise filled the small office at once. "I got the taste for this mixing my father's Sazeracs," he said then. He sipped thoughtfully. "No sense messing up its purity with whiskey and bitters. Eh?"

He glanced at Rynders and saw that the man was nodding off in his chair. Edmund sipped again, then set down his drink and carried the three vials of crude to the window. In the early-morning light the dark green oil had a sheen, an inner life like that of the water as absinthe turned it into white swirls.

Outside, people were walking to work. It was nearly eight o'clock. Most shops had already opened for the day. Edmund glanced at the passersby. Someday they would pause in this square of Carondelet and point to this second-story window and say: "That's where Edmund Crozat cornered all the oil in Louisiana."

The old lopsided smile distorted his lips. Eight years in the making. Eight years of secrecy and defeat. And now, at last, victory.

He held the stoppered bottles against the morning sunlight. Iridescent magic swirled inside them. Oil was a genie that would answer Edmund's prayers. In a matter of a few years, Louisiana would step forward into the full roaring tumult of the industrial revolution. This sleepy little state of his, this town that ran at Mediterranean half-speed, would be dragged out of the agrarian past, out of ways that had hardly changed in two centuries, to become a major industrial power.

Louisiana crude, Edmund mused. Owned, drilled, pumped, and sold by Great Southern and no other. There he goes, Edmund Crozat. You know, the Great Southern man. The banking Crozats? Oh, there may be some connection. But Edmund Crozat is *the* Crozat.

There was a knock at the door. Edmund turned. Clem Rynders was fast asleep, head on the table, cheek pressed against the great sheaf of deeds. Edmund stood the vials of crude on the windowsill. He opened the door to a boy in the dark blue uniform of the Postal Telegraph Company. "Great Southern?" he asked, reading from a folded and sealed sheet of paper.

Edmund put a half-dollar in the boy's hand, took the telegram, and watched the messenger run off down the hall. Rynders' heavy eyes opened. "Whu's matter?"

Edmund ripped open the telegram:

REQUEST COURTESY VISIT YOUR OFFICES WEDNESDAY 8 A.M. DETER-
MINE GREAT SOUTHERN PLANS, OWNERSHIP. LOUISIANA STATE LEGIS-
LATURE COMMITTEE ON TAXATION, CHAIRMAN JACK BUNCH. SUBCOM-
MITTEE ON LAND USE, CHAIRMAN MIKE LEATHERS.

"Son of a bitch," Rynders muttered.

Edmund looked past him to the windowsill. The three stoppered bottles glittered strangely, their contents seeming to shift and wink in the sunlight. He reached for his absinthe.

13

If you wanted everyone in the French Opera House to see you, Kate Blood thought, and you weren't a performer on the stage, you would choose one of the four *loges d'avant scene*, boxes which half projected out onto the stage from the side walls of the elderly theater.

It was to one of these boxes that Jed Benjamin had ushered Kate and Olivia. "It's Edmund's box. He's due later," the impresario murmured as they settled themselves and every single theatergoer that December evening craned forward to make note of, and pass along to those on either side, the fact that the questionable Miss Blood would be enjoying tonight's performance by the New York Philharmonic Orchestra.

"Just like that Benjamin to invite her," the echo would follow along.

"But she's . . . um, retired, so they tell me," one gentleman would murmur behind his hand to another.

"Shameful," a dowager would hiss.

"*And* in the Crozat loge."

"Not *the* Crozat loge. The son's loge."

"*La même chose. Incroyable!*"

It did tend to enliven the preconcert period, normally spent comparing jewelry and clothes, and perhaps add sparkle to the program as well. The Philharmonic's very German conductor, Theodore Thomas, planned to ladle a large amount of Beethoven down his audience's throat. But after intermission, one of the city's favorites would set the audience afire. Pablo Sarasate had chosen well. The French-Spanish composer Lalo had written Sarasate a *Symphonie Espagnole* for violin and orchestra. After the castor oil of Beethoven, the audience would be treated to nectar.

None of this did Kate know. Benjamin had told her little when he had called on her one afternoon at her father's home. Kate was finding leisure hard to take. She had begun to read books, and by coincidence, the impresario had brought a book as a gift. He stayed barely long enough to invite her to the concert—"not one of my own presentations, I'm afraid."

Now, as she sat in the dark red plush armchair, she was interested only in the fact that Edmund Crozat was expected later. She had seen and heard nothing of him since that evening in September at the musicale. No one, in fact, had any news of Edmund at all. The invitation had been accepted because Kate hoped Jed or Olivia might shed some light on matters. But so far they had spoken almost entirely about music and, of course, the effect of her presence tonight.

"I do believe," Olivia murmured behind her fan, "that to these people you are something of a scarlet woman."

"Indeed."

"To those of us who know you better," Jed Benjamin added, "you are still, in fact, a woman of mystery."

Kate sat back, the better to watch both of them. At first she had felt Olivia's presence to be a reassuring one. Now she wasn't sure. Whose game, she wondered, was being played, Jed's or Olivia's? Or was the glib impresario courting both of them, willy-nilly?

"Despite the sensation you think I've created," Kate said in her sweetest tones, "I do thank you for the invitation, Mr. Benjamin."

"Please. Jed."

"And for inviting me as well," Olivia chimed in. "Do you know, this is the second time in my life that I have sat in Edmund's loge? I am usually sequestered in my parents' box, like a chick still being hatched."

All three of them laughed quietly, but it was enough to attract the eyes of the entire dress circle. "Dear me," Jed breathed. "I feel like Gulliver in the land of the Yahoos. With two such dangerously attractive women, how can I remain anonymous tonight?"

"As if, dear Jed," Olivia cooed, "you had ever in your life craved anonymity." She turned to Kate. "But he's right on one point. The public will never let you pass unnoticed."

Kate's chin went up. "I could not care less."

"Good for you," Olivia said.

The two young women smiled at each other, and Kate once again felt reassured by Olivia's presence.

"But someday," Jed Benjamin said then, "you may care about the opinion of others. When you consider marriage, for example."

Kate's smile came and went quickly. Her father, her family, now even mere acquaintances, all wanted her married. It didn't seem to matter to whom. "I have not considered it," she said in a low voice, "so much as had it shoved under my nose."

Olivia laughed and touched Kate's hand with her fan. Benjamin frowned slightly. "You're a strong woman, then." He sighed. "But a wise one."

He turned his back on the audience and spoke in an undertone that could not be heard beyond the loge they were in. "Behind me you see marriage, New Orleans style. The men hate being dragged here. They will fidget through Beethoven and fall asleep with Lalo. But this is the price they pay for enjoying their freedom on other nights. An evening here buys a man six nights of bliss in the District. And this is New Orleans marriage."

"From what I see of the wives," Kate remarked, "he's not wrong to get out of the house as often as possible."

"No, these women were once attractive enough," Olivia said. "But marriage does something to them, Kate. In this town marriage is arranged for the man's convenience. He's married at home, but single everywhere else."

"And when he comes home after a night," Kate said, "no explanations."

"Absolutely," the impresario agreed. "Never asked for, since the wife is too well trained."

"But what about the *médiatrice?*"

He smiled and nodded. "That's for the occasional sinner, not the typical New Orleans husband. The man—the rare man—who has only one night out in a blue moon, he will buy a 'peacemaker' to take home to his wife. An oyster-loaf poor-boy sandwich does nicely. The poor deluded woman accepts it, and once again, no questions asked. This is marriage à la New Orleans."

Kate looked at Olivia's smooth, calm face. "Is it so?"

Olivia nodded. "Utterly so."

"Is it different elsewhere? I have never set foot outside New Orleans," Kate admitted.

"It's much the same everywhere," Benjamin said flatly. "But it's more blatant here. I don't pretend to understand how normal women feel, since most of my experience has been with divas and actresses, but this state of affairs cannot make wives happy."

The oboe sounded an A and the orchestra began a flurry of tuning noises. "I had thought Edmund would be here by now," his sister said. "Lately, there's no telling what he'll do. The oil."

"I beg your pardon?"

"He's run into a great deal of opposition in Baton Rouge. Apparently—and here I get the story from others, not Edmund—he has bought oil-producing land upstate. The legislature wants to revoke the sale. The land went too cheaply, perhaps. There's talk of taxing anyone heavily for removing from the earth something that cannot be replaced. I don't pretend to und . . ." She stopped. A ripple of applause had begun in the parquet below.

Glancing across the stage from the angle of the box, Kate could see the conductor making his way to the podium. "Till intermission," Benjamin said, turning resolutely toward the orchestra.

"Does Edmund know you invited me to share his loge?" Kate whispered.

"Sh."

Kate sat back baffled. The man was evidently not going to talk during the music. Everyone else had quieted, too, as Thomas gave the downbeat and the orchestra launched into something very martial. But within moments people were whispering discreetly behind their hands. Benjamin was not.

A strange man, Kate thought. She was not quite innocent enough to miss the connection between his invitation tonight and his artless talk about marriage. Wouldn't her father turn purple to learn that one of her suitors was a Jew? It must have taken Benjamin a while to nerve himself to this, Kate realized. He was perhaps ten years older than she, and although he dressed well and entertained lavishly, was known to be hovering forever on the brink of bankruptcy, like most show folk. He depended so completely on the favor of the same dowagers and betrayed wives with whom he had been sympathizing a moment before, that it must have taken a lot of nerve to think of proposing to Kate Blood.

She grinned demurely, holding her fan before her face for an instant. So keyed up was the audience, she saw, that half of them instantly flashed a glance at her, attracted by the movement of the fan. Woman of mystery. Dear God, yes, Kate thought. It's a mystery to this woman what she'll do with herself now that Billy O'Hare's doing Da's books. Supervise the house staff? She already did that. Sit at home and read books? Not for long.

So Edmund was in trouble. The lone wolf at bay.

Her mind seemed to somersault endlessly back and forth as the music grew slow and sad, then martial again. The orchestra was directly under her, particularly the men who played the big copper kettledrums and crashed the brass cymbals.

Married to Jed Benjamin. If he converted?

It wasn't as if a proposal from Edmund Crozat arrived every afternoon by mail. The lone wolf had disappeared into the wilderness. Marriage to him would be worse than marriage to one of the fat, pompous pigs sitting there in the audience tonight, eyelids slowly lowering.

Crash! Ba-ta-boom! Eyelids . . . *up!*

Kate hid another smile. These sleek little swine trotted off to the excitement of Basin Street and lived fantasy lives by night, paying for their sex, their drink, their food, their drugs. Married to them, you had only two worries, she thought to herself. One was if Mr. Oink gambled. You might awake one morning in permanent poverty. The other worry was that your particular porker might bring home a disease.

The chancres and carbuncles were everywhere. Neil Blood's girls got a weekly checkup from a doctor, but as Doc Strawn had confessed to Kate once: "That gives a girl at least six days to spread it around."

"And from whom did she get it, Doc?" Kate had flashed back.

The whole idea of the women being the carriers infuriated Kate. The pigs who trotted back and forth so industriously, had they no responsibility for any of it? When they brought it home and infected Mrs. Oink, whom else could she blame?

Cases of paresis were everywhere, too, Kate recalled. If it went.on long enough, she knew, it affected the brain and people went mad. But that was a known evil, wasn't it? Marriage to Edmund Crozat would be like a blindfolded stroll through a haunted forest.

She watched Jed Benjamin's face from the side. Except for the rate at which he was losing that carrot-colored hair on top, he looked respectable enough. Of course, even if he converted, she really wasn't interested in marrying Jed.

And what would Crozat have to do to become acceptable as a husband? Get down off that horse, for one. Pension off that quadroon, for another. Learn how to behave in polite society for a third.

Once again Kate raised her fan to hide a mischievous grin. Below her, the sleek porkers were beginning to snooze again. As if aware of the possibility, the percussionists suddenly . . .

Ba-ta-boom! Boom! Boom!

She felt quite pleased with herself. Six months ago Edmund Crozat had been a hectic fever in her blood. Now she could take him or leave him. Not indifferent, she told herself, just more realistic. It's not that I can't have him, she thought. It's that I'm no longer so sure I want him. He needed housebreaking, did Crozat.

Having trouble in Baton Rouge. Too bad. Let him stay home, go to his father's office each day, and learn behavior, the way she had.

Finally, not soon enough for some of the audience, Beethoven thundered to a close. Kate found herself wishing it would go on. There was something—what was it? uplifting? encouraging?—about the music that seemed to give her confidence. She could do anything to that music and do it well.

Jed Benjamin sat back during the applause and consulted his program. "The next is by that Debussy Olivia writes to," he whispered. "It's called *Printemps*. Springtime."

"I do manage to limp along in French myself," Kate told him.

"Jed cannot believe," Olivia whispered, "that anyone with whom I correspond can be a serious composer."

The first strains of the music began. The impresario turned his back on the women, but Kate leaned forward for a last word in Olivia's ear. "I think he's a very good composer."

"Sh." Benjamin's glance was intimidating.

"Perhaps we young people," Olivia whispered slyly, "can appreciate Debussy better than an older listener."

The impresario turned around. His frown was magnificent. Suppressing giggles, both young women settled back to enjoy the sliding grace of the music.

At intermission a messenger who had been waiting outside the door to the loge opened it and poked his head inside. "Miss Crozat?"

Olivia took the envelope and tore it open. She read the note inside and glanced up at Kate. "It's from Dr. Amabile."

"I beg your pardon?"

Olivia was reaching blindly for her cape. "I must go. Edmund . . . it seems he's had a collapse."

"Where is he?" Kate demanded.

"At the Pontalba. I must go."

Kate reached for her own cape. "I'll go with you."

"Kate!" Jed Benjamin looked hurt.

"Olivia can use my help."

"Kate, this is too much."

Olivia paused in the doorway. "I'd like Kate to come along."

The impresario's jaw tightened. "I am not missing Sarasate because Edmund's let himself break down over this fool business of his."

"By all means stay," Olivia urged him. "Come, Kate."

"This is really most—"

"Rude," Kate finished for him as she shrugged into her cape. "Awkward. Even insulting."

Mouth open, Benjamin could only nod as the two women left the loge and made their way unescorted out of the theater.

14

When it began, it was not a massive parade by any standards, particularly those of the Mardi Gras, whose route it borrowed. Apparently the marchers—some newspapers next day wrongly referred to them as "drunken rabble"—had arrived in three keelboats. One boat had come from as far away as Shreveport, but the people from the other two had started at Baton Rouge with a march on the capital, then added forces along the way south by river.

Most of the newcomers who streamed off the keelboats that evening onto the Washington Avenue docks were young men, countrified in denim overalls and mud boots. Some had come a long way to speak their piece. Few had ever been off their farms. None were black.

They had learned a bit about political rallies from their march on the capital. Along the way south, the keelboats would pull in to shore to cut pine-knot torches wherever a likely stand of trees could be reached.

In December the city can be chilly. Tar barrels had been lit on all the keelboats, and now horizontal poles were lashed to them so that two men could carry the bright light as they marched.

Someone with a sense of humor had chosen the route, probably Mike Leathers himself. It mimicked the Mardi Gras parade closely, moving along St. Charles from Washington to Canal. If sophisticated New Orleanians had considered the farm costumes as Mardi Gras maskery, the illusion would have been improved, but no one did.

Ned Blood came out of Strong's Saloon, next to the new St. Charles

111

Theater. He stood under its colonnaded gallery for a while, drawn by the shouting.

Following a tar barrel, two men carried poles from which a banner proclaimed in red paint: "THOU SHALT NOT STEAL THE EARTH."

Ned frowned and tried to make out what the passing men were chanting. They broke into a confusing babble of voices until someone began clapping his hands to establish a rhythm.

"Cheap cotton," they chanted.

"Cheap soil.

"Steal the cotton.

"Leave the oil."

Ned stepped out into the street. An open buckboard wagon was being dragged by four men. Standing on the back of the wagon, a tall young man in a black frock coat and knee-high boots was waving to the throng. Now and then he would beat his hands together to emphasize the shouted words.

"Cheap cotton!

"Cheap soil!"

Ned could read a bedsheet tacked to the side of the buckboard. "Hear Mike Leathers, Jackson Square. Tonight." He waved at the tall man in the boots. This had to be Mike's fracas about Edmund Crozat's oil lands.

"Steal the cotton!

"Leave the oil!"

Fascinated, Ned began walking with the marchers, as others had done, swelling their ranks considerably by the time they reached the border of the French Quarter at Canal where St. Charles Street changed its name to Royal.

What had at first been a few hundred backwoods rubens had now become a horde of about a thousand people wildly waving torches in a town where fire was a constant danger. The city lads like Ned lent a lightfooted air to the event, jumping about and brandishing their torches while the farm contingent plodded steadily on.

From somewhere to the west, in the District, a spasm band materialized to add its jerky brand of music to the march. Stalebread Charley sawed at a violin made from a cigar box. Cajun made his harmonica wail and chuff like a cow in heat. Chinee played a bull fiddle made out of a barrel. Warm Gravy produced shrill piping from a tin whistle.

None of them had yet reached the age of ten, but they did well for themselves on nickels and dimes drunks would toss them. Harking back to the old river songs and chants, they shouted "hi-de-ho!" in time to the marchers' slogan. Seeing that no one was tossing coins, however, they dropped away at St. Peter Street, where the line of march turned right along the side of the old *cabildo* toward Jackson Square.

"Cheap cotton!

"Cheap soil!

"Steal the cotton!

"Leave the oil!"

Ned dashed along Pirate's Alley between the *cabildo* and St. Louis Cathedral to reach the square ahead of the throng. Another crowd of perhaps five hundred was waiting for the arrival of the parade. They had a band of their own, a small one, in which Ned could make out the face of the cornetist, Buddy Bolden. They had begun playing a slow, somber tune punctuated like a funeral march by the deliberate single beats of a bass drum. Bolden's silver tone arched up over the trees in Jackson Square had seemed to rally all of New Orleans.

Now the buckboard rattled into the square and halted beside the statue of Old Hickory on his horse. "Howdy!" Mike Leathers bellowed. "We're here to save the earth!"

A shout went up from the crowd. Marchers continued to pour into the square. Ned managed to scramble up over the barrier that ringed the Jackson statue. Finding toeholds, he pulled himself up to the top of the pedestal and stood there holding onto Old Hickory's left boot and stirrup for support.

The square was filled now. Tar barrels had been set up at either end of the buckboard. Men with torches advanced from the perimeter of the square until they ringed the wagon. Light flaring up into his face, Mike Leathers turned a barrel on end and mounted it.

"Friends!" he shouted. "And I think we can count on you fine New Orleanians as friends!" The crowd shouted unintelligibly. "We're here to tell you about a crime taking place in our sovereign state of Louisiana."

Hawkers were moving into the square, pushing their wheeled carts. In the distance, Ned could hear an old woman cry: "*Belle cala! Belle cala! Tout chaud.*" He sniffed and could already smell the odor of the deep-fried rice balls flavored with nutmeg and cinnamon.

"Up home," Mike Leathers told his audience, "we grow the cotton you folks ship all over the world. So we're in this together, us'ns and you'uns. Cotton is how we make a living. Or try to."

"*Belle cala!*"

The crowd hooted. Mike raised his arms for silence. "It's a hard buck, friends, and ain't that God's honest truth?"

The crowd roared its approval, and this time Mike let it roar awhile. Finally: "But the earth is fertile. You work hard and you harvest, year after year. The earth is bountiful, friends. That's why they're trying to steal the earth from us."

Catcalls. "There is a thing called petroleum," Mike went on after a pause. "You don't need it. I don't need it. You take it and it's gone. It ain't like cotton. There is only one harvest, and then . . . desolation.

And they are stealing the earth cheap," he shouted. "They are paying as low as four bits an acre for land, tax-free. They intend to harvest those acres just once and then let them run wild. But we've got a few pieces of legislation up at Baton Rouge that'll put a stop to it. That's why we're here. To ask for your help. The help of your legislators."

The crowd howled its approval. The bass drum boomed ominously. Men began to throw torches high into the air, like fireworks. The lighted pine boughs turned end over end like catherine wheels, then fell in a shower of sparks, to be snatched up, still flaming, and thrown again.

Ned's glance swung across the square from one side to the other. In December the ground was damp and chill. Even so, he could see a bush catch fire as one of the torches landed squarely in its branches. Evidently Mike Leathers had seen it at the same time. He took a prodigious jump off the barrel and buckboard and landed on the path, already running.

Dashing toward the bush, Mike pulled off his frock coat and began slapping at the flaming branches. Soon other men joined him, and in a moment the crisis was over. Mike turned back triumphantly to the crowd. "That's the way, friends!" he roared. "That's how we're gonna snuff out the oil fire!"

Ned climbed down from the pedestal and began to mingle with the crowd. "You going to ask your legislator about this?" he asked one man.

"Don't rightly know who the hell he is," came the frank response.

To another: "How do you feel about this oil?"

"What oil?" the man responded.

Finally, feeling a little foolish at having been carried away by the enthusiasm that only Leathers and his country lads seemed to have, Ned moved off toward his newspaper's office. You could always collect a crowd in New Orleans, he thought, but as for trying to peddle an idea to them . . . When the shouting died down, they moved on to the next excitement.

Already the *cala* women were pushing their carts away. "*Tout chaud! Tout chaud!*" Somewhere else in the city folks would gather tonight for some other reason, toss nickels to the spasm bands, buy the hot rice balls. Here everything was ending.

As if to speed the departing guests, Bolden's band struck up a lively two-step, his cornet sending bright jabs of staccato notes out over the city. Ned turned once more to stare at Jackson Square. Most of the people had left. Four men were dragging away the buckboard. Mike Leathers was nowhere to be seen.

Ned watched a lighted window in the corner apartment of the upper Pontalba building, nearest the river. On the second floor, screened through the florid outdoor iron lacework galleries with their intertwined P-and-A motif, a curtain that had been pulled aside was slowly let fall.

Whoever had been watching the protest from Edmund Crozat's apartment had turned away from the window. Ned found himself wondering whether Leathers and his up-country bumpkins were serious enough someday to start burning effigies. If so, he knew who one of the straw figures would resemble.

15

Dr. Fortunato Amabile turned away from the window of Edmund's apartment. *"Che peccato!"* he said mournfully. He was speaking aloud to himself, since his patient was in bed at the rear of the apartment and the sister was in the front foyer talking earnestly with another woman. Of the parents there was no trace, which Dr. Amabile found astounding. Not to be here when the son and heir is stricken?

He went to the foyer door. Miss Olivia and a taller woman with reddish-blond hair broke off their conversation. "How is he?" Olivia Crozat asked.

"There is no change. He rests comfortably," Dr. Amabile reported. "And your *papa . . . maman?* How will they get through that maddened horde below in the streets?"

The taller woman frowned. "Most of those men have left the square," she said. "The rally is over. Can I . . . ?" She stopped herself, but not for long. "Is it possible to talk . . . to him?"

The doctor's head had started shaking negatively even before she finished her request. "He is asleep, mamselle. It is a question of the nervous system, nothing more serious."

Olivia's smile was a lopsided replica of her brother's. "Nothing more serious," she echoed with a mocking tone. "Have you, perhaps, read of the new Vienna school of mental disorders, doctor?"

"What about his nerves?" the taller one persisted.

Dr. Amabile threw up his hands. "I am a simple family physician. I know exhaustion when I see it. And I know that bed rest is the cure in ninety-nine cases out of a hundred."

Olivia turned to her guest. "I expect my parents at any moment."

The taller woman sighed. "Yes, I understand. Well, it was only a thought, Olivia. If there had been anything I could do to help . . ."

"I appreciate your concern, dear Kate. Perhaps you can return to the opera house for the last of Sarasate. I know Jed would be pleased with your company."

"Oh? Has he discussed . . . ?" Her voice died away.

"No. But I'm aware that Jed has been thinking of . . . ah, companionship for some time."

"Really? Then he . . ." She paused and pointed a finger at Olivia. "You don't mean he's . . . ?"

Olivia nodded, and both young women began to giggle. "Enterprising of him," Olivia said at last. "And one simply has to admire his taste in choices."

For some reason not known to Dr. Amabile, this produced a second attack of giggles. He watched the two women bid each other good night. When the taller one had left, the doctor put a sharper tone in his voice. He had been attending the Crozat family since Edmund's father was a lad. "*Votre papa . . . maman!*" he said.

"Any second now. But if Edmund's sleeping, what possible use can they be here tonight?"

"That is for your father and me to decide."

"Without consulting Edmund?"

"Edmund is a very weak boy," Amabile told her. "He will recover much of his strength by tomorrow and think that he is well again. But he will be fooling himself. He needs discipline and patience. Otherwise I have known this exhaustion business to lead to worse. Influenza, even."

"He has discipline and patience," Olivia retorted. "He doesn't need yours, and he can certainly do without Papa's. Simply tell him what he must do. He will take care of the rest himself."

Dr. Amabile rolled his eyes upward. "With the same efficiency he has displayed in letting his physique run downhill for months now? No sleep. Constant trips upriver to Baton Rouge. Horseback travel. Strange food in strange places. And, always, the absinthe."

Olivia's eyelids twitched. She marched past Amabile into the parlor and threw open the *escritoire*. The absinthe bottle stood half-full next to the cut-glass bourbon decanter. "That is the same level of absinthe as a week ago," she told the doctor.

"But is it the same bottle?"

She stood silently, her lips tight. "What are you telling me, doctor?"

"He is no addict, but the signs are there. The . . . the pores of the skin *exude* an aroma of anise. And the speech is delirious. There is a flush of fever without an elevated temperature. And the tremors in the extremities. I know the signs, mamselle."

"Except for the anise smell," she told him, "these are the signs of someone undergoing an emotional crisis."

"Except," Amabile agreed sleekly, "for the anise smell."

The doorbell rang. Olivia opened it to her father, who was alone. "Maman?" she asked.

"I preferred not to trouble the poor woman with the tragedy of her only son. She is, to the best of my belief, enjoying the melodious performance of Sarasate, as was I until your imperious summons. Who were the strangers sitting in Edmund's loge with you?"

"Friends of ours, Papa. You must have recognized Mr. Benjamin."

Crozat *père* frowned importantly. "I knew his father. A great patriot, Livy, despite his race. But who was the woman with him? Everyone seemed to be whispering. Of course, no Crozat listens."

"That was Miss Katherine Blood, a schoolmate of mine," she added quickly, "from the Sacred Heart Convent."

Her father still seemed dissatisfied. "But Edmund must not let people use his loge," he persisted doggedly. "It is not proper unless Edmund himself is there. There is a punctilio in these matters. It is a question of hospitality . . ."

Olivia's ears shut down automatically. How strange, she found herself thinking. His son lies ill and he must deliver a sermon on something that is of no importance whatsoever. She found herself wondering if she, too, would have such a rigidly shut mind when she reached her father's age.

"Father," she finally managed to interrupt. "Dr. Amabile is waiting for you in the parlor."

"Ah, yes." Crozat *père* permitted himself to be led into the next room, where he and the doctor performed their own extended form of punctilio.

Olivia finally left them alone and went to the kitchen, where she set a kettle of water to boil, opened the blue-enameled Creole coffeepot, and pulled off its cuplike upper section. She filled the top with ground dark-roast coffee and returned it to the main pot. Then she placed the whole thing in a shallow pan of warm water. When the kettle came to the boil, she patiently let the hot water drip slowly through the top opening.

The business about the absinthe was new to her. Edmund kept it around, as far as she knew, for Sazeracs or frappés, which guests sometimes requested. She had rarely seen him drink the bitter green liqueur.

Customarily it was added in small quantities to a glass of crushed ice. One placed a cube of sugar in a perforated teaspoon and trickled water through it. When liquid reached the absinthe, the whole glass turned milky. Even thus diluted and sweetened, Olivia found the drink too bitter for her taste. It did produce delusions and convulsions, as Amabile said. That much was true. But only if persistently taken in large quantities. Edmund, she felt sure, would never want to dull his mental processes to that level.

When she returned to the parlor, she found her father and the doctor staring dejectedly at their boot tips. "*Un peu de café, messieurs?*"

Crozat *père* looked up. "You heard? The absinthe?"

"I have never actually seen Edmund dr—."

He stopped her by an impatient wave of the hand. "The evidence is overwhelming. But I shall see for myself."

"He's sleeping, Papa."

The doctor grimaced, hands outstretched at his sides in a silent apology to Olivia. "We shall be very quiet," he promised. "If he still sleeps, I believe he should not be awakened."

"That," Crozat *père* told him, "is for me to decide."

"*Bien sûr*. Of course."

"Father," Olivia said sharply. "The doctor has said—"

"But I *am* the *father*," Crozat *père* reminded her, his thin mustache quivering with his own sense of himself. He started for the rear apartment.

If he had been sleeping at all, Olivia saw when she entered her brother's bedroom, it had been badly. The sheets were bunched up. Edmund's eyes opened a moment after they came through the door. "Out!" he rasped. "All of you."

"Silence." His father stared at him with a cold smile. "Before me lies the end result of indulgence. Of independence. Of undisciplined hubris." He gave the word a French intonation.

Edmund closed his hot eyes. The skin around them looked bruised. He seemed to Olivia to be trying to switch off his father's voice as she had a few moments ago.

"And what a *grande pagaille* you have made of your independence," Crozat *père* continued, still smiling mercilessly. "You have squandered your inheritance. You have gone down to defeat with those Kaintock thieves and swindlers at Baton Rouge. You have alerted every political and business enemy to your plans. You have so mismanaged this affair that you have undoubtedly lost whatever commercial advantage you possessed from the start. It will now become an area of haggling between white trash with an inflated idea of the value of their land and cheapjack entrepreneurs seeking to fleece them. Moreover, this miasma of doubt, ill will, uncertainty, and suspicion of the Crozat name will continue to exist for years to come. You, sir, have done a grave and irreparable injury to the family whose proud name you are not fit to bear."

Olivia could see Edmund's jaw showing white through his flushed skin, as if he were gritting his teeth.

"Now, sir," Crozat *père* continued in a tone of mournful satisfaction, "like the owner of a fine china shop, I have to examine the damage and determine what can be mended. To begin with, I have consulted with one of our upstate managers, the man from Whiteacres, Waddell, about the character of this Leathers person who has inflamed his constituency to such a point that even tonight my vehicle was impeded in its progress here by drunken mobs brought down to rally support against you."

Edmund's eyes, behind closed lids, seemed to Olivia to shift sideways. But he continued to listen—if that was the word—in silence.

"Waddell tells me you can expect no mercy from Leathers. He is one of these *nouveaux populistes* who promise fools their freedom. And he has the confidence and support of a very powerful colleague, Representative Bunch. Your business, sir, is finished, if indeed it ever could be said to have begun."

Edmund twisted slowly in bed, as if trying to turn away from the sound of his father's voice.

"I went a step further," Crozat *père* continued. "I consulted with M. Badger, of the cotton-mill company. He is knowledgeable about the pack of liars and drunkards we call the state legislature. He confirms Waddell's estimate of Leathers. He tells me Leathers cannot be bought.

"But, I am not without compassion," Jean-Paul Crozat thundered, slamming his hand down on the footboard of the bed with such violence that Edmund's body was jolted. "I try like a father to see what can be done so that a life will not be ruined forever. I ask Badger whether the British mills can support you in this matter. Surely Leathers is their enemy as he is yours."

Edmund's face was pressed into the pillow, eyelids still clenched as shut as a fist.

"And that is when I learned your scheme was totally dead. Badger told me the mills support Leathers," his father continued with a kind of relentless glee. "Oil money distracts farmers in the area from growing cotton, so he opposes your plans. You have no hope, sir. Now, then, I am not without heart. What can be done with this miserable failure who happens to be my only son?"

"Who happens to be ill, Papa," Olivia cut in.

"You are forbidden to speak."

"Who needs quiet, not gloating tirades," she told him.

"Who has drank himself into idiocy already, perhaps," Crozat *père* roared back at her. "You are forbidden to speak!"

"Whom you will kill this way, Papa. I warn you."

"Forbidden!" he almost screamed. "Forbidden to speak!"

His face had grown scarlet. Turning, he grasped Dr. Amabile's shoulder for support. "My children are murdering me, doctor," he muttered.

"Come. Come." The doctor led him out of the room. "Sit down, sir," Olivia could hear him say in a soothing voice, growing more distant. "Perhaps a bit of absinthe to relax your tension, eh? It can do no ha . . ."

At last she could hear him no more. She cleared her throat. "Edmund," she said then, "I'm going to turn down the lamp and let you try to sleep. Is there a draft the doctor left, a sleeping draft?"

He opened his eyes and stared at the ceiling. The pupils were dilated, Olivia saw, so that the entire iris seemed as black as night, staring, unfocused, at nothing. "The old devil is right," he said then in a weak voice. "I'm finished."

His deep tones sounded more like a croak. Olivia turned down the gas jet until the room was almost in darkness. "We'll talk about it in the morning, if you wish. I'll try to get him out of here."

He nodded, but said nothing more. "Oh, you had a visitor, Kate Blood." Edmund lay silent, as if he had not heard. "I have been thinking," Olivia said then. "She is a good friend, Edmund. Perhaps . . . in this matter . . . her father . . ."

16

Christmas 1888, a holiday the Bloods would later have reason to remember well, began weeks ahead of time with open warfare.

Traditionally, Christmas dinner was held at Cornelius Blood's rather somber three-story home on Chartres, in the square bounded by Esplanade, the northern limit of the Quarter. It was prepared by Julia, the black cook Neil Blood had employed for more than a decade, on whose cuisine all the Bloods had been raised. Her style had begun as Creole French, but Neil had over the years weaned her away to dishes he considered more fitting, roasts of meat and potatoes in an endless variety of preparation. Kate assumed she would again supervise the feast this Christmas.

She was surprised when Mary insisted that her new house, only two squares away on the grand expanse of Esplanade, was the obvious choice.

Mary pressed home her arguments with breathless ferocity. "You've only been to my place one time. It's not nice."

Kate responded in murmurs.

Life had become exceedingly dull of late. Edmund had suddenly left town. His sister believed he was in Chicago or New York. Running her father's house took little of Kate's time or energy.

She understood Mary's reasons for wanting to have the dinner at her home. In the undeclared but permanent war between them, Mary had very few weapons. She was not particularly bright, nor attractive. In her

122

the fair Blood coloring had washed out to a series of beige-grays. But she did have two children and a third pushing her belly proudly out, and a grand new home, none of which Kate could claim. Sighing with boredom, Kate surrendered the first round.

There followed hectic preparations. Julia would do the cooking in her own kitchen. Walter would carry over the pots that noon. To Mary's one Irish maid would be added Neil's two Negro women. And so the battle lines were drawn.

"It will be a simple meal," Mary promised them, "the sort Abner and I usually enjoy when he has his many important political and financial friends over for Sunday dinner. Just family-style. Nothing grand."

Her weak blue eyes, milky with subdued malice, peered from Neil to Kate to Father James, her oldest brother. He and Kate shared the same birth year, having been born ten months apart. Otherwise they shared little else. James's coloring resembled his garments, drab gray as benefitted a Jesuit scholastic teaching grammar for the next five years to Ignatius Loyola students.

But James had always been dark, like his mother, with the same look of muted anger in his eyes as in Mary's. The two of them gazed out at what they both seemed to feel was a hostile world. Kate, like her father and other two brothers, looked squarely at what was in front of her, expecting little but hoping for a pleasant surprise from time to time. Agnes, the youngest, could not get leave from the Carmelite convent where she served as a novice. It was a strict order and even Christmas was not considered an excuse for a visit home.

"A simple meal," Mary repeated several times. "Let Julia do the turkey. I'll do the rest."

Kate understood that a trap lay there. The enemy was undoubtedly preparing something immensely grand, and when the trap was sprung, would sit modestly collecting a garland of compliments, like the laurels placed on the winner's brow. Let's see poor spinster Kate do anything remotely as wonderful as this.

As she feared, the holiday dinner began at two o'clock and continued till long after five, with an array of dishes that swamped the most heroic eater at the table. To start, Mary had boiled a peck of shrimp, to be munched with *rèmoulade* sauce. This was followed by a clear turtle soup with sherry and, still bubbling inside their parchment-paper papillotes, baked pompano stuffed with crabmeat. Saffron rice attended the fish, as well as a cold cauliflower salad tangy with lemon juice. Six bottles of Neil Blood's finest hock were served.

Kate glanced around the table. Patrick and his new wife, Nelly, were packing it in. She supposed they didn't eat half as well on the sergeant's salary he drew from Police Chief Hennessy. James ate small, priestly portions, but saw to it that he refilled his plate often. Abner, their host, a stringy man next to Patrick's thick beefy frame, matched his brother-in-law serving for serving.

Ned, who was engrossed in a private conversation with their guest, Mr. Badger, whose daughter Daisy had returned to England, seemed hardly to eat at all. He was still nibbling shrimp by the time the pompano was cleared away. He had commandeered his own bottle of hock. The Englishman did well enough, Kate saw, holding his fork all wrong, with the tines down, and pushing bits of food on top of it.

Walter cleared the empty hock bottles, slim and long-necked, from the table, to replace them with six opened bottles of claret, one of which Ned promptly appropriated. Walter then returned pushing a cart on which Julia's large turkey rode, an imperial visitor, flanked by its own company of giblet dressing, Cumberland sauce and candied yams topped with spun sugar. A chorus of ah's and too-much's produced a wan smirk of satisfaction on Mary's face.

This widened to a weak grin when one of the maids brought in the glazed ham drenched in bourbon sauce, and another arrived with hot string beans and tomatoes cooked in garlic. A platter of potatoes au gratin made an appearance, as did another of mashed, in which a gob of butter the size of a fist was slowly swimming.

Kate's appetite had been poor for some time. It was one thing to know that Edmund was in New Orleans and, eventually, reachable. It was another to have him mysteriously vanish. She would have to make a decision, she told herself now as she passed up the ham and its accompanying dishes. Her father had a saying that covered the situation. She would have to "cut her losses."

Sick or well, here or somewhere else, Edmund showed no interest in her. Jed Benjamin, on the other hand, continued to escort her to concerts and operas and had even taken the daring step of inviting her to a New Year's Eve ball sponsored by one of the prestigious Mardi Gras krewes, an all-Creole, upper-class affair at which she was certain no one would speak to her except poor Jed.

She had a clear idea of his strategy. If he was to propose marriage, he first had to surround her with as much acceptance as he could muster. Seen often enough in society, Kate Blood would begin to lose her scarlet sheen and be taken for granted. At that point a proposal was sure to follow.

She watched the maids carry off the debris. Then her father cleared his throat portentously and said, "Lovely meal, my dear." Mary simpered. Neil winked at Kate as he launched into his favorite genteelism: "I have enjoyed an elegant sufficiency," he announced. "Any more would be a superfluity."

As it always did, this brought chuckles from some of his children. But

Mary failed to smile. "I hope you've left room for desserts," she said in a worried voice.

"Mercy," Ned groaned.

"My dear hostess," Alexander Badger began in his broad style of flattery, "seldom have I enjoyed a more truly Lucullan repast. Surely the nectar of coffee alone could follow the abundant ambrosia of this triumph."

But Kate knew better. Sweets began to arrive like the cars of an exceedingly long freight train. Plum pudding rattled in with its side dish of hard sauce. This was followed by fruit cake soaked in bourbon and a large platter of blackberry turnovers. Serving plates of pecan lace cookies were passed. Silky tan pralines appeared. As a kind of caboose, a train of nuts and hard candies rumbled into view.

Walter uncorked Château d'Yquem dessert wine. Five kinds of liqueurs arrived, with port displayed on the sideboard. And finally a silver tureen of spicy *café brûlot* was wheeled in, blue flames flickering over its surface.

It was just as well, Kate thought, that Agnes hadn't been able to come. The Spartan fare of the Carmelites would have left her poor stomach defenseless against this occasion of gluttony.

Kate lifted her glass. "Mary, you win."

Her sister's milky eyes widened in pain. "What does that mean?"

"I suggest we make this a permanent institution," Kate said in her kindest tones. "From now on, every Christmas at Mary's."

"Hear, hear," her father chimed in. He lifted his glass to Alderman Abner Hinckley. "And to mine goodly host and his new reform government. May 1889 produce wonders of honesty in our fair city."

"And to the new Hinckley," Father James added, lifting his glass. "May he be all that you hope for, Mary." The choice of pronoun had been clearly made. After two daughters, the Hinckleys prayed for a son.

Ned got slowly to his feet, his small, lithe body a bit unsteady. By grasping Badger's shoulder he managed to hoist himself erect. Spilling the dark amber wine a bit, he lifted his glass. "And to the great port city of New Orleans," he announced, or meant to. It came out "T'th'gr'porsity v'Nawlins."

Everyone's glass went up. "To its shippers," Ned continued, nodding to Badger, "its protectors," he went on, nodding to his brother Patrick, "and let's add a special prayer for the continued health of Massimo and Peter Provenzano."

Sudden silence.

His father was the first to speak. "And what business does them dagos have at my family Christmas, may I ask?"

Patrick looked glum. "It's not a fittin' subject for dinner talk, Pa."

"My point exactly."

Patrick glowered at his younger brother. His frown, Kate noted, had become an instrument of intimidation, a prime weapon for any policeman to carry, especially if he were, like Patrick, one of the city's few honest ones. "Did you have to spoil the meal?" Patrick inquired of Ned in a menacing voice.

"Just a prayer for their health," Ned retorted, making his face look as innocent as possible. "You *are* looking after their health, I hope."

Kate glanced at her father. This would never do. The Provenzanos controlled loading and unloading at the docks. They happened to be personal friends of Police Chief Hennessy as well. But lately Tony Matranga had been muscling in on the docks, hoping through his Black Hand organization to take over the Provenzano monopoly. And Tony Matranga was a friend of Neil Blood's.

"That's enough toasting," Kate said in a cheery voice, getting to her feet. "I think it's time we all . . ." Her glance wandered. We all what? Any diversion would do. "We all moved to the parlor to hear Mary play the new piano. Will you, Mary?"

Nothing would have pleased her sister more. She jumped to her feet as Ned, still brandishing his glass, said, "And while we're drinking healths, here's to missing friends." He hiccuped solemnly, as if this were part of the benediction as well. "And a prayer for the well-being of Edmund Crozat."

Ponderously his father remarked, "Mary, start playing." His glance darted sideways to his oldest daughter, a look that said: "Can't nobody control him?"

"Sit down, Neddie," his brother Patrick told him in his best cop voice.

"And no more toasts," Alexander Badger chimed in, regaining his seat. "Let there be a moratorium on encomiums." He laughed with such violence that Ned turned to stare down at him.

"Then a last benediction," he said, raising his glass over Badger's head. "To our friends from o'er the seas. May they come often, stay well, and keep their bloody noses out of our business."

With that he gently tipped the dessert wine in a delicate stream over Badger's unprotected head. Patrick leaped to his feet so quickly that his hefty torso rammed the table and wineglasses crashed to the floor. He began sponging at Badger, turning his hair into a revolting mess which suddenly came off in Patrick's hands.

"Paddy!" Neil Blood thundered. "Lay off'n him!"

Badger clasped his bald dome in both hands. "Where? What?"

Kate sat down again and watched her sister Mary standing in the doorway. The big musical moment had passed. Sweet revenge. "Ned," Kate called. "Can you think of anyone else to offend?"

"To our all-wise spinster sister!" Ned retorted instantly. "May she remember that old Irish saying."

"Ah, shut your gob!" his father shouted.

"No, not that one," Ned countered.

Kate started to laugh. Just a happy Irish Christmas, she thought. "What's the saying, Neddie?"

"Dear Kate. There is only one thing worse than not getting your dream."

The assembly grew suddenly silent. "And that is?" Kate asked.

"Getting it."

17

Neil Blood had christened the brothel the House of Blue Lights because it pleased his often perverse sense of humor to own such a place in the red-light district.

The facade of the three-story mansion was outlined in gas lights set in blue-glass cups. And inside, on the second floor, ran a series of rooms in which customers and house girls performed under blue lights. A peephole into each room was available for other customers at a price. In this way, with the customer's knowledge, Neil got two fees for each girl, one from the man who got a kick out of being watched and one from the watcher.

Tonight Neil sat at a corner table of the main parlor, the house's only semirespectable room. In another corner a piano player pounded an upright next to a small stage on which the more talented girls sang and, within limits, danced.

The rest of the room was in perpetual dusk. Here Neil's clients would drink, talk, watch the show, and when moved, head upstairs for other pleasures. But here, in the vast parlor, everyone behaved.

It was a typical night for the House of Blue Lights, Neil noted. On this thirtieth of December he had a party of six visitors from upriver, St. Louis they said. He had two judges, five state senators, four planters, half a dozen local merchants, a U.S. congressman and his party, a few brokers and factors, a group of Central American *finca* owners spending their banana- and coffee-crop money, several sea captains in civilian garb, the French ambassador, a table of bankers, and as his own guest, Tony Matranga.

"Nice," Matranga grunted, sipping a glass of red wine. "Nice place, nice wine. This is Lombardo's *vino rosso,* no? He give you a good price?"

Inviting Matranga here had been Matranga's idea. The man made Neil nervous. He had a way of looking at everything with his dark, heavy-lidded eyes, as if pricing it for later sale. He reminded Neil of an undertaker who measures you alive for what he will eventually have to do for you dead. For a price. Always a price.

"It's not easy, running a place like this," Neil told the Sicilian. He assumed, having been in a few business deals with the Matrangas and their associates, that they coveted such Blood operations as the Wicklowe and the House of Blue Lights and would one day make their move.

Till then, he had to keep them convinced that the management of such establishments was an art, a mystery few had mastered. Playing with tigers, was the way Neil put it to himself. He wasn't sure exactly how he had gotten involved with the Sicilians, but the game of holding them at bay was an exciting one.

Tony Matranga finished his wine. "I go upstairs now. That Stella. She's free?"

"For you, anytime. Madam Consuelo will give you her room number."

Matranga got to his feet. "You know how to treat a guest, Signor Blood. And Tony Matranga, he knows how to treat a good friend." Soberly he made his way to the madam's table near the entrance, and a moment later was climbing the stairs to the third floor.

It came to Neil as he watched his friend leave that he had gotten mixed up with the Matrangas over a matter of price. Normally he bought his fruit and vegetables wholesale through an affiliate of the Provenzano family. Melons, that was it. He was paying two cents apiece for the fine green melons from Costa Rica. Tony Matranga had made him a one-cent offer. Then the lettuce, also at half price. Finally Neil was buying all his produce from the Matrangas. Considering that he had four restaurants and served food in at least six of his houses, he was saving himself quite a bit of cash. So price was at the bottom of it.

A rangy girl got up on the stage, dressed in the low-necked, pinched-waist style of a lady of fashion. Her long, full skirt ended in ruffles that swept the floor, the pleats in front coming to a rosette centered at about the place where her legs joined. In the fashion of the day, her hair was curled in thick ringlets from a middle part, pulled into a high chignon and also allowed to flow freely over her neck. She had a wide mouth, which she contorted comically as she sang one of the newer songs of the day.

"You're so ugly," she sang, pointing at the black piano player.

"Um, you're ugly.

"You're some ugly chile.

"Now the clo'es that you wear

"Are not in style.

"You look jus' like an ape

"Ev'y time you smile."

The pianist was accompanying her at a medium drag tempo, heavy chords in the treble, and in between, mock gestures of defense against her verbal attack.

A shorter girl mounted the stage with the intent of singing her own song. She gestured to the piano player, but he continued pounding out the drag. The rangy girl turned on the newcomer as her new target.

"Ooh, how I hate ya,

"Ya alligator-bait, ya;

"You're the ugliest thing I ever saw.

"You're five by five and box-ankled, too.

"How'd they ever get a pair of shoes on you?

"Your hair is nappy.

"Who's your pappy?

"You're some ugly chile."

Neil stopped listening when the short girl, getting into the spirit of the thing, turned the lyrics around and aimed them at the rangy singer. The proprietor of the House of Blue Lights gazed around the room, his glance coming to rest at Madam Consuelo's table just as the doorman ushered in a new guest.

Edmund Crozat.

Neil felt the skin across his shoulders prickle. The Crozat lad hadn't been seen in New Orleans for weeks. Nor, in his prime, had he ever been seen at the House of Blue Lights. He was no man for the sporting houses. Neil looked him over closely. The reports of his physical breakdown seemed exaggerated. In fact, the lad looked to be in good shape. He paid his compliments to Consuelo and took a step into the room, handing his hat, gloves, and cape to the Negro attendant.

Just as Neil had done a moment before, Edmund Crozat now surveyed the parlor. He nodded to one man, gestured politely to a second. Then he made his way to the table of the French ambassador and presented himself with a ceremonial bow. A few moments of polite conversation and he moved deftly between tables to greet the congressman with a firm handshake. Politely refusing a drink, he strolled to the table of bankers, where he greeted each in turn. Here he accepted an invitation to sit but again refused a drink.

Back from the dead, Neil thought. And no Lazarus ever made a handsomer return. It was as if, instead of putting an advertisement in the paper, Crozat had chosen this way of announcing his return, undamaged, sleek as a snake and with a new *bonhomie* that seemed a far cry from his old standoffishness.

He was hobnobbing with the judges now, but Neil had figured out his itinerary. The last stop would be the proprietor's table. Neil wondered how the boy would handle it, since they'd never formally met.

He found out a few minutes later when, having bid a pleasant adieu to the planters, Edmund Crozat approached the proprietor. "Have I the honor of addressing Mr. Blood?" he asked.

"Mr. Crozat, you do."

"May I sit with you a moment, sir?"

At close range, Edmund's dark eyes seemed to smolder. It was, Neil saw, as if the fires behind them were banked and carefully tended, well under control. But fires, nevertheless. He was handsome, no doubt about it, Neil thought. He understood what Kate saw in the lad.

"You may." Neil indicated his own glass of beer. "What's your pleasure?"

Edmund shook his head. "Thank you. I have been ill."

"Beer is a great builder of body."

Edmund's crooked smile seemed regretful. "I have just returned to town today," he said then. "How is Ned?"

"Still mongering scandal."

"And your daughter, Miss Katherine?"

"Fine. Just fine."

Edmund seemed to relax very slightly in the upholstered chair. He sat back and stared for a moment at his long, narrow fingers. "I said I had been unwell. But the truth of it is this. The doctors in Chicago called it a case of poisoning."

"Dear God."

"Absinthe poisoning," Edmund added with his ironic smile.

"Ah. I see."

"I would appreciate your keeping it as a confidence."

Neil Blood nodded almost sleepily. In this room of half a hundred men, he was privy to the secrets of many. That was the damned thing about people. As Ned put it with such nasty precision: everybody has something to hide. To journalists and blackmailers such secrets brought a price. Neil Blood was neither; he had mastered the even more lucrative profession of keeping his mouth shut.

Across the room, still with one arm in a sling, sat a living example of the power Neil Blood had found in being closemouthed. Representative Jack Bunch had only recently come out of enforced seclusion. His accident with the McCormick reaper had brought him a lot of joshing, but not the kind that hurt a public figure. And no whisper of the real truth of his accident had reached his wealthy wife, Miz Eulalia. Between Neil Blood and Christy Leathers, the fat, perverted Carolina Duffy had been eased out of the District to a house in Milneburg, on the shores of Lake Pontchartrain. Patrons with a taste for pain could take "Smokey Mary," the elderly train that ran to the lake, and enjoy themselves in screaming seclusion.

No one had connected the important Jack Bunch with the murderous Miss Duffy. No one would. There were a lot of rewards in silence. It, too, had a price.

"You have my word," Neil said then.

"I believe I'm over it now," Edmund told him. "The doctors think so. Of course, the success of it lies in my hands."

"Which can no longer reach for an absinthe," Neil said in a joshing tone.

Edmund stared at his fingers. "Or any drink. One leads to another. And eventually one is calling for absinthe."

"True."

"It would be fair, would it not," Edmund went on, "to say that I left New Orleans under something of a cloud?"

Neil found himself wondering why a lad who had been a stranger until a few minutes ago was abruptly unburdening himself. And not merely a stranger, but one with a reputation for playing a lone game.

"It would be fair," Neil agreed.

"In Chicago," Edmund continued, "once the doctors allowed it, I moved about the city rather extensively. Our family has connections there."

"And not only there."

"But word of my disgrace had not yet reached Chicago."

"You are very frank."

"This will be an extremely candid conversation, Mr. Blood." Edmund's dark glance raked across his face. "It may have come to your attention that I have a problem with the legislature concerning my oil explorations."

"If you call a dead stop a problem, yes."

"I cannot admit to a dead stop." Edmund looked back at his fingers. "More than my health is in my own hands," he confessed. "I hope it is still within my power to overcome this political opposition and move forward with my business plans."

"I hope you're right," Neil said in a doubtful tone.

"But"—Edmund grinned crookedly—"you wouldn't bet on it."

Neil sat back. He was beginning to like this lone wolf. "Let me guess," he said then. "You've managed to drum up financial backing in Chicago."

"That's most astute of you."

"And now you'd like to drum up political backing right here at this table."

"If that is not beyond the bounds of possibility."

Neil reached inside his breast pocket for a small leather case from which he half-pulled two thin panatelas. He extended the case to Edmund, who shook his head. Neil scratched a match on the table's ashtray and got his cigar drawing to his satisfaction. Then he sat back, a picture of ease. "Why?" he asked then.

"I beg your pardon?"

"Why should I back you up politically?" Neil sat forward, intent on the young man. He watched the fires behind Edmund's eyes flare as he straightened in his chair.

"Because the destiny of this state is oil," Edmund told him in a low, intense voice. "As is the destiny of the world. I have devoted most of my adult life to learning about oil. To finding out what it can do. I have nearly ruined my health in the service of this dream, sir."

The candle at their table flickered wildly in Edmund's hot, dark eyes. "Today it is a curiosity. But very soon," Edmund said, "it will become a necessity more precious than cotton or sugar or rice. More costly than wheat or corn. A mineral more valuable, sir, than silver or gold. Oil will become the prime mover of our world. Of this I am absolutely certain."

Neil felt a chill across his shoulder blades. The boy was damned convincing. The utter conviction in his voice had to come from either madness or truth. For the sake of the little deal he had in mind, Neil hoped the boy had told of the truth, not some nightmare illusion.

"Do you share that dream, sir?" the younger man asked him. "If you share even a piece of it, you must help me."

"Everything is possible, Mr. Crozat," Neil said in a lazy voice, realizing what the deal was going to be. "We're men of the world, however. We know that at the bottom of every possibility lies a price."

Edmund's dark face seemed to grow in intensity. Thoughtfully he touched his long fingers to his small, prudent mouth. "And what," he asked in a careful voice, "is yours?"

"Mr. Crozat," Neil purred, "this is the first time you and I have discussed business. It may come as a surprise that I am known as a generous man."

"Sir, I have heard nothing but good of you. That is a fact."

Neil nodded appreciatively, the accolade of one master flatterer to another. "Consider your situation," he went on then. "What you ask of me is nothing less than the complete reversal of a trend that has already been established in the legislature. Already pieces of legislation against your position are heading toward a final vote. You are asking nothing less of me than that I stop the mighty Mississippi in full spate. And then cause it to run backward in its course. You ask a miracle, something outside the laws of nature or man. Let me speak frankly: you ask the damned near impossible."

Edmund sat gravely for a long moment. Then his mouth warped in that peculiar smile of his. "*Near* impossible," he repeated with changed emphasis.

Neil Blood inclined his head to one side. "As near as makes no nevermind. I must salute your judgment, young fella. There is nobody else in the world you could have come to with this proposition. But by the same token, I am in a position to demand a most terrifying price, am I not?"

Crozat's face grew pale. "Name it, sir," he responded.

Neil laughed softly and clapped the young man's forearm. "Not so gloomy. I told you I was a generous man. You have met my eldest daughter, Kate?"

Edmund's dark eyes blinked suddenly, then took on a hooded look. "I have had that honor, sir."

"She is, I think you will agree, both an attractive and an accomplished young lady."

"Indeed, sir, one of our city's finest ornaments. And a childhood friend of my sister, Olivia, as well."

The older man sat forward in his chair. "She hasn't lacked for suitors. Some fairly important men have popped the question. But, speaking frankly again, I just didn't feel they were right for my Kate." He slowly sat back. "But now," Neil went on, "I believe I have met the right one. Tonight. At this table. Do you take my meaning, Mr. Crozat?"

Edmund sat perfectly still, a statue carved in a pale stone. After a long moment he seemed to let out a breath he was holding. "I do indeed, sir. And, speaking for myself, I say this is no price to pay at all. It is a magnificent gift from a man of great generosity. But . . ."

Neither of them spoke. "But," Edmund continued at last, "speaking for my family, I believe there would be . . . impediments in the way of such a marriage."

Neil Blood nodded sagely. "If the matter were to run its normal course, posting of banns, the usual delays, yes, I am certain a pretty formidable logjam would be thrown up in our path. But there are ways and ways. And Cardinal Contreras will know them all."

The younger man sat silently for a long time. "Have you thought how Miss Kate would take this?" he asked then. "My impression of her is of an exceedingly modern young woman with a first-rate mind of her own."

The father of the bartered bride smiled sweetly. "I see you two are not strangers. Then it must not have escaped your attention, Mr. Crozat, that my daughter has some feeling for you. Damn me if I don't think she likes you."

"And I her," Edmund rushed to confess. "She is . . ." He stopped himself. "She is so . . ." He paused again. "Miss Kate is . . . different," he said at last. "She is as different from the Creole girls my family would pick for me as the red-hot sun of day is from the pale light of the moon. I . . ."

"A poet, sir!"

Edmund sat back, nodding thoughtfully. Neil Blood considered himself a fairly astute reader of faces, but he had no idea what was going on behind those hot black eyes and that small, careful mouth.

"Am I to understand," Edmund began finally, "that if I marry your daughter you will reach forth and reverse the mighty Mississippi in its course?"

"Turn the legislature ass-over-teakettle? Something like that, yes."

"You believe it can be done," Edmund persisted.

"*I* can do it," Neil said, quietly accenting the pronoun.

In the pleasant intimacy of the big room, dusk pinpointed by candles, the two men sat watching each other. Wary, missing nothing, black eyes stared deeply into blue.

18

The Reverend Mr. Luke Leathers had inaugurated the year-end memorial service some time back. Folks liked it. On the last night of the year, before they went off and raised hell or took themselves quietly to bed, they remembered those who'd died.

The clapboard church was about half-full, Mike Leathers estimated. He had brought Luanne to the service because of her paw dying earlier in the year, his land being the cause of all that oil ruckus and snarling and dirty fighting.

But Mike judged they had the bastards licked for good. He sat back in the pew and let Luanne hold his hand. It was normal for courtin' couples to try that in church. But there was no way you could call Mike and Luanne courtin'. Not unless you had a definition of it as broad as the Mississippi.

"In Jesus Christ's name," Luke finished. "Amen."

"Ay-men," the congregation echoed.

"Well, we done it proper," the minister said after a pause. "We laid those good souls to rest. But we don't just remember people. The good Lord puts a lot of other things on his earth for us to notice and remember." He drew in a breath, and some of the more experienced listeners flinched in advance.

"That's *right!*" Luke Leathers thundered. "For it's written in the good book that he who forgets his *mistakes* is *doomed to repeat them!*"

136

His brother frowned slightly. What good book, he wondered, was that?

"Which is why on this *last day* of the year," the preacher soared, "we try to remember what we done wrong. *Think* about it now! Come forward and *resolve* in your *heart* never to make *that* mistake again. Who's first?"

He paused, and in the silence one parishioner spoke up. "I done made the mistake of not selling that hardscrabble of mine to the oil man," he said in a slyly innocent tone. "Mebbe I better remember that one, huh, preacher?"

Luke Leathers grinned at him. "What was he offerin', Calvin?"

"Buck'n acre."

"Hoo-ee!" Mike shouted, getting to his feet. "Here we go again. One miserable dollar for land that can be fruitful forever. For your children and their children. And you'd pawn their birthright for cash on the barrel."

"Ain't nawthin'd ever grow on that mess," Calvin retorted. "You are plumb talkin' th'ough a hole in your head if you call that hardpan fruitful."

"I call it your children's birthright. Tell me I'm wrong."

"They try farming it, they ain't gonna thank me a whole lot."

Mike shoved his fingers through thick black hair. "Calvin, I am sorely troubled that you folks don't get the true meaning of them snake-oil salesmen."

"You done said it," his neighbor persisted. "Cash on the barrelhead."

Mike Leathers shook his head slowly from side to side like a bull being tormented by flies. "I will be eternally damned if I can't make you people understand. First off," he said, holding up one finger, "you got a right to do whatever in tarnation you want t'do with your own land. Keep it. Sell it. Burn it over. Walk off and leave it for taxes. This is America, where free men own their land free and clear. All right? That is point one. Are you with me?"

Calvin nodded. "So far, a hundred percent."

"Two," Mike shouted, waving two fingers at the congregation, "is that the land has value in it and under it. From the topsoil you grow crops. Underneath there is mebbe some oil, mebbe not, which some fellers want to drill for. They offer cash. For taking away the oil? No, sir! For the whole kit and kaboodle, topsoil and all. So point two is this: keep the land; make 'em lease the right to drill for oil. Are you still with me?"

"Keep a-goin', Mike," another neighbor said.

"Three," the legislator cried out, "is money. The money they should pay you, per barrel, for draining off *your* oil. The money they should pay the state in taxes, per barrel, for removing a natural resource from Louisiana. Are you—?"

"You done lost me," Calvin cut in. "What the hell—pardon me, preacher—does anybody care about all that? I am speakin' for most of us," he went on, "when I tell you the news, Mike Leathers, that they is more'n a few of us *needs* cash on the barrelhead. Not tomorrow or next year or whenever some oil trickles in. But right *now*, to pay the company store and the doctor and Lord knows what else."

"Don't fall in that trap," Mike warned him.

"A man holds out cash money to me? All right, sure, mebbe he's pullin' a fast one. Mebbe if I leased it at so much a barrel I'd end up makin' more over the years. But I am hurtin' right *now*. *Now* is when cash looks mighty good to me."

Leathers sighed heavily. "That's the whole point, Calvin. It's that *now* thinkin' that pawns your kids' birthright."

"Shee . . ." Calvin stopped himself in time. "And that's another thing. Them taxes. Who gives a hoot in hell—pardon me, preacher—for sending money to Baton Rouge? You fellers got enough as it is."

"How long does it take you by buckboard from Winnfield to Shreveport?" Mike asked suddenly. "A whole day's ride? Why? Because they ain't no proper road. That's what tax money would build, or put in a school for your kids to get their proper learnin'. A man that don't give a hoot about taxes is a man who don't give a hoot about his kids."

"If that don't take the rag right offen the bush," Calvin exclaimed. "Pardon me, preacher. But here is this bachelor brother of yours lecturing me about kids. I swear I don't know whether to laugh or spit."

"It's a free country," Mike Leathers snapped back. "Do whatever you've a mind to do. Sell. Get that cash now. Pay your bill at the company store. Next year you'll have a bill just as big, and what land you gonna sell then, Calvin? Is that how you look after your future?"

He started pacing the center aisle of the church, clearly disturbed and forgetting the niceties an elected representative has to maintain with those who vote him in. Or out.

"You people," he complained."You're like kids yourselves. No wonder you don't plan for your own children. You want it all now."

"Mike," his brother called from the pulpit. "Calm down."

"I'll calm down. I just want to hear somebody tell me I'm not a voice hollering in the wilderness." He stopped pacing and tried to collect himself. "All right," he said at last, sitting down next to Luanne. Nobody spoke for a long moment.

"Where is that voice?" Mike asked in a softer tone. "Where is that person who will tell me I ain't crazy? That I'm doing the right thing."

He waited, but no one spoke. Mike patted Luanne's hand. He had fought the battles of Baton Rouge. He'd managed to hold off the oil people, knowing his own voters didn't approve of what he was doing. Knowing he was truly a voice in the wilderness. Knowing he had Jack Bunch's help only out of gratitude for when the man was flat on his back. Knowing that without Jack, he'd have lost on the first roll call.

"That's what this service is for," Luke Leathers began in his medium-range voice. "That's what any service in this church is for. You stand up and you speak your heart! And when it's over, you thank God for his blessings."

And, Mike added silently, thank Jack Bunch.

19

On the last day of 1888, Eulalia Bunch counted off solid sterling silverware (three forks, two knives, four spoons per guest) and supervised the
rewashing of her Royal Doulton, hand-carried by her daddy from London on one of the first clipper crossings twenty years ago. Tonight was
going to be a real do, the whole of her own Clapp family and a few of
Jack Bunch's more presentable relatives. If there were a score, it would
run Clapp, 18; Bunch, 4.

She was well aware of the discrepancy, but what could you do with
Jack's kin? He came from the improbable town of Zylks, at the upper
edge of Caddo Parish, where Texas and Arkansas meet Louisiana. The
Bunches were trash, croppers for the most part. Only Jack had risen
above his clan, and sometimes Eulalia wasn't too happy about that,
either.

On the whole, though, she did enjoy the marriage. Under the "American" laws, she held on to her money and still put a "Mrs." in front of
her name. Jack was seldom in Shreveport to remind her of her married
state. He was often away for months at a time, which suited Miz Eulalia
just fine. That thresher accident of his, for instance. He'd had the good
sense to spend most of his mending time out of Shreveport. Who needed
a bandaged husband around, looking like a prize fool for having somehow tangled with a piece of machinery? If there was anything Eulalia
despised, it was looking like a fool. Having a lot of money was some
protection, but you never knew.

Smoothing her brocaded dress down over her fat hips, Miz Eulalia supervised the drying of the Royal Doulton and its placement on the long mahogany table her daddy had bought in Paris as a wedding present for her.

The front doorbell chimed charmingly. Her daddy had bought it in Rome, a series of bells that played a tune whose name he and Miz Eulalia had forgotten. But it surely was appealing.

She supervised the two Negro women who were laying out damask napkins and silverware. "Each setting looks like this, girls," Miz Eulalia explained, placing a model at the head of the table. It was her seat, actually. Jack thought his, at the other end, was the head. But Eulalia knew better.

The groom-butler came to the door of the vast dining room. "Gemmun here with a telegram, Miz Eulalia. It's for Miztuh Bunch, ma'am."

Eulalia looked up, startled out of her comfortable domestic routine. Telegrams were a novelty, and usually not a pleasant one. In the front hall a young man held a folded blue-bordered paper in his hand.

"My husband won't be here till sundown." Miz Eulalia twitched the telegram from his hands. "That will be all."

"But—"

"Show the gentleman out, Jesse."

Miz Eulalia glanced down at the telegram and hesitated only an instant before tearing it open. What was Jack's was hers, always had been. She stared at the message inside: "WHY MIKE LEATHERS SPREADING NEW RUMOR?"

Miz Eulalia's pudgy face, normally as smooth and untroubled by thought as an egg, puckered slightly. She hated to feel like a fool, but something was going on that she knew nothing about. The message was peculiar and troubling. She had heard of Mike Leathers, a troublemaker over to Winn Parish way. But who was the person who had signed the telegram?

"CAROLINA DUFFY."

20

Five hundred minims of laudanum. Madame Fleurigant hurried away from the tiny pharmacy on Royal Street just at closing time, the words of the proprietor echoing in her mind. Her daughter Ynes had purchased enough laudanum to reduce a regiment to slumber. Since the girl took no drugs, obviously the tincture was for her patron. Just as obviously, he had returned to New Orleans.

In such roundabout ways did Madame Fleurigant keep up with the doings of her daughter. True, she had a key to the tiny cottage on Rampart, and Ynes was not one to keep her mulatto mother from public view. But she was reticent when it came to matters between her and Edmund Crozat. By resorting to gossip, by putting together bits of news, Madame Fleurigant tried to remain *au courant*. It was not easy. And now this alarming purchase.

Surely Edmund's preference had been absinthe, not the opium tincture called laudanum. But the Lord only knew when one weakness led to another. Madame Fleurigant bustled through the dark streets, returning to her home, where already a small group of clients would start to gather in advance of midnight.

At the pharmacy—well, not quite the kind of shop proper Creoles patronized—she had secured a few of the materials needed for the New Year's incantation. A dram of gunpowder, dried laurel leaves, a powder made by crushing the skull of an infant dead at birth, an extract from the male organs of the caiman. The rest of the paraphernalia, the fowls and pig innards, she had already assembled at home.

The New Year's incantation was an important one for a *mama-loi* like Madame Fleurigant. While a priestess of voodoo can, in her trance, see into the future when required, the ceremony at New Year's was much more powerful. Her clients depended heavily on tonight's prognostications, as well they might, to help them arrange their lives to best advantage in the coming year.

But what she saw tonight, Madame Fleurigant knew, was more important to her own life than to any of those participating in the ceremony. What the future yielded up in her tranced state was for her benefit alone. It took a bit of clever rearranging to make the visions fit anyone else's future.

Five hundred minims of laudanum. The small, birdlike woman quickened her pace. She decided to stop by her daughter's cottage. One needed no voodoo to read trouble in such a purchase.

It lacked a quarter of an hour before midnight as she arrived, out of breath, at Ynes' door. The house lay in shuttered darkness. She rapped lightly, first on the door, then a window. Finally she let herself in. The instant she stepped into the hall, the sweet reek of laudanum was everywhere.

"Ynes?" Silence. She groped on the hall table for the silver match container, found it, struck a light, and touched it to a candle. "Ynes, *ma p'tite?*"

The drug's candied stench hung in the air like a thick mist off the river. Holding the light aloft, Madame Fleurigant moved through the parlor and turned the corner into the bedroom. She could see her candle flame repeated in the immense mirror that covered most of the wall over the bed.

Ynes lay across the covers as if dropped from a great height. Madame could feel her heart knock against her ribs. She set the candle on a table and knelt beside the bed.

"P'tit chou, dis-moi." She turned her daughter's face up from the covers. Carefully she opened one eye and stared into the immense blackness of a pupil so dilated it seemed to have swallowed the iris.

She turned the slender girl over on her back and pressed her ear to Ynes' breast. Nothing. No . . . something. A faint whisper, sluggish, retreating. The accursed drug was killing her even now.

Madame Fleurigant sat back on her heels. Her glance swept the room, came to rest on a thick, folded wad of paper. She snatched it up from the floor. "I, Edmund de Brossac Almonaster-Nunes Crozat, do hereby transfer, bequeath, and endow in its entirety the hereto attached deed of ownership to the property known as Number 31 Rampart Street to Ynes Marie-Claire Fleurigant, colored, of that address and . . ."

Madame rose to her feet. Surely this could only mean . . . ? She shook her head. Later. Now time was of the utmost importance. She lifted the girl's limp body by her armpits and slid her off the bed.

Panting, the tiny woman half-carried, half-dragged her daughter to the basin stand in the corner of the bedroom. She bent Ynes' head over the creamy porcelain bowl. Calming herself, Madame Fleurigant slowly inserted two fingers in the girl's mouth.

"Give it up, *bébé*," she murmured. "Give back the poison, *ma p'tite*." She managed to stroke the back of her daughter's throat and felt a weak spasm of gagging shake the girl's body.

"C'est ça," she told her. "Now. Now. You will not die for that wastrel, *bébé*. You will live. And he," she added, the candlelight catching her eye whites in a flare of anger, "will die."

21

Kate ran a tortoiseshell comb through her long, straight reddish-blond hair. She never curled it, after one disastrous occasion in her teens when the hot irons had turned her fine hair into a frizz that had to be scissored off.

Watching herself in the long mirror of her father's entrance hall, smoothing down the fine brocade pattern of her long dark green dress, she knew that the other women would be curled and ringleted. In their ivory gowns they would be dark and petite, not bright and colorful. They would be mostly Creole, few of them Irish. And, single or married, they would find Miss Katharine Blood invisible.

She had pressed Jed Benjamin for details of the New Year's ball, hoping that there might be one among the guests on whom she could rely. "Do you think Olivia will be there?"

"Edmund is a member of the krewe," Jed told her. "But you know him. It's an honor secured for him by his father, so Edmund can't be bothered with the thing."

The thing, as the impresario called it, was the delirium that infected New Orleans from shortly after Christmas until that doleful day late in February or early in March, Ash Wednesday, when the Lenten season began and—at least for the pious among them—the largely Catholic city bid *"carne vale,"* farewell to the excesses of the flesh for the forty days preceding Easter.

Shrove Tuesday, then, was the last day on which to kick up one's

145

heels. It went by the name of Fat Tuesday, Mardi Gras, but the heel-kicking started long before. Tonight, New Year's Eve, Kate knew, was the beginning of the revelry, followed on Twelfth Night by the three Kings' Day balls and an almost unbroken series of such events until the climax was reached just before and during Mardi Gras, with parades and yet more parties.

Of the four grand krewes who by tradition staged the most prestigious parades and balls, Kate knew little other than that membership was secret and male, but pretty much dominated by the politicking of wives and daughters. The men of the krewe selected their elderly king each year to foot the bills. But then came the furious infighting to name someone's nubile daughter queen. It was a struggle, Kate was aware, that often began a decade before, girls being groomed as carefully as brood mares for the expensive one-day honor.

How Jed Benjamin came to be invited to one of these exclusive affairs, Kate only suspected. The haughtiest of the krewes requisitioned the French Opera House's foyer for their parties, and Jed had something to say about the house's schedule, being the chief supplier of its cultural events. Even so, the demands of an ancient and lofty krewe like Comus, Momus, Proteus, or Rex could often override the commercial requirements of a mere impresario, at least in the decisions of the opera house's management.

It was much like one of those high-wire acts in the circus, Kate decided. Jed Benjamin needed his wealthy Creole patrons, and they, in a more rarefied way, needed him. Somehow he kept his footing on the tightrope, but it was obvious that any random breeze could topple him.

She heard his carriage roll to a halt outside on Chartres Street. A moment later he rang the bell, and Kate waved off the advance of Walter, who normally answered such summonses. "Good evening," she said, opening the heavy door inset with diamonds of bezel-cut glass.

The impresario made a very theatrical gesture, throwing back his opera cloak to reveal its brilliant crimson satin lining. *"Mamselle! Charmante!"* he cried, doffing his hat. The air outside was chill and damp. Kate took a strong sniff of it and detected a sandalwood cologne as well.

"Don't we look good?" she agreed. "And smell divine." She curtsied and picked her own cloak from the hall rack. Benjamin took it from her and helped settle it on her shoulders. "Sables," he murmured, stroking the dark brown fur so lightly that Kate couldn't feel the pressure. *"Quelle richesse!"*

She waved to the groom. "When I see you again," she called, "it will be 1889. A happy new year to you, Walter."

"And the very same to you, Miz Kate."

Benjamin ushered her down the short flight of steps and into the waiting brougham. It was typical of Jed, Kate thought as he settled her in the seat, that he would have the last brougham in town and, moreover, one with a collapsible top, almost a barouche, so that in every weather except rain his progress, and that of his guests, could be prominent through the city.

"There's quite a bit of the performer in you, Jed," she remarked as the carriage moved off along Chartres. "Were you never an actor? A singer, perhaps?"

"Enough to know what stage fright is," he muttered.

"I have heard it's quite terrifying."

He smiled grimly at her. "In other words, you don't feel it tonight."

"Should I?" Her green eyes grew wider with mock interest. "You mean, at the prospect of meeting the wives and daughters of all the men who frequent my father's places?"

The impresario laughed. "Not so much the prospect of meeting them, but rather the likelihood of being rudely treated by them out of sheer guilt."

"If I'm snubbed," she retorted, "I'll leave. These people mean nothing to me."

"Brave words."

The passing gas lamps threw his face into shadow. "It will be an interesting experiment," he said then. "This is not one of the fussiest krewes. It includes a good many younger men. I don't expect too much of them or their womenfolk, but I do expect common courtesy. We are, after all, their guests."

"You are."

"I made it well known in advance whom I had the honor to escort tonight."

"And?"

Benjamin gestured helplessly. "No one let out a yelp of pain."

"Or threw up?" Kate asked mischievously.

He frowned at her. "You have picked up all of Ned's worst verbiage. Young ladies do not know the meaning of that phrase. Young ladies, if sorely pressed, regurgitate."

"This one may," she agreed. "Why do you play the ancient Polonius? Your proper work is not giving me moral instruction. Quite the contrary."

He managed a sickly smile as he turned to her. He was about to blurt, Kate saw. In advance of getting the results of tonight's experiment, he was about to ask a question from which there was only red-faced retreat. "Never mind," she said abruptly, patting his arm. "We'll have this talk another time."

A sign of great relief showed in his face. The averted blurt, Kate thought. Just as well. She was even more interested in the "experiment" than he was, and she had no intention of entertaining any possible commitments until she knew the outcome.

The New Year's Eve ball was, Kate realized after they arrived, designed from the ground up to provide suitable moments and tableaux for snubs. It was devised, in fact, to enhance any natural or accidental moment in which communication could be ended, intentions misread, anxiety heightened, and advances fended off. It was, in short, a thoroughly French confection.

The form of the ball had been arranged to keep casual social intercourse to a minimum. To begin with, everyone was masked. Jed had brought a particularly attractive pale green satin domino for Kate to put on as they entered.

As a second aid to disruption, men were separated from women shortly after arrival. Women sat on rows of upholstered gilt chairs, a gleaming smile glued beneath each domino.

Finally, the usual informal manner of dancing was replaced by an impossibly complex system. Members of the krewe committee, lists in hand, circulated among the seated women, calling names and matching masked women with masked men who had issued a "call-out" card for the ladies of their choice.

Kate decided that it gave the men the best of it. They knew the identity of their partners. And perhaps, Kate decided, some of these women could identify their partners, dominoes or not, but if any of them were newcomers like her, the anonymity of the man gave him a clear edge in the encounter. How typically New Orleans.

She glanced about her at the rest of the women in time to catch two of them surveying her rather closely. Another, watching Kate over her fan, was busy discussing the newcomer with several friends, all their mouths equally masked by spread-out Japanese paper or ivory fans which they made only a slight pretense of fluttering.

Then a tall man with carrot-colored hair was calling her out. His mask gave him no advantage, Kate thought as she and Jed began to waltz. She was a bit surprised that the krewe had accorded him the privilege of calling out a lady. Guests normally sat in the balcony and waited until midnight to dance.

"Mamselle," the impresario said as he led her through a series of backward swoops, "your hair interests me. It seems to interest the other ladies, I notice."

"They consider me a rare specimen for their zoo," Kate replied.

"Surely not. Your hair's red, like mine." They waltzed for a moment without speaking, Jed Benjamin maintaining the fiction that they were unknown to each other.

"A lovely color, mamselle. Is it yours?"

Kate stifled a hoot of laughter. "Tell me, who would choose such hair in a shop? It is unmanageable."

"I take a personal interest in redheaded people," he announced.

They danced on to a melody Kate found very pleasant. "I have never heard this before."

"This is the new Strauss, from *Der Zigeunerbaron*," he informed her. "It's the *Schatz* waltz. Very popular in Europe too."

"Try to think of our waltz in a less businesslike way."

"Music is my business, mamselle." They pivoted more animatedly for a moment. "I have suggested your name to a few acquaintances in the krewe. You will be called out again."

"I was wondering about that," Kate admitted. "After all, I couldn't expect you to dance every dance with me. People would talk."

Behind his crimson domino, Benjamin's eyes seemed to grow fierce for an instant. "Do you think so? Really?"

"A compromising situation," Kate went on in an innocent tone. "I am most grateful that you've arranged for other partners. What did the trick? Bribery? The threat of physical violence?"

"On the contrary. They all know you behind your mask. And they're all anxious to . . . ah, make your acquaintance."

"Sweet are the uses of masking," Kate murmured. "Later, at home, as they listen to their wives upbraid them, their excuse is simple. 'What, you mean *that* was Kate Blood? Heavens!' And Mrs. Oink simply has to accept it."

"Mrs. who?"

"Never mind." They whirled in place for a moment. "The *Schatz* waltz? What an odd name."

"Means 'treasure.' In the operetta these Gypsies find a treasure hidden in a tower."

"Hidden treasure." She glanced at the seated rows of masked women. "There they sit. But I don't see anyone who looks like Olivia."

"On the contrary. In their dominoes they all look like Olivia."

"You see Olivia everywhere? And your heart quickens."

He was silent, spinning her this way and that for a while. "Why did you say that?" he asked at length. "Do you imagine my heart beats for Olivia?"

"Perhaps I have it backward," Kate suggested mischievously.

Stunned, Benjamin stared at her as they waltzed. "You," he said, "have Crozats on the brain. You see the world through a haze of Crozats. You hanker after Edmund, but it's useless. So you'd like me to waste my time pursuing Olivia, is that it?"

She moved herself a full arm's length from him. He was right, of course. Imagine, all the time and torment she had put into it. A novena to St. Roch! She smiled condescendingly at the memory of how foolish she'd been. The poor saint would be hard-pressed. He had only till midnight to work his miracle.

"You're wrong," she told Jed. "I've forgotten Edmund. With so many bachelors panting at my doorstep, why worry about him?"

Kate felt certain her partner was now thoroughly confused, particularly about Olivia's supposed interest in him. She watched conflicting emotions flicker rapidly across Benjamin's freckled face: surprise at her frankness, fear that someone else's proposal would be accepted before he got his own trundled into place, jealousy at her thinking of Edmund as a potential husband.

"Jed, you are a magnificent performer," she told him then. "Whatever you think shows on your face. Even masked."

At that moment the band swooped to a dashing conclusion, fiddles joyous, horns ablare. The impresario applauded politely and escorted Kate to her seat. "A pleasure, mamselle," he said rather warily. *"À bientôt."*

But she detained him a moment. "Can you tell me the time?"

Benjamin consulted a slim pocket watch. "It lacks an hour of midnight."

"Dear, dear. But you *will* be my partner when the clock strikes twelve?"

"Bien sûr, chère mamselle."

She watched him stride off. Some of the other women were watching him as well. Masked or not, he was certainly no mystery to most of them. Once he'd gone out of sight, they turned their attention, more covertly now, to Kate. If she had been a slightly unknown quantity before, she was now neatly pigeonholed for them. That curious Mr. Benjamin had brought her. Probably the woman was a performer of some sort, singer perhaps. My dear, you mean you don't *know* who that redhead *is?* Buzz, buzz. Fan, fan. Oink.

The call-outs Jed had arranged now began to appear. The men ran to a carefully selected type: older than the impresario, and much duller. They would spend the time of their dance hinting broadly that they "had a pretty good idea" of her identity. Or, throwing caution to the winds in hope of God knew what favor, they would launch into boring descriptions of their own identities, pastimes, bank balances, and worldly states.

"Ach, wunderbar," one gentleman more elderly than the rest said as the band struck up yet another waltz. *"Brüderlein, Brüderlein, und Schwesterlein,"* he crooned near Kate's right ear as he marched her through a boxlike step.

"Strauss?" she guessed desperately.

"Die Fledermaus," he explained. "Can you guess, *Fräulein?* I am German."

"No."

"Really?" Behind his plain shiny black domino he seemed to radiate warm glee at putting one over on her. "Herr Muckermann at your service, *schönes Fräulein.* I have eight hundred acres at Des Allemandes, mostly in rice. And turpentine forests to the west of town. You have heard, perhaps, of Muckermann's turpentine? The heart and soul of the pine?"

"Who has not?"

"Exactly. *Brüderlein und Schwesterlein und* Turpentine." He subsided into humming, his gait permanently locked into his own box figure.

"You know what that means?" he asked after a while. "That we are all brothers and sisters under the skin."

"Yes."

He was holding her closer now than the usual foot or two of space that convention called for. "Fräulein Blut," he murmured feverishly, "there is for us to live one life."

"Yes."

"And we therefore must seize the moment." His grip became fiercer.

"Mr. Muckermann?"

"Yes?"

"You are hurting my hand."

His face went scarlet as he loosened his grip. "And my waist." He let his right hand flutter uselessly from his wrist as he continued leading them through the eternity of the box step. *"Verzeihen, gnädiges Fräulein."*

"You are a very interesting man, Mr. Muckermann."

He brightened. "I am a bit of a philosopher."

"But in your turpentine camps, you have surely heard the American philosophy expressed?"

"Perhaps. Which, ah, philos—?"

"The one that goes, 'You can't win 'em all.' "

He threw back his head and guffawed loudly. *"Sehr gut! Ganz richtig! Ach,* wait until I tell my wi . . ." The word stuck in his throat. "Well," he said more calmly, "you are a most entertaining young woman, Fräulein Blut. Remember me to your fath . . ." Again his throat closed alarmingly. "Ah, that is . . ." He shook his head. "The music has me all confused." He chuckled. "Only the music, mind you."

A few minutes before midnight, waiters began to pass tall, narrow glasses of champagne while the band took a brief rest. Jed Benjamin rescued Kate from the harem section by bringing two glasses over to her. They went to a corner of the immense room and stood under glittering chandeliers.

"It's gone better than I imagined," she said. "And thank you for Herr Muckermann."

The impresario lifted his glass in a mock toast. "The heart and soul of the pine," he quoted. "Muckermann and the German colony buy season tickets to my productions. *And* they don't fall asleep at Beethoven." He pulled out his watch. "A minute. Less."

Kate raised her glass slowly. "To the experiment."

"You think it's a success?" he asked in an anxious voice.

"As far as the men are concerned. I haven't had anything but looks from the women."

He nodded glumly. The snare drummer began a press roll of deafening loudness. The bandleader, holding his fiddle by the neck, raised his free hand. *"Mesdames et messieurs,"* he began. "I give you . . ." He paused and looked at the ball chairman, who was staring at his watch. "I give you . . ."

The chairman looked up and nodded.

"Eighteen hundred and eighty-nine!" the bandleader shouted.

Cymbals! "Happy New Year!" someone called.

Jed Benjamin turned to Kate. They raised their glasses and clinked. As they did so, a third glass touched theirs.

They turned to see the young man in a black domino who had joined their toast. Behind the slits in his mask, dark eyes flashed. Kate felt something squeeze hard inside her, pushing the air from her lungs. "You!"

Edmund Crozat tore off his mask, grinning wildly. He reached across and gently lifted the green satin domino from Kate's face. "Jed," he said in a low voice that sounded almost hoarse, "please excuse us a moment."

Stunned, the impresario seemed unable to move. People were throwing confetti. He stood there, still masked. Someone shot a long spiral of paper past his ear. It draped over his shoulder.

"Katharine," Edmund said slowly, "this is unmannerly, and I apologize. But I had to see you." He stopped and turned back to Benjamin. "Jed?"

Benjamin brushed confetti from the front of his jacket. "What the devil is this, Edmund?"

Crozat shrugged. "Then stand there." He took Kate's hand and moved off quickly through the crowd, which had begun to swirl in little circles. Someone was tooting a horn. People were singing off-key.

He moved her rapidly across the center of the floor to the far corner. She could see Jed Benjamin's glance follow them, stricken. "Kate," she heard Crozat murmur in her ear. "I've been away. I've not been well, but I'm recovered now. And all the while I thought only of you."

People were shouting to each other. The drummer was making a racket. The voice in her ear, close, intimate, sounded like distant thunder.

"I've wanted to ask you this for so long. But until now I had nothing to offer." His hoarse voice crackled. "Just a dream, and a failed one at that. But everything's changed, Kate. I have the dream again, and this time it *will* happen. But it will mean nothing"—his voice dropped to an electric growl—"if you can't share it with me."

Champagne corks exploded. Horns blared. "I was so afraid of losing you," the voice in her ear continued more urgently. "I've known for so long how much you meant to me. But I knew someone else . . ." His voice died away. "*My* hands were tied. Now I'm released, Kate! I'm my own master."

She turned to stare into his hot dark eyes. "Kate," he said, "I have no time for the usual amenities. Will you do me the honor of becoming my wife?"

Wild drumming and shouts of laughter. Kate saw Jed Benjamin coming across the floor. Too late, Jed.

And just in time, St. Roch.

❧ Part Two

22

The morning of January 15, 1889, dawned damp but coldly sunny. The flow of the Mississippi, in its massive curve around New Orleans, was broken by serried rows of wavelets kicked up by a thin, sharp wind that swept in off the Texas plains to the west.

In the long, white-tiled kitchen of Edmund Crozat's apartment in the Pontalba, the master of the establishment stood over an enameled coffeepot, slowly dripping hot water into the top, as he had watched his sister, Olivia, do. Edmund had shaved and dressed for the day, but wore a long embroidered silk dressing gown over his shirt and trousers.

He finished pouring water, put down the copper kettle, and filled his cup. As soon as he tasted the coffee, his nose wrinkled. It was lukewarm. He had neglected to keep the pot in a bath of boiling water. This morning, his first as a married man, Edmund vowed, would be the last time he let his wife sleep late.

Moving quietly through the parlor to his dressing room at the rear of the apartment, Edmund wondered if the daughter of the Shadow Mayor of New Orleans even knew how to boil water. He knew so little, after all, about his bride. Like the principals in most arranged marriages, they came to each other as relative strangers.

Well. He smiled crookedly as he hung away the silk gown. Not quite strangers anymore. She had been incredibly tight to force open. In their mutual pain they had quickly found a kind of camaraderie. And Edmund also knew that she was a very neat person, as was he. She had

157

insisted, although it was past midnight, on removing the bloodied sheets and remaking the bed.

You see, he told himself, you are beginning to know her quite well after all. She *can* make a bed. And the second time, she had made him quite content. Although there undoubtedly was still pain for her, he could enjoy their encounter quite as pleasantly as any with Ynes.

He frowned as he carefully buttoned his vest and shrugged into his jacket. Poor Ynes. The rumor was that she had tried suicide. Stupid girl. She was a landowner now, and of a valuable property. Let her be satisfied with what very few *gens de couleur* could claim in this day and age.

It wasn't as if he hadn't taken the time to explain the situation to her. It wasn't as if she had any right to expect him to remain unmarried. It wasn't even as if children were involved. No, thank God, it was a clean break and a lucky one for Ynes. The Rampart Street cottage had more than an acre of land attached to it. She could easily divide it into any number of building lots. Damned generous gift, if he said so himself.

Edmund picked up his topcoat and hat and paused in the doorway to the bedroom. He eased the door open a few inches and saw that his bride was still fast asleep. In the darkened bedroom a thin ray of light had slipped past the side of the curtains and fell on the outer fringes of her red-blond hair, spread across the pillow.

Really, he told himself, this wasn't the fate he'd planned for himself, but it wasn't exactly hard to take.

He grinned his crooked smile, turned, and tiptoed through the parlor to the entrance foyer. At this hour the coffee in the French Market would be hot and the *beignets* powdery crisp. Edmund let himself out the front door and locked it behind him. As he descended the stairway, he hummed softly. It was a tune he had heard Yancey Morgan play one night at Mahogany Hall, but Edmund would not have remembered that. He did not, in fact, realize that he was humming at all.

At the click of the front-door lock, Kate got out of bed, her pale beige nightgown flowing behind her as she moved on bare feet through the parlor to the windows overlooking Jackson Square in one direction and the French Market in the other.

After a moment she caught sight of Edmund Crozat striding briskly to the coffee stall. She rested her elbows on the windowsill and watched him sip his coffee and munch his *beignet* like half the husbands in New Orleans. Then he strode off in the direction of his tiny office, where, Kate knew, he was to meet this morning with Christy Leathers. It was the first part of the dowry Kate had brought to the marriage, the first move in turning the legislature 180 degrees around.

Her back ached as she stood up straight. So did her knees and thighs. So did her buttocks and groin. Parts of her she rarely gave much thought to were reminding her of the rude awakening they had had last night.

Kate wandered into the kitchen, surveyed the abandoned wreck of the coffee, and began heating a pan of water. So that was the thing the girls on Basin Street sold so matter-of-factly. The thing brides gave up so dearly. There had not been too many surprises, except for how quickly the pain passed and how—what was the word?—shocked . . . unnerved Edmund had been to find her a virgin. A little pain for both of them did no harm.

She was glad he hadn't let the first stand alone. The second time, if you could judge by his stifled moan of pleasure, had been much better for him. And that was that. Some of the girls in the District said there was more to it for the woman, but Kate was on unsure ground, not having pursued the matter with them.

She put the coffeepot in the boiling bath of water and padded across the cold tile floor to the cupboard. Inside she found a jar of marmalade and a tin box in which Edmund kept plain white biscuits that looked about as durable as hardtack. Kate arranged a tray for herself, and when the coffee was hot, carried everything into the parlor and sat down by a window.

Married.

She felt swept up in one of the near-hurricanes that blew through New Orleans in early fall. It was as if she had been whirled about and set down in another place. Cardinal Contreras, in his capacity as diocesan bishop, had issued a dispensation that avoided the need for posting banns. He himself, with her brother James assisting, had managed the early-morning nuptial mass at St. Louis cathedral so swiftly that Kate could hardly remember the details of what for most girls would be a lifelong memory.

Had there been flowers? She remembered now. Her father's Sicilian friend, Matranga, had arranged a drayload of lilies and baby's breath, fit more for a funeral than a wedding. Kate shook her head as she sipped the coffee and managed to crunch a biscuit between her molars.

Somehow Edmund had cozened Jed Benjamin into being his best man, surely an act of thoughtlessness Jed had no business accepting. Olivia had been Kate's maid of honor, and . . . and had there been anyone else? Da, of course. Ned? Oh, and that peculiar husky little man who worked for Edmund, Mr. Rynders. And no one else. The cathedral doors had been bolted. In the early morning, banks of candles had flickered brilliantly. As they knelt at the prie-dieu she could feel the stiff, almost mechanical rigidity of Edmund's body.

The wedding reception at the Wicklowe had been another exceedingly private event, doors again locked. Only a hundred people, all of them her father's friends and associates. She and Olivia had been the only women.

By sundown last night, word of it had undoubtedly spread all over New Orleans. She had wanted them to embark on their honeymoon directly after the reception. A steamer bound for Havana would have been preferable to remaining in town while news spread until it reached Edmund's father.

But the honeymoon had had to be postponed, both Edmund and her father agreed, because of today's oh-so-important meeting with Christy Leathers. And somehow, no word had yet arrived that news of the marriage had reached Jean-Paul Crozat or his wife.

In the morning chill, Kate shivered. It would only be a matter of time. Olivia, who had returned to her parents' house last night, would be the first to know. And the moment she did, she would—

Someone knocked on the door.

Kate jumped up, ran into the bedroom, threw on a robe, and stepped into her slippers. Wildly trying to shove her hair into some semblance of order, she ran back to the front door. "Yes?" she called.

"Package, miz."

Kate opened the door. The black porter from downstairs was holding three cartons wrapped in thick brown paper and tied with heavy white cord.

"Goodness. In here, please." She watched him lower the boxes to the foyer floor near the entry to the kitchen.

"What is your name?"

"Jimpson, Miz Crozat."

"Thank you, Jimpson."

She locked the door behind him and turned to the packages. All bore tags in different handwriting addressed to Mr. and Mrs. Edmund Crozat. Kate found a knife in the kitchen and cut open one container. The heavy paper crackled as she unwrapped a large cubelike white pine box with a hinged lid.

A thick envelope had been affixed to the lid by a wax seal. Kate broke it open and unfolded the stiff paper inside. "With profound good wishes and heartfelt hopes for happiness," the calligraphy said, its thick and thin strokes like twists of a rich black ribbon. The note was signed, somewhat scratchily, in another hand: "Alexander Badger, Esq."

Kate swung open the pine lid. Embedded in dried moss lay half a dozen objects swathed in tissue paper. She unwrapped one and saw that it was a Royal Doulton teacup of a design she found fussy and old-fashioned. But . . .

The packages kept coming for most of the morning. By noon Kate had opened thirty in all. Every important person in New Orleans had sent a token, usually expensive and ugly, of his respects: a Ming pug dog, a Waterford punch bowl, fourteen sterling creamers and sugar bowls, four dinner-table bells of Venetian glass, a large cuckoo clock (Herr Muckermann, the heart and soul of the pine), a small brass carriage clock with beveled glass sides, six pairs of . . .

Married.

Kate sat down by the window that overlooked the river and sipped coffee. She spread a dab of bitter orange marmalade on a shard of hardtack and dutifully munched away at it.

She called herself fairly hardheaded. Could it have been otherwise, considering her life? But getting married—to the man she had always dreamed of marrying—now seemed less a romantic fantasy than a cut-and-dried business deal. She stopped chewing to consider this as hardheadedly as possible.

It was indeed business. Start from that premise, she reminded herself. And yet it was between human beings who had feelings, expectations, dreams. Who could be hurt and could inflict it as well. In a business deal, what mattered was profit and loss. At the end of the bargaining, at the signing of the contract, one had a good idea of what one had.

She had no idea. Today, which should have been the first of her honeymoon, was only another business day for Edmund. He had dressed and left for the office as if this were the tenth year of their marriage, not the first morning. Yes, there were reasons, extenuations. In that sense, everything was in order, even to the consummation last night.

Kate watched a short string of barges moving swiftly downriver, a hefty little steam tug shoving them along. She sighed. This event, this culmination of a Catholic girl's highest ideal, was just another of those self-proclaimed landmarks by which people set such store.

Did one, after all, *feel* a year older on one's birthday? No more, she supposed, than one felt married the morning after the wedding.

The mysteries of the physical, unveiled in a night, turned out to be no more mysterious than a cook's recipe for some fancy dessert. All those veiled hints over the years, those discreet allusions of the Madames at the convent, those blushing giggles of the schoolgirls, had painted it as something so supernal as to defy description, the mystical power of Original Sin condoned.

Pouring herself another coffee, Kate decided that the girls in the District had gone too far in the other direction. For them, the act of love was too physical, about as important in the scheme of things as a sneeze.

And here I sit, she told herself, neither transformed nor purged. Just here. Another of life's great mysteries stripped bare.

She started to bite a piece of biscuit and stopped, realizing that this was her home now, at least until Edmund found more permanent quarters, and it badly needed to be stocked as a working home. There was nothing in it but scraps of food and a few bottles of wine.

She would shop and prepare something small for supper tonight, a light, spicy fish soup perhaps, and a fluffy soufflé and a bird for each of them with braised vegetables. She had seen pheasants at the butcher shop only yesterday. Saffron rice, and for dessert some lacy cakes topped with praline. A light meal, really.

Kate stood up. The parlor was overflowing with open boxes and wrapping paper. She wondered if the porter could clear away the wrappings. Edmund liked a neat appearance, that much she knew. Whether he liked fish soup and pheasant, she had no idea. She supposed a lot of marriage was simply finding out.

The little office in Carondolet Street looked like what it was, a place for Edmund Crozat to hang his hat, nothing more. No secretaries worked here at the new writing machines. No file cabinets lined up in rows. No telephones jangled. A squat iron safe stood in one corner. That, a flat-top desk, and three nondescript chairs were the only furniture in the place, and they needed dusting badly.

Tall jars sealed with corks and wax stood here and there, the dark green and brown liquids within lying in levels, as if carelessly mixed by a bartender and left to settle. Labels on the jars spoke in cryptic numbers and letters that meant something only to Clem Rynders, to whom the contents of the heavy safe—maps and deeds, mostly—also had significance.

Edmund, sprawled back in an oak armchair, his boots on the desk, gazed across at the thin, sunburned neck of Christy Leathers. The older man scratched uneasily at the stubble just above his collar, where he had neglected to shave.

"Not easy," Christy was saying for perhaps the dozenth time that morning. "We're going against the sentiment of the legislators. And against the routine of the oil people over in Texas."

Edmund nodded. "I just don't think it's good business not to own where you drill."

"Granted." Christy looked past him to the row of glass jars on the windowsill behind him. "But this is a new world for you. It's a world where a fella compromises. He don't ride down the opposition. He cozies up to him."

Edmund smiled slightly. "The normal procedure is to lease the land and give the owner an eighth of the value of what's produced. I don't mind that. I mind that a lease must specify when drilling begins. I mind even more that once oil or gas starts flowing, the lease can continue in perpetuity, not the five or ten years it specifies." He shook his head. "That's giving away too much. It's putting too much of your fate in the hands of others."

"But," Christy demurred, "if you own the land and all you come up with is dry holes, you're stuck with a lot of useless real estate."

"That's a business risk," Edmund agreed. "I'm willing to take it."

"Just to keep that one-eighth for yourself?"

"Just to keep the drill-start and pumping schedule in my hands, yes." Edmund swung his boots off the desk and sat up straight. "Just to keep the inner workings of Great Southern private. Just to keep my plans and production figures to myself. When you lease a man's property, he has the legal right to know every detail of what you pull out of the land. I won't operate that way."

Christy Leathers sat quietly for a moment, his small eyes in their freckled pockets of skin concentrating on Edmund without actually locking glances with him. "You are something," he said at last, "some kind of throwback to the big-time robbers like old John D. hisself. That Sherman Antitrust Act they're gonna pass will put a gravestone on the kind of operation you want to start up."

Edmund's grin was crooked with malice. "You are beginning to sound like your son Mike, Mr. Leathers."

Christy held up both hands. "If there is anything with two sides to it, Mike is always gonna be on the one opposite to his paw, you can bet on it." He hunched his skinny frame forward and planted his elbows on the dusty desk top. "I will be level with you. We'll try, Neil Blood and me. We'll try real hard. But it's like drilling a well: no guarantees."

"You have already done quite a bit," Edmund said.

"Taking Jack Bunch off your back?" Christy's shrug conveyed modesty. "Him and Mike was never natural allies. We've got Jack so upset now he's cut off any access Mike ever had to new legislation. And he's dismantling what laws have been passed. But when that's all finished, we're only back where we started. We won't have made any progress toward what you're asking."

"How did you manage Bunch?"

"Easy."

"I'm interested. How?"

Christy looked vaguely ill-at-ease. "Now, look. If you knew that, you wouldn't need Christy Leathers, would you?"

Edmund thought for a moment. "Is all your work for me going to be in the dark? Like a sleight-of-hand man?"

"It has to be that way," Christy assured him. "What you don't know, you can't be expected to tell." The older man got to his feet and began pacing the small room. "In legislative work, I do what I have to, make what deals I must. And in case something blows up nasty, you want to be able to say, 'Why, hell, I had no idea that kind of stuff was going on,' and sound convincing."

Behind him, someone knocked on the door. Leathers flinched at the sound. "You expecting company?"

Edmund went to the door and called through the frosted glass, "Who's there?"

"Open up. It's Ned."

Edmund glanced at Christy Leathers. "A problem for us?"

"Sure as hell is," the older man whispered.

"Ned, can you come back in half an hour?" Edmund called.

"No." The figure dimly seen through frosted glass seemed to turn away for a moment. "I'll see you at the Wicklowe for lunch," Ned Blood said, and walked off without saying good-bye.

Edmund walked to the window. He stared down at the street a floor below until he saw Ned leave the building. "He's standing outside."

"Damned little snoop."

"No, there he goes. He's off." Edmund turned back into the room. "It was a mistake to keep him out. I know Ned."

"So do I." Leathers took out a bright red bandanna and wiped his forehead, although the day was still quite chilly. "I know about sons that go against their fathers. Neil Blood has as much control over that kid as I have over Mike." Christy's eyes narrowed. "Or your father over you, for that matter."

Edmund's smile flickered. "It's a disease of the age," he said then. "The old patriarchal patterns are breaking up. Young men no longer are content to wait till their middle age to inherit power."

The politico's answering smile was a study in soft dissembling, a calculated compromise between humor and hatred. "You're not there yet," he said in a quiet tone. "And to get there, who do you turn to, young man?"

Edmund tried to warm his grin into a genuine smile. He reached across to shake Christy Leathers' gnarled hand. "You, sir," he said, "are absolutely right."

Christy nodded slowly. His handshake felt cool. "And don't," he suggested softly, "ever forget it."

After he left, Edmund stood at the window and watched passersby along Carondolet, some of them on their way to lunch. Shaking Christy Leathers' hand had recalled the cool, dry, faintly scaly feel of handling a snake.

He found himself wondering why he had to do business with sinister old men. He craved the companionship of Ned Blood, with his open, slangy talk and jokes. Thinking of Ned, he suddenly thought of Kate.

Edmund blinked against the cold winter sun. He was married. Another's life had been grafted onto his. Slowly he moved jars aside and sat on the windowsill to stare down at the street, feel the faint warmth of the sun through the glass, and wonder what his bride was doing.

It felt strange to Edmund. Married.

23

A chill rain fell on Winn Parish. The surrounding cottonfields, strag-
gling rows of dried stalks harvested of their fleecy pods, began to run
red as rain mixed with orangy dirt poured through deepening crevices.
Washout weather.

Mike Leathers looked out the back window of the clapboard church
in Winnfield. This was his brother Luke's room, but since yesterday,
when Mike had moved out of his own law office because he couldn't
afford the rent, he had been using the back room of the church to store
papers. He watched the cold rain for a while until it seemed to be falling
on his own bare bones. Then he shuddered and turned back to the
room.

Luanne knelt beside two rickety chests in which a messy array of
briefs, deeds, wills, and certificates of sale were shoved together aim-
lessly. "I purely don't know where t'begin, honey," she complained.

He grimaced. "The things tied with blue ribbons," he said. "Get
them together in a pile and sort 'em out by last name. They're wills.
Like, if it says 'Luanne Grimes,' you put that under G for 'Grimes.'"

Luanne's shawl began to slip from her shoulders. She drew it more
firmly around her neck. The church was damp and cold this time of
year. But there was a certain air of defiance in the movement. "You
sure as hell know I can't read nor write, Mike Leathers."

He paused in the act of prying open another box. "That ain't quite so,

166

Luanne. I learned you the alphabet, didn't I? And that's all you need to file them papers."

In silence the two of them worked, making piles of documents until the wooden chests were empty. Luanne got to her feet and stretched. "You don't expect nobody to come see a lawyer in the back room of a church?"

Mike brushed dust off his hands. "I expect to get a proper office soon enough. It'd have to be smaller, though. The legislature gave me money for the old place. Now . . ." He looked down at the floor.

Luanne moved up against him and patted his shoulder. "You knew nobody was gonna vote for you, honey. So it don't come as no shock, losing the election."

"By four to one?" Mike asked bitterly. "That ain't losing, it's getting skunked." He frowned. "And by that bastard Waddell, too."

"Ringo's a mean old boy," Luanne agreed. "I hear tell he's got himself some kind of private army over there to Whiteacres."

Mike carefully lifted a pile of wills and stacked them neatly in an empty box. "The Knights of the White Camellia," he said after a moment. "Fine bunch of God-fearing cowards."

"Right pretty name, though."

"Prettier'n Ku Klux Klan?"

"Huh?"

He kept adding documents to the box. "The Knights are like a plague. You think it was stamped out, say, ten, twenty years ago. No sign of it. Then all of a sudden it flares up again." He turned to her, a pile of wills in his hands. "And don't think I don't know how much I have to thank that bunch of night-riding polecats for losing the election so bad."

Her big eyes, with their thick, sooty lashes, flickered. "Ringo did that?"

"He's slick. He hasn't lynched a nigger or burned a cross. But him and his Knights have talked. You know what I mean, talked?"

Luanne nodded. "You mean talked."

"I mean it's nine P.M. and you're getting ready for bed and they's a knock at your door. In stomps Ringo Waddell and three or four mean-looking shit-kickers carrying double-barreled twelve-gauges. Sometimes they talk a whole lot about how much they want your vote for Ringo. Sometimes you don't need no talk because you already hate Mike Leathers. But if you love Mike Leathers like a brother, you sure as hell don't open your mouth to such a posse. You keep your trap shut and go to bed in fear and trembling, hoping them bastards believed you when you swore you were voting for Ringo Waddell."

Luanne's arm went around his waist and squeezed him comfortingly. "Honey, folks still know you're a good lawyer. Don't fret none about not being no legislator."

"I'm thinking they're afraid to come to me, afraid the Knights would take it unkindly."

Silently they continued repacking the boxes. When the last one was filled, Mike hammered the lids shut. "That's the lot." He turned to Luanne. "I thank you. You'n Luke'r about the only friends I have left in this place. Would you think that goo that oozes up from the ground would make such enemies for me?"

Luanne looked away from him. She pulled the shawl across her breasts. " 'Pears as though you'll be losing me, too, honey."

"What?"

She shook her head. "They's no place in Winnfield for me. I been living on what you gave me. You ain't got what to give no more. I'm gonna head down for New Orleans, Mike. Try my luck there."

"Luanne."

She glanced sideways at him. "I ain't gettin' no younger."

"You're seventeen."

"It ain't as if I'm a virgin."

Mike grabbed her by the shoulders. "New Orleans will chew you up. Two bites and you'll be gone. Do I have to tell you what's waiting for a girl down in the city?"

"Good pay."

"While her looks hold out."

"Good pay," Luanne insisted stubbornly. "I can save a mite."

"Listen, Luanne." Mike shook her gently. "Things are bad for me right now. But maybe they'll pick up sooner'n we think. I might take my pride in my hands and go see what my father can throw my way. What I'm asking is . . . well, don't do nothing rash. Wait awhile. See if my luck don't turn."

"And then?"

In the sudden quiet, both of them could hear rain drumming on the window. Mike let the unspoken thoughts go by. And then what? Neither of them had ever talked about marriage. However much Luanne might have thought of it, she'd held her tongue. Mike glanced at her now, trying to guess what she was thinking. He had given her enough to live on in return for her favors, as they were called. Now she wanted to outright sell them, and for a lot more money, too. Who was he to go all high-and-mighty moral on her?

But he had to. The life was no good for any of the girls in those downstate houses. They burned out fast from booze and drugs and handling a different kind of maniac every night, men who weren't having fun till blood flowed. In that respect New Orleans hadn't changed since the days of the keelboatmen. It had only gotten smoother. But there were still plenty of men like his former colleague Jack Bunch, who—as the story now came out—liked to punish his girls more than somewhat.

Mike supposed he should have fought more against what they'd done to him, pretending to Jack that he'd whispered the nasty secret in the ear of Bunch's Miz Eulalia. Maybe he should actually have told Miz Eulalia the truth, and taken his revenge on her treacherous husband. But when Mike learned, at last, that his own father had put him in this corner, the heart had gone out of him.

"You're too damned pure for the legislature anyway," Christy Leathers had told him. "Time you woke up, Mike. If it starts hurting too much, drop down and see me. I might have some work for a lawyer who can take orders."

Mike had agreed with his brother, Luke, that they would starve hollow before taking charity from their father. But Luanne's welfare was another matter.

"Don't do it," Mike urged her. "Hang in with me. I'll make it right."

They stared into each other's eyes now. In the feathery depths of Luanne's dark irises, Mike could see the moment of knowledge, coming as surely as Christmas, the knowledge that it was a choice between being used by one man or by the randy studs and errant hubbies of New Orleans. Either way, used.

"No, honey," she said at last. "It ain't gonna be no picnic being with you. It's New Orleans for me."

24

"You leave the okra, *ma p'tite*," Madame Fleurigant chided her daughter. "There is much power in the okra, chile, as much as in the gumbo filé."

Ynes lay back on her pillows and stared listlessly at the bowl of soup in her mother's hands. "Not hungry, Maman."

"You must eat."

Ynes seemed to think about this for a long time. She had been in and out of bed now for several weeks, no longer feeling the effect of the laudanum but not interested in getting out of bed or out of her little cottage on Rampart Street. She needed for nothing. Her mother brought food twice a day. But Ynes rarely touched it except for the soup.

"Why must I eat?" she asked.

Madame Fleurigant shook her small head quickly from side to side like a bird splashing water in a basin. "*Non, non, non,* no more of that talk, *bébé.*" She stirred the gumbo and advanced a spoonful toward her daughter's lips.

Ynes sighed and took the feeding, heavy with okra bits. She chewed for a moment, her pale olive face impassive, her aquiline nose moving faintly, nostrils flared for a moment. When she tried to swallow, she began choking. Eventually the mouthful ended up in a towel her mother hastily produced.

170

"Nothing goes down my throat," Ynes murmured somberly. "It is closed."

"You should have let me do what I wanted to do," Madame said darkly. "By now the treacherous one would be dead and my baby would be free of his spell."

Ynes shook her head feebly. "No spells. Leave him alone, Maman. It is finished."

Madame Fluerigant put the bowl of soup on the table by the bed. She sat back and considered her daughter as matter-of-factly as she could. Her color was unhealthy, she noted, but that could be lack of sun or more likely the time of month. Her behavior was weak, still, though surely no more opium tincture flowed through her veins. Madame's opinion carried weight. She was perhaps the most skilled midwife of color in New Orleans, the confidante of a dozen physicians of color. And she knew her daughter well. It was mostly in her soul, this weakness.

She poked into her black beaded reticule and brought forth a sheaf of legal papers. "I have had my lawyer look at this deed," she said. She watched a faint flicker of interest come and go across her daughter's face. "He says it is valid. He suggests that you could have an income from this land if you could put houses on it."

Ynes gestured faintly with one hand. "Enough, Maman. I have no interest in this."

"In how you are going to live?" Madame asked sharply. "You had better take an interest, ma p'tite."

"How I'm going to live," Ynes echoed feebly. "Does anyone care?"

Her mother bit down hard on a caustic retort. Instead she sat there and surveyed Ynes' face again. The girl must be helped in spite of herself, the mother decided. If only she looked healthier.

"Is it perhaps that time of the month?" Madame asked then.

Ynes sighed listlessly. "Yesterday it was over, I think."

Madame Fleurigant nodded sagely. She got to her feet and carried the soup bowl out of the room, closing the bedroom door behind her. Around the edge of Ynes' pretty washbasin she found three long fine black hairs. She rolled them on the little finger of her left hand, like spare thread. Then she began searching the small cottage for what she knew had to be there.

She found the stained rags in the outside jakes, where Ynes had left them in a wooden bucket with a fitted cover. Frowning with concentration and handling the rags only with her left hand, Madame Fleurigant carefully rolled up the hairs in one rag, then wrapped everything in some palmetto leaves and tucked it away in the bottom of her reticule.

Inside the cottage, Madame glanced in on her daughter again and found her asleep. Carefully, lifting to avoid a squeak of wood, the mother opened several drawers in the bedroom dresser until she found a set of summer-weight underwear she knew belonged to Edmund Crozat. She added the thin cotton garment to the items in her handbag, cautiously slid the drawers shut, and let herself out of the cottage.

Hair, wax something of the man's, and blood of her daughter's womb—these would be enough, she thought as she hurried through the streets. If Ynes wouldn't help herself, her *maman* would have to do the job.

25

In the long, narrow Crozat house on Royal Street, the air hung damp and unnaturally silent. Thick walls kept out the clatter of carriage wheels on Royal's rough cobbles, but this silence was more penetrating than usual. It lay over the pleasant little inside courtyard that separated the front of the house from bedrooms in the rear.

Servants moved silently. If they had to speak, it was in hushed voices. The cherrywood clock standing in the front parlor showed that the time was already noon, but no one had yet left the house, certainly not its master, Jean-Paul Crozat. He lay in his own bedroom, off the dressing room he shared with his wife. She sat in a chair by his bed, and as she watched him, her eyes occasionally dropped to the crocheting in her fingers. The needle dipped, hooked. Her large dark eyes lowered, raised. The door opened softly.

Olivia tiptoed to her side, bent over, and whispered, "Is he awake?"

Ana Almonaster-Nunes Crozat shook her small, neat head. The needle dipped, twisted, hooked, lifted. "Dr. Amabile says he will not awaken until noon," she murmured. "It is a very strong sedative."

"But it is noon already."

Madame Crozat's eyes flashed down to her crocheting and up to her daughter's face. "Let him sleep. Amabile called it a kind of stroke."

"All that shouting."

"Screaming," her mother corrected her softly. "His face! Scarlet!

Your father's temper is renowned, Livy. Thank God you did not inherit it."

"Does he know . . .?" Olivia let the thought remain unspoken.

"That you were the maid of honor? No. Never, if I can help it."

Olivia bent down and kissed her mother's cheek. "You are so good, Maman."

Madame Crozat shrugged neatly, without the gesture affecting her crocheting. "What choice did I have?" she asked her daughter in a low voice. "I only thank *le bon Dieu* that Edmund in his final hour had the solace of another family member on hand."

Olivia smiled slightly. "You think Edmund was dragooned into this? I assure you his bride is a very accomplished, resourceful, attractive girl of good heart, Maman, and equally good manners. She—"

"Enough." Her mother gave her a severe look. "This girl is your friend. She is now my daughter-in-law. What choice am I given but to think well of her?"

Both women eyed each other for a long moment. On the bed nearby, Jean-Paul Crozat sighed thickly and stirred but did not wake. It was the mother who finally broke the silence. "I will meet this paragon someday?" she asked.

"Kate? Today, if you wish."

"My place is here today. And for as long as Dr. Amabile tells me. Your father may have done himself a grave injury, indulging in such paroxysms of rage. I think if Edmund had been here, his father would have run him through with his saber."

"Not if Edmund had also been armed."

"Sh, girl, sh! What an idea!"

"But surely, Maman, you can see, you have always seen, that Father's own worst enemy is himself?" Olivia's glance moved back and forth across her mother's face.

Madame Crozat's glance dropped to her crocheting. Dip. Spin. Hook. Draw. Head down, she said, "My duty is here. I pray Amabile is wrong and that your father is not seriously injured. But at the last, when his mouth contorted but no words came forth, when his eyes bulged but did not see . . ." She looked up. "I pray he will be himself again."

Olivia was about to reply, but thought better of it. She moved to the bed and carefully laid the palm of her hand on her father's forehead. The upturned ends of his waxed mustache quivered slightly. "He has no fever," Olivia whispered.

Her mother nodded. "Will you be good enough, child, to go to the kitchen and see if Gri-Gri has prepared the gumbo of chicken soup as I directed her? With okra? When he awakes, he must have nourishment."

Olivia started for the door. Her mother's voice came to her, low but clear, across the room.

"As for your friend, my daughter-in-law. There will be time enough one day for us to meet."

Olivia flashed a smile at her. "Thank you, Maman."

"You paid her every kind of compliment. Did you say if she was a strong girl? With great patience?"

"I am sure she is."

"She will have to be," Ana Almonaster-Nunes Crozat murmured. "To be married to my son will not be an easy task."

26

Ned had wandered morosely from Carondolet Street along Poydras in the direction of the river. He had told Edmund that he would see him for lunch, but it was bravado, a casual remark to hide the fact that Ned felt hurt.

As if Edmund could hide the fact that he was closeted with Christy Leathers. Or somehow dissemble the reason for the private meeting. As if Ned wouldn't know what was going on behind that closed door. Or couldn't be trusted to treat it in confidence.

Ned increasingly believed that a journalist in pursuit of the truth was better off without a family. Especially one connected to so much chicanery and corruption. Already Neil Blood and Christy Leathers had defeated Mike Leathers at the polls. They had poisoned Jack Bunch's mind against Mike, as well. And this was only the beginning of Kate's dowry, as committed by her father to her bridegroom.

Ned crossed Constancy and Tchoupitoulas. Ahead he could see the customhouse building and the post office. Beyond lay the depot for the Louisville and Nashville Railroad, and beyond that, where Canal and Poydras almost met, lay wharves and steamboat landing slips. Ned paused at the river and watched the Canal Street ferry slanting quickly through the Mississippi's flow to Algiers across the river.

No, he thought, you have to travel alone when you start trafficking in the dirty underside of life. Otherwise you run into too many friends and relatives with nasty secrets they expect you to help them keep.

But hadn't he already kept a few in his time? Edmund's quadroon, for instance. He'd never told Kate about her, nor had anyone else. She probably knew because Kate knew the city and the Quarter. But it was amazing how, without being asked, Ned was already keeping Edmund's secret for him.

A barge heavy with carrots, celery, and cabbages was being butted into place by a steam tug. Swarthy dockhands helped warp it tightly into the wharf. The thick ropes were secured around massive iron cleats, and the tug steamed off downriver to another job.

Ned watched the dockhands begin to unload. They were Provenzano bravos, muscles gleaming with sweat on this chilly day as they worked in sleeveless vests loading sacks of vegetables on a waiting two-horse wagon. By nightfall the vegetables would be steaming hot and ready for the patrons of New Orleans' best restaurants.

Ned watched idly, his mind on his own problems. He had checked at the Illinois Central depot and learned that there were two trains a day that got him to Chicago. From there an overnight express would bring him to New York.

He had been corresponding with a few of the magazines there and had received replies from *Harper's* weekly and *The Nation*. He also had a letter from the private secretary of someone named Joseph Pulitzer, at the New York *World*, not too encouraging but suggesting he might drop in "next time you find yourself in our city." It would take two and a half days to get to Pulitzer's city, but Ned had already decided he must make himself known to some of these moguls of the printed word.

Ned watched two men in a small double-ended rowboat glide noiselessly up under the barge of vegetables. Deftly they opened the bilge drains. As quietly, with quick flicks of their sculls, they dashed away downriver without any of the Provenzano workers seeing them.

Ned rested his elbows on the railing and watched as the barge began to settle in the water. The movement was slow but steady. "Hey!" he called to the Provenzano foreman. "Hey, Luigi!"

A squat bald man with powerful shoulders looked up. "Wha's a matta?"

"The barge is sinking!" Ned called.

"*Porca miseria! Venga subito! Presto!*" He pulled in workers with sweeps of his long arms. They redoubled their unloading efforts, moving with wild speed. Each moment the barge sank lower beneath their feet. It was now almost impossible to hoist the sacks as high as the level of the landing.

The barge was starting to tilt, its great weight forcing its outer gunwale down while the hawsers held the inner gunwale fast to the dock. Cargo started to slip sideways. In a moment, the river was filled with vegetables floating downstream on brisk wavelets.

Only by some agility did the dockhands manage to stay dry. They climbed up the hawsers and stood on the wharf, watching produce disappear in the direction of Cajun country. and the Gulf of Mexico.

Luigi Bosco, the foreman, stalked over to Ned. "What you see?"

"Two fellows in a rowboat. They opened your bilge drains."

"Wha' kinda two fellas?"

"Tall with mustache. Short with light hair. Like mine."

The foreman grimaced. "The tall one. He's skinny?"

"Yes."

"Ettore Matteo." He nodded once. "The Matrangas again."

"They give you this much trouble all the time?" Ned asked.

Luigi was silent for a moment. Then he said, "Trouble? What trouble?"

Ned laughed, stood up straight from the railing, and patted the foreman's heavily muscled shoulder. "You people always keep it in the family, huh?"

Luigi winked and returned to his work gang. Ned wandered slowly along the dock in the direction of the Old Quarter. He stood for a moment at the corner of Bienville and stared back at the sinking barge. Luigi and about a dozen Provenzano workmen were loading the wagon with the hurriedly salvaged produce.

As Ned watched, a one-horse buggy with a top went flashing by. The man at the reins flicked his whip smartly. The passenger reached down beneath the dashboard. He brought up a package about the size of a magnum bottle.

Ned's eyes narrowed, staring at the length of smoking fuse. The man drew back the package and let it fly across the street. It hit the cobbles between the dock and the wagon the Provenzanos were loading.

A brilliant flare of orange-and-yellow light broke forth. An instant later Ned heard the roar of dynamite. Smoke rose in a thick gray cloud. The dockers went sprawling in all directions, as the horses hitched to the vegetable wagon keeled sideways, dragging the wagon over with them.

Ned saw Luigi's body hurtle past one of the massive iron cleats. His head remained impaled on the metal, a bright red pool around it. The buggy with the top rattled along the docks and turned right at Customhouse Street.

Ned broke into a run. As he reached the corner, he saw the buggy swerve left on Decatur. No one on foot could follow it now. It was lost to view.

He turned and ran back to where the bomb had landed. The air stank of excrement. He was sliding through a bloody mass of horse's entrails.

He stepped onto a clear area of the dock and counted bodies. Three dead. Two groaning in pain. And the bald head of Luigi Bosco, eyes wide, mouth open in silent accusation.

But he still won't talk, Ned thought, reaching into his pocket for a pencil and a sheaf of paper.

27

At six o'clock, dusk had settled along the river. The lamplighter was making his rounds, leaving a trail of glowing circles around which the night seemed to condense. Edmund Crozat alighted from a horse-drawn cab at the corner of Jackson Square nearest his entrance to the Pontalba. He paid off the driver and was walking through the lobby when the porter, Jimpson, greeted him.

"Congratulations, Mr. Crozat, suh," he said. "Nobody tole me."

Edmund stopped on the first tread of the stairway. "Thank you. Have you been a help to Mrs. Crozat?"

"I sho'ly have. All them packages!"

Edmund nodded, his curiosity piqued. But he was due for dinner and cards at Jed Benjamin's apartment and he had barely half an hour to change clothes. In any event, one didn't give house servants the dubious advantage of supplying gossip.

He opened the door to his flat and immediately smelled something delicious. As he paused in the foyer, his eye caught neat stacks of wooden boxes. On the foyer table, a half-circle of highly polished rosewood, stood the cards and letters of good wishes that had come with the packages, as well as a few letters and telegrams.

Edmund riffled through the mail. It was pleasant to have someone arrange things in such an efficient manner for him. He sniffed the air. Two delicious aromas, he decided, some sort of soup and a baking bird.

180

He let a card drop from his fingers. Dear God, she expected him to eat dinner with her?

He listened to faint noises from the kitchen and realized that the sinking feeling in his heart was unworthy of Kate.

"*Bon soir,*" he called. "*Personne ici?*"

The woman who came to the kitchen door was dressed for dinner in a long dark green gown, much ruffled and gored, cut low at the breast with a collar that stood up behind her neck, outlining it. She had pulled her reddish-blond hair up high, and the steam of the kitchen had turned the ends to ringlets. Over her dress, Kate had tied a linen kitchen towel, which she was hastily removing.

"No proper apron," she was muttering. "I didn't expect you till . . ." She paused and smiled at him. "But it's so nice you . . ." She stopped again and came forward. "*Bon soir,*" she said.

Neither of them moved for a moment. Edmund realized that the moment was as awkward for her as for him. In some ways it was far more awkward than last night's encounter in bed, where each of their roles was preordained. He put his hands out to either side and started to take her waist.

Her own arms darted forward around his neck. As they kissed, he could feel her breasts pressing against him. He drew back an inch, then started another kiss. Her lips felt soft and warm, like her body. How could he tell her he was due elsewhere this evening?

"My dear Kate," he said then, stepping back half a pace, but still holding her waist. "I had no idea you cooked."

"You still have no idea till you taste it," she responded. "And it's ready right now, if you wish."

"But you've been alone all day cooking?" Edmund frowned. "We must find you a cook. And a maid."

"For this tiny place?" Kate placed her palm on her forehead, as if testing her own body heat. "You will sit down to dinner when you wish, and I shall serve. I think the table at the parlor window will do."

Edmund's frown deepened. "I have never served a meal here."

"It's only a little light dinner, hardly a meal."

Slowly Edmund's mind filled in the blanks of Kate's day. "You shopped, then?"

"Yes. Not for the wine. I borrowed some of my father's hock. It's been cooling in the back hall."

Edmund let her go. "I shall make a telephone call and wash my hands. Then we can eat. But no wine for me."

"None? Really?"

Edmund gestured uneasily. "I did tell you of my problem with drink."

"With absinthe."

"Yes. Well . . ." He turned away uncertainly. "For the present, I take no alcohol, not even wine. Someday my character will have been restored to the point where I can drink wine with impunity. But not yet."

"Your character," she said, "is in small need of strengthening."

"You barely know my character." He picked up the telephone and jiggled the hook. "Hello? Hello? Ah, *bon jour*. M'sieur Benjamin, *si'l vous plaît*. He's number twenty-eight, I believe."

"You're not inviting Jed—?"

Edmund's grin stopped her. "Quite the contrary." He stood listening to the telephone's clicks and buzzes.

"Jed, Edmund. You'll have to play with four tonight, old man." He listened for a moment. "My bride has prepared an amazing dinner," Edmund explained. The color across his cheeks, always high, seemed to burn still more hotly. His glance swiveled sideways to Kate. He winked. "You must remember, old man, that I am now a married man." He paused. Then: "Hello?" He jiggled the hook. "Hello?"

"He's rung off," Kate said.

"He damned well has, the old devil." Edmund replaced the telephone in its ornate cradle.

"You mustn't torment him, Edmund." She spoke almost hesitantly, for Kate, as if not sure she had the right to make the suggestion or, oddly enough, to call him by his first name.

"Torment Jed? We're the best of friends."

"And asking him to be your best man, too."

"He accepted."

Kate folded the linen towel and held it behind her. "Were you supposed to dine with Jed tonight?"

"Yes." Edmund's grin shifted off center. "But the aroma of your cooking has swept everything from my mind."

"You know . . ." she said then, and stopped.

"Yes?"

"You know, Edmund," she said, hesitating again on his name, "I am not one of those little New Orleans wives who says"—and here her voice suddenly swooped into a falsetto soprano—"*mais certainement, cher mari*, you may dine where you desire. And you need never give me advance notice, either."

Edmund burst out laughing. "An absolutely vicious parody, dear Kate." He started through the parlor to the rear of the apartment. "I shall join you at the table in five minutes."

Kate felt her cheeks. They seemed to be on fire. Was it her usual reaction to being on intimate terms with Edmund Crozat? If so, she could look forward to a life of blushes. Or was it that she still felt ill-at-ease with him?

At half-past seven, the candles on the table had burned to a more comfortable height. The night outside the parlor windows pressed in on them as they sat playing with their cake and sipping coffee.

The meal had been a success, at least as food. As a pleasant interlude of talk between husband and wife, it had not gone too well. Kate could see that Edmund was not in the habit of discussing his affairs with a woman.

For the fifth or sixth time that evening she started to recount her day to Edmund, complete with small shopping successes (finding the two guinea hens had been a triumph) and her adventures in locating his kitchen utensils (the butler, for some reason, kept the mixing spoons and spatulas in a bottom drawer in the dressing room); and for the fifth or sixth time, she muzzled herself.

"I heard the clang of the ambulance bells around noon," she said at last. "They seemed to come from your part of town. Was there an accident?"

Edmund seemed to consider this for a while. "Not that I know of."

"If it's anything immense, Ned will have been there."

This seemed to trigger a recollection. "You may be right. He was to meet me for lunch at the Wicklowe and never appeared."

They sat silently for a while. Kate turned the candles slightly to let them gutter in the opposite direction. Finally she could stand the silence no more.

"Is this what happens at newlyweds' dinner tables?" she asked.

He looked up. "You are asking the wrong man, my dear."

"We are still too much strangers," Kate told him. "And you are not in the habit of discussing your affairs with strangers."

His off-center grin flickered. "Quite true." He started to say something more, stopped, then went on. "But even when we are an old married pair, I doubt that I will burden you with business conversation."

"That is your life," Kate burst out. "Until now it has been your only life. Surely—"

"No," he cut in. "I have very conventional opinions on that score. Business is too much like politics, dear Kate. One cannot speak of either before any decent woman."

The thought seemed to bounce off her like a thrown stone. "My father—"

"Spoke often of it to you," Edmund finished for her. "In my opinion, he was wrong, although I can understand his need to do so. But you do not work for me and I have no need to sully your ears with the kind of low cunning and disreputable morality that underlie most events in the business world."

"My husband involved in low, disreputable events?"

"When necessary."

"Edmund, you need not fear shocking me. I will have heard worse in my time."

"Possibly, but not of me." He tapped the linen tablecloth with its lace edging. "A man does what he must in business and politics. But he hates to appear any less than righteously moral to the mother of his children."

Kate shook her head in amazement. "I love my husband, Edmund. I can overlook, explain away, forgive, and forget almost anything he does, so long as news of it comes to me from him. First," she added, smiling.

He sat without speaking for a moment. Then: "Those are brave words for a wife. You are a very spunky young woman, Kate. It was almost the first thing about you that attracted me."

"Almost the first?"

"Your beauty came first," he said. "You have spoken before of that day when we were children and Ned was taunting the Yankee soldier. But you have forgotten the reason I happened to be at the levee then."

They stared at each other, remembering. Candle-points flared in Edmund's dark eyes. "I had followed you there, in fact." He lifted his hand to stop her response. "You had literally turned my head that afternoon. I little realized how permanent a turn you gave it."

After a while he took her hand and rose to his feet. Kate got up. Holding hands, they moved slowly back through the apartment to the bedroom. Behind them, standing against the night, the candles burned brightly.

28

Charity Hospital, on Tulane, had been the closest to the docks when the bomb exploded. Ned Blood had visited the wards twice that afternoon, but none of the survivors had regained consciousness. He filed his eyewitness account with his own weekly newspaper. Then he prepared a shorter version and telegraphed it to the Pulitzer fellow in New York whose secretary had casually invited Ned to "drop in."

Instead of eating dinner, Ned wrote a more ambitious version, including some of the background of the Black Hand in New Orleans, and put it in the last mail for the man at *Harper's* weekly who had responded to his original letter of inquiry.

It was a local fracas, Ned knew, but perhaps there was enough gore in it to warrant some interest. At seven o'clock he returned to Charity, where he ran into his brother Patrick.

The two Bloods stood in the carbolic-smelling anteroom of the hospital, Patrick tall and beefy, Ned small and light.

"What's Hennessy's verdict?" Ned demanded.

"Jaysus, Neddie, you know I can't tell you official police business."

"Don't play copper with me, Paddy," his younger brother snapped. "Anytime one of your boys is blessed with an idea, it's so rare he has to trumpet it to the world."

"Lay offen me, will you?"

"And your esteemed chief is a pal of the Provenzanos, too," Ned persisted. "I understand Chief Hennessy and Massimo Provenzano break bread regularly."

"Is that some kinda crime?" Patrick asked.

"Did I say it was?" Ned parried. "Far as I know, Massimo is a respectable businessman, whatever that means. And nobody's died eating his produce. But this isn't the first time the Matrangas have come down heavy on his neck. It shouldn't take Chief Hennessy too long to figure out who chucked that pineapple."

"Whoever it was," Patrick agreed in a gloomy tone, "you can be sure his name wasn't Matranga. It'll be some other dago, fresh off the boats from Palermo, that Tony Matranga sent passage money."

"Not this time." Ned glanced around him and saw that the anteroom was empty of other visitors. "Your usual Matranga import is lightning with a knife or a garrote. But this gentleman was a specialist, Paddy. I trust the coppers have duly noted it."

"Specialist?"

"That pineapple was fused to a split second. And the man who threw it had an aim like Davy Crockett."

This time it was the heftier brother who glanced around the room. "Enzo Balestreri," he murmured in an undertone. "He's the one been blowing up shops on the American side of Canal Street. The ones who don't pay protection money to the Matrangas."

Ned silently cursed himself for having filed all his stories before learning the name of the bomber. "My God, Paddy," he said at last, "you have suddenly turned into an asset after all."

His brother's jaw took on a mulish set. "What's that s'posed t'mean?"

"Have you brought in Balestreri?"

"No witnesses."

"Shit to that!" Ned pounded his right fist into his left palm. "You mean there's no formal charge? Maybe you can sweat something out of the man who drove the buggy."

"Can you describe him?"

Ned shrugged. "Not too well. Clean-shaven. Bowler hat. Big hands." He closed his eyes, remembering. "The hands. He whipped up the reins in a funn . . . Paddy! He was left-handed."

His brother leaned his bulk against the cold stone wall. "That'd be a small-timer named Aloi. We found him floating off Audubon Park, near the Walnut Street ferry slip. We wondered why. Till now."

Both Bloods stood silently for a while. "No witnesses," Ned agreed at last. "And the lads upstairs are still out?"

"We got a watch on them," Patrick assured him. "Anybody comes to life, we'll push for a statement in any language they speak."

"What I need is a statement in English from Dave Hennessy."

"Can't do it, Neddie."

Ned eyed him. "Let me buy you a dram to keep out the cold, Paddy."

"Not on duty."

"A beer, then."

Some of the monumentality of Patrick's chin softened. "A beer, then." He followed his brother out onto Tulane and a place called Brannigan's in the block between Howard and Liberty. As far as Ned knew, he had never been in the place before, but the name was reassuring.

"Let me ask you," he began after both of them had taken their first sip of the warmish beer. "If you were Dave Hennessy, and you had all that information, what would stop you from making a public accusation? It isn't as if this was New York, where the big crooks all have high-priced lawyers. And it isn't as if Dave Hennessy fears being gunned down."

"You're damned right about that," Patrick assured him. "No braver man walks the streets of New Orleans than D—"

"We all know that," Ned interrupted. "So why does he take the coward's way out and pretend he doesn't know who bought and paid for the biggest mass murder in this city for—what the hell?—half a century?"

"You're calling the chief a coward?"

Ned patted his brother's arm. "It's only a figure of speech, Paddy. A coward would remain silent. Dave Hennessy is standing mute."

The beefier of the two Bloods looked sullenly around Brannigan's, as if hoping to spot someone who, less fleet-footed with words than Ned, would come forward, call Chief Hennessy a coward, and get his face smashed in. At last he turned his frown on his younger brother. "How would you like to make that statement in front of the chief himself?"

"Take me to him."

The frown thickened. "The man who calls the chief a coward to his face is gonna get quick comeuppance," Patrick warned him. "Being my brother won't help you. He already knows what a scandalmonger you are."

"I don't want scandal. I want facts. Take me to him."

"Ah, shut yer gob," Patrick growled in an unconscious imitation of his father.

"Now who's the coward?" Ned prodded. "Take me to him."

By nine that night they had tracked Chief Hennessy to his home on

Prytania, in the newer Garden section of the city where "Americans" with money were building a community to rival the Creoles' fanciest neighborhoods. Near the corner of Washington, the Hennessy house was nowhere as grand as its neighbors, but its dozen or so rooms gave it a respectable heft. Ned found himself wondering how a police chief with such a reputation for honesty could afford even a modest home in this area.

The night chill had gotten into his bones by the time they rang the bell on the front porch of the two-story, straight-sided house, with its double rows of ironwork trellises set back from an iron fence in a style the locals called "Greek Revival." Ned shivered and cupped his hands to blow on them.

A black face stared haughtily at them through the lace-curtained door. Patrick Blood turned back the lapel of his coat to show a star pinned there. The door opened reluctantly. "Detective Blood. Is the chief free for a few minutes?"

The Negro servant seemed to consider the idea. "Wait there," he said at last, and firmly closed the door.

Ned shifted from foot to foot. "Cold work."

"You'd never make a policeman, Neddie," Patrick told him.

"Give me another fifty pounds of suet," Ned assured him, "and put most of it between my ears, and I'd work out just fine."

"Damned little blatherskite."

Thinking about his story to the New York *World*, Ned wondered how late either of the telegraph offices would be open tonight. A quote from the chief would give the story a needed touch of official reaction. Or, if he could dig up some more information, Ned realized, the quote would go well as the opening of another dispatch tomorrow.

The door opened. "Five minutes," the servant said, leading them through a center hall to what was evidently meant as a library.

David Hennessy got slowly to his feet, a man shorter than Patrick Blood but easily as well-muscled. His collar was unbuttoned and the celluloid had been allowed to flap sideways. "Paddy, what's up?"

"You know Ned Blood, chief." Patrick stood to one side so as not to obstruct the view. "I just found out he was an eyewitness to the bombing."

The chief stared through pale blue eyes at Ned. He scratched his close-cropped head. "Ned, you're only now coming forward?"

"I——"

"He wasn't that close an eyewitness," Patrick cut in hastily. "He was standing at the corner of Bienville. But he'd been talking earlier to the foreman. He saw the fellas who sank the barge."

"Sit down, both of youse."

"And he chased the buggy Balestreri was using," Patrick added.

The chief frowned massively. "And who the hell would Balestreri be?" he demanded angrily.

Both brothers sat silently. "I have no idea, chief," Ned spoke up then. "I'm here to help all I can. I gave Paddy a description of the driver."

"Aloi, chief. The floater off the Walnut ferry dock."

Hennessy nodded, but his heavy face didn't lose its stony, bulldog look. "You two Bloods have been running your own investigation, that it?"

"Chief, I——"

"Never mind." Hennessy settled back in a dark red armchair. "Drink?"

"Not on duty," Patrick snapped briskly.

The chief's nostrils flared. "Beer don't count, huh?" he asked, sniffing. In the awkward silence, he looked from one brother to the other. "As a father," he said then in a slightly lighter tone, "I don't envy your da bringing up a brood like youse two." He lifted a crystal glass half-full of amber liquid and drank. The level of fluid went down considerably.

"I'm waiting," he said then.

"Chief," Ned began, "I'm looking for a statement." Hennessy's massive head began swinging from side to side. "It seems to me there is no reason to pussyfoot around like this. There's a history of Matranga harassment of the Provenzanos. Massimo Provenzano is a legitimate, respectable member of the community. The way the thing was done points to a particular criminal on a particular payroll. To my mind, this isn't a moment for silence. It's a time to stand up and point a finger."

"To what purpose?"

Ned's hands churned wildly. "To the purpose of justice. The purpose of——"

"Hogwash," the chief cut in unceremoniously. "The purpose is to give Ned Blood a headline for his story."

He hitched himself forward in the easy chair with such violence that the wood frame squawked in anguish. "The man who points the finger at the Matrangas has got to be able to go into court and put the Matrangas behind bars. That's justice. Otherwise, pointing the finger is just doing the almighty press a favor." He gulped down the last of his drink. "Dave Hennessy don't do nothing that stupid for any man, let alone the runt of Neil Blood's litter."

There was a long tense silence. Then the chief chuckled. "The look on your two faces!" He sat back, pleased with himself. "Were you maybe after discussing this idea of yours with your da?"

"No reason to."

Hennessy nodded with slow power. "Yes, there is."

His cold glance locked with Ned's. The young man sat motionless, bearing up under the glance and trying to return it in kind. "Tony Matranga is a pal of Neil Blood's," he said in a flat voice.

"So are you. So is half of New Orleans."

The chief nodded again, ponderously. "And the other half don't count a fiddler's fart. But Tony Matranga is more'n a pal, young Ned. You'd do well to have a few words with your illustrious da before you start trying to pry accusations out of a poor, hardworking copper."

"I see."

"Do you?"

Ned said nothing for a moment. Then he got to his feet. "Thanks for your time, chief. I appreciate it." He jerked his thumb at his beefy brother. "Don't go too hard on Paddy here. He didn't know I was looking for a denunciation. He just thought he had a friendly witness."

Hennessy stood up. "I hope he was right," he said, sticking out his hand. "I hope we can count on your testimony if we need it."

Ned took the chief's hand and promptly got his fingers pressed to a pulp. "Is that 'if' or is it 'when,' chief?"

The cold blue eyes turned to Patrick. "Get him out of here, will you?" he ordered. Then he smiled slightly, but only slightly.

The two brothers walked briskly through the cold night, Ned scrambling to keep up with Patrick. "Never again," the bigger one promised. "You're lucky as hell the chief don't take you serious-like."

"Oh, he don't, don't he?" Ned said, mimicking Patrick's imitation of their father's brogue. They paced along in silence till they reached Jackson Street. Without saying good-bye, Patrick slewed right and started off toward the river.

"Where y'going?" asked Ned.

"Down to the channel," Patrick called back. "A few of the boys may have heard something."

"In the Irish Channel?" Ned retorted unbelievingly. "Are you mad? This is a Sicilian affair entirely."

"The boys hears things."

"Be off, then." Ned turned his back on his brother, and walking more slowly now, headed north toward the main part of town. The chief's refusal to make a statement hadn't been surprising. What bothered Ned was the way he'd thrown dust over his trail by implying that a reporter named Blood was making a mistake attacking the Matrangas.

A chill wind swept up Terpsichore Street from the river. In the distance Ned could hear the clanging of the ambulance bell. It seemed to him that his native city, always a violent place, was churning more furiously. Maybe it would overheat and blow up like a volcano. In any event, it was a perfect place for an ambitious young journalist.

29

In the dark fastness of the *hounfort*, Madame Fleurigant knelt before her cast-iron brazier. A strong spice of burning herbs filled this small room where she held séances for herself alone. None of her clients had seen this private temple, its walls covered with *vévé* drawings and symbols. In this place only one mambo-priestess served the *loa*, good and bad, who controlled the life on earth of all human beings.

Bade, the *loa* of the wind, moaned in the eaves. A true *hounfort* could never be sealed against the wind. Bade was the carrier. The other *loa* rode forth on Bade's shoulders to work their will.

Madame added a small, withered twig to the glowing coals, and a sharp aroma something like cathedral incense filled the *hounfort*. The *mama-loi*'s short, thin fingers worked a ball of wax, punching deep indentations in it. Within the pink mass could be distinguished the ingredients of the *wanga* that she had selected. Slowly—one must never hurry in summoning *loa*—Madame Fleurigant shaped the ball into a manikin smaller than her hand. Its stubby arms and legs sprawled sideways like a starfish with only four points.

She worked with the economy of a professional. In each of her arts—healing, midwifery, voodoo—Madame was the consummate professional, the initiate whose knowledge was utterly secure.

Moaning softly the song Bade was singing in the eaves, Madame pulled a fifth point outward to become the doll's head. She drew a long hatpin from her bodice and rotated it slowly over the brazier.

192

Her muted song took on syllables now. Of all the *loas*, only one could do what had to be done for her daughter, Ynes. He was Baron Samedi, in his tall black plug hat, his high white collar and black bowtie, Baron Samedi, lord of the dead, lord of pain, and most of all, lord of the urges that coupled men and women.

She glanced upward, her eyes open but her vision turned inward. In front of her, unseen, a *vévé* drawing of Damballah decorated the wall, Damballa, the serpent who swallows his tail, symbol of the earth and everything in it, endlessly repeating.

"Ba-ron," she chanted, "Sa-me-di."

The wind rose suddenly in intensity. The brazier embers glowed fiercely in the abrupt breeze that swept through the temple. Madame continued her chant, knowing that Bade would soon bear Baron Samedi to her on his strong shoulders. The music of the wind was like low flutes.

No drums. This was no rustic *bambouche*, given over to drinking and sexual games. Nor was it the fevered *banda* in which the *mama-loi* danced herself into a sweaty trance. This was an elegant ceremony between individuals of power. Baron Samedi had the power of a god, but Madame Fleurigant moved and worked with the confidence of power at another level. It was not a meeting of equals, but it was the next thing to it.

Madame lifted the hatpin, glowing red now, and darted it three times into the head of the doll. The wax spit and fried. Smoke curled up. Three clear holes remained in the head, two eyes and a mouth. The *mama-loi* put her hatpin back into the brazier and watched it reheat.

"Ba-ron Sa-me-di," she enunciated clearly.

Lifting her face again, sightless eyes wide open, she saw his form coalesce out of the darkness before her, obscuring the drawing of Damballah on the wall behind. She nodded three times.

She saw Baron Samedi gravely nod once in return. He folded his arms across his chest. Over the high collar, his skull face glistened rosily in the up-from-under light of the brazier.

"Cro-zat, Ed-mund," Madame intoned. She held up the wax figure for a moment, letting it catch the same glow. Then she placed it on clean sand beneath the brazier. Lifting out the red-hot hatpin, she plunged it deep into the manikin where his legs came together. Wax hissed.

"Cro-zat," she said in a quiet voice, "Ed-mund."

Abruptly she froze into a position of complete rest. Beneath her small fingers the doll lay impaled through its groin to the sand below. Her eyes stared unmoving into the bony sockets of Baron Samedi, lord of living and dying, lord of pain and pleasure.

At last her glance broke contact and dropped to the doll. The hatpin, frozen in wax, stuck up out of the manikin like an immense erection, ending in a pearl ball like the engorged head of a penis.

Finesse was important now if the *wanga* was to succeed. Madame Fleurigant slowly lifted the doll by its penis, which held firm in the wax. "Cro-zat, Ed-mund," she intoned for the third and last time.

She dropped the doll into the hot heart of the brazier. Clouds of smoke erupted. The room filled with eye-stinging fumes. Flames burst forth from the brazier. In a few moments, the wax with its contents was consumed.

When she looked up, Baron Samedi's skull face seemed elegant and grave. Then as she watched his body began to break up before Madam's gaze into bits and pieces of light and shadow. Behind him, she could again see the symbol of Damballah.

Madame Fleurigant rocked back on her feet and nodded three times in farewell. It had been a thoroughly professional ceremony. The *wanga* would succeed.

30

The early thaws had sent tidal floods thundering down the Mississippi, boiling with tan and red earth. At Baton Rouge, where a lot of tall tales were told, someone reported that the river was running so thick a politician could tiptoe across to Port Allen without getting his spats wet.

Even taller tales were whispered about the kind of money being spent in the name of Crozat's Great Southern to diminish or scissor from the books any law more bothersome to oil drilling than mud to a pig.

Downstate the gossip was also of Crozat, not Edmund but his father. The two men who knew the truth were Dr. Amabile, who visited the silent house on Royal Street every afternoon, and Alceste DuBois, the partner in DuBois, DuBois, and Penhaligon charged with looking after the elder Crozat's affairs. Although neither doctor nor lawyer had a word to say on the subject, before the Mississippi's waters had started to clear, such phrases as "apoplectic seizure" and "cataleptic trance" had already given city gossip a frosting of classical Greek.

Alceste DuBois had summoned Edmund early in February, when it became obvious that Crozat *père* was not coming around as expected. "As Dr. Amabile has told you," he informed Edmund, "your father can neither move nor speak. This is most unfortunate."

Edmund nodded. "Is there pain?"

"Most unfortunate," DuBois continued without having heard, "since the very morning of his seizure he had summoned me to Royal Street with a view to changing his will."

"Did he say why?" Edmund asked smoothly.

Alceste DuBois gave him a pained look. "It was while he was explaining the matter that he succumbed to the seizure, young man."

"Then I imagine I'm thoroughly disinherited."

The pained look deepened. "Try to put on a show of grief, Edmund. There is a great deal at stake here."

"Since it is lost to me, I can hardly mourn it."

"The point is . . ." DuBois shot his cuffs in a fussy manner, then toyed with the solid-gold placer's nuggets that formed his cufflinks. "The point is, the will was never changed. There was no time. And although I have a good idea of his wishes, if I were to draw them up, who would sign such a codicil? Surely not that poor man lying on his bed in Royal Street. Even if he were to regain the use of sight and speech, how would it be possible for him to sign anything that testified to being of sound mind and body when he made the change in beneficiary?"

"To Olivia?" Edmund asked.

"To . . ." The attorney stopped himself. "There is a list of eleemosynary bequests which needn't concern us. The will can effectively dismember the Crozat empire into a dozen institutional holdings."

"When he regains control of his body," Edmund began, "he will—"

"Amabile is not sure that will ever happen."

The two men mulled over the idea in silence. Edmund's small, finely molded mouth pursed. "How long can control of the Crozat holdings be left suspended?"

"A long time." Alceste DuBois shook his head morosely. "The proper solution would have been to establish a special committee under your chairmanship as heir apparent. But knowing what he intended doing with his will, I am reluctant to sanction such an arrangement."

Edmund got to his feet. "Nor am I interested in sitting on such a committee. Good day, Alceste. Thank you for telling me this news."

"At the same time," the lawyer went on as if Edmund hadn't spoken or moved, "I cannot allow leadership of the Crozat concerns to flounder about awaiting dismemberment."

"Can you not."

"DuBois, DuBois, and Penhaligon," the attorney reminded him, "is also counsel for Crozat et Cie., and all its subsidiaries, including the Louisiana and Mississippi Land Corporation." He fingered his nugget cufflinks again, as if the touch of gold reassured him, which indeed it did.

"Our firm is also obliged to supervise audits of the brokerage accounts that manage Crozat securities investments. You see my point,

Edmund." The lawyer flashed a brief smile in which, somehow, the upper corner of his mouth remained suspended in a sneer that hung on for moments after the smile had vanished. He watched Edmund, whom he had known since birth, turn slowly from the direction of the office door and with equal slowness sit down again.

"Alceste," the younger man said at last, "Father lives, but it is as if he had died intestate, am I right?"

"In a vulgar manner of speaking, yes."

"Oh, I have become quite vulgar," Edmund assured him. "I hobnob with politicians. I have married into a whoremaster's family. I have quite sunk," he summed up on a faint note of sarcasm, "to the depths of depravity."

Alceste DuBois's face turned bright red. "I meant no offense, *cher* Edmund."

"Then why, do you imagine, did I so take it?"

"B-but, consider. There is none among us who does not pay homage to the beauty and careful upbringing of your bride, Edmund. She is a paragon." The lawyer's look of anguish relaxed, to be replaced by a reminiscent smile. "Who of us does not remember the fair Kate Blood making her rounds of the District with her bodyguard, like an angel among the foulest of fiends? How we smiled with pleasure."

Edmund sniffed. "I have no such memories, Alceste, having rarely frequented the fleshpots of Basin Street in my youth."

He could see something quick and cutting form on the attorney's lips, then die there, some remark, Edmund thought, having to do with Ynes Fleurigant. Instead, DuBois said smoothly, "Edmund, you are what? Twenty-seven? And from what I hear, you have spent your grandparents' legacy well on oil-bearing land. You are mature enough to understand what a brouhaha your father's indisposition has left us. The same sword hangs over you as the rest of us."

Edmund chuckled, not very kindly. "You are damned either way, eh, Alceste?"

"How so?"

"If he never regains consciousness, you must deal with the very difficult Edmund as sole heir. If he succeeds in changing his will before he dies, you are stretched between a mixed group of faceless institutions. On the whole," he concluded more softly, "you will find it easier to deal with me."

"Quite so. But you speak of end results. We must now live—for an indefinite period—with a situation whose end cannot be foreseen. We are . . ." He paused, groping for a phrase.

"My geologist, Rynders, would say you are between a rock and a hard place, Alceste."

DuBois nodded unhappily. "I am of a mind to form the interim committee of which I spoke. But its work cannot go forward without you as chairman."

"I have no time for committees. Do you know how many employees I maintain at Great Southern? Rynders and two field assistants. A woman who comes in three afternoons a week to typewrite my letters. No more."

Alceste DuBois made a rotating motion with his hand, as if spinning out the list still further. "You are forgetting your . . . ah, legislative representative and his associates. You are overlooking your father-in-law. No, Edmund, you may abhor committees, but in this day and age no serious businessman can work alone. There are too many details. *Écoutez-moi*: if we let you name some of your own people to the committee, will you head it?"

"How many? Half?"

"Certainly not. No more than a quarter."

"No."

The attorney sat forward. "Very well, a third. But they must be men who meet our approval."

Edmund got to his feet again. "No." He started for the door.

"Edmund, please."

The younger man paused in the doorway. "It is you who want to bring order out of this chaos, Alceste. So it is you who will have to yield. Good day."

"Edmund," DuBois called, "you'll think about it, won't you?"

"Not too much," Edmund called from the carpeted hall outside the door.

Edmund walked along the fumed-oak corridor to the public waiting room, where two clerks on stools worked at high slant-top desks in a Dickensian atmosphere of scratching quills. Both put down their pens and bade him a respectful adieu.

Without responding, Edmund let himself out of the office and went quickly down the stairs to the street. He stood for a moment at the corner of Exchange and Canal streets and watched the morning pedestrians moving past in ones and twos. So the old man had done himself in, had he?

Sweet were the uses of an ungovernable temper.

31

The offices of the *Weekly Almanac* were not, strictly speaking, offices at all. The owner had rented a long, dingy floor-through loft in an elderly building on the "American" side of Canal Street. Windows at front and back gave the tunnellike area what light it had. At the rear, Ned Blood shared a desk with three other reporters and Archer, the illustrator. This noon, they had ordered poor-boy sandwiches from a Greek restaurant around the corner on Rampart.

They sat, each with his boots on the battered desk, slowly chewing their long hard rolls stuffed with slices of sausage and bits of pimiento. "What I could do to a beer about now," Archer remarked.

"The Greek's sandwiches are dry work."

Ned spoke absentmindedly while holding up to the dim light the latest issue of the *Almanac*, in which another Blood-Archer effort had been featured. "Venereal Disease Reaches Epidemic Proportions." The article went on to use this brave medical assertion as an excuse for salacious descriptions of the women who carried the diseases, and the ways in which they spread it.

"I didn't write this paragraph," Ned announced. "Moser must've stuck it in. Listen to this, will you? 'Medical authorities are quick to point out the good fortune that human diseases such as s------s and g-------a cannot be transmitted to the donkeys, mules, trained dogs, and geese used by these scarlet women in the performance of lewd and unnatural acts of bestiality.' Talk about titillating the readers!"

199

Archer's narrow face, with its wide-set eyes, gave him something of the look of an ostrich as he craned his neck to see the paragraph in question. "Nobody," he said in a low voice, "can beat old Moser when it comes to ticking the privates with words." They both glanced down the dingy tunnel to the far end, where the owner sat at his desk, opening mail.

"But it's *my* name on the article," Ned complained in a near-whisper.

"It's Moser's pay in your pocket."

"But he can't put down words under my name, dammit."

Archer guffawed. "What're you, Ned, a professional virgin? You've written worse innuendos than that."

"Fine," Ned agreed angrily, "but I won't take the blame for Moser's cowflop. Suppose on the way to the engraver's he put mustaches on all your sketches of the girls? How'd you feel?"

"On Friday afternoon?" said Archer patting the change pocket in his trousers. "Just lovely."

"This town is one big whorehouse," Ned said. "We're all selling our backsides." He started to gesture at the sketcher, but Archer had begun drawing him on a pad of paper. "Cut that out."

"You get that messianic glare in your weak little eyes," Archer teased. "I am going to have to try oil paints someday." He put aside the sketch. "Have you . . . ?" He stopped, knowing he was treading on a sore spot. "You know . . . the New York thing."

"Not a bloody word." Ned put down the remainder of his sandwich. "You'd think somebody'd have the decency to sit down and write some kind of reaction. But in New York they think the country stops at the Hudson River."

"The what?"

"Never mind. It's been a month. More. Not a word."

"Your big trouble," Archer said, "was that you didn't send some of my sketches along. It would have made all the difference, my boy."

Ned chucked his sandwich across the desk, hitting Archer's chest. "Maybe you could have worked a few titties into the scene of carnage."

Archer made a fastidious face as he brushed crumbs from his vest. "As it happens, I did a few sketches before the ambulance arrived. Want to see them?"

"Not on top of one of the Greek's poor boys."

"Blood!" Moser, a former barkeeper, stood up at his desk. "Who told you to use this place for getting mail?"

Ned swung his boots off the desk. "What now, Moser?"

"Here!" The owner slung an envelope in his direction. It was heavy enough to land halfway down the office.

Ned got up and retrieved the manila packet. He stared at the return address. "Hey!"

Moser looked up. "Tell your doxies to send their dirty underdrawers to your home, Blood, not here."

"Hey!" Ned was ripping open the envelope. A fat, folded wad of paper fell out of it. Ned stooped and lifted it from the floor. It unfolded into a news magazine. "Hey!" Ned yelped.

Moser looked up. "What the hell is that?"

"Didn't you ever see *Harper's* weekly before?"

Archer was on his feet. "Don't tell me."

Hastily Ned swung the paper open. "Page seven. 'Black Hand Terror Grips New Orleans.' By Edward M. Blood." Ned laid back his head and let loose a banshee Rebel yell. "Eee-ha! Hoo-eee!"

Standing beside him, Archer stopped and picked a slip of greenish paper off the floor. With great solemnity he handed it to Ned. "My boy," he said, "you have the simple bastards hoodwinked."

"Twenty-five dollars!" Ned turned on Moser. "I would have to turn out five stories to spring that much kale loose from you."

Moser's round face looked bland. "Every week," he reminded his reporter.

Ned examined the check closely. "Moser," he said at last. "Start getting more advertising from the brothels. My price is about to go up."

"Seven-fifty a yarn, Blood, and that's my limit."

Ned looked at Archer. "I wonder," he mused, "what's taking so long for the check from that Pulitzer fellow?"

32

It was to be a gay Sunday outing for the four of them, but it looked like rain. Jed Benjamin's open barouche seemed the wrong vehicle. It picked up Kate and Edmund at the Pontalba, then trundled down Royal to pause for Olivia. Kate glanced at the second-story window of the Crozat house to find a small oval face looking down.

"Edmund . . ." She indicated the window. Slowly Edmund raised his hat to his mother. She nodded, then pushed aside the filmy lace curtains to get a clearer look at him. Edmund, hat in hand, gestured first to Kate and then to his mother, as if in silent introduction. Kate rose to her feet and smiled politely to the mother-in-law she had officially yet to meet. The open carriage rocked back and forth as the horses stamped their feet.

Gravely, a dark smile formed on Ana Almonaster-Nunes Crozat's small, full mouth. Ceremoniously she nodded.

Olivia, who had stopped on the sidewalk to watch, clapped her hands and darted aboard the barouche. Still staring upward at Edmund's mother, Kate touched her lips and blew a kiss.

The small dark woman reacted by stepping away from the window. Her fingers clutched the edge of the curtains for support. Then, abruptly, she neared the glass again and blew a kiss in return.

"That," Edmund said as the driver snapped the horses into motion, "was a very daring thing to do, my dear."

202

Kate's cheeks burned with color. "Was it?"

"Your wife is a courageous young woman," Olivia told her brother. "Just to have married you is enough proof of that." She poked her finger into Edmund's ribs. "And you are growing fat on it."

"She expects me for dinner at home every night," Edmund complained. "And what is more, I am there."

"Who would have thought?" Olivia asked no one in particular. "Edmund Crozat has become a gourmand."

"When I moved into the apartment," Kate told her, "I found a package of hardtack. And nothing else."

Both of them giggled. The chill damp of late February made Olivia shiver and pull her sable-collared coat closer around her neck. "This was to have been a sunny day."

"Kate has packed a heart-warming picnic." Edmund sat thinking for a while as the carriage jogged over the pavement. "Is there a way you can spirit Maman from the house one evening soon, Livy? For dinner with us?"

"Do you imagine Papa can monitor anything in his condition?" His sister glanced sideways at him. "It is Maman who keeps Maman a prisoner."

"Then urge her to visit us," Kate said. "Tell her winter is over and . . ." She glanced up at the leaden sky. "Well, think of something better than that. Tell her Edmund is not being well-fed. She must come and see for herself."

The two young women eyed each other. "Housewifery becomes you," Olivia said then. "A surprise."

"To me, too."

The barouche pulled up at the French Opera House. Jed Benjamin, in a full coat of beaver with astrakhan collar, his freckled face pale in the dull light, stood beside one of the great square pillars at the edge of the banquette. He greeted them rather formally and then turned to the driver.

"I can manage, Henry. You trot on home."

The small Negro handed the reins to Benjamin and climbed down. "The bay's done gone skittish again, suh. You gotta keep her headin' left a mite."

"Very well."

The impresario climbed into the driver's seat and snapped the reins. The carriage jolted off along Toulouse Street, heading up from Bourbon, away from the center of the Old Quarter toward the newer areas north and west of the turning basin for the old canal that had given Basin Street its name.

"Jed," Edmund called over the rattle of wheels and the clatter of hooves, "we'd like to see the Esplanade property first."

Benjamin glanced back over his shoulder. "You won't like it half as much as the land in Elysian Fields. I've seen both pieces."

He turned right on Rampart. Both plots of ground were already among the Crozat family holdings. Edmund wanted to start construction of his house as soon as the weather permitted, so that, with luck, they could move into the new place by late summer. But he had no great hopes that the lots they would view today would be right for them.

The city's residential life lay in several places, sharply delineated by income and even more sharply by whether one was of Creole or Kaintock origins. Both of today's plots were thoroughly Creole in provenance, but neither appealed much to Edmund. Married to Kate, he supposed he was no longer much of a Creole anyway.

The barouche rattled past the corner of Urselines, and like a lucky arrow loosed by a blind bowman, headed along the square in which stood the cottage of Ynes Fleurigant.

Damn Jed, Edmund thought. It couldn't be that much of a coincidence. Jed had his own subtle bag of tricks, didn't he? And it still rankled that before he could get his own mind made up to pop the question, Edmund had stolen Kate away. As if he'd ever had a chance, Edmund added silently.

The cottage looked . . . occupied. Edmund had been avoiding it since that night just before New Year's when he had handed over the deed to the place and, with it, the news that he would never visit Ynes again. Passing it made something cold stir across his shoulders—a ghost walking on one's grave, so they said.

"Are you chilled?" Kate asked him.

He turned on her, sensing sarcasm. But her glance was clear of malice. Edmund's glance had started to follow the cottage as it retreated behind them. He forced himself to look straight ahead. Kate knew, or she didn't know. But it was too much to ask any wife to watch her husband openly ogle the place he had squandered so many glorious hours with his mistress.

Why dwell on it? Edmund asked himself. It's successfully over. He thought of Ynes now and then, certainly. It would be strange if he didn't. But that was a book of his life on which the last page was turned. And locked away.

He realized that the barouche had stopped in front of the Esplanade property.

Jed Benjamin eyed him. "Deep in thought our Edmund lies," he announced in a mocking basso.

"And lies and lies and lies," Olivia added.

All three of them were watching Edmund. Had a man no privacy, even in his thoughts?

"Stop teasing Edmund," Kate said at last. "He has had a lot on his mind lately."

33

In one corner of the first-floor parlor sat a man rumored to be Mark Hanna, Ohio political boss, and a portly gentleman who was supposed to be something big up North, governor or senator perhaps, named McKinley. But no one in the House of Blue Lights stared at them. The real celebrities of the evening were neither of these drab Yankee politicos but three opera singers, a tenor and a baritone who had daringly brought along a soprano.

Women were not barred from the parlor floor, but Neil Blood discouraged the idea. In any event, the matter sorted itself out by midnight, when all three vocalists moved upstairs to one of the larger rooms, where three of Neil's finest whores were waiting. The rush by others to pay for spectator rights was instant.

By two A.M. things had returned to normal at the House of Blue Lights and Alceste DuBois had descended to the parlor for a nightcap before tottering home, visions infesting his brain of what couplings were possible among six people.

He bowed to Neil Blood and was invited to sit at the owner's table. "No," Blood said, holding up the palm of his hand like a traffic cop, "I don't want to hear about it, Al."

"*Sensationnel! Merveilleux!*"

"Spare me the details." Neil signaled a waiter. "What'll it be?"

"Something soothing. *Crème de menthe*." The lawyer sprawled back in his chair.

"You randy old goat," Neil Blood said after the green drink had arrived. He waited until the lawyer had calmed himself with a sip of mint. Then: "Al, have you solved that estate problem yet?"

Alceste DuBois was too exhausted to blink in surprise. "Is it too much to ask how you knew?"

"Even if I'd heard nothing, common sense tells me you have a problem with the old gentleman's holdings."

"Your son-in-law is very difficult," DuBois admitted grudgingly.

"After the way his father treated him?" Blood shrugged. "Edmund is a proud young man, Al. And he's going to be a very wealthy one even without a sou of his father's money."

The lawyer sipped his drink. "That is no excuse for the cavalier way he treats me." He paused. "How do his chances look in Baton Rouge?"

Neil Blood made an expansive gesture, as if spreading out an immense stack of hundred-dollar bills on the table between them. Both men stared down, as if seeing the same illusion. "He's winning," Blood said.

"At what price?"

"Anything worthwhile costs."

"His funds are not unlimited."

"Perhaps not, Al. But his credit is."

The bland face cracked slightly, like an egg, with a faint horizontal line meant for a smile. "I know this boy well," he said. "He is a very conservative person, very old-fashioned, one might even say ignorant of the methods of modern business."

"We've seen that in the demands he's making on the legislature." Blood sighed heavily. "That's why the price has gone so high."

"But Edmund neither understands nor trusts the idea of credit," the attorney explained.

"He'll have to."

"He'll balk."

"We'll just have to keep leading him to the trough till he drinks."

"He'll die of thirst first."

"Thirst," Neil Blood repeated. "That's a good word for what's going to happen, Al. Right now he's land-rich and cash-poor. And he keeps buying more land. So it won't be long before his cash runs out."

"I'm surprised it hasn't already."

The owner of the House of Blue Lights sat back and pondered the question for a long moment. Down the stairway from the second floor trooped the three opera singers, the tenor and baritone holding on to the soprano to keep her from stumbling. They tipped the madam and called for their cloaks. As they did so, they received a polite round of applause, discreet but wholehearted. A moment later they were gone.

Neil tapped the table in front of him, as if to focus Alceste DuBois's wandering attention. "The boy has commercial rivals."

"The Standard Oil people have been buying up leases?" asked the lawyer.

"There's an outfit in Pennsylvania called Equity Petroleum. Nobody knows who they represent. But they're picking up ten times as many leases as the Standard boys." Neil sighed in exasperation. "You see, *that's* the way to operate. You don't tie up a lot of cash in land. When the time comes and Edmund's ready to buy drill rigs and hire men, he won't be able to pay for it."

"Your fatherly concern does you honor," the lawyer murmured.

"Fatherly hell," Neil burst out. "I hate to see him outmaneuvered by a bunch of Yankee sharpsters. Great Southern means a lot to New Orleans, Al. It's more than a name. It's the idea that, maybe for the first time since Reconstruction, we can develop our own resources for our own profit, not some Yankee combine's balance sheet."

DuBois made a noise like a gas flame going out. "Whoof! Such patriotism. I see Edmund has made a convert of you. Mind you, he is not wrong. If he can get away with it, his way of doing business makes the most sense. *If* he can do it."

The proprietor of the place gave his parlor a long, careful glance, not missing the two Ohio politicos or the visiting royalty or the clusters of Washington legislators and local businessmen.

"Al," he said at last, "I think hard times are coming. Sugar's never been higher, because the supply from Cuba has been all but cut off. The way the Spanish are treating the Cubans, it's no wonder they keep revolting. It'll be a permanent insurrection one of these days, and we'll have to do something about it. But until then, Louisiana sugar is riding high. The same," he added, "can't be said for cotton."

The attorney shifted uneasily in his chair. "As you know, this strongly affects the holdings of many of my clients, particularly the Crozats."

Neil reached across and gently patted DuBois's hand. "It strongly affects Alceste DuBois, my friend. You and Badger and the rest of you boys speculating in cotton futures for your own account."

"Then it affects Cornelius Blood as well," the lawyer suggested.

"We're all in it together, Al. And we're in a lot of other investments as well. Of all the syndicates in this town, I think our little group is the most powerful."

"Indubitably."

"Now, our land investments are solid. Cash businesses like this house are even solider. So are the taverns and restaurants, the barge companies, the steamers, the factoring companies, the . . ." He stopped. "What I'm saying is, we're spread nicely. But our biggest hunk of risk is cotton futures. Badger hasn't let us down, but all Badger knows is cotton. The rest of us have a feel for the general situation. That means we have a responsibility, Al. We should be asking ourselves: 'If we have to dump cotton, where should we put the money instead?' You follow?"

The egglike face managed to look pained. "Easily. You are preparing to suggest we get out of cotton and into oil."

Neil Blood nodded firmly. "That I am."

"But how?"

"That we will know soon enough."

The attorney eyed his host calmly and said nothing. If Neil Blood had a way of making Edmund Crozat accept credit, who was Alceste DuBois to say no?

At that moment the front door opened and the soprano came in, alone. She stood in the vestibule next to the madam, her dark eyes surveying the room quite as calculatingly as had its proprietor a few moments before. The singer let her cape fall to the floor. She took two long strides to the staircase leading upstairs. Then she paused on the first step.

Alceste DuBois rose to his feet. "Excuse me," he said as he moved across the floor of the parlor room. He reached the soprano, kissed her hand, and led the way upstairs.

34

Mike Leathers had hoped to reach New Orleans before sundown. It had been a long trip, nearly a week. He'd done much of it on horseback, his gladstone case tied to the saddle. Then, in Baton Rouge, he had sold the horse for enough cash to buy passage downriver, with a few dollars left over to keep himself alive in New Orleans until . . .

Until what? he wondered now, as he stepped off the *Rogue Queen* near the foot of Canal Street. He hefted his tightly packed gladstone and stood for a moment watching the light go out of the sky to the west. His father would have left his office by now and be somewhere in the Quarter, taking a drink with this one and that as he pursued his evening routine.

Mike had arrived in town too late to find him. It seemed like a symbol to him of his whole life. He let the gladstone thump to the wooden dock, and leaning back against the iron railing, thought over his chances. He decided they were slim.

He ran his fingers through thick black hair. He'd fought hard on the side of the yeoman farmers and sharecroppers in Winn Parish, and they'd voted him out of office by what amounted to a landslide. Broke, Mike had lost Luanne, too. She was here in the city somewhere, God knew where, up to God knew what tricks. It was because of Luanne that Mike had finally swallowed his pride and come running to Paw, something he'd sworn he'd never do.

But even if the Leatherses weren't a family in the tight way the

210

Creoles knew it, they were still blood kin, weren't they? And when times got bad enough, who else could you turn to? Mike asked himself.

He groaned at the idea, then pushed himself forward and picked up his gladstone. Along the railing, half a square away, another man seemed to imitate his gesture. He'd been leaning on the railing watching the river, too. Now he started toward Mike.

"Mike," said Ned Blood. "Last time I saw you was on top of a wagon between two tar barrels. They were dragging you to a rally in Jackson Square. Something about oil."

"That was me, all right."

"That's right," said Ned. "I've been hearing about you, though."

"Like what?"

"Like how you were euchred out of your seat in the legislature."

Mike frowned. "As Neil Blood's son, you should know."

"I was afraid you'd feel that way." Ned took back his hand. "What brings you to the Crescent City?"

"Looking for work. But as Neil Blood's son, shouldn't think you'd care."

Ned shook his head. "My da and I don't always see eye to eye on things."

Neither of them spoke for a moment, looking each other over. Mike found the slight young man almost too physically inconsequential. In the boondocks, size and heft were everything. Mike supposed that half-pints like Ned Blood were bred special for city life. "You still a reporter? Make money at it?"

"Not much." A longish pause. "Enough to buy you dinner if you aren't a monstrous big eater."

Mike Leathers grinned. "I never expected to break bread with no kin of Neil Blood after what happened. But thank you kindly, I will."

"You mad at him for doing you in at Baton Rouge?"

"Sure am."

"Then how do you feel about your own dad?"

Mike said nothing for a moment. "You are a sharp little sawed-off carbine, ain't you?"

"But loaded for bear."

Mike looked him over again. "You still want to shake hands?"

Ned stuck his out. "I'll risk it."

Mike crunched down hard on Ned's fingers, but found them too bony to do more than hurt his own hand. "Prickly, ain't you? What's on your mind, wanting to talk to me?"

Ned retrieved his hand. "I figure a legislator who's been diddled as bad as you might have a few things a reporter could use."

"And you been waiting at the dock for me all this time?"

Ned started laughing. "I'm here a lot. The best story I ever got happened right here. This is my lucky dock."

Mike banged him on the back and headed them off along Canal Street. "You may be a whole hell of a lot luckier," he told Ned, "than you suspect. Tell me, is it hard to find a runaway girl here in New Orleans?"

"Your girl ran away?"

"More or less. You know your way around the District?"

"Do I know my way around the District?" Ned led the way up Canal Street, laughing.

35

The apartment in the Pontalba looked different now, especially by candlelight. When they ate dinner at the table in the parlor, Kate insisted on turning down the glaring gas mantles. Edmund would do this as she lit the candles. Between them tonight they had finished the last of his father-in-law's hock, a delicate straw-colored wine that Edmund could drink like water, it tasted so fresh.

He had been drinking a little wine now for about a week. Kate's magnificent dinners demanded it, and Edmund had come to a further conclusion about his drinking. When he and Kate were alone, he could trust himself with alcohol. More important, he trusted Kate. If he drank wine, she would make sure he didn't move on to absinthe.

The parlor looked rich in the candlelight. Kate had bought only a few new things, a chair and a small table for a lamp. But she had put pictures on the walls from her room at home, watercolors of houses and squares in the Quarter. And she had done something with the window draperies that Edmund didn't understand but approved. The light seemed more moderate in daytime; the windows seemed less black at night.

He watched her across the table as she concentrated on cutting into a small pecan pie she had baked. The crisp, pralinelike interior, thick with nuts, resisted the blade of the knife, and she frowned as she pressed the knife down. A wisp of aromatic steam drifted across the table from the coffeepot beside her.

How long their honeymoon had lasted. And how wise they had been to spend it here in their home and not some unfamiliar hotel or resort.

Outside, a tug hooted softly, its horn muted by river mist. Edmund pushed back the thin voile curtains and watched a tiny red light swing sideways, blink out, and be replaced by a green one. Late for a tug to be abroad. He pulled the watch from his vest pocket. Nearly ten o'clock. They dined later and later now, or else the dinners took longer, what with the wine.

Edmund stretched his arms and yawned. "Shall I light a fire?"

Kate looked up. "Perhaps in the bedroom."

Edmund padded noiselessly to the bedroom at the back, where the butler had laid a neat stack of wood, crumpled shavings at the bottom, then twigs, then chunks of fatwood and slender staves of oak. April was warm this year, but the nights were still cool because of the damp. Edmund struck a match and watched the flames catch and spread.

He wondered to what other use Kate put Thomas. He'd been with Edmund ever since he'd moved into this apartment, but only as a day servant, doing what shopping and cleaning and valeting Edmund needed as a bachelor. Perhaps he wasn't adequate to the demands of two people. Perhaps a housekeeper was needed. But Kate had postponed such questions until they moved to a house.

Behind him Kate entered the bedroom, carrying a tray on which the coffee and pecan pie stood ready. "Dessert in here?" she asked.

"God, you are spoiling me, Kate." He took off his jacket and stood for a moment, looking at the way her fair coloring grew rosy in the firelight. He loosened his tie and popped open the top collar button.

"Domesticity," he pronounced slowly, sinking into an upholstered armchair.

Kate glanced worriedly at him. "Too much of it?"

"If I am drowning in it, it's a lovely death."

But this didn't satisfy her. "Too . . . smothering? Men like you start to feel tied down."

"From whence comes this fund of knowledge about men?" He kicked off his slippers and accepted pie and coffee.

"From growing up with a houseful of them. And . . ." She stopped herself. "Cream?"

"No, black." He wondered what she had not said. But after a moment, he forgot to think about it. And later, when she took off his collar and tie and hung away his vest and jacket, he lay back on the bed and watched the shadows dance over the ceiling. Domesticity. It had a fat sound to it. But he didn't at all mind.

The shadows were putting him to sleep. He felt the bed sink under the weight of another body and glanced sideways to see Kate on her hands and knees beside him on the bed. She leaned over to kiss him lightly on the lips. When he reached for her, she dodged back, and when his arms dropped, she pounced, biting his ear. His hands darted out for her, but she was too quick.

She jumped off the bed and stood between him and the firelight, hands behind her, slowly unbuttoning the back of her dress. It slid to the floor, and he could see her ankles now as she unfastened her slip from behind and let it drop beside the dress.

A small comb had fallen from her hair. She pulled out three ivory pins, and the long blond-red tresses fell about her face and neck. Edmund sat up on the edge of the bed. She removed her chemise. He could see her legs now, and as she slowly removed her brassiere, her breasts burst into the firelight like bright ripe fruit. She unfastened her stockings but left them on as she drew off her garter belt. A moment later she removed the last of her underthings. She stood naked before the fire except for her stockings and small pointed shoes with spoollike heels.

Edmund sank forward to the carpet, kneeling before her. He wrapped his arms around her legs, stroking the wicked sheen of the silk stockings. Her bright red mound of hair pressed against his mouth. His hands cupped her buttocks.

"Do I give you pleasure?" she asked.

He nodded, silently rubbing his face against her pubis.

"Does that give you pleasure?"

"It does." He could feel her fingers sink into his hair, pressing him against her. Then she let her grip loosen.

"I can do that for you," she said.

He sank back on his heels. "What?"

She reached down, and he let himself be helped to his feet. "Lie back," she said. As he reclined on the bed, she pulled his suspenders down over his shoulders, then began to unbutton his fly. "Kate . . ."

"No, lie back."

He could feel himself stiffening. A moment later she had opened his trousers and underpants. His penis rose into the air like a serpent testing the wind. "Kate you don't—"

"I know I don't." She was kneeling on the floor in front of him. His legs straddled her as she took his penis and began stroking it upward.

"This is the way," she said. "You don't have to tell me. I can see it in your face."

Edmund lay back, his brain whirling. She had never before done this. He had led the way in everything. He felt her gently bite the inside of his thigh and then the skin below his navel. Suddenly he could feel her teeth on his penis. He flinched.

"Oh. That's wrong," she said.

He could feel her lips now. "Kate . . ."

He sat up and pulled her on top of him, sinking back on the bed under her body. Her nipples stood out, gem-hard. She sank back, burying his penis inside her. There was a faraway look on her face, as if she were listening to something in the distance.

Edmund's mind fizzed with images, bright explosions of her face, her breasts, her eyes shutting tight, her hair swinging wildly . . .

Dark hair. Aquiline nose. Ivory skin. Ynes rocked forward and back, increasing the tempo. Edmund shut his eyes, opened them.

Kate's hands moved along his arms to grasp his fingers, pinning him to the bedspread. Her cheeks burned rose and pink. She . . .

Smiled, and Ynes let his hands go. Her fingers pinched his nipples. Her immense eyes in their shadowed caves stared deep into his.

"Kate!"

"Yes."

"Kate!" The line of fire burned upward through him and exploded.

"Yes," Ynes said, tightening her muscles until he reached the edge of pain. He climaxed again, and the jolt seemed to rock the bed under him.

"Yes," Kate said. "Oh, yes."

Later, as she lay beside him, Edmund stared into the fire. It needed stoking, but he had no strength to move. He watched the black wood collapse.

"*Fais dodo,*" he said.

Kate muttered something unintelligible. It had been his game with Ynes. The child going to sleep said its prayers, kneeling by the bed. That was how he pleasured Ynes and she him. So many times. *Fais dodo.*

What had gotten into Kate to do that to him? It was not something a wife did. A husband could do what he wished. He was a creature of the outside world, and all its ways were known to him. No wife knew such ways, or thought of them, or tried them.

The fire was breaking up. Edmund's eyes smarted, as if from smoke, but there was no smoke. God, it had been a hallucination as real as if Ynes had been in this bed, or he in hers under the huge mirror that doubled them over and over again.

She had come back to him with the force of a blow, riding him like a jockey, forcing him to a final orgasm only she knew how to summon. She had been here! He would almost swear to it.

He moaned and tried to look away from the fire, his eyes misting. Tears, he realized.

The fire was breaking up.

36

The summer had been dry, which kept down the mosquitoes. It pleased Kate to have the weather so comfortable. By the time she began to show, it was already September. She could face with equanimity the prospect of being awkwardly with child in the cold months.

Dr. Amabile was certain her son would be born in January, "always a salubrious season for births," as he put it. But then, Kate recalled, he was equally certain it would be a boy.

The workmen had finished most of the masonry walls of the house. Almost daily Kate and Olivia would make an inspection trip. One could begin to see what the final shape would be, broad across the facade and set well back from Livaudais at the corner of Washington. A block below, running along the river, was Tchoupitoulas, a wider thoroughfare, which made coming and going to this part of the Garden District much faster.

Both Edmund and Kate would have preferred living in the Quarter, where they had spent their childhood, but a house with the scope of Edmund's ambition was not possible in the crowded Creole section. Only in the Garden District, among the "American" homes built since the war, with their broad lawns and separate servants' houses, was sufficient space to be found.

Kate, who was used to making important decisions *en famille*, found it strange and a little frightening that Edmund went his own way in

218

such matters as choosing the land and building the house in which he and Kate would raise their own family. She longed to discuss it with her father, but he and Edmund were mysteriously on the outs these days. Edmund refused to tell her the reason, but warned her not to discuss it with Neil Blood.

He hadn't warned her against Ned, however, and so, on this pleasantly warm September afternoon, her youngest brother was sitting in the parlor of the Pontalba apartment, the windows open, a river breeze lazily shifting the voile curtains. Ned had put his boots up on Edmund's footstool and was sipping a cool beer from a tall, fluted champagne glass.

"Never had beer from one of these, Kate."

"A peace offering."

Her brother frowned. "From Edmund? He's at war with everyone else. I didn't know the hostilities extended to you."

"He's a lamb with me, Neddie. Don't stir up trouble." She held the lovely French glass to the light. "No, it's from *chère* Maman. Oh, yes, once she learned she was to be a grandmother, she dropped that cloistered existence she'd been leading by the bedside of the famous invalid. Olivia brought her over for tea, and Maman gave me a dozen of these."

"How is the prostrate one?"

"He lives on gruel and soaked biscuits. He has lost weight, but Dr. Amabile tells me his heartbeat and respiration are quite sound."

"He lives and Edmund dangles."

"I warned you not to stir things up, Neddie."

The journalist gestured rather grandly with his glass of beer. "That is my method. When things remain at equilibrium, no one's interested in telling me secrets. When things start to shift and topple, people with a grudge suddenly want access to my ear. And this has been a great year for instability. Starting with old Crozat's terribly inconvenient stroke."

"Edmund and I don't discuss it. You can stop pumping *my* handle, Neddie-boy."

Ned laughed appreciatively. "Nobody ever got a nickel's worth of secret out of you. Da trained you well, indeed. As a matter of fact, I have an associate bloodhound helping me sniff the trails of this fair city. There's enough work for both of us."

"Who?"

"You wouldn't know him. I managed to do him a favor, and now he's a pal for life. He was the one put me on that filibuster story."

Kate shook her head. "What would anybody find interesting about that? Those men are nothing but highwaymen, if you ask me. They don't want to liberate Cuba from the Spaniards so much as loot it for themselves."

"Dead right," Ned agreed. "But the people in New York thought it was worth fifty iron men, Katie. I sent along some of Archer's sketches as well. Damned impressive, a regiment of men boarding a cutter in the dead of night bound for Havana, or so they said."

They sat in silence, surveying each other with something approaching fraternal satisfaction. The bond between them had always been stronger than with their brothers and sisters. Kate, the oldest, had been the only mother Ned could remember. Now that she was on her way to a child of her own, Kate realized, she was getting more visits from Ned, bragging as always about his peculiar exploits, like a cat bringing home a dead bird.

"And how," she asked, breaking the silence with a question she had carefully considered for some time, "is that busty young lady with the thick black ringlets?"

Ned looked blankly at her. "Who?"

"It was a week ago. I was leaving Gambetta's meat market and you two were sitting in the window of that coffeehouse across the way, chatting like two lovebirds."

"Luanne?" Ned looked absolutely astonished. "She's no ladylove of mine. She's . . . she's the friend of a friend," he concluded somewhat mysteriously.

"No entanglements?" Kate persisted.

"None."

"Then, Neddie, what do you do with your evenings? Skulk around like a retriever in the bush?"

Ned stretched out comfortably in Edmund's favorite armchair. "You have the Irish gift for language," he said then in a less self-satisfied tone. "I suppose that's exactly what I do, retrieve. Sniff out the grislier secrets of this corrupt little village and bring them back to show everyone."

"Is that what you like doing?"

He glanced up at her. "Yes. No." He shifted uneasily in the chair. "I don't like finding what I find. I do like looking for it. Does that make sense?"

Kate got up and spread the curtains a few inches to let the breeze into the parlor. "You're a romantic, Neddie." She was staring at the river's gentle curve. "You are quite sure the people before whom you lay your secrets are the better for knowing."

"Kate . . ."

She turned back to face him. "I can only admire you, Neddie. And hope it doesn't break your heart."

He rubbed his face slowly, as if he had spent a late night and expected the massage to invigorate him. Kate noticed that his face seemed narrower. Faint half-circles, no more than tiny wrinkles, lay beneath each eye. Below his cheekbones, where his light beard needed shaving only every other day, the curve had hollowed a bit inward. She supposed he was simply growing up. Experience was marking him. But, really, Ned was barely twenty-two years old. Should there be the beginnings under his eyes of those pouches their father had, those great imposing badges of terrifying experience that Cornelius Blood showed the world?

"You don't always sleep at home anymore."

"I have a place on Marais. I work there. Sometimes I work too late to go home. Who snitched on me? Walter?"

She nodded. "I don't care where you sleep, Neddie. I just want to be sure you get enough of it. You look tired."

By way of answer he sprang to his feet, waving his arms in the air. "I am a fount of energy!" he exclaimed. "I have enough for two of me! Stop worrying about Neddie-boy."

"Since the day Edmund saved your skin, I have stopped worrying about you. You're . . . you're incorrigible, irrepressible, irrational, and not even very good-looking. Sit down, you jay!"

When he came to rest on one of the brocade-covered couches, Kate sat beside him and took his hand. "What's the trouble between Da and Edmund?"

"God, he *did* train you right. Get a fellow all worked up, then hit him when his guard's down." Ned frowned. "Any more of that beer?"

"As soon as you've talked enough to raise a thirst."

"It's one of those gloriously tricky Neil Blood muddles. You can see some strands of sense running through it, but he's blown so much smoke that you never get a clear look at it. It has to do with Edmund not cooperating with his father's lawyers to help them administer the estate while the old gent is lying doggo. It also has to do with Edmund refusing to let Da's pals finance Great Southern's expansion."

"Edmund doesn't need financing."

"No, of course not. What a thought!" Ned grinned sarcastically. "The man owns half the oil-bearing real estate in Louisiana outright. He's spent his last cent on it. His next-to-last cent he's squandered on Baton Rouge bribes, making sure he pays almost no tax on the land he owns. Then there's his antepenultimate cent. It went for a one-acre corner lot in the Garden District, or did you think someone gave it to him as a present? And if there is a preantepenultimate cent left, it is going to the contractor who's building the house. Oh, did I tell you, this man is expecting to be a father fairly soon? Does he need financing? Tell me."

She squeezed his hand hard. "Surely he has family sources."

"Edmund is a friend, not someone I keep a watch on, Katie. But there was a trust left him by an uncle. He liquidated it. Also one left for Olivia, which she let him cash in. He has been back to Chicago twice now to see the bank that gave him his first loan a year ago."

"That was not his reason. He went to Chicago to look at a new drilling device," Kate assured him. "It is faster than the cable-tool method. It uses a rotary bit. He told me all about it. You see, Edmund does not keep his wife in the dark, Neddie."

Her brother laughed. "You don't let him get away with it, eh?" He patted the hand that held his. "All right, he looked at drill bits in Chicago. But he also went there to refinance his first note, and the bank said no. Originally they lent him the money on the strength of the family name, not knowing it was for the oil business. Now they know, and they want to be cut in. To get more money from Chicago, Edmund has to trade Great Southern stock. He won't."

"Is that the way Da's group wants to lend him money?"

"Cornelius Blood is another man on whom I don't keep a regular watch," Ned told her. "Someday I will. Right now I'm too weak to go up against the Shadow Mayor of New Orleans."

Kate felt her anger rising. "That's a funny way to describe the man who put the shirt on your back and the meat in your stomach."

"And sent me to the right schools," Ned agreed, "where the Jebbies pounded way too much sense into me, Kate. They taught me logic. It was fatal, so it was."

"Blaming the Jebbies for the way you think of your father?" She let go of his hand and stood up. "Neil Blood is something we all have to live with. But none of us is skulking around looking to demolish him."

He got to his feet, standing an inch shorter than his sister, and looked her in the eye. "He is a sly, shifty, evil man, Katie. The only reason I stay away from him is because I love him, you booby."

Her arms shot around him, and they hugged. "Promise me you always will," she demanded.

" 'Always' is too big a word."

"Don't quibble, Neddie. If you love him, stay off him forever."

"Always? Forever?"

"Promise."

He stepped back out of her embrace. "No promises."

"Ned, please."

"You know," he said, sidestepping her as he moved toward the door to the foyer, "when you hugged me then, I could feel the baby. I mean, it was either that or you swallowed a melon. Which is it, Katie?"

"Where do you think you're going?"

"To a bar where they serve beer without demanding promises."

37

The pains had begun that January morning, shortly after Edmund had left the apartment. Olivia, arriving around noon to escort Kate to the site where the house was being built, found her huddled in a goosedown comforter, face pale, hair disheveled. At that time the pains were coming every half-hour or so.

By midafternoon they were coming faster. Olivia had gone for Dr. Amabile. When they returned at five, Kate's skin had an unhealthy, greenish tinge to it.

"Perhaps quite soon," the doctor said. "Perhaps not. I shall send for Mrs. Groark."

Kate made a face. "Not Biddy Groark. She never washes her hands."

Amabile's luxurious pepper-and-salt eyebrows went up and down. "Madame Lescot, then? I have employed her often."

Kate tensed, her back arching slightly, as another pain built, peaked, and retreated. "I've never heard of her. But send for her now. Please?"

Amabile's glance slid sideways to Olivia. "She lives on Touro," he murmured. "Would you be good enough to . . .?"

Olivia nodded. As she left the bedroom, the doctor followed her. In the entry foyer they conferred in lowered voices. "I do not like her complexion," Amabile said.

224

"It's her behavior." Olivia let him help her into her coat. "She's like a different woman. I have never seen Kate so . . . so . . ."

The doctor nodded somberly. "Fearful," he supplied. "But there is no reason to fear. She is a healthy young woman. All goes normally. Please," he added, pressing Olivia in the direction of the door. "The corner of Touro and Villere. Second-floor front. And hurry."

Olivia stared at him. "You, too, seem perturbed."

"Not at all."

"Edmund will be home shortly," Olivia promised him. "Kate will feel much better then."

The doctor's gray-topped head swung quickly from side to side. "Madame Lescot, please. *Tout de suite.*"

At seven the pains were coming every eight minutes, according to the fat gold watch on Dr. Amabile's chain. Olivia had not returned. Edmund had not returned. The doctor had watched Kate's expression grow steadily less controlled. She was making every effort, but she was beginning to panic.

"Come," he said. "A cup of tea, perhaps?"

Her eyes opened wide as the jolt of pain passed through her. Then they narrowed almost maliciously. "Can you make a cup of tea, Dr. Amabile?"

"I . . . There is surely a servant we . . ." He paused. "Olivia will be here at any moment."

"With Edmund?" Kate retorted angrily.

"*Bien sûr,*" Amabile said in a soothing voice. "Both will be here soon."

"Really?"

"Of course." He patted her hand. "With Madame Lescot."

"And if she can't come? Can you . . .?"

The doctor shrugged eloquently. "I have myself never attended a birth, dear girl. It is the proper duty of midwives only. Their experience, their skill . . . and, after all, they are women like yourself." He waved a finger negatively from side to side. "No, it is not given to physicians to participate in this miracle, dear girl. It is a . . ." He coughed delicately. "A feminine *mystère, n'est-ce pas?*"

Her torso convulsed. The hand he was patting suddenly turned upside-down and grasped his. She squeezed fiercely for a moment, her palm wet. Beads of perspiration were forming on her forehead. With his free hand Amabile whipped out a large silk handkerchief and patted her face.

Kate sank back on her pillows as the spasm passed. Weakly her eyes opened, and she stared at Amabile. "Where are they?" she whispered. "Where is Olivia? Where is Edmund?"

Amabile started to shrug, but thought better of it. Panic was all around them. One had to move cautiously, if at all.

At a quarter past eight Kate could hear footsteps coming through the apartment, one pair lighter in sound than the other. "Edmund?" she called.

Olivia appeared at the bedroom door. "I have someone," she told Amabile. "Your Madame Lescot was not at home. Her daughter gave me the name of a Madame Taliaferro on Claiborne Street. But she had another *accouchement* to attend. She gave me this woman's name, and I finally found her after some searching."

Olivia moved aside. In her heels, she stood perhaps an inch over five feet. But behind her, hidden until now, was a dark, birdlike woman, her hair hidden under a squat black grosgrain hat from which hung a veil. In her black coat she looked like a small raven. She bobbed her head.

"Madame Fleurigant, at your service," she said.

38

Outside, New Orleans shivered on this January night. The wind off the river carried a chill that got into a man's bones. Inside the Wicklowe, its gas mantles pulsing like implacable suns refracted through cut glass, the air was warm with the rich aroma of beef, oyster stew, Creole shrimp, and hot fresh-baked bread.

Patrick Blood, all 220 pounds of him, sat at the corner table looking vaguely embarrassed as he waited for his dinner companions. He hadn't ordered anything, either, to drink, since his own chief, David Hennessy, was to be his host at dinner. He was not certain whether he was on duty or off, and resolved to make no move on the matter until Hennessy himself produced a clue.

The room sparkled before him, the great main hall where the general public ate. For special parties, or for regular patrons who wanted privacy, there were smaller rooms upstairs. But most visitors to the Wicklowe preferred this barn where one could see and be seen.

Bulky mahogany tables were set with brilliant glassware and gleaming silver. The waiters had a trick with the napkins, folding them just so, like a bishop's mitre, and standing them up in a row of four with a silver band around each.

Warmth radiated from the immense fireplace, where a pair of shoats turned slowly on a spit. The small Negro boy who revolved the crank seemed almost asleep from his proximity to the great heat of the fire. Patrick watched him doze off, wake with a start, give the crank a turn, and fight to keep his eyes open. An assistant chef from the kitchen bustled in, dipped a brush in sauce, and deftly painted each shoat a bright orange. As the liquid dripped into the fire, it filled the room with a pleasant acrid smell.

Patrick sniffed mightily. Not fair of the chief to keep him waiting this way, not knowing what this dinner meeting was all about. Not knowing, really, if he was invited to dinner or only to get his instructions and leave. Hennessy was a hard, taciturn man most of the time. And being Cornelius Blood's son didn't exactly help Patrick.

Across the room, at another corner table, sat four aldermen. Patrick recognized Sidney Story, the man who was always agitating to make prostitution legal. Well, not exactly legal, but contained in one redlight district where you could keep an eye on them.

Not much given to analytical thought, Patrick Blood found himself wondering how the Shadow Mayor of New Orleans and acknowledged master of the Tenderloin felt about Story's plans. Would the plan help Neil Blood or hurt him? And what concern was it, after all, of Detective Sergeant Patrick Blood? If the law went on the books, he would have to uphold it. Simple. Or at least seem to uphold it. Even simpler.

He looked up as he saw Chief Hennessy enter the main room with Captain O'Bannon beside him. As they made for the table, Hennessy told O'Bannon in a loud voice, "You see, it pays to eat with the owner's boy, so it does. Corner table and all."

Patrick was on his feet. "Evening, chief. Evening, captain."

"Sit," O'Bannon ordered, as if addressing an obstreperous mastiff.

The two older officers flanked Patrick as they took their seats. Hennessy arched an eyebrow as he surveyed his detective sergeant. "Where's your da?"

Patrick's eyes went wide. "Is he expected?"

Hennessy signaled a passing waiter. "Three beers," he said.

"What kind of meeting is it, then?" Patrick wondered aloud.

The waiter reappeared almost at once, carrying three heavy glass steins. Behind him was the patron himself. "Good appetite to you gentlemen," he said. "Evening, Paddy."

"Sit down, Neil," the chief suggested.

Cornelius Blood's cool blue eyes over their imposing pouches blinked comfortably like a lizard's in the sun. "The truth of it is, chief, I find myself in a lather for time. I am due elsewhere, not"—he held up a cautioning hand—"to a meeting as august as yours."

"We had an appointment for a little talk." Hennessy's voice had chilled suddenly.

"Little, is it? Then let me stand here and palaver awhile."

The two senior policemen exchanged disgusted glances. Captain O'Bannon cleared his throat. "The dagos are riled up, Neil. A lot of new ones coming into town. There's a rash of knifings. We think a gentleman whose name you may know is getting ready to take over a certain docking operation."

"Does any of this blather have Christian names to it?" Neil asked in a mild voice.

Hennessy's eyebrow crooked alarmingly. "Is it names you want, Neil Blood? Let me put it to you straight. You and your pal Salvatore Antonio Matranga are hereby on notice. The first move—the *first* move—no matter how small, against the Provenzanos, and we will clamp down on Matranga like the lid on a garbage barrel. Do you understand?"

"I understand what you're saying. What has it to do with me?"

"If you want to play that game, fine," the chief snapped. "Let it be a message, then, from me to Tony Matranga. Tell him he won't be able to *breathe*. Tell him tonight."

Neil Blood pulled for a moment at the tip of his blond mustache. "Davy Hennessy's errand boy," he said to no one in particular. "It's a strange world filled with strange coppers." He bent over the chief. "To hell with your message, chief. And to hell with you."

Patrick Blood was halfway out of his seat. His father glanced at him. "Sit!" he commanded in almost the same tone O'Bannon had used. "You made your bed with these fine gentlemen. Now lie in it."

He started to turn away, but Hennessy's voice detained him. "Neil."

"I'm in a hurry. Make it quick."

"Neil," the chief said gently, "maybe my tone was out of line. Let me put it as a request, if you will. *Please* give Tony that message?"

The chef at the fireplace painted a fresh coat of sauce on the turning shoats. Clouds of smoke wafted through the huge hall and disappeared in the rafters.

"Since you put it that way," Blood said, "I will."

Hennessy nodded. "Tonight?" he suggested softly.

"Not tonight." Neil Blood heaved a great sigh, and his glance shifted to Patrick. "Tonight I am with my daughter, gentlemen. She is in childbirth, or so they tell me."

All three policemen got to their feet. Chief Hennessy lifted his beer with a solemn look to his bulldog face. "*Slainte!*"

"*Slainte!*" the others echoed.

"Thank you, gentlemen. One of my daughters has already given me three granddaughters. Here's hoping I'm blessed with a grandson." He favored them each with a broad smile, turned, and disappeared from the Wicklowe.

"What do you say, Blood?" asked Hennessy. "Will he deliver the message?"

"Sir, when my father promises something . . ." Blood paused to steady his voice. "It's as good as done."

"Damn," Hennessy muttered, "you'd better be right. One hell of a lot of lives hang on it."

39

"Push!" Madame Fleurigant urged. "Now."

Kate bit her lip and tried to do as she was told. She bitterly resented all of it, of which the pain was only a part. She resented Edmund not having come home. Amabile washing his hands of responsibility. Olivia not finding a midwife of repute, but this mangy little bird of a woman who surely attended only blacks and mulattoes, great strapping girls who popped babies as champagne popped corks.

"Now," the little woman ordered.

She had rolled up her sleeves and was kneeling on the bed beside Kate, her big avian eyes staring intently into Kate's as if trying to mesmerize her. Where on earth had Olivia found this strange person?

The pains were coming rapidly now. There had been a very sharp one a while ago. Kate's recollection was hazy. And blood. Not a lot, but . . .

"Bear down, missy!" Madame Fleurigant demanded. "You must help more."

"The blood."

"Only natural, missy. Part of life. You have seen blood before, have you not, missy?"

Kate felt unable to respond as she wanted to, sharply, telling this little crow to leave her alone. Behind her the closed door to the bedroom opened a crack and Olivia peered in. She gasped, seeing the blood, and turned quickly away. "Dr. Amabile?" Kate heard her call.

"Bear down, missy!"

Beyond the half-open door Olivia and the doctor conferred in mumbles. The gas mantle flickered. Kate watched it lower and rise, as if gauze fluttered before it. Strange movements in the walls. Undulating like snakes.

Half of Amabile's face appeared at the door, eyes averted from the bed. "*Vous permettez, madame?*"

"*Mais non!*" the tiny midwife exploded. "Out! Out!"

"*Vous permettez*, Madame Crozat?" the doctor persisted.

"Yes," Kate called. Her voice seemed to be coming from far away.

Face still averted, Dr. Amabile sidestepped into the room. "Mamselle Livy has asked me . . ." He stopped, thoroughly panicked at the sight of the stained sheet. "What is the problem, Madame Fleurigant?"

"There is no problem."

"But surely . . ."

"*Tout va bien, m'sieur,*" she assured him smoothly.

"But surely there is unusual strain."

The midwife shrugged her small, bony shoulders. Her thin nose seemed to raise loftily like a bird's. "*L'enfant se présente à l'envers, m'sieur.*"

"Dear me."

"Quite normal."

"What is it?" Kate demanded. She could see their heads, but the focus kept shifting. "Tell me."

"The baby . . ." Amabile bit his lip. "The baby is presented backwards."

"But then . . ." Kate felt another pain mushroom inside her, a fire that had nowhere to go.

"Bear down!" Madame Fleurigant demanded.

"No!" Kate could hear herself screaming. "No!"

"Push!"

Thrashing her head from side to side, Kate began to sob. "If the b-baby is backwards," she moaned, "I must not squeeze this way."

"Surely, madame," the doctor murmured in the midwife's ear, "there is something to relieve this situation. Some drug? Massage?"

The tiny woman in black straightened up from the bed. She was straddling Kate's legs. "You must leave this room, m'sieur. It is wrong for you to be here. This is women's work."

"I underst—"

"What's the problem?" Neil Blood's voice boomed through the doorway.

In silence, the doctor and the midwife turned to see the blond giant filling the space from floor to lintel. "Who in God's name is that?" he inquired.

"She was the only midwife we could get at short notice," Olivia explained. "Madame Fleurigant."

Nothing stirred in the tall man's face. He turned slightly to stare down at Olivia. "You don't recognize the name?" he asked almost gently.

"No. But she was recommended."

"You, Doc?" Blood demanded.

Amabile had hurried toward him and was now wringing his hands. "She is qualified, sir. I have heard of her," he quavered.

Blood stepped into the room, grasped Amabile's shirtfront, and lifted him over the threshold to deposit him outside the doorway. Then he closed the door and put his back against it. "Kate, how're you bearing up?"

"The baby is coming out b-backwards." She began sobbing softly again.

"Do you know this woman?" her father asked.

"No."

The midwife in her black dress had gotten off the bed and was standing beside it, drying her hands with a towel and leaving streaks of blood on the fabric. She glanced boldly at Neil.

"Now, then, Madame Fleurigant," Blood said in a low, penetrating voice. "You are going to do this right at last, are you not?"

"M'sieur . . ."

"You *are*," Blood assured her, his voice as heavy as a ton of stone. "Oh, yes, Madame Mambo."

Muddy white showed around the midwife's irises. "*Hunsi-bosal?*" she asked.

"*Hunsi-kanzo,*" Blood told her contemptuously. His hand shot out and wrapped around her right wrist. The tan skin began to grow yellow with pressure. "You will do it right, *mama-loi.*"

She tried to extricate her arm, but it was no use. "*Laissez-moi.*"

"*Vous rencontrez un hungan grand, madame. Un boko hungan.*"

"Let me go!"

"Never." The syllables were heavy in Neil Blood's mouth. "Even after you do this right, I will never let you go, *mambo.* You will forever be in my hands."

For the first time, the little woman seemed to lose spirit. She stopped twisting and let her arms go slack. Blood released her. "Do it now," he commanded, "and do it right."

"There is truly a danger, *papa-loi.*"

"Yes? Then use all your skill."

"The danger is not of my making. I swear it."

"No? But when the Baron comes for you, it will be of my making," the tall man promised her.

Madame Fleurigant's mouth set in a straight thin line. Her face looked more birdlike now, her cheeks drawn.

"Hold the girl's hand," she said. "This will be difficult."

"Da? Are you still here?"

Crouched on the bed, the midwife was massaging Kate's belly in slow upward strokes, gently but firmly. Kate could feel the movement soothing her. The tension was not as painful. She closed her eyes. Then . . .

"Christ!" she screamed.

The tiny woman had plunged her skinny hand inside. Blood welled up around her wrist. "Christ Almighty!" Kate shouted in agony.

Her arm moving in and out, the midwife was doing something horribly painful inside Kate's womb. She could feel it like a tiger clawing at her insides.

"Da! Stop her!"

Deftly Madame Fleurigant withdrew her arm and swabbed away the blood. "Hush, *bébé*," she crooned. "It goes well now. You see?" she asked the tall man. "*Voilà, la tête.*"

A convulsion wracked Kate's body. Suddenly a small white dome appeared, and a moment later, with a second thrust of her muscles, a baby slid out into the welter of blood between her legs.

The midwife scooped it up and patted it dry. With quick fingers she twisted the cord, bent over, and bit it through between her teeth. Working deftly, she knotted the cord and tucked it into the infant's belly. Then she laid it across her lap, facedown, and patted it vigorously.

An angry wail came from the baby. Olivia threw open the door. "Oh!" she cried. "Isn't he beautiful?"

The midwife wrapped the baby in a towel and laid him in Kate's arms. Face streaming tears and sweat, she cuddled the baby at her breast and searched its face. He looked like no one, except perhaps a very small monkey. But across his head was a faint fuzz of red hair.

"*Hungan,*" the midwife told the tall man, "he would have died. I have saved the life of your grandson."

He eyed her coldly. "And your own life as well, Madame Fleurigant."

40

New Year's Eve had come and gone. January's damp, chilling grip held the city prisoner, keeping the streets empty except in the District and those parts of the Quarter where parties prepared the way for the great 1890 Mardi Gras festivities. It was a month of anticipation.

The man huddled in the doorway on Dauphine Street looked out-of-place. No sensible person was abroad tonight, unless from one Basin Street establishment to another, and then well fortified by alcohol. He seemed a stranger to New Orleans, gangling, hair in need of trimming, wearing ill-assorted clothes and an overcoat too thin for the weather.

From time to time he stamped his feet in their rundown boots. Wrapping his long arms around his chest, he tucked his hands under his armpits for warmth. Even so, he managed to remain in the shadows as he watched the house across the street.

It was a lovely old two-story edifice, narrow, with a parlor facing the street. The curtains were drawn, but a faint rim of interior light outlined the parlor windows and spilled out into the entry hall, behind its ornate front door inset with plate glass.

The man blew on his hands and jammed them in the pockets of his coat. He seemed miserable enough at his lonely station, but he remained where he was, careful to keep out of sight.

* * *

Winter being a slow time for cotton buyers, Alexander Badger had taken himself back to England for a personal report to his superiors at Fiddoch, Larned.

From there he had taken his daughter, Daisy, on a pared-down version of the Grand Tour. They spent a week in Paris, followed by Vienna, where both were personal guests of the emperor at the Sylvesterabend Ball on a snowy New Year's Eve. They fled south, seeking the sun in Venice and Rome and finding it at last in Palermo, where Badger delivered several letters Neil Blood had given him on behalf of his friend Tony Matranga.

Now the brilliant sun of Sicily was only a memory as Badger sat disconsolately in the parlor of his house on Dauphine Street.

He shivered. Would he ever be warm again? he wondered. Or was it also that he missed Daisy? For a plain, gawky girl, she was certainly a pleasure to travel with. When he had Daisy with him, all sorts of interesting people seemed to join his party, especially young Europeans who liked fun, dancing, gambling, and staying up late.

Still, tonight he had made elaborate plans for warming himself in a memorable fashion. He had arranged with Madame Lulu to send Josefa to his home at ten o'clock after Badger's housekeeper retired for the night. And together he hoped to try out an item recommended to him by one of Daisy's friends.

Badger smiled and rubbed his hands before the fire. Life wasn't really as bleak as it had seemed yesterday on his return to the chill damp of New Orleans. The year 1890 would be fine. And if all went well, Daisy would make a permanent move from London in the spring, to keep house for her father.

Badger got up suddenly, went to the sideboard, and poured himself a small glass of whiskey, an unblended malt Scotch he imported by the keg for his own private use. As he sipped the cognaclike drink, he reflected that, really, life had worked out remarkably well. His coming-home depression seemed to be lifting. The whiskey was doing him a world of good.

He was a rich man, with nearly half a million pounds sterling now resting in a vault under Threadneedle Street in London. Before taking this trip he had cashed the larger portion of his New Orleans holdings into gold pieces. They had filled two small but exceedingly heavy trunks, which had sailed with him to London.

Never mind your greenbacks or your bits of paper with the good old queen printed on them. The two trunks, padlocked, reposed sedately in a vault behind steel bars and two-holed Chubb locks. And the matching keys the bank needed to open the vault were residing now in Badger's

New Orleans safe-deposit box. Oh, it was foolproof. Better yet, no notes or letters of credit or what-have-you lay around attesting to the transfer. Fiddoch, Larned's man was as discreet as they came.

Badger smiled and poured himself another sip against the cold. He'd been careful to leave himself enough cash in New Orleans with which to take advantage of whatever new suggestion came his way through Neil Blood. The old blackguard was talking oil these days. Very well, Alexander Badger would invest in oil.

Mrs. Fenwick came to the parlor door. "Is there anything more you'd be needing, sir?"

Badger pulled his pocket watch from his vest and consulted it at some length. Ten o'clock, less ten minutes. "You may retire for the night, Mrs. Fenwick. I'll lock up."

"Very good, sir." She curtsied and left.

Badger waited until he heard her climb the stairs to her room in the rear of the second floor. Then he swung open the bottom doors of a great fumed-oak sideboard and withdrew a small flat box wrapped in brown paper. With the cigar knife attached to his watch chain, Badger cut the cord and opened up the wrapping. Inside was a plain cardboard container. He lifted off the flat top.

Within, wrapped in pale tissue paper, lay a curious sort of belt, liberally studded with brass nailheads along its ornately scalloped edges. The leather itself seemed unusually thick, and Badger could see a fine horizontal network of thin copper wires in and out of the leather. The belt-like item closed with an unusually heavy brass buckle on which, in raised letters, could be read the name "Heidelberg, Mk. II."

A booklet in German lay at the bottom of the box. Badger lifted it out and, beneath it, found another booklet printed in English. "Heidelberg Mk. II Electrical Health Stimulator. Owner's Manual," read the booklet cover.

There was a faint knock at the front door. Badger hastily stuffed everything back in the box, closed the lid, and dashed out into the hall. Beyond the beveled plate-glass windows stood Josefa in a long coat and heavy veil.

Touching his fingers to his lips, he let her in and led her into the parlor. "Here, my dear," Badger whispered, helping her out of her heavy caracul coat. "See what I've brought from Austria?"

The tall young woman stood revealed in a low-cut evening gown that displayed her *café au lait* throat and the cleavage between her generous breasts. Josefa's mother had been Italian—"from the north," she was always quick to remind her clients, "not one of those southern pigs"— and her father, to judge by the face behind the veil, had been an unusually handsome black man. All in all, Badger thought, a very thrilling, very dominant personality.

"I heard tell of these," she said in a normal voice.

"Shh." Badger indicated the study off the parlor, where he installed them both on a large overstuffed sofa and carefully locked the only door through which someone could reach them. "Mrs. Fenwick may still be awake."

"You put this on or something?" Josefa inquired, holding the belt up to the gas mantle light. The brass studs glittered. "How does it . . . ?" She laughed. "Poppa, look at that." She flicked with her fingers a sling of fine copper wire braided with silk threads that looped down from the belt. "This goes under the *cojones*, eh, Poppa?" she asked, grinning.

Leafing through the English manual, Badger nodded. "So it would seem." He flipped pages. "Instant rejuvenation. Total restoration of youthful powers. Dear me."

Josefa removed her veil. As she turned down the gas mantle, its light flashed wickedly in her dark eyes. "My little Badger and me, we're gonna have fun."

Her client embraced her in the half-dark, pressing his face between her big, perfumed breasts. "You don't link the belt together until you're ready," he murmured, half-smothering himself. "When you link it together, the electrical current begins to flow."

Deftly Josefa freed herself from his embrace and in a matter of moments had stripped off Alexander Badger's trousers, shoes, socks, garters, and underwear. She settled him on his back on the overstuffed couch and worked the Heidelburg Mk. II up behind his buttocks.

"Pretty little thing," she said, slipping the loop of copper wire under his scrotum. "Oh, Poppa, you're gonna outstud the biggest mule in town."

Moving with a kind of inexorable speed, she whisked off her own clothes and bent over him, her long, muscular, dusky-skinned body poised in the air. "Ready?"

"Ready," Badger squeaked, voice high with tension.

Josefa's long dark fingers snapped the belt buckle closed. Badger was breathing with difficulty, his lungs filled with her aroma. He could feel a faint tingling in his groin. "It's not . . ."

"Wait a second, Poppa."

Josefa opened the belt and jammed it closed again.

Badger's body doubled backward like a bent bow. His mouth opened in a silent scream, eyes popping. Josefa hastily clamped the palm of her hand over his lips. He was biting her flesh. Scrambling in the dark with her other hand, she managed to open the buckle.

His back collapsed against the upholstery. Worried now, Josefa took her hand from his mouth. A great sighing exhalation shook Badger's small frame. His potbelly wobbled. His eyes closed.

"Poppa? Say somethin'."

"Uhhh!"

Carefully Josefa opened one of his eyelids. "Poppa, speak t'me."

His breathing began to grow calmer. "Perhaps we ought to read the manual again."

Josefa sat down next to him and patted his cheek. "Again? You a game little rooster, Poppa."

"I would hate to think they had cheated me," Badger told her in a thin voice. "At that price, one expects complete satisfaction."

"Don't you worry none," she told him. "At my price, that is exactly what you gonna get."

At eleven o'clock Josefa let herself out through the front door, pausing on the steps to adjust her veil. Then she set off at a long, athletic lope for Mahogany Hall. The night was young and her funny little friend with the electric belt no longer required her services. If she was any judge of Poppa, he'd wake up tomorrow morning on that sofa after the best sleep of his life.

Across Dauphine Street, in the shadows of a darkened doorway, Mike Leathers stirred. He took his hands out of his thin overcoat pockets and rubbed them together as he watched the tall mulatto stride away.

He doubted very much if what Ned Blood needed was a diary of Alexander Badger's jousts with the livelier ladies of the Quarter. Ned expected something big to happen, now that the Englishman was back in town. It was his notion that Badger was the key to the situation. If they knew who came and went, who met with him late at night, they would have a better idea of what was going on.

Mike had spent last night until midnight freezing in this doorway as Badger, fatigued from his long Liverpool crossing, slept the night away. On this, his second night, Mike had come up with nothing more than Josefa, who Luanne told him had the nerve and strength to tackle any trick in the District.

He shivered again and found himself wondering how many members of the Louisiana bar were freezing in doorways tonight, living off handouts from a friend and the earnings of their woman.

It had been going on far too long. What kind of man had he turned into? He'd come to rescue Luanne, not live off her whoring. If he could somehow damp down his pride and ask his father for work, this whole demeaning life would come to an end. He'd been tempted often enough, but each time he decided to do it, Ned had come through with another ten dollars. This idea of digging up information Ned could turn into dollars went only so far, and although Ned split the take fair and square, it didn't go far enough.

"Stake me to a new suit, boots, and a few new shirts," Mike had told him just tonight at dinner, "and set me up in Baton Rouge. That's where I can cut the mustard, Ned, not here. Turn me loose where I really know the territory."

"You talk like I had the ready to grubstake an army," Ned had complained. "If I didn't tap my old man now and then, I'd be as stony as you."

Fair enough, Mike Leathers told himself now, blowing into his cupped hands. You tap your old man, Ned, my boy, and I'll tap mine. First thing tomorrow, bended knee if necessary.

For some time now there had been no lights showing in the Badger house. Hearing the bells ring midnight Mike sprinted up Urselines at a country boy's long-legged pace, heading for the place on Marais where Ned paid the rent and Mike slept. Luanne, too, on her day off. Otherwise she slept with the rest of Miss Harriet's crew of whores. He hardly saw her except for that one day. If he wanted more, he'd have had to pay for it.

At the corner of Rampart he started to turn left in the direction of the District, thinking to go up Bienville to Marais. Nearer to Basin, the streets would begin to fill up. Here they were empty, as the sturdy bourgeoisie snored behind their own shutters.

He saw a flicker of movement behind him. A man was leaving one of the small cottages and a woman was kissing him good night. Then she closed the door, blacking out the scene.

Sex was more than a business in New Orleans, Mike Leathers told himself as he continued walking south along Rampart. Sex was the air this city breathed. Selling it, buying it, giving it, taking it, sex was the commodity far and away beyond cotton or sugar that kept this city rattling along like a kettle on the coals.

Behind him a horse trotted neatly along Rampart, ridden by the blood who'd bid his ladylove such an affectionate adieu. At St. Ann the rider turned left as he passed a streetlamp. Mike saw the grave, sharp profile of Edmund Crozat.

He watched the horseman move off toward the river, Jackson Square, and the Pontalba Apartments.

Ned Blood's friend. His brother-in-law. The man who had bought Mike Leathers' downfall.

Mike made a face and plunged on in the night. He was cold and tired and ill with self-loathing. If Edmund Crozat with his oil-dirty millions wanted to leave his redheaded wife at home while he spent an evening with a jade in a Rampart Street cottage, that was Crozat's business.

But Mike would remember to mention it to Ned.

41

Clem Rynders kicked the half-frozen ground with the heel of his boot. The night wind whistled across the knife-edge brim of his Stetson hat. His own breath was condensing in his mustache and dripping down over his upper lip.

Rynders cursed and ducked into his tent. A small vertical kerosene stove gave off heat, but not enough to gain much on the wind, which whipped away the air as fast as it was heated. Crouched in the triangular entrance of the tent, back to the heater, he squinted through the dark at the row of holding tanks. One was finished and ready for crude. The rest were still in the framework stage. They would not be usable for months. But Edmund Crozat had ordered drilling begun.

Luckily, Rynders told himself as he stared past the tanks to the two drill rigs in the distance, the boring wouldn't reach oil—according to his guess—for some time. The tried-and-true cable-tool rigs were shorties, not more than a hundred feet bottom to top, with a narrow base some twenty feet square. They worked in tandem off one donkey engine, its walking beam lifting and falling monotonously, transferring motion to a great cast-iron flywheel.

From the wheel, belts and pulleys transmitted the motion to cables that rose to the top of each rig and wound down through the top crown block, dropping inside each derrick until they disappeared in the ground. Far below—at least fifty feet down, the last Rynders had checked—the ramlike cutting edge would drop into the earth, hammer loose a bit of it, and scoop it up out of the way to make room for the next down-dropping fall, like a pile driver.

Torches flared in the wind. This was a twenty-four-hour operation. The earth beneath Rynders' feet shook almost imperceptibly, and there was a strange, disturbing rhythm to the pounding.

He shrugged violently to warm himself, then fastened the tent flap behind him. The younger geologist at the makeshift drafting table looked up. "About time you stopped letting in the wind."

"Just thinking."

"There's something new. A thinking oil man."

"If we knew what was good for us," Rynders continued, "we'd slow the drills even more than they are. Because when we hit crude, there's only the one tank for storage."

The younger man gestured airily. "We just cap it off and wait for the other tanks to be built."

"Crozat won't like that."

"Then Crozat should have come up with more cash. He's trying to build storage on pennies. So the work goes slow."

"He's counting on selling the crude to pay for more tanks."

"That's a terribly thin shoestring, Clem."

Rynders stepped nearer the heater. "Maybe he's got another source of money, but I doubt it. He's cleaned out till we start pumping crude."

"That will be months."

"Try to sound a bit more unhappy," Rynders told him. "If Crozat don't get crude soon, he goes under."

The younger geologist sat back on his stool and stretched his arms, yawning. "Standard Oil is hiring down around Baton Rouge," he said at last. "I hear they need geologists and surveyors."

Rynders made a disgusted face. "I been in this with Crozat since the beginning. I can't walk out on him now."

"Loyal, eh?"

Rynders' look of disgust deepened. "I don't know. Maybe just curious." He laughed unhappily. "To see the man hang himself, I suppose."

"Why wait? They say the S.O. boys are planning some kind of refinery across the river from Baton Rouge. The money's good. And I hear tell they pay regular. Not like some employers I know."

Rynders held his palms out to the heater. "When'd you get paid last?"

"What is this, middle of January? Say, middle of November. My pocketbook thinks they've stopped printing greenbacks in Washington."

In silence they heard the sudden sound of hoofbeats. Rynders looked up. "Riders coming." He opened the tent flap and peered out into the torchlit night. "Dozen of 'em. Oh-oh."

"Shee-yit," grumbled the younger man. He reached down for a short carbine as Rynders turned down the wick on the kerosene lantern and blew out the flame.

"Sons of bitches ain't even wearing hoods," the younger man said as he knelt in the tent entrance and steadied the carbine.

"The lead man is."

Rynders pushed past him and knelt behind a scrubby growth of bush. He had pulled a six-shot, long-barrel Colt from his holster.

"Clem, I'd swear the masked one is Ringo Waddell."

"Sits his horse like Ringo." Rynders squinted along the barrel. "I hate waiting for them to fire the first shot."

"So far, none of them has done nothing more than sort of ride around awhile trying to spook us."

"Like we was heifers or something." Rynders laughed softly. "Long's they stick to that, I don't mind a little break in the routine now and then." His right arm steady, he was keeping the masked leader of the horsemen in his sights.

Slowing to an easy walk, the troop of mounted men circled the well-site once and began a second circuit. They held their rifles and shotguns easily, some across their chests, some in their laps. The finicky clip-clip of the horses' hooves added a new rhythm to the beat of the drilling rigs.

"You know," the younger geologist said at last, "if they was to open up, Clem, they'd wipe us out in ten minutes. They got more weapons. They're more mobile. And compared to the two of us, they have got to be better shots."

"Mighty funny. I am gonna smile about that. Maybe tomorrow."

"I seen that Waddell shoot at a county fair over to Winnfield."

"So did I. He's the joker in this pack, far's I can tell. He's the man they sent to the legislature, sure enough, but what he lives on is his salary as manager of Whiteacres."

"So?"

"Whiteacres is Crozat land."

The younger man chuckled. "A Crozat manager spooking Crozat drill crews. Don't make no sense, Clem."

"Like I said."

The horsemen paused now between two torches. They had reined themselves into a tight circle, as if ready to resist attack from all sides. Then, with a wild "ee-haw!" the masked leader led them off into the darkness.

"I reckon," Rynders said at last, lowering his revolver, "if you set up in business as a night rider, well, sir, comes nighttime, you gotta ride."

"There's wisdom somewhere in there, Clem." The younger man ejected the shell in his carbine, caught it in midair, and snapped it back into the magazine of the short rifle. "Hot damn! You got any of that Monongahela rye left under your bunk?"

"If you been leaving it alone I have."

Inside the tent, they sat on opposite sides of the heater and passed the jug back and forth awhile. "What call has Waddell to menace us poor oil men?" said Rynders.

"Cotton men just naturally hate oil men, Clem. Everybody knows that."

"So they say. But why does Crozat cotton hate Crozat oil?"

"Maybe—"

A faraway yell cut through the night. Both men grabbed their guns and ran out of the tent. "Over there!" Rynders shouted.

"Yo, Clem," someone cried. "Come a-runnin'!"

"What's up?"

"Crude!"

"What?"

"At sixty feet," the man in the distance called.

"Couple of months yet, eh?" shouted Rynders. Then a troubled look crossed his face. "Now what do we do?"

"Tell Crozat?"

"That lucky bastard."

42

The moment he let himself in the Pontalba apartment, Edmund knew something had gone wrong. A small dark coat that looked like Olivia's was carelessly thrown over the love seat in the foyer, its sleeve trailing on the floor. He walked into the parlor and found Cornelius Blood asleep in the armchair.

The immense bulk of the man looked menacing even in sleep. Edmund stared down at his father-in-law. In the next instant, he understood. From the direction of the bedroom, a baby cried.

Edmund removed his hat, shrugged hastily out of his coat, and dropping it on the floor, dashed through the apartment. He opened the bedroom door. Olivia sat in a chair pulled up to the bed. A tiny mulatto woman was handing a swathed baby to Kate, who sat up in bed, supported by pillows.

Carefully the mulatto woman guided the baby's mouth to Kate's full left breast, its nipple big, the smooth skin distended. "Just rub it against his mouth, missy. He don't need more learning than that."

He! Edmund took a step into the room, but none of the women looked up. Kate took the baby in her arms. The little mulatto woman cradled his head with its scurf of red fuzz and pushed him until his lips met the nipple. A moment later, his tiny lips drew back and he seemed to push himself forward the necessary half-inch more.

"Look at that," Kate marveled. The baby was sucking greedily. "Will you look at that?"

246

"Now we got to know," the midwife said, "is he getting what you have got to give him." She poked a tiny finger into the corner of the baby's mouth. A pearl of liquid ran out. "Good." She stood back from the bed and nodded. "All is in order, missy." As she turned away, her glance fell on Edmund.

"*Mon Dieu!*"

Olivia and Kate looked up. "Edmund," his sister cried out. "A fine time to put in an appearance."

"Is he . . .?" Edmund stopped. "Can I . . . ?"

"He's busy now," Olivia snapped. "In fact, you'd best leave the room."

"How long . . . ?"

Olivia turned to the tiny midwife. "How long will he nurse, Madame Fleurigant?"

Edmund blinked. "Madame Fl—"

"My work is finished here," the small woman said with sudden briskness. She bustled about the room, piling bloody towels in a corner. Then she picked up her coat and veiled hat. "I shall return in the morning, missy, but I doubt you will be needing me. All goes well."

She seemed not to want to look at Edmund, yet her big eyes kept swerving in his direction. With a final burst of energy she left the room. "I must see her home," Olivia said, following her. "Edmund, please leave your wife and son to themselves."

"In a moment."

When she had left, Edmund slowly closed the door and stepped to the bed. "He looks so small," he said then.

In the silence that followed, the only sound was the greedy pulse of the sucking baby. Kate's glance remained on her son.

"Are you all right?" Edmund asked. "The blood . . ."

She said nothing. "Why did you call Madame Fleurigant?" he asked.

Kate shifted the baby an inch but did not reply.

"Kate, I am talking to you." Edmund's voice sounded uncertain. Still she was silent.

"This is intolerable!" he burst out. Pacing away from the bed, he glared at her from a distance. "I am not to be punished in this childish way, my girl. Tonight I had business to attend to. You seem to have done well enough without me, in any event."

Kate's glance shifted a moment from the baby to him. The sucking noises had come to an end. She lifted the baby to her shoulder and pulled her gown over her bare breast, nestling the baby's head next to her ear and gently patting his back.

"Kate! Dammit!"

For a long terrible moment, the silence held them. Then, by way of answer, the baby let out a small thorough belch. Kate held his head as she lifted him down. "Are your hands clean?" she asked suddenly.

Startled, Edmund looked down at his hands. There were so many ways a man could take that question. "Clean?"

"Here."

She held the baby out to its father. "Hold his head this way."

Frowning, Edmund approached the bed. Waves of guilt seemed to flush up through his body like the flames of a great fire. How in God's name, he wondered miserably, had Kate managed to make him feel this way?

The baby was warm and wet. Eyes shut, he lay in Edmund's arms like a not-very-well-designed doll. "He has your hair," Edmund heard himself saying. He tried to fight the feeling of inadequacy that overwhelmed him. He had no business handling this infant. He was unclean in every way.

"This Madame Fleurigant . . ." he began in an unsteady voice.

"Without her," Neil Blood said from the doorway, "this boy and this girl might not be with us now. The woman is a master of her art." He took the baby from Edmund. "Look at that face," he crooned. "It's the handsomest face this side of the New Orleans Zoo, so it is." He swung the baby up in the air. "Katie-girl, what're you going to call this monkey?"

"Da! Don't swing him that way. He's full of milk."

The tall man settled his grandson in Kate's arms. His cool blue eyes swung sideways to Edmund. "Let's let 'em rest," he muttered.

In the parlor, the two men touched glasses and sipped Château d'Yquem. "To himself," Neil Blood said. "May he prosper and grow big."

Edmund set down his glass. "Kate is quite all right?"

"We think so." The tall man sat in the armchair where he had been dozing. "None of these women," he said then in a low voice, "knows who Madame Fleurigant is."

"I beg your pardon?"

"You heard me, Crozat," Blood snapped. He stretched his long legs before the fire. "She's good. There was a real problem with himself, presenting his bottom instead of his head. Madame is good at what she does, Crozat, but I want to tell you, if I hadn't been here, it would've gone different. That's water under the bridge now. But if it had gone the other way, I'd've blamed you, you bounder."

Edmund's face felt hot. "What is the meaning of that?" he demanded.

"Did you think I wouldn't know?" his father-in-law asked, keeping his voice low.

"Is that why Kate is out of sorts with me?"

"Hell, she suspects nothing. You'll be back in her good graces soon enough." Blood sat forward suddenly. "Where the deuce were you till midnight, man?"

"I beg your pardon?"

Neil Blood got to his feet. "The arrogance of the Creole is beyond belief," he said softly, more to himself than Edmund. He looked about him and found a heavy blue cape. "I'll be going now. You . . ." He paused before pulling on the cape. "You play husband, Crozat. Play it properly."

He started out the room, then stopped and turned in the doorway. "My daughter is a forgiving lass. Her heart is full of the baby boy. She's not one for holding grudges, Crozat. But the same," he said, "is not true of her da."

He turned and left. In the fireplace, embers broke and dropped in a shower of sparks. For a long moment Edmund stared into them. Then he sank down in the armchair and covered his face with his hands.

43

Rynders was waiting on the makeshift dock at St. Maurice, holding the reins of two horses. The Shreveport steamer surged into view and with three hoots of her whistle signaled a landing. Peering across the river, Rynders could make out Edmund Crozat at the bow railing, a Gladstone bag at his feet.

The steamer barely touched the pilings as Edmund leaped off and the boat swung neatly to port and headed back out the river's main channel.

Edmund stood there for a moment staring at Rynders, searching his tired, ugly face for confirmation of the news the geologist had telegraphed. "Then it's true?" Edmund said at last.

"Meaning no offense, but would I of telegraphed otherwise?"

Edmund clapped the stocky man on both shoulders. "Not you. But someone wishing me mischief."

"Not in our code."

Edmund saw that the man was bone-tired. "When did you last sleep?"

"Nobody's getting sleep. And the number-one tank is nearly filled." The geologist held Edmund's horse while he swung into the saddle, then wearily climbed aboard his own mount. "You have to see the flow to believe it. It's on the order of ten barrels a minute."

"Clean?"

"Cleaner than I hoped for." Rynders snapped the reins, and his horse trotted off along the rutted track that led north to what both men privately thought of as the Grimes field. Edmund followed. The horses needed no guidance over this well-beaten path. Edmund surveyed the reddish-brown sweep of hardscrabble dirt and pebbles.

The telegram had come at an opportune moment. The arrival of crude, so quickly, would give Great Southern a much stronger position with the drilling and storage people who supplied the equipment Edmund so badly needed. In this respect, the telegram was a lifesaver.

But it had also come at a moment when Kate was being difficult. The tension between them had heightened when Edmund decided he too would remain silent. With Kate and the infant using the bed, Edmund had spent last night on a parlor couch. Olivia had dozed in the other, almost as accusingly mute as Kate. Edmund was beginning to understand that the two of them intended to keep him under a cloud for as long as possible.

Of course, he had a right to see his son, which he exercised that morning at sunrise. To indicate that he was paying Kate back with the same coin, he spoke only to the boy. Overnight the tiny thing had already begun to change. Gorged on milk, he was quite at home and not half as simian as he'd appeared at birth. The fringe of fine red hair seemed darker, too, more auburn. There was still no telling whom he resembled, Edmund saw, but at least he had stopped looking like he belonged in a tree.

As Edmund jogged along on the horse now he wondered how long it would take Kate to live up to her father's prediction, to forgive and forget Edmund's absence at the crucial hour.

But, dear God, he reminded himself, what a shock finding that Ynes' mother had been the midwife. He had never actually seen the old woman before, except from a distance. How like Ynes she looked, an aged Ynes, aquiline nose beginning to hook down toward her mouth like a proper Judy to some unknown Punch. Would Ynes look that way someday?

All in all, the telegram had been most welcome. Rynders really didn't need him here. Edmund's time would be put to better use in New Orleans, dickering for storage. But the whole thing was an admirable excuse to get away long enough for Kate to come to her senses.

After all, what he had done was no different from any other Creole husband in town. Come home late. Only his father-in-law suspected what had actually happened and his lips were sealed. This was an area of information no gentleman shared with a lady, much less a father with his daughter. Of course, Edmund thought, Cornelius Blood is no gentleman.

The thought brought him up so short that he reined in his horse. Rynders was yards ahead of him before he realized what had happened. "Are you all right?" he called.

Edmund didn't answer.

They reached the Grimes field at sundown. Edmund listened to the donkey engine at work, pumping now, not drilling. The storage tank loomed into view as the sky in the west turned crimson and began to darken. A man in overalls sat on the upper rim of the tank, lowering a long pole through a hole in the top. He waved at them and let the measuring rod come to rest. Then he cupped his hands around his mouth. "Another hour and she's full up!" he called.

Rynders glanced sideways at Edmund. "And then what?"

They swung out of their saddles. Rynders opened the flap of one saddlebag and pulled out two cartridge belts with holsters. "You better get into this rig," he told Edmund.

Edmund frowned, then buckled on the belt and silently accepted a long-barreled Colt revolver. Pointing the muzzle to the earth, he pulled .44 cartridges from the belt and fed them into the cylinder. For a long sunset moment there was no sound but the ratcheting of turning cylinders. Then both men holstered their guns.

"Anyone shot anybody?" Edmund asked.

"They just sit there on their horses and look ugly. Nobody's bothering with hoods no more. Just the leader. But that's because . . ." He paused and shifted the weight of the gunbelt. "Well, meaning no offense, but it looks like it's your manager at Whiteacres, that Waddell fella."

Edmund tied the reins of his horse to a nearby bush. "He's not my manager. I have nothing to do with my father's holdings. I thought you knew that."

"Well, but ain't that a technicality? I mean . . ." The geologist gestured uneasily. In the years they had worked together, he stopped calling Edmund "Mr. Crozat" or "sir." But he had not yet found anything to take the place of those words of address. It put unnatural pauses in the normal flow of his talk. "I mean, your father being under the weather, as they say, and all," Rynders finished lamely.

"That's got nothing to do with me."

"But maybe if you was to ride over to Whiteacres and talk t—"

"Waddell's a stranger to me," Edmund said. "Now that he's a legislator as well as a hooded coward, I suspect he has taken pains to get all the information he can about the Crozat holdings and their relation to Great Southern. The lack of a relationship, I should say."

"So you'd cut no ice with him, huh?"

Edmund led the way into the tent, where the kerosene heater was humming away. He took off long gauntlet leather gloves and held his palms to the heat. "What sort of law do we have in this parish?"

"There's a sheriff in Winnfield. Waddell appointed him."

"I see. What about Shreveport?"

"Different parish. What law we got here is what we're wearing."

"Are the men armed?"

"Half a dozen carbines."

Edmund pulled on his gloves and went to the triangular tent opening. "It will be black outside in a few minutes. We need some kind of perimeter defense."

"I've got a picket at each trail. They're supposed to let out a yell if we get visitors. But I don't have to tell you the main business of a picket is sleeping."

"Torches?"

Rynders joined him at the entrance. "Charlie!" he called. "Get the torches going." The men began moving through the underbrush, and Edmund could see them bind torches to the few leafless trees that formed a kind of ring around the drill towers and the tank. One by one, matches were struck. The torches flared wildly for a moment, sending up billows of black smoke before they settled to a slower burn, making the night a reality.

"Great Southern Number One," Edmund said in a low voice. "All the work you and I did here. All the planning and scheming. All the times it seemed to be lost. But we hung on. I imagine you never pictured it this way when we first started poking around here."

"I never pictured these damned night riders."

"It's the last gasp," Edmund assured him. "They lost their fight in the legislature to keep this land for cotton. Now oil is a fact of life. Their hope was to keep the yeoman farmers and tenant croppers dependent on cotton. But once we were able to buy the land outright, why would a man break his back chopping cotton when he could sell and collect cash?"

"I follow you there," Rynders agreed. "But Waddell don't."

Edmund stared out at the torchlit scene. The cold was getting to him. He retreated inside the tent. "Do we sleep here?"

The geologist made a kind of apologetic gesture toward the pile of blankets on the pounded dirt floor. "Not much in the way of mattresses."

"And to eat?"

"We cook up a stew. The boys should have it ready in a while."

Edmund thought for a moment of the dinners he and Kate had shared at the Pontalba apartment. All that was ended, he supposed. With the arrival of the boy, they would be moving into their house in the Garden

District as quickly as possible. And meanwhile, Kate would have no time for cooking. Nor would she in the new home, since Edmund would be engaging a cook, maids, and a butler. The old, comfortable ways were a thing of the past.

"To keep the cold out?" Rynders was asking.

Edmund's thoughts returned to the present. He saw that his geologist was offering a small stone jug and a not-too-clean glass. "I'm no longer drinking spirits. But you go ahead."

"It gets powerful cold this time of year."

Edmund walked to the makeshift drawing board and looked over the plans. Once the rest of the holding tanks were built, Great Southern One would resume drilling. They were nestled at the base of a range of hills known as the Kisatchi, which Edmund guessed would give them enough grade to lay a steadily down-dropping pipeline from here to either St. Maurice or Clarence, on the banks of the Red River across from Natchitoches. Tank barges could load there and float downriver fairly easily.

All this would take time. And money. But no man carries so much assurance of success as one whose well is already pumping crude. In a matter of days, work would begin all along the line, from building more storage to laying pipe. By Mardi Gras, Great Southern One would be delivering oil to a dozen waiting buyers.

The stew had been abominable, its ingredients prudently undisclosed. Edmund folded a blanket under him and spread another over him. By nine o'clock he was almost asleep.

Flap tied shut, the tent was warm. Drowsily Edmund could hear a night bird hoot in the distance. Somewhere horses whinnied softly. He turned sideways under his blanket and his body bent at the waist, the way he would lie pressed to Kate's back. Beneath their comforter the two of them would generate a kind of primal warmth that comforted Edmund. Edmund missed his wife. He missed being able to talk to her. But she would come around soon enough. He had his father-in-law's word for it that Kate didn't hold a grudge.

Rynders sighed, a heavy sound, full of woe. In a moment he was snoring, but too softly to bother Edmund. A horse stamped his feet and whickered.

The shot came an instant later.

In a spasm of motion, Edmund doubled over on his knees and jumped to his feet. "Eee-haw!" someone hooted in the distance.

Edmund ripped open the tent flap and stepped outside, pulling the Colt from its holster. Staring into the night, he could see his breath in the chill air.

Then he heard hooves. In the scrub a quarter-mile away a line of hooded horsemen approached at a gallop, carrying their own torches. Flames spewed out from behind them like comets' tails.

Rynders was beside him, coughing as he reached for his gun. "Charlie!" he called. "Rouse the men."

As if it had been a command to the night riders, they began to fan out sideways until their line curved like a sickle blade. "A dozen," Edmund said. "We're outnumbered."

He raised his Colt and began tracking the horseman in the center, trying to keep his bobbing head at the top of his front sight.

Rynders was tracking another rider. "That's him," he muttered. "The one without a torch. Waddell."

"No shooting."

The ends of the sickle were curving inward now. A shrill whistle sounded. The night riders reined in their horses. The leader lifted a pump-action Winchester rifle and took aim.

The Winchester cracked once. Edmund's glance flicked sideways, following the apparent path of the bullet. A hole opened up in the storage tank. Dark crude spouted out in a wide, down-dropping arc.

Edmund took a breath, held it, fired twice. The man with the Winchester twisted in his saddle, pumped off a wild shot at Edmund, then whistled again.

Now the night riders began to circle the camp. Edmund saw the storage tank, riddled with holes, spouting dark oil.

One of his men atop the tank began firing at a steady clip until a bullet caught him in the chest. His body lifted sideways and began to topple, sliding off the rim of the tank. Edmund saw him thump onto the red soil. A spout of crude covered his face with blackness.

Rynders plumped down behind a saddle and steadied the barrel of his Colt on the smooth leather. Carefully he fired twice. One of the night riders jerked hard. His horse kept galloping. The man's body slammed against the horse's flanks. His heel caught in the stirrup. A random bush tore at his hood. Now his head was banging against the earth.

Edmund held his Colt in two hands and tracked the horseman without a torch. He squeezed the trigger, and a red patch spread across the leader's shoulder. He grabbed his arm and wheeled his horse out of the circling line of night riders.

Three bullets whistled past Edmund, and he dropped to the dirt next to Rynders. Steadying his revolver, he fired at the nearest horseman. The man seemed to explode from his saddle, arms shooting out wide, as if the horse were bucking him off. Edmund watched him pull back his torch and send it roaring through the air, tumbling end over end.

It landed in a puddle of crude formed by two jets of oil spouting from new holes in the tank. The crude caught fire smokily.

Now the other night riders galloped in to fling their torches at the oil-damp earth. Fires began to ring the tank.

Edmund squeezed off another shot, only to hear the firing pin click against a spent cartridge. He rolled on his back and began reloading. The hoofbeats grew fainter. He stared out at the night. The horsemen were retreating. But the scene was brightly lit by the burning storage tank.

Edmund jumped to his feet, running for the tank. He got within a few yards of it and had to draw back. The fierce heat was like a furnace.

Attackers gone, men were circling the fire now, drawn to it like moths. But none of them could get close enough to try putting out the flames. The body of the man who had dropped from the roof burned furiously.

Now flames completely ringed the tank. It flared like one giant torch, a single fireball. Rynders came running. "Back off!" he shouted.

Edmund began hauling men away from the pyre. They found refuge behind pieces of equipment or piles of logs. "Get back!" Rynders screamed.

The explosion was surprisingly quiet, a "wumpp!" sound. Edmund saw the circular top of the tank go up in the air like a giant wheel.

A moment later the sides of the tank gaped open in great jagged rips. Crude spilled out into the flames.

"Back off!" he shouted, pushing men farther from the fire.

Flowing more quickly as it heated, the crude shot out rivers of orange flame. Like lava it began to send fiery fingers through the campsite. One reached a pile of logs that instantly caught, as if mere kindling.

The men were screaming now. A channel of fiery oil darted past Rynders, outlining him in orange-white. Edmund dashed forward, grabbed the burning man by the collar, and dragged him backward through the dust. He whipped off his coat and began batting at the flames. A moment later Edmund saw a new runnel of fire approaching. He pulled the heavyset geologist out of range and finally smothered his burning clothes.

Kneeling, he stared into Rynders' face. The geologist coughed. Edmund bent over him. "Speak to me, Rynders."

"I'm okay," the man gasped.

Edmund sat back on his haunches and watched the bonfire that had been his drill site. Burning crude covered the ground for fifty yards in every direction. The derricks burned like Christmas candles.

The donkey engine tilted sideways as its wooden supports gave. A moment later it keeled over into red dust.

An evil stench of burning crude hung over the bonfire. Men were struggling to move still farther from the heat. A horse, shackled to a tree, whinnied horribly as fiery oil engulfed it.

Edmund's eyes burned. But he found it impossible to blink as he watched the total destruction of Great Southern Number One.

❧ Part Three

44

"No," Kate told her youngest brother. "Not a word. It's been most of a week."

Ned stood in the parlor of the Pontalba apartment, the sheet of telegraph paper in his hand. "This arrived Monday morning?" He glanced up at his sister. He had been prepared for her to look drawn and tired. He had wormed out of his father a highly censored version of the baby's birth and was prepared to see the results of it in Kate's face. But the way she looked now was not what he had expected at all.

Physically she seemed fine, he told himself. Her figure seemed flat and trim, quite as he remembered it from before the baby. Her hair was washed and brushed to a gloss. Her complexion was radiant, no lines, no dark smears under the eyes. But the eyes themselves seemed haunted. She no longer looked at him directly. Her glance darted this way and that, often toward the foyer and the front door. The slightest sound from that direction and she would jump from her chair.

He reread the telegram: "CRUDE FLOWING. COME AT ONCE. RYNDERS." So much was clear. The Great Southern adventure was paying off. But where? The Shreveport address on the telegram was less than informative. Ned folded the piece of paper and tucked it into the inner breast pocket of his jacket.

"I'll take whatever steamer's leaving this morning, Katie. I should be upstate by tomorrow morning. Did Edmund tell you where he was going? A particular place?"

"We . . ." She stopped, as if listening, but Ned could hear nothing. Automatically, as if unaware of her motion, Kate was gently bouncing the infant on her left arm. She moistened her lips. "We weren't speaking," she said at last.

"Lovers' quarrel." Ned put it as a statement, not a question. He watched her glance slip away from him to the windows overlooking the river. "I would've thought . . ."—he gestured helplessly toward the baby—"being new parents and all, that . . ." There was no way to finish the thought.

Kate looked down at the infant. "Has Da told you?" she asked in a low voice. "Edmund was out all that evening. Returned at midnight after everything had been accomplished. I . . . I was angry. Of all the nights of our life, for him to play the Creole husband."

"Did you tell him that?"

"Do I look like a loon?"

"Then why did he button his lip?"

"Did I say that?" she retorted. Her glance lifted to his. "Why are we asking questions and not answering them?"

"Is that what we're doing?" Ned laughed, trying to jolly her. "It was you did the clam, was it? And Edmund who was able to take on the ceremonial robes of the injured party. Ah, me."

She nodded, still moving the baby gently up and down. His eyes had closed some time ago and his breathing indicated he was fast asleep, but Kate had not looked to verify this. She glanced at the door. "I appreciate your help, Ned," she said in that same hushed voice.

"You'd like him back so you can refuse to speak to him some more, is that it?"

"Because I'm going mad without him," she burst out.

The silence that followed was broken, but only for an instant, when the boy in her arms shifted to a new position and picked up his dream where he had left it. "I went into this marriage," Kate said then, "with very wide-open eyes, Ned. You know I had gotten over my early infatuation. I really had. I saw him with all his flaws. And he has as many as the next man. I was well aware what kind of game Da was playing on my behalf. It's not exactly love's romantic young dream to find yourself the price of a business deal. But I was no longer a young romantic girl, was I? Especially when it came to Edmund. So, there having been contracts and deals related to the marriage, I laid down my own as well. I think the bride is entitled to make a few conditions of her own, don't you? And God knows, they weren't that onerous, Neddie. I was happy to hold up my part of the contract till the end of time, cook his meals, bear his son, even wash and iron his shirts like a black woman, if that was needed. But in return I was not to be treated like a Creole wife. I didn't marry Mr. Oink. I was not going to become Mrs. Oink."

"What the hell are you talking about?"

"You get my meaning, Ned. Where there had once been such a silly outpouring of romantic foolishness on my part, there was now a very practical, businesslike marriage. Do you know," she went on in a suddenly higher voice, "just how foolish your sister was over that man? Do you know I did a novena to St. Roch for him?"

"No," Ned lied. "Really?"

"*And* it worked."

"So it did."

She laughed softly. "I can be just as superstitious as any other Irish lass, you see. And just as stubborn, Ned. But it worked. You saw how well it worked. Home for dinner every evening. Early to bed. A loving pair if ever there was one. All last fall, with himself here on the way and me puffed out like a balloon, Edmund was . . ." She stopped and thought.

"Attentive," Ned supplied.

She sat silently for a long moment. "It was in November, I believe, that he first began having these business dinners. I was in no condition to cook by then, anyway. Walter was bringing casseroles from home." She thought for a while again. "November and December he was rarely home till nine o'clock, having already dined. It didn't seem anything worth pointing out to him. I . . . I said nothing because I didn't feel adequate to defend such a complaint, being in the condition I was."

Ned turned away and stared out the window. The pull of conflicting loyalties was growing sharper. He loved his sister and respected his friend, now his brother-in-law. It wasn't fair of Kate to . . . But her call on him would always be greater than anyone else's.

". . . later and later," she was saying. "Ten o'clock he'd show up, in a distant sort of mood, as if checking into a strange hotel, Neddie. And me getting closer to my time. And him seemingly not aware of it. And me . . ." She shook her head to stop herself.

After a silence she took a long breath. "I *am* going mad," she said then. "Because in the face of all that, I miss him like an arm that had to be cut off. I worry if he's all right. Instead of sleeping, I wonder what sort of trouble he's in. Why there's been no word."

"Kate . . ." Ned knelt down by her chair and patted her hand. "I'm going to set your mind at ease. I'm off this minute, Kate. When I know something, I'll send a telegram."

"Thank you." Her voice was pinched down to the edge of audibility.

"So." He stood up. "You stop worrying. Take care of himself here. Don't upset him with your problems. Promise?"

She tried a smile that failed. Dumbly she nodded.

The *Shreveport Flyer* was scheduled to leave at noon; Ned had two hours to spare. He left the docks and wandered back into the Quarter, looking for a place to sit, sip a coffee, and get his thoughts together. Where Urselines came to the river, at Gallatin Street, he stepped inside one of the French Market stalls and stood at a counter sipping the hot black chicory-tasting brew. Suddenly, without saying a word, he left his half-full cup and sprinted out of the place.

At Rampart, winded, he walked up the front steps of the small cottage set on its own abundant grounds. The shades were drawn. He tried peering in a side window, without luck. Then he wandered around the back of the house. A clothesline stretched from the rear door to the jakes. On the line hung a pair of mud-spattered gray serge trousers, narrow cut, stylish, but spotted with dark blotches. Ned sniffed the pants. Oil.

He moved silently along the back porch and tried the rear door. It opened inward. Tiptoeing through the tiny kitchen, he reached a closed door that must lead into the bedroom. Ned sniffed again. There was another aroma in the air, not the tarry stench of crude oil.

Anise.

Gently he eased open the bedroom door, lifting it to take the stress off its hinges. The room beyond was dark. Ned could see his own face reflected in the corner of an immense mirror that formed one wall, its rim encrusted with gilded cupids. The air reeked of anise. It seemed to lie in layers like smoke.

Neither of them was clothed, and both lay fast asleep, Ynes Fleurigant with her pale olive skin glowing softly in the faint light, one arm thrown over Edmund, whose face pressed into the pillow, skin pasty white, breathing congested.

No longer tiptoeing, Ned walked to the nearest window and raised the shade. The sudden white of winter sunlight had no effect on Edmund, but Ynes' great eyes twitched a moment behind closed lids, then opened wide. Her mouth formed a silent O.

Ned raised the other shade. He slid his hand under Edmund's face and lifted it from the pillow. The bedclothes felt damp. His hair was matted in a sweaty tangle. Ned waved the air in front of him as if to make the anise stench go away.

"Edmund, wake up."

Ynes sat up slowly, her firm breasts catching the brilliant sunlight. *"M'sieur,"* she asked in a small voice, *"vous êtes . . . ?"*

"His friend," Ned retorted. "How long has he been out?"

"Out?" Her eyes lowered, took notice of the fact that she was unclothed. She pulled a sheet over her breasts.

"The absinthe," Ned suggested. "How long?"

"What is today?"

"Friday."

"Two days . . . three . . ."

Ned let out a sharp sigh of exasperation. His glance shifted from Ynes to take in the rest of the room. The slender bottle on the dresser was empty. Another beside it held about an inch of the pale liquor.

"Get dressed," he said then. "Help me move him."

Ynes seemed to think about this for quite a time. Her reactions were slow, Ned saw, but not dazed. After a while she gathered the sheet about her and slid off at the foot of the bed.

As she walked to the basin, Ned saw for the first time that she was pregnant.

45

Jed Benjamin's house was a small, ancient one on Royal, barely a square from the more imposing home in which the elder Crozats resided with Olivia. The Benjamin house had once belonged to a mysterious rogue named Malfois, rumored to have been the secret agent of that dread sea rover Jean Laffite. It was Malfois through whom the pirate chieftain sold certain items of loot—jewelry, gold plate, and the like. It was also Malfois, so the story went, who interceded with the corsair on behalf of the beleaguered American troops under Andrew Jackson. Laffite's cutthroats joined them in defending New Orleans against the British.

The impresario had changed little when moving in some years before. The most recent owners had remodeled and repaired the house completely before being carried off by yellow fever in the epidemic of 1885. The second-floor parlor faced south, which filled it with light on this January day. Another set of windows to the rear of the parlor overlooked the tiny inner courtyard, where wisteria vines covered the walls with a network of branches.

Benjamin, in a high-collared red velour dressing gown piped with gold braid, sat at the tiny round marble-topped table. Legs crossed, feet in slippers, he looked supernally at home as he poured coffee from a blue enameled pot into two demitasse cups. He passed one to his visitor, who responded by dropping two small lumps of sugar into both his cup and hers.

266

"Capital," Jed Benjamin said, smiling. "Another muffin?"

The woman shook her head daintily. She too wore slippers, open-backed with slight heels and puffs of maribou at the toes, the kind of slippers quite popular in Paris and called—no one knew why—"mules." The rest of her was hidden beneath a brocaded silk boudoir gown with long, full sleeves and a design in smoky bugle beads faintly observable along the cuffs and up the arms. It was a gown no one else had ever seen Olivia Crozat wearing, not even her parents.

The impresario glanced over Olivia's head to the mantelpiece clock. "I'm afraid . . ." He let the thought die away.

She turned slightly in her chair and saw that it was almost noon. "I'm off!" she cried, jumping to her feet.

"Your coffee."

She paused indecisively. "I promised to feed Papa today so that Maman could go shopping. But I don't suppose he'll . . ."

"No, he won't know the difference if you're five minutes late."

Benjamin delivered this with such a beaming look of indulgence that Olivia promptly sat down and sipped her coffee. "I must say . . ." she began, but said nothing.

"Comfortable arrangement, *n'est-ce pas?*"

"*Tous les conforts.*" She stirred her drink for a moment. "It requires only that one of these Royal Street busybodies see me entering or leaving once too often. The tongues will buzz. And Maman will be told. For her own good, of course."

"At least your father will not throw himself into any new paroxysms."

They smiled at each other with sly humor. "And anyway," the impresario went on, "the little side door is invisible from the street. Old Malfois made sure of that. You could be coming along the passage from the cathedral, for all anyone knows."

"After my daily confession?"

Jed Benjamin placed his hand over his heart. "My dear, sweet, innocent Livy. What sins have you committed?"

"Other than adultery," she replied with some briskness, "there would be lust, of course, and gluttony for certain, and some of the things I have learned from you would certainly qualify as . . ." She paused, searching for the word. "I found it in Freud several times, and Sacher-Masoch as well." She frowned, trying to remember.

The impresario gave her a pained look. "Neither of us is married, Livy. How can we commit adultery?"

"That is not very Hebraic of you, Jed. How could you not understand that if I am not yet some husband's property, I am still the chattel of my poor mute, paralyzed father. The Old Testament is full of it. To have seduced me is to have adulterated his property. Do you follow, heathen?"

"Heathen? To a member of the senior faith you cry 'heathen'?"

"Well . . ."

"And what about this seduction business? Who is supposed to have seduced whom?"

Instead of replying, Olivia slowly finished her coffee. "We both like our convenience, Jed. You know nothing could possibly have happened between us if we lived farther apart than one square." She glanced critically at him, examining his carrot-colored hair. "I shall have to invent a better way of combing it, my dear. The . . . er, backward flight is far too apparent."

"I'm afraid to comb it anymore," Benjamin said dolefully. "I lose too many with each stroke. If . . ." He stopped, hearing a noise outside on Royal Street. He glanced out through the heavy voile curtain and saw the lacquered top of a cab. "Odd hour for a visitor." He got to his feet. "Good Lord."

Olivia jumped up. "Who are they? They can't be coming here."

Jed stepped to the edge of the window, hiding himself to one side as he peered out. "It's Ned Blood and that friend of his. And . . ." He stepped back. "Livy! Into the bedroom quickly! Lock the door."

"Are they . . . ?"

"It can only be here they are coming. I'll get rid of them as quickly as possible."

He watched her sweep through the room, picking up her bonnet, cloak, and reticule, then dash along the hall to the rear of the house. He heard a door slam, then almost at once a pounding on his front door.

Adjusting his robe, the impresario rushed downstairs and looked through the cut-glass window of his front door. Between Ned and Mike Leathers hung a limp body in blotched, mud-stained clothes. Edmund!

Jed swung open the door. "Inside, quick!"

He shut and bolted the door as they carried Edmund into the front hall. "What in God's name has happened?" The reek of anise filled his nostrils. "Never mind. I smell it."

He and Ned stared at each other over Edmund's head. "So he's back on it," Benjamin said in a dull voice.

"Can we get him upstairs to your bedroom?"

"Yes, of course. *No!* Out of the question."

Crimson with confusion, the impresario glared widely at Ned. "Where did you find him?"

"Later," Ned promised him. "We have to dry the boy out, Jed."

"Why here?"

"My room's a mess, and anyway, Mike's staying there. I hope you're not suggesting I should take him home to the Pontalba?"

Benjamin pursed his lips, calculating. "I see the problem. But can't we clean him off first? He seems to have been rolling about in oil."

Mike Leathers relinquished his grip on Edmund and let him slide into a hall chair, draped sideways like a sack of old clothes. "Have you got some nightclothes?" he suggested.

"No!" Jed snapped. "Yes! The very thing! Wait here. I'll just run . . ."

He dashed back up the stairs and along the corridor to the rear rooms beyond the courtyard. He tapped quietly on his bedroom door. When she opened it, Olivia was fully dressed in street clothes. "Can I get to the side door?" she whispered.

"Yes. The most ghastly thing . . ."

She stared at him. "You're dead white."

"It's Edmund."

"What?"

He pushed past her and began rummaging in the dresser. "They've brought him here because he's positively passed out on absinthe."

"Oh, dear God."

"You must leave," he said, ripping out a long, pale blue nightshirt. "Follow me."

He sped along a side passage and down a rear flight of stairs. Next to the first-floor kitchen stood a door. He opened it and glanced both ways along the narrow outdoor passage beyond. "Clear," he whispered.

"But what about Edmund?"

He gazed down into her wide-set brown eyes. "I don't know, Livy. I'll send word as soon as I can. Oh, one thing." The impresario could feel his face flushing with shame. "Not a word of this to Kate."

46

The building spree which had visited New Orleans, sending up dozens of office structures on the American side of Canal Street, had hardly touched Lafayette Square, near the old *cabildo*. Here, the former Spanish seat of city government, the tiny tree-lined park remained a soothing bit of country amid the ever-more-feverish comings and goings of the Crescent City's business life.

Mike Leathers stood for a moment across the square from a block of office buildings, savoring the peace. Most of the trees were bare of leaves on this January afternoon, but the spaciousness was balm to his spirit. God knew, it needed balm.

To be down and out in the country, Mike told himself, was never the grim, demeaning thing that being broke in the city had become. A man always had something to pleasure the eye in the country. Money he might lack, but never vistas. Here he lacked both.

And the ultimate insult was playing nursemaid to Edmund Crozat, the incarnation of all the oil-rich spoilers who had paid enough in bribes to undo Mike Leathers and put oily new laws on the books. Whatever harm the absinthe had done to Edmund, Mike Leathers hoped it would finish the job.

His long jaw tightened as he stared across Lafayette Square at the second-floor window on which was lettered the simple legend "INSURANCE." Then he crossed the street, walked upstairs, and knocked on a

270

door whose lettered sign was a bit more informative; "INSURANCE. Christy Leathers."

"It ain't locked," his father called from inside.

Mike strode in and closed the door with more noise than necessary. His father's glance jumped from his desk. "Tarnation!" He got to his feet. "If this don't beat the bugs t'bitin'!" he shouted, coming around the desk.

He would have hugged Mike, except that his son stepped back slightly and held out his hand. Christy Leathers shook it hard and long. "What the devil did it take t'bring you down here to Sin City, young fella?"

"Just the pleasure of laying eyes on you," Mike responded with smooth insincerity. He glanced down at the tips of the new boots to which Ned had grubstaked him. His coat jacket was worn but clean. The shirt was new, and so were the breeches. The only scars from the life Mike Leathers had been leading in New Orleans were internal. He would take care they didn't show.

"You rascal!" Christy thumped his son on the back. "Set a spell." He resumed his seat behind the desk and began rummaging through a drawer. "Little hair of the dog?" he asked, bringing out an unlabeled bottle of whiskey. He glanced around him with mock surreptitiousness. "Ain't nobody here but family." Lifting the bottle, he took a swig from it, wiped off the neck, and handed the bottle across the desk. Mike tasted the smooth sour-mash whiskey. "Tennessee?" he asked.

"No other." Christy leaned back and thumped his boots on top of a pile of official-looking papers on his desk. "You are a sight for sore eyes, boy. How y'holding up?"

"Surviving."

His father's smile vanished. "Things bad up to Winn Parish way?"

"Now, Paw."

"What's that s'posed t'mean?"

"You know good and goldarned well things're bad up Winn Parish way. You went to a lotta trouble to badden the hell out of 'em."

"That so?" Christy muttered. "You in trouble, son?"

"What could be my trouble, Paw? No clients. No work. Nobody I can turn to but Luke. How much help can a poor preacher give? He's the next thing to stony broke. But I go him a tad better. I am as impoverished a pauper as God ever put down here to suffer."

He had not yet finished when his father's hand was delving in his pocket. Out came a roll of greenbacks roughly the diameter of a hoe handle. "What d'y need, son? Fifty? A hundred? If I got it, it's your'n."

"Put that away," Mike said, "before you sprain your wrist."

"I'm serious, boy."

"No charity, Paw. I . . . The thing I . . . What I need is work."

Christy Leathers put his roll away. He rubbed the palm of his hand across his chin, making a soft grating noise. "Doing what?" he asked at length.

"I'm a lawyer. I know my way around Baton Rouge. There are half a dozen ways such a man could make himself useful up there."

Christy's glance moved gravely from the desk top to his son's face, lingered there a long while, then shifted to a stack of documents. "What do you think about representing?" he asked.

"The kind of thing you do?"

His father gave him a look of disbelief. "Son, ain't nobody does what I do. I'm talking representation of interests. An interest needs a fella in Baton Rouge to put forth a certain point of view. Make friends with the legislators."

"Lobbying?"

"Call it what you want, boy." Christy Leathers thought some more, scratching the stubble on his chin. "Something might open up most any time."

"Who for? What interests?"

His father held up his hand cautioningly. "Son, I don't have to tell you Lou'siana's in a state of turmoil. You been the victim of it yourself. We all have. There's a new interest unleashed in this state that has the drive to turn Lou'siana upside-down. It has the power cotton and sugar once had. But it's got more shekels. And it don't mind spending to get what it wants."

Mike Leathers deliberately sat back in his chair and hooked an arm over the back, the very picture of easy disinterest. "If you mean oil, I guess I have noticed one or two clues."

His father laughed appreciatively. "Glad you don't harbor no injury, son. Because it's just a game. And they ain't no reason your turn can't come."

"Lobbying for the oil interests?"

"Whew! You young folks do like to call a spade a spade."

"This young folk likes to know where he's at," Mike drawled. He could play cat and mouse as well as his father. It didn't matter that he desperately needed work. To win this game, he had to stay cool and a little distant. "I'm a simple country lawyer, Paw. That high-powered stuff is beyond me. Just throw a few wills and contracts my way. Give me some mortgage closings and purchase deeds. That's my speed."

Christy sat forward with a powerful shrug of his shoulders. "Michael, you are your own worst enemy, boy. There is no sense working for dimes when you can work for dollars."

"What do I need, Paw? Give me a roof over my head and spoonbread on the table and a little sour mash to wash it down. I'm happy."

His father shook his head sadly. "You used to have ambition, boy." He grumbled wordlessly for a while, then settled back in his chair. He rubbed his turkey-red neck and blew out a breath of air, making his cheeks bulge. Then he gave his son a disgusted look.

"There *is* work," he admitted at last. "People I know been looking for a likely young fella to help them in Baton Rouge. But it can't be known I'm naming someone for the job."

"Least of all your own flesh and blood." Mike stood up. "Paw, it's been right nice setting a spell with you. You're looking downright pert, so you are. Be seeing you." He put on his hat and started for the door.

"Hold on!" Christy Leathers thundered.

"For what?"

"Come back and sit down!"

"Jesus, what did I do to get yelled at now?"

"Michael, sit back down," his father said in a more reasonable tone.

He waited until Mike was back in the visitor's chair. "Here's the lay of it, son, but if you blab a word outside, I'll deny it on four Bibles. What I tell you has to drop down a bottomless well. It didn't come from me. Understand?"

"I can keep a secret, don't fret none."

"Friends of mine," Christy went on, lowering his voice. "Oil people. Yankees. You know, Crozat's drilling. Any week now, he should hit crude. When he does, it'll set off the damnedest stampede you ever saw. These friends of mine . . ."

"These anonymous friends."

"They aren't waiting for oil greed to start churning everybody's gut. They are moving in on Crozat right now. Naturally, they came to me first."

"Naturally."

"And, naturally, I had to turn them down."

"Oh?" Mike hooked his arm behind him and crossed his legs, dangling one new boot in the air. He hadn't figured out yet whether news of Waddell's attack on the drill site had trickled downriver. Maybe his paw knew and maybe he didn't.

"A matter of . . . um, ethics," his father said in a delicate tone of voice.

"Hallelujah. Christy Leathers is saved."

"Yeah, well, laugh. It's better than crying over missed chances. How would it look, me taking the Crozat dollar and representing his business rivals behind his back?" Leathers hitched forward in his chair. "Now, it is well known you and me, we don't get along. Oil and water, you might say." He cackled suddenly. "Not bad. Oil and water."

"So no one would suspect you put me in touch with your friends."

"Ain't nothing slow about your brain, boy."

"I must take after Maw," Mike said, deadpan. He let his crossed leg come down, boot heel hitting the floor. "What's in it for you, Paw?"

Christy Leathers reached for the unlabeled bottle. "You ever hear of a finder's fee, boy?"

"Ten percent?"

"Try fifty."

Mike pursed his lips and produced a thin whistle of astonishment. "You are *all* gator. Them jaws could chomp up a water buffalo and not leave a bone behind. Twenty."

"Not a lick less'n forty percent."

Mike reached forward and picked up the bottle. "Let's drink to thirty-five." He upended the bottle and let the whiskey course down his throat. With a sharp sigh, he handed the bottle to his father.

"Done." Christy Leathers took a swig. "Pleasure doing business with a sharp road agent like you. I take note you ain't too unhappy about helping to dig Crozat's grave."

Mike said nothing, watching his father while trying not to seem attentive. He had no idea it would be this easy. But then, he had no idea what these "interests" would demand of him. Not that it mattered. His real work in Baton Rouge would be for Ned Blood.

He got back to Jed Benjamin's house by six o'clock and let himself in by the side door. In the kitchen, Benjamin's housekeeper, a chubby black woman with almost white hair, had been sitting on a stool, thoughtfully puffing at a thin, crooked cigar, short and almost black in color. Hastily she hid it behind her and patted the air free of smoke.

"That's all right, Aunt Mae," Mike Leathers assured her. "You like those horrible Sicilian ropes, don't you?"

"Mighty refreshing, Mizta Mike." She got up. "No idea it was gettin' so late. I best be on my way."

"How's the patient?" Mike's eye lifted ceilingward.

"Sleepin'. Mumblin.' Then sleepin' some more."

When she had left, Mike went upstairs to the rear bedroom. Aunt Mae had aired out the room. It no longer stank of anise, but Edmund Crozat still did. Stretched out under the covers, his shoulders protected by Jed Benjamin's light blue nightshirt, he lay on his back, eyes closed, face pale, a small spot of color like a clown's daub on each cheekbone. One hand lay outside the covers. As Mike stood there, the fingers twitched.

"Crozat?"

Edmund frowned in his sleep. The uncovered hand jerked wildly.

"Crozat, can you hear me?"

The closed eyelids twitched open. Dark brown, almost black eyes stared up directly into Mike's. "Wh-who . . . ?" Edmund stopped. Feebly he licked his lips.

"I had a notion you'd be coming around," Leathers said. "Try sitting up."

Edmund moistened his lips again. "Where am I? Who are you?" Even in his weakened state, the questions still had a faint flash of the true Crozat arrogance that echoed in Mike Leathers' head like a knife scraped shrilly across a plate.

"You're in Jed Benjamin's bedroom."

Edmund's arms trembled as he helped himself up against the pillows. Sweat stood out on his forehead. His mouth tightened in a thin line as he grasped one shaking hand with the other and squeezed hard. "And you?"

"You don't remember me?"

"You have the advantage, sir."

Leathers snorted. "Last time we met you were running under the alias of Captain Nemo. That ring a bell?"

Edmund's eyes, rimmed in red, seemed to widen slightly. The deep half-moon shadows under them thinned for an instant. "You're . . ." He paused and once more moistened his dry lips. "My mortal enemy," he said mockingly. "To what do I owe this honor, sir?"

"Absinthe, mostly."

Edmund took in a tentative, almost hesitant breath. "And before the absinthe? How did I get downriver t . . ." He stopped, remembering. "The wells!"

Leathers gestured reassuringly. "That was the first thing you told Ned and me. Matter of fact, we was hard put getting you to stop talking. The fire. Old Ringo Waddell's troops. Then you petered out again."

"How long have I been here?"

"In New Orleans almost a week. Here, getting on for a day and a half."

Edmund seemed to sink back into the pillows as he tried to remember the passage of days. He badly needed a shave and a bath, but Mike was damned if he'd do that for the arrogant son of a bitch. In fact, Mike decided as he watched remorse slowly shadow the Damascus-steel mask Creoles like Crozat habitually wore, he was damned if he'd make life any easier for this miserable specimen than it already was.

"You and Ned . . . ?" Edmund's voice died away. He took another testing breath. "You found me . . . where?"

"You know where's well as I do, Crozat."

The man on the bed stared into Leathers' eyes, then gave it up. "I see. Does . . . ?" He almost sat up again, so sharp was the pang of remorse that shook him. "Has Ned told . . . ?"

Mike Leathers grinned, enjoying the man's torment. "You better ask him, Crozat."

"My wife . . ."

"Ask Ned."

Edmund's glance fastened on Mike. "You are being deliberately cruel, Leathers. I imagine you think I deserve as much."

"You imagine right."

Edmund's lips twisted to deliver a crushing retort, then softened and went slack. "I believe you are the injured party?"

Mike squinted at him. "Injured? How about 'left for dead'?"

"I speak of the dueling code, sir. If you consider yourself injured, you have but to call me out."

The rural lawyer leaned back in his chair and guffawed. "Me call you out? The way your hands shake, you couldn't hit the rear end of Miz Eulalia Bunch at ten paces."

"Name your weapon, sir." Edmund uttered the words with such force that he went into a coughing fit. Tears streaming, he settled back on the pillows. "When I am my own man again, I will give you satisfaction."

"Crozat, I am getting a whole slew of it right now." The two men eyed each other. "You imagine . . ." Mike laughed. "You Creoles think whatever you do to a man, standing up at fifty paces is going to square it. The hell with that, Crozat. The satisfaction you're going to give me is watching you go down in the mud and your cheating schemes with you. I know," he went on, holding up his hand, "nobody held a pistol to their heads and made them farmers take Great Southern gold. Nobody forced my fellow legislators to take it, neither. I am an expert on human weakness, Crozat. I got it in my blood, considering who my paw is. But just because a lot of people are weak in the face of strong temptation don't mean the tempter gets gets off scot-free. In the ocean," he added cryptically, thinking of the job his father had offered, "there are always bigger fish waiting for their dinner."

"Did Ned tell my wi . . . ?" Edmund stopped himself and for a long moment lay in silence. "Deliver me," he muttered, "from the holierthan-thou. You and your brother have an unpleasant habit . . . preaching to people who have no recourse but to suffer in silence."

"Preaching's wasted on you, Crozat. You're the kind of man who only understands a kick in the head. It pains me more than somewhat that a white-livered coward like Ringo Waddell was the one to launch the kick. It's like thieves falling out, the two of you. But it's real nourishing to know that the Lord ain't choosy who he makes his instrument."

"It took a kick in the head to bring you down, too," Edmund said. "Does it bother you that your own father did the job?"

Mike's arm went around the back of his chair in a pose of offhandedness. "Quite some," he admitted. "But I play with a full deck, Crozat. The game between me and my paw ain't over till the fifty-second card is dealt."

"I do not understand you reformers," Edmund retorted with sudden strength. "I cannot understand any man who puts the welfare of his neighbors ahead of his own. It is self-destructive. It is dangerous. It flies in the face of nature and her laws."

"Don't excite yourself none, Crozat. Mike Leathers knows how to take care of his own skin. Like I said, it might take the whole deck, but I don't aim to end up a loser."

The fire died out of Edmund's eyes. He lay back, his body slack, his eyes slowly closing. "Kate . . ." he mumbled.

"How's that?"

Edmund was sleeping. A tic on the right side of his face, underneath his eye, pulsed, paused, then kicked three times. Behind him, Mike Leathers heard the bedroom door open. He turned to find Ned in the doorway with a short, dark young woman. He stood up.

"Mike Leathers. This is Olivia Crozat. Livy, Mike has been a big help in this, though God knows why." Ned stood at the foot of the bed. "Any change?"

"He offered to fight me a duel," the lawyer said, grinning. "I guess he ain't in as bad shape as he looks."

Both men stood silently as Olivia sat down next to her brother and patted his damp face with a small lace handkerchief. "He looks much worse than . . . than a year ago," she said in a small voice. "I hardly know what to do. Dr. Amabile is no use in these matters. The doctors in Chicago . . ." Her voice died away.

"Will you excuse us a moment, Livy?" Ned asked.

Outside the bedroom, he turned to Mike. "Did your paw have a job for you?"

"In Baton Rouge, where I want to be."

"Nothing honest."

"Lobbying for the Yankee oil barons. The ones who want Crozat's head in a hatbox."

"That shouldn't make you too sad, working for Edmund's enemies."

Mike Leathers stood silently for a moment. "You'd think so, wouldn't you? Paw said the same thing. But, a duel! I can't tell you . . ." He stopped. "Ned, these Creole bucks are unbelievable. And this one is the prize of the pack, though you have to sort of admire the bastard." He sighed. "Still, I am going to take the Yankee gold. I'll be able to get Luanne out of this pigsty. She can come live with me in Baton Rouge. Meanwhile, I'll be the ear you need in the capital. Piece by piece, Ned, you'll get the whole damned thing together and blow it sky-high."

"Marvelous." Ned eyed the closed bedroom door. "I'm going to see my sister now and break the news."

"Is that smart?"

"I sent her a telegram saying Edmund was all right. She thought it came from upstate. Now I'll tell her the whole story. Oh, not . . ." He paused, smiling grimly. "I'll say I found him upstate *non compos mentis* from the green stuff. I'll say he'll be back in New Orleans as soon as he can be moved. Then, in a day or two, we'll bring him back to the apartment and Kate can nurse him."

"She'll buy the tale?"

Ned glanced uneasily at his friend. "They were on the outs when it happened. Maybe it'll bring them together."

"And how," Mike asked, "are you going to weave the expecting little quadroon into the story?"

"That part," Ned replied, an ugly look on his face, "I am going to leave to my miracle-working father."

47

Cellini's was not one of New Orleans' larger restaurants, but it was among its most private. It was a bit out of the way for a leisurely business lunch, deliberately so, being located around the bend of the river almost at dockside between Piety and Desire.

Tony Matranga had spared no expense and certainly no imagination decorating Cellini's. Almost no window area fronted on the river. One had to step inside, pass a doorman, and be announced before a second door was opened into the dimly lighted interior. Tables stood far apart, massive round oak tops fully three inches thick. It took at least two waiters to move them. The walls, from the oak dado upward, had been decorated with brilliantly gaudy views of the harbor at Palermo, the strait of Messina, and, perhaps as a concession to those customers who did not originate on the island of Sicily, a view of the harbor at Naples.

The menu featured seafood. The fish, fresh from boats that tied up in front each morning, was served in unusual ways, layered with spinach leaves, garlic cloves, clusters of oregano blossoms, and steeped in the heavy red Segesta of the motherland. For the more adventurous were delicious scungilli, baby octopi, and the tiny fish called *biancomangiare*, which the English called whitebait, dusted in flour and quick-fried in hot oil.

The menu listed steep prices for those tourists who prowled New

Orleans, especially in the weeks preceding Mardi Gras. But if one were a regular customer, a lower range of prices prevailed. And if, like Cornelius Blood, one were a close personal friend of Tony Matranga's, the check went out the window. The only price a friend could ask of another friend was the continuation of friendship.

Behind Cellini's one-story building stood a two-floor house whose entrance was on Piety. It looked from the outside like any other prosperous middle-class dwelling. The heavily curtained windows excited no special attention, nor did the fact that it sat alone with fully fifty feet of lawn separating it from its nearest neighbor and from Cellini's.

There was, however, a connection with the restaurant past the steamy kitchen reeking of herbs and garlic. A customer might exit in that direction along what seemed like a fifty-foot corridor. It was, in fact, a tunnel. He would end up at last on the ground floor of the two-story house.

Here he would be greeted by the dwelling's mistress, the obscenely fat, magnificently painted Madam Carolina Duffy. After she had been removed from New Orleans at Christy Leathers' request, Carolina had prospered enough in her new location on Lake Pontchartrain to be able to buy her way back into New Orleans within a year's time. As the more knowledgeable residents of the Crescent City often said, not without pride, there were no rules for New Orleans politics except the one rule that there were no rules.

On this particular night, late-running tugboats scurried downriver past Cellini's on their way to tardy dockings. The mists of late January swirled up off the waters of the Mississippi and rolled over the bulkheads onto the street that ran past Cellini's unmarked door. A lone cab rattled up on cobblestones. Neil Blood's tall, bulky figure alighted on the banquette. He opened the front door and was immediately ushered within.

Neil glanced around him. Each table had a sterling or vermeil centerpiece whose swooping curves and lavish use of human figures was expected to evoke the name of the celebrated Florentine whose name had been attached to the restaurant. The place was only half full at this early hour, which suited Neil. He could count on the discretion of the regular Cellini customer, but tourists who arrived later were not to be trusted.

Not that it was a criminal act to dine with Tony Matranga. But in the event something happened later, Neil Blood did not want some feckless stranger coming forward to testify that a dinner meeting had, in fact, taken place.

Neil watched the wine steward approach with a large bottle of red.

Normally Neil drank beer with his meals. Having to drink wine, however, was a small price to pay for the Matranga connection. It had continued to be a profitable one for Neil Blood. Tony Matranga had made himself useful in so many ways the Shadow Mayor could no longer keep track of them, a mistake he rarely made.

When he needed men to run confidential errands, perform unusual services, convey important messages, Matranga provided them under an iron discipline that assured the secrecy of these tasks. Their employer, if that was the right word, was himself a man of some substance, now that he had secured his grip on the city's underworld. It would not be an exaggeration, Neil reminded himself, to say that no crime was committed in New Orleans without Matranga's permission.

This control worked in both directions. Celebrated and well-to-do visitors were left in peace, to carry back glowing tales of how safe the city was, while Blood had to contact only one man when dealing with the criminal element.

That man was now approaching the table in the wake of the wine steward. "*Buon appetito*," Tony Matranga said in his low, careful voice. He shook Blood's hand but remained standing while the steward presented the wine for the Shadow Mayor's approval.

"A special *vendemmia*," Matranga explained. "My own vineyards in the hills above Agrigento. This is the *vendemmia* of 1880. It's ready to drink, *amico*. But you must give me your honest opinion, no?"

Blood smiled expansively. The steward pried up the cork, sniffed it, and gently laid it within Blood's reach. Then he carefully poured half an inch into a large bulbous glass. Neil held it to the light and made an appreciative noise at its dark ruby color, then he swallowed some. To him it had the same heavy taste as all of Matranga's wines, but he nodded and broadened his smile. In dealing with Sicilians, he knew, if the wine was at least drinkable, one had the duty of praising outrageously.

"*Capolavoro!*" Blood exclaimed. "*Meraviglioso!* One of the great ones."

Matranga's tight, private face, with its deep-cut lines, seemed to grow easier, and he ordered their dinner.

After prawns broiled in an olive-oil-and-lemon marinade, the two men were served a superb red snapper baked in parchment paper. Finally the waiter brought a great iced mound of cassata for dessert, carved two wedges, and poured cups of espresso to which a few drops of Sambuca had been added. The licorice aroma seemed to Neil Blood to put a pleasant end to the meal.

"Hennessy," he began without preamble, "is a very nervous man."

Matranga took his time replying. "The Provenzanos have him in their pocket, my friend."

"No."

Matranga blinked. Few people had the power to contradict him to his face. "No?"

"Dave Hennessy wears no man's collar. He's a strange fella, but in his own way, he's honorable." Neil Blood considered his remark for a moment. "For a cop, that is."

"I have been told," Matranga said, his voice still low, "there's a message he wants to give me."

Neil continued playing with the dessert. So he had informers in his own Wicklowe, he mused. Waiters or busboys or God knew who, taking his money and Tony Matranga's as well. And Tony wasn't too shy about saying as much, was he? A fine kettle of fish.

"If you know that," the Shadow Mayor said in an equally low voice, "then you know the message as well."

"It ain't no surprise, *gumbare*."

Blood nodded slowly. His mind was at work going over the list of his own people who might be selling information to Matranga. Anybody with an Italian name, he knew, could be blackmailed into such a job. Or forced under threat of maiming or death. That sort of leverage didn't work as well with non-Italians, who hadn't yet learned to quake at the name of the Black Hand. But in time it would.

He sat back in his chair and held his wineglass to the light again. "Do you have a message for Hennessy?"

Matranga's lower lip curled. "I don't talk to errand boys for the Provenzanos."

"Hennessy would like to know that you're easing off on them." Neil sipped his wine. "Otherwise he plans a crackdown like you've never seen."

"Him? Crack down on me? It's a joke, *amico*. He don't have ten men he can call his own."

"Well, then . . ." Neil Blood said in a lighter tone. "Poor Davy."

"Let him be content with what is," his dinner companion stated flatly. "You and me, we know what's best for the city. Hennessy must sit back and let it happen, my friend. Otherwise he gets . . . ah, caught in the middle. *Capish, gumbare?* Out there in the middle, it's no place for a man to be."

"Tony, let me tell you what I think." Cornelius Blood leaned forward. "Peace and quiet is what business thrives on. Visitors don't want to read headlines about fellas having their heads blown off by pineapple bombs. They want to enjoy themselves in the District. Discreet. Private. They don't want to worry what would happen if they're injured or forced to be a witness. It's bad for business, Tony, is what I sincerely believe. Bad for my business . . . and yours."

Matranga lowered his eyelids. "What you tell me is one way business gets bad. I understand. But it is not the only way."

He looked around the room, now slowly filling up with customers. The silver epergnes and centerpieces glittered in the candlelight. The walls between the murals were covered in a dark red velour on which a pattern of leaves and vines had been cut. At the next table, four portly gentlemen were spooning up a steaming, spicy *zuppa di pesce*, aromatic with oregano and rosemary.

"Another way business gets bad," Matranga went on in his low voice, "is when there is no leader. No discipline. Or when the leader has enemies. When he has close friends who prove false." His hooded eyes had a look of measuring and pricing a man that Blood had noted before. The undertaker look.

"That," Blood said with some emphasis, "is something I understand perfectly. And no one appreciates more than I when the leader is strong and secure."

"That is wisdom," Matranga intoned. "One leader . . . to another."

The fattest of the four men at the next table caught his eye. Matranga nodded gravely. *"Scusi, per piacere,"* he murmured, getting to his feet. At the other table he inclined his head barely an inch, a gesture that silently said: "Yes, I recognize you as important men, almost my equal."

"Tony, my boy," the fat man said, pumping Matranga's hand. "Your fish soup is a hymn to gluttony." His glance swept the table. "Gentlemen, may I present our host, Signor Matranga. Senator Beaulieu, Judge Hanratty, whom you know. And this is a visitor from far away, Alderman Grieskowski of Chicago.

"Piacere, signori."

"We're giving him Cellini's and a little light amusement at Madam Duffy's. Do you think you could prepare the good lady for our visit? It's just for the alderman. He's never sampled our New Orleans specialty."

Something froze in Matranga's face. The lines seemed to cut deeper into the dark skin around his tight-held mouth. "You take that up with Mario," he advised the fat man in a cold tone of voice.

"Oh, certainly, certainly. We onl—"

"Your friend," Matranga interrupted, "he's got a taste for that?"

"He wants to find out." Anxious to appease his host for what seemed to have been a gaffe, the fat man went on hastily, "I tell Grieskowski he's not a man till he's tried it."

Matranga's steady glance seemed to pin the Chicago alderman to his chair. The newcomer shifted uneasily. "If it's too much troub—"

"I send Mario over," Matranga snapped. When he turned back to his table the Shadow Mayor was getting to his feet, dabbing his napkin to his lips as he did so. "I'm on my way," he murmured. "Thanks for a magnificent wine, my friend."

Matranga walked Blood to the entrance and whispered something to Mario, the headwaiter. Then he escorted Blood outside. A cab, waiting a few yards down the square, came to life as Matranga snapped his fingers. "The Wicklowe," Blood called.

"Yes, sir, Mr. Blood, sir."

At the table for four, dinner progressed in a leisurely manner from soup to crayfish salad and a seafood thermidor. Wine flowed. With dessert came brandy. When they got up to leave, only the fat man seemed interested in accompanying the out-of-towner to the rear of Cellini's.

Moving at a ponderous rate along the tunnel, the two men reached the entrance of the house behind the restaurant. The fat man rapped on the door. A small peephole opened. Through it they could see an eye outlined in kohl with beads of blacking clinging to its upper and lower lids.

"Why, Congressman, we've been expecting you," a woman's voice said.

The door opened slowly and both men stared at the owner of the eye and voice. She stood a bit over five feet, teetering on spiky heels. Carolina Duffy's face had once, perhaps, been pretty in a Kewpie-doll pattern, round, big eyes, tiny nose, and rosebud mouth. The features were still to be seen, but only in the form of rouge, kohl, and other cosmetics, as if a sidewalk artist had scrawled a face on the blubbery mass of her flesh.

Gruesome as it appeared, there was a fascination about the overlay of faces, a kind of pentimento effect, but as if the artist were unsure which was the old and which the new version of Carolina Duffy. Her thick, puffy hand, stubby fingers covered with rings, shot out to grasp the congressman's.

"Mighty pleasing," she said, clamping down hard. Her rings bit into his fingers and he flinched.

"Th-this is Dr. Johnson," he said, introducing the alderman.

"Doctor." Carolina Duffy's rings chewed into his flesh with such startling effect that Grieskowski yelped in pain. "For shame," Carolina said. One of her eyes winked through its camouflage. There was a curiously sinister delay as the drawn image of the eye slowly caught up with the movement of the flesh beneath. "Big strong man like you." The Kewpie mouth widened. "Top or bottom, Dr. Johnson?"

Grieskowski's small eyes blinked. "Beg pardon?"

The congressman intervened. "He's a novice, Carolina. But I think he'd like to have the whip hand, so to speak, his first time around."

The madam's heavily muscled arms trembled with delight as she laughed. Her neck, as thick as a wrestler's, bulged dangerously over her crimson gown. Her stubby fingers dug mercilessly into Grieskowski's biceps. "Strong's a bull," she announced. "I better match him up with something solid. This way, gentlemen."

They followed her through a small parlor crammed with Victorian knickknacks in ormolu and onyx, tasseled curtains, and amber-shaded gas mantles. Unlike the usual bordello, no women lounged here, chatting and smoking short cigars. Nor did a piano player enliven the atmosphere. No drinks were being served. These niceties the madam's clientele did without.

Carolina Duffy ushered them into her office. "It's the same as always," she told the congressman.

For a moment he failed to understand her. Then he started, nodded vehemently, and dug into his pocket for a roll of bills. "Fifty, is it?"

"In advance, thanking you so very kindly." She chucked the bills in a desk drawer and indicated one wall of the office. A collection of whips hung from hooks.

"This quirt here," she said, taking it off the wall, "hurts real smart, but it's more of a finisher-offer. It ain't for the long haul. This mule whip here," she went on, "will give you a good half-hour of fun, guaranteed. And this cat," she said, brandishing a long-handled whip with a dozen thin strips of rawhide fastened to one end, "cuts like a razor. You being a doctor and all," she told Grieskowski, "maybe you acquired a taste for blood?"

Her eyes rolled sideways, with that sinister tandem movement, first the flesh, then the makeup. "I think he needs a little introduction," she told the congressman. "Don't you?"

"Now, Carolina . . ."

She grasped Grieskowski's hand and brought the cat down sharply on his palm. He yelped again. "It's to familiarize you," she explained pleasantly. "So you know what you're doing." She reached for the quirt, but the alderman backed off.

"Hey, nobody told me . . ."

"All right," the madam agreed good-naturedly. "You experiment on your own, then, doctor." She looked him up and down. "Chunky little devil, ain't you? But more muscle than fat, I'd judge. You're going to need a girl with a lot of natural padding."

"Like you?" The congressman snickered.

Carolina Duffy's face turned to stony blankness. "Watch it, Claude." She brought the quirt down hard on her own palm. "In this place, I'm top man. Anytime you've got another fifty simoleons, I'll prove it to you."

"Now, Carolina, you know I don't play the game that way."

"You dagos never do. But the Froggies and Limeys love it. You'd be amazed how much they can take. And beg for more." Her immense breasts jiggled as she laughed again. "How about this sawed-off Polack here?" she went on. "Maybe he'd like to play bottom after all."

Grieskowski looked hurt, in advance, so to speak. "That ain't no way to talk," he grumbled.

The madam stopped laughing. "I'm getting bored with the pair of you," she said. "Let's get on with it."

At that moment a chime rang in another part of the house. "Paco!" Carolina Duffy bellowed. Then, to the new arrivals: "Pick a whip, Dr. Johnson, and let's proceed to one of the private parlors."

They were starting up a broad, curving flight of stairs when the doorman, Paco, interrupted them. "It's that farmer," he told his mistress.

"What farmer?"

"Miss Luanne's friend."

"Tell him to go to hell. Tell him Luanne ain't here tonight."

"He has to see her."

"Get rid of him, Paco. What do I pay you for?"

"He says if—"

"You!" Mike Leathers shouted as he strode into the hallway. "I want Luanne. Right now, fat woman."

Carolina Duffy simpered. "Didn't she tell you, farmer? Luanne never showed up tonight. Far's I know, she's home."

"That's a lie," Mike retorted. "I want her out of here. Her and me is leaving this town for good."

"That's wonderful," the madam cooed. "I'd love to help you. But she plain ain't here, sweet daddy, and that is the whole, entire truth of it."

Leathers frowned. He took a step toward the madam and her customers. At that moment, standing behind him, Paco lifted a cosh and swung it down on the back of Leathers' head. He pitched forward onto the carpeted floor.

"Clean it up, Paco." The doorman began dragging Mike Leathers away as the fat woman mounted the stairs, her buttocks rolling in the tight red dress. Eyeing this spectacle, the congressman and Alderman Grieskowski climbed the stairs behind her. At the top they paused while she caught her breath.

"Now, then," she said, coughing. "It's the first door on your left. And the lucky lady's name is Luanne. You'll get along swell. She's a novice, too."

48

"It was terrible, Mrs. Crozat," Clem Rynders said, his glance avoiding Kate as they sat in the parlor of the Pontalba apartment. The geologist looked tired. He had been rubbing the palm of his hand over his face, as if squeegeeing off moisture or pain. It had begrimed his face quite thoroughly.

"The men was scattered to the four winds. I still haven't rounded up all of them. I just hope they're alive. It gets real cold out there at night without a tent and a fire. For a while I thought your mister was among the missing as well, which is why I came downriver. I could picture him wandering in that wilderness and maybe running into some of the very night-riding sons of . . ." Rynders sighed unhappily. "Then I heard a rumor he'd shipped down by the *Rogue Queen,* so I followed along, and here I am."

He slapped the palm of his hand on the arm of the chair as if to reassure himself that he was not only alive but securely in this place. Kate shook her head understandingly. He had been fearfully formal when he'd called half an hour ago. Kate had no idea what he was expecting, probably a cool little Creole belle, all manners and starch. But in short order she had him talking to her like a fellow human being.

In the bedroom at the back of the apartment, Dr. Amabile closed the door carefully. "He sleeps," he hissed. "The recovery is quick enough in a person of his age. So quick he will believe himself truly well again. But that is a dangerous illusion. He must remain in bed for at least another week."

Only then did the doctor realize a stranger—and a dirty-faced one at that—was sitting in the parlor with Kate. "Mr. Rynders is a friend of the family," Kate assured him. "He is Edmund's right-hand man."

Rynders painfully hoisted himself to his feet and stuck out his hand. "Clem Rynders."

"Please," said Dr. Amabile, ignoring the offer, "be seated. You look quite fatigued."

"We had a hard time upstate." The geologist paused a moment, hesitated. Then: "How bad are his injuries?"

The doctor's eyebrows flew up. His glance swung to Kate. "Injuries," he echoed, as if never having heard this particular word before. "Injuries."

Kate's expression was blank as she considered her choices. Rynders could be trusted, but she understood a man like the doctor even better. Once he had her permission to discuss Edmund's condition with an outsider, he might feel free to talk about it to others.

"We're not sure yet," Kate said at last. "Doctor, can you come back tonight after dinner?"

"*Bien-sûr*, madame." Much relieved, Amabile was already looking about him for his coat and hat.

When he left, Kate returned to the parlor. The baby would be due for a feeding soon. But she didn't want to send Rynders on his way. The short, stocky man, even in his present state of exhaustion, was a comfort to have by her side. When Ned had brought Edmund home this morning, both of them had been in such a high-strung state that Kate wanted none of them. It was just as well Edmund slept so soundly.

She sat down across from Rynders. Her lips framed questions, rejected them. Finally she asked, "What do you know about absinthe, Mr. Rynders?"

His tired eyes swung toward her face but stared past her out the window at the river. "He wasn't drinking up at the drill site. He even refused a shot of rye. The man was on the temperance wagon, Mrs. Crozat. Has been for a long time now."

"Was there any absinthe in the camp?"

"That's not a proper drink for workingmen. And it's costly. Rye we had, and sour-mash whiskey. Maybe some of that local white stuff. No absinthe." The geologist reluctantly turned back to her. "Is that the problem?" he asked, cocking his head in the direction of the bedroom.

"That is the problem."

"Beats me where he'd get any."

She smiled slightly. "It's a city drink. One doesn't find it in the country. Well . . ." She got up. "I must attend to our son now. If you'll make yourself comfortable on the couch, I'll be back with you in half an hour or so."

Rynders lumbered to his feet. "I'd better go."

"Please stay."

He eyed the couch. "If it wouldn't be too much of an inconvenience, ma'am."

"It would be a favor to me. We haven't really talked about the problem, have we?"

"I've told you the whole story."

"But there are things you should be doing upstate. Things my husband is in no condition to plan."

"Like what?" Rynders asked, a thin edge of peevish fatigue in his voice. "Build new tanks? Where's the money? And if we build them, Waddell and his gang burn them again. As far as I can see, the only plans would be for bankruptcy."

Kate stared at him for a long moment. "You and I don't know each other very well, Mr. Rynders," she said at last. "But I have an idea you are a man of character. Not a quitter. You might say I am the same way. I don't see either of us giving up that easily."

"No?" He considered this for a moment. "But we're both smart enough to know when enough is enough."

"I don't think we're anywhere near that point yet."

"An expert on oil, are you?" Rynders asked. He was careful to smile when he said it.

She returned the smile. "No," she admitted. "Just a person who won't give in. The same kind as you."

He spread out his hands like a man on a crucifix. "Give me a prayer of a chance and I'd follow it. But what is there?"

"I was thinking." Kate had stopped at the entry to the dressing room, where the baby lay in his cradle. "If we had the money to build new tanks, what would be wrong with putting them underground?"

The geologist frowned. "Underground? You mean . . . ? That's real hardpan there. You'd need buckets and drag lines and an army of mules. Or you'd have to ship a steam shovel downriver from St. Louis. Or . . ." He stopped himself. "That's dreaming, Mrs. Crozat. First, tell me about the money."

"I'm working on it," Kate promised him.

49

Patrick Blood moved carefully through the muddy freight yards of the New Orleans and Northeastern depot at the head of Press Street. His partner, Jerry Mulcay, moved toward him from the opposite end. At each boxcar, the plainclothes detectives stopped, slid open doors, and peered in. Slowly they drew nearer each other until they met near the wharf end of the yard.

"Not a sign of 'em," Mulcay said. "You s'pose it was a bum steer?"

Patrick shook his head. "They were shipping out half a dozen men. And nary a one do we find."

"Maybe Matranga's paying full passenger fare for 'em."

Beside them, filtered weakly through the barn-red wooden wall of a freight car, came the sound of a groan. Patrick Blood stepped back. "That rattler was empty. I checked it myself."

Mulcay pulled a short-barreled .38 from a slim holster on his hip. "Whoever he is, he don't sound too healthy."

"Help me," a man's voice begged.

"Don't sound like a dago, neither." Blood pulled open the freight-car door and peered inside. "Whoever is making the racket, give us a look at your ugly mug, and make it slow."

There was a feeble scratching sound. In the shadows at the end of the rattler something moved. After a moment Patrick Blood could see a long body painfully crawling toward him. He pulled out his own gun. "Easy, mister. Identify yourself."

"Leathers." The man crawled into the weak winter daylight. "You're Ned's brother, aren't you?"

"And if I am?"

"The bastards sapped me," Mike Leathers said in a hoarse voice. He sat up and dangled his long legs over the doorway. The effort made him wince. "They must've dragged me over here, hoping the freight would move out in the night and take me with it."

"Who's 'they'?" Patrick demanded.

"The crusher at that damned Carolina Duffy's."

The detective put his gun away and indicated that his partner do the same. "You go for flogging, eh, Leathers?"

"I do not. My girl . . ." Mike Leathers stopped and thought for a moment. "Can you take me back there? When I called to get her, they did me in."

Patrick eyed Mulcay. "Got anything better to do?"

"Naw."

At the house that stood on its own grounds between Piety and Desire, they pounded on the door for five minutes without rousing anyone. "Closed up tight," Patrick Blood announced. "You didn't dream it, Leathers?"

"I didn't dream this," Mike said, indicating the lump at the back of his head.

Patrick's intake of breath was short and sharp.

"Look that bad?" Leathers demanded.

"Pulpy. Still bleeding a bit. We'd best take you to the Hôtel Dieu."

"What time is it?"

"About four in the afternoon."

"Then take me to Ned's office at the *Almanac* on Canal."

"Suit yourself."

The hardest part of it, Ned thought in retrospect, was getting his own thick brother Paddy to let go of the "case," as he called it. After an hour, he and Mulcay finally left. Ned and Mike then boarded Smoky Mary, the train that ran to Lake Pontchartrain, where Carolina Duffy still maintained her original house in Milneburg. That place, too, was locked up, although it seemed that it had been occupied as recently as this morning. Now it was sundown.

Ned made a face as he jabbed with a stick at the garbage in the trash barrel out back. "Eggshells," he announced. "And they're still wet to the touch."

Mike Leathers stood over him, thoughtfully rubbing the soft spot at the back of his head, now bathed in arnica and perfuming the air with a hospital smell. "You ought to be working for Hennessy, same as your brother. Where'd you learn all that Sherlock Holmes stuff?"

"Elementary," Ned muttered. He straightened up and looked about. Like the house behind Cellini's, this one stood on its own grounds, far from neighbors. Its windows, too, were blinded by heavy draperies. "You could ask at that house over there," he suggested, not too hopefully.

Ned watched the lanky man pace across a hundred yards of muddy turf to the next house. When he had knocked and a woman holding a lamp had come to the door, Ned noticed something in the trash.

He bent closer to examine a tangle of long black hair. It seemed real enough. Someone had hacked it off with quick slashes of a coarse shears. Some of the hairs had not been cut. They had been pulled loose. Bits of pale white skin clung to their roots.

"What're you looking at?"

Ned casually brushed eggshells over the hair and a wad of rags over the eggshells. Then he stood up, glad the darkness was settling around them. "What'd the neighbor say?"

"She saw nothing," Mike reported. "Heard nothing. Knows nothing."

"Like one of those three monkeys." Ned watched Mike's face closely for any sign he had seen the hair. "My guess is Luanne's not in a mood to be carted off to Baton Rouge. You might as well take the night steamer. I'll send her along."

"When you find her," Mike pointed out.

"When she wants to be found." Ned banged the lanky man on his forearm. "She's a grown girl. She has a mind of her own."

"That she does." Mike frowned. "But I can't help thinking—"

"No good ever came of that," Ned told him. "Why don't you catch Smoky Mary back to town? I'm going to catfoot it around, ask a few questions."

"The neighbors have nothing to say."

"To you, maybe not. But to Old Sherlock . . ."

They shook hands. Ned watched the tall man disappear in the direction of the Milneburg depot. When he was out of sight, Ned glanced at the nearest house. No one seemed to be watching him through the windows. He kicked over the trash barrel and began going through its contents with a stick again. The darkness made it difficult.

If a woman wanted to disguise herself, she might begin with a wig, he thought. But there was no need to cut off her real hair, was there? And even if there was, would she be so frantic that she literally tore strands loose?

He hunkered down, examining the trash without finding anything more than the sinister tangle of dark ringlets. He wished fervently that Milneburg was in Hennessy's territory so he could call on Paddy to help him.

As blowsy and debauched as Luanne Grimes had become, as slack as her flesh had grown on a diet of booze and abuse, her thick head of shiny black ringlets had always been her trademark, her promise to Mike that she could still go back to being the fresh young girl who had run downriver from Winnfield to try her luck in the wicked city.

It would take a lot to part her from those ringlets.

50

At three in the afternoon, as the sun wheeled slowly from south to west and dropped lower in the March sky, light flowed directly into all the windows of the Pontalba apartment. Cartons and boxes lay everywhere, some open, some already hammered shut.

The draymen would arrive tomorrow and carry everything away, including the furniture, wrapped in old quilts. The Crozats' new home in the Garden District was finally finished. Finally all the windows fit properly and snugly against the damp river air. Finally all the floors had been sanded and stained and waxed and polished with rottenstone and rewaxed and repolished. Finally the stairways were carpeted, the gas outlets in place, the plumbing connected to the city water supply. It had taken almost a year.

Standing in the window of the apartment bedroom, combing her hair, Kate wondered if it had been worth it.

She glanced over her shoulder at Edmund, napping. As always, he looked crumpled, feverish, bedclothes knotted around his limbs as if he had thrashed and turned in a high temperature or in the grip of strange nightmares. And yet, Kate thought, watching his sleeping face, all the symptoms of absinthe poisoning had vanished. His limbs and fingers were steady now. His temperature was quite normal, his speech quite clear.

She could see his eyes move behind closed lids, as if in a dream he were watching objects pass by. It was not a restful sleep. Her husband hadn't seemed to sleep soundly for some time. Only in those early honeymoon months had he awakened rested.

Fine sweat beaded his forehead. A bad dream. Should she waken him?

Not yet. Her son needed his afternoon feeding. He had a name by now, of course. Edmund had, in fact, really taken himself in hand and snapped out of his absinthe induced illness almost two weeks ago on the occasion of the christening at St. Louis cathedral. It had been quite an affair.

Maman Crozat had behaved herself remarkably well, sitting beside Cornelius Blood, if not like an old friend, then at least an acquaintance. The only other invitees were family and a few close friends like Jed Benjamin. But the cathedral had been mobbed by people who wanted to see if Edmund Crozat were still alive, walking under his own power, and managing to hold his son without dropping him in the baptismal font. There were probably some who wanted to know what such a celebrated mating of Creole and Irish money would look like. And perhaps a few of the more malicious wanted to search the baby's face for a hint that he was not, actually, Edmund's.

The object of this scrutiny, now christened Edmund Cornelius Crozat, no longer resembled a redheaded Barbary ape, as his Uncle Ned had once termed him. He had smoothed out into a rather handsome baby, in the opinion of more observers than his mother alone. With the passage of weeks, the telltale Crozat cheekbones had begun to show up through the baby fat. The wide-set eyes completed the picture. He was nobody's son but Edmund's.

Kate turned away from her husband. That was, perhaps, part of the problem, she realized. The shock of being a father, on top of the shock of losing the drill site, had seemed to sap Edmund's energy to a remarkable degree. He had never been a man for afternoon naps. Yet here he was, at almost four o'clock, feverishly dreaming the afternoon away.

Kate finished her hair as she looked out the sunstruck window at the dazzling ripples on the river. She had been letting her hair grow all through the pregnancy. Not that it had grown very long, hardly past her shoulders. In school, she'd had much longer hair. And shinier, too. With her son inside her, the fine reddish-blond hairs had lacked luster. Now they were shining again.

Small Edmund liked to grab handfuls of the gleaming strands. The feel seemed soothing to him. He would sigh and give a contented gurgle once his pudgy fingers were buried in her hair. And he had a grip already. Putting him down to sleep was not easy.

"Lovely long hair, full of sun," her husband said behind her.

Kate turned. Edmund had raised himself on one elbow. The hectic spots of red were dying across his cheekbones. He almost smiled, but his small, perfectly formed mouth seemed frozen for a moment in time.

"Rested?" Kate asked.

He shook his head. His black eyes still looked sleepy. It had been a long time since Kate had seen them blaze the way they used to. "I seem to have done myself a permanent injury with the green stuff." He produced a weak version of his crooked smile. "Once too often, perhaps."

"Nonsense. You have too much on your mind, Edmund."

"You and Olivia subscribe to the latest Viennese theories?"

"I know nothing of them."

"This cunning Dr. Freud Olivia talks about." He yawned and sat up on the side of the bed, stepping into his boots. "He has a theory that people's minds can cause sicknesses."

"Worries do."

"I have no worries. I have a beautiful wife and a handsome son. I am blessed of all men on earth."

Kate could hear the odd note in Edmund's voice. It was not sarcasm. Insincerity, yes. From disbelief, she decided. He does not consider himself blessed, by a long chalk. He thinks himself under a kind of curse.

Stepping around two packing cases, Kate leaned over the cradle. "This Crozat has no trouble sleeping."

"Then let him sleep. Don't wake him yet, Kate."

She had begun to unfasten her bodice for the feeding. Instead, she stopped and turned back to her husband. "Do you want to talk?"

He was standing by the bed, slowly knotting his cravat. "About what?"

"Anything. Money."

He laughed, a short, almost angry noise. "To say 'anything' is to exclude everything else. Money. Money. If you say it enough, it begins to sound meaningless."

"Olivia," Kate began, choosing her words with great care, "has mentioned that you have refused several offers of financing." The news had come not only from Olivia, but Kate knew her husband would accept that source more than any other. He had a queer temper lately. She never knew what would anger him.

"Olivia is a goose."

He checked his reflection in the pier glass and shifted the cravat a quarter-inch to the left. Kate told herself that his behavior could have been worse. He could have let himself slump into slovenliness. She wondered how long she might be able to stand living with a man who was intemperate, moody, haunted, depressed, *and* slovenly.

"Have you talked with Rynders lately?" she asked then.

"Regularly. Why?"

"He had some idea . . ." She gestured, as if in confusion. "Something about burying the storage tanks, although I may have it wrong."

"He's talked of little else." Edmund shrugged into his vest and carefully buttoned it. "Apparently he's mentioned it to you. It's quite a good idea. Out of my reach financially."

"But if you accept new financing . . ." Again she made the same movement with her hands, as if not really understanding her own words.

He pulled on his jacket, checked it in the pier glass, and turned to her. For a moment, in the powerful glare of sunshine reflected off the wall onto his face, he looked as he had when they were first married. But only for a moment. Then his face went slack.

"Kate, if you don't know me by now, you never will." He tried to straighten himself into a more commanding posture, but something was missing in his backbone. "I must do things my way. I must install my wife and my son in our new home. What money I have goes for that. The rest I will work out later." He grinned. "If at all."

"Edmund . . ."

She came toward him, arms out. He held her weakly for a moment. "Brave and idiotic words," he muttered in her ear. "But to be brave is to be an idiot."

It was almost as if he were not really holding her. The fierce pressure of his body didn't seem to exist. She was being held by a ghost. Kate's arms went around him and pressed his body against her.

"I won't hear such words," she told him.

"If not from me, then from half of New Orleans."

"Edmund . . ." She was almost shaking him.

Behind them, the baby awoke, hungry. His sudden wail made them start back from each other, as if now that they had finally touched, they must part at once.

"All right, young man." Kate was fumbling with her bodice, freeing her heavy breasts. She picked up the baby and sat in the sunshine next to the window. His eyes still closed, her son was making greedy sucking noises. She guided his lips to her nipple, and he began feeding instantly.

Kate was aware that fathers were not supposed to witness such scenes. In this small apartment, now loaded with boxes and crates, there was really no way of hiding from the man who had sired this infant. And, to tell the truth, it bothered Kate not at all for Edmund to watch her.

She turned to smile reassuringly at her husband. But he had his back to her.

51

Mike Leathers looked around the small upstairs room at the Red Pole. It was the one where he had sat one night commiserating with that traitorous Jack Bunch, and him full of opium for his whip cuts.

They'd removed the bed and bureau and put in a long pine table and a few ladderback chairs. It was a place for confidential meetings away from the curious eyes of Baton Rouge regulars who frequented the big glittering taverns in the main part of town.

And confidential was the name of this meeting today. Mike had made contact weeks ago with the man whose name his father had given him, a mean old cuss, as long and lanky as Mike himself, named Harry Pilcher. Some kind of Yankee, although the man was picking up a Southern twang faster than a mule picked up ticks.

Harry Pilcher and Mike Leathers had gotten off to a slow start, in Mike's opinion, mainly because the idea of Nigger Mike representing oil interests was a novelty Baton Rouge didn't swallow all at once. It took a few mighty gulps before most of the legislators and lobbyists got the message that this was the new Mike, anointed by his father.

Greenbacks began changing hands. A slush account was set up for Mike at the State Bank of Baton Rouge. Things moved right smart after that. Today, Pilcher told Mike, was the moment when the knight about to joust would learn whose colors he wore on his arm.

In his green ignorance, Mike had naturally assumed that the Rocke-

300

feller colors, whatever they were, emblazoned on a Standard Oil of Indiana shield, would be forthcoming at this point. But Harry Pilcher managed to surprise him.

He arrived at the Red Pole with two short, heavyset fellows in dark business suits and bowler hats who had just disembarked from the St. Louis steamer. That was one of the Red Pole's advantages: you could bring in a guest fresh off the steamer without the whole town seeing him.

"Mike Leathers," Pilcher said as he ushered the two newcomers into the upstairs meeting room, "say hello to Mr. Gough and Mr. Cudlipp."

The men shook hands, with much pressure and a few extra shakes. Mike found himself wondering how a pair of twins had ended up with different last names. Then he realized that behind their city faces with the dark mustaches and long sideburns, one man was sallow and tired while the other had a tan. Mr. Inside seemed to be Gough. Mr. Outside, Cudlipp.

"Gents," Mike began, "if you'd care to cut the dust a bit, this is right promising sour mash here." He lifted one unlabeled bottle. "And this dark stuff is Barbados rum."

All four sat down at the table, named their choice, touched glasses, and drank. "Yeh!" Gough coughed. "Whuh!" He shook his head and turned to Cudlipp. "That dark bilge is number-seven fuel oil. Go kind of careful on it."

The men settled back while Harry Pilcher spread out neat piles of paper. "This here," he began without further preamble, "is the list of Great Southern land holdings. What counts is this here column." He pointed with a long, hairy finger. "That's Great Southern's own forecast on yield. You add three zeros to the number. Follow me?" Both newcomers nodded.

"Nobody upriver has any idea how much Crozat's expecting to pump."

Mike sprawled back in his chair. "When you say Crozat's expecting," he said in an offhand tone, "he's about as far from pumping as a rooster is from laying eggs."

"So we hear," Gough agreed. His glance strayed toward the Barbados rum. Instantly Mike filled his glass. Gouch sipped the dark liquid this time instead of gulping it.

"So we can take our time," Harry Pilcher said, "and do the job right."

Gough smiled, his pallid face losing its tired look for a moment. "I have always found it hard to believe that the legislature can be pointed in so many different directions. First they tied him up in knots. Then they gave Crozat everything he wanted. Now you're saying we can tie him up in knots again."

"Gents," Mike spoke up, "welcome to Louisiana, where money talks real loud."

"We did remember to bring it," Cudlipp assured him. "Once you fellas spring the trapdoor on Great Southern, we're ready to move right in. The minute his purchases are ruled illegal, we step up and offer each shit-kicker a nice lease."

"You have the sound of a confident man," Mike told him.

"Equity Petroleum stresses the positive, Mr. Leathers."

Mike relaxed still further in his chair, absorbing the fact that his employer was still unknown to him. Whoever in tarnation Equity Petroleum was, they walked and talked and spat like real winners.

"Right comforting to know that," Mike responded. "It would help me a lot with the legislators if I could know the source of that confidence."

Gough finished his rum. He and Cudlipp exchanged glances. "But you already know that," Gough said at last. "You said how far Crozat was from pumping? He's stony. Great Southern Number One was his only chance at cash. When it burned, he lost the whole game."

This time it was Pilcher who glanced at Mike. "We hear work's started up at Southern One. They got drag buckets and mules working day and night. They're burying the storage tanks this time."

Cudlipp absorbed this information. "What's he using for cash?"

"We got no idea," Pilcher admitted. "The place is ringed by a passle of boys with carbines. Ain't nobody gets within a mile of it."

Both newcomers turned to Mike Leathers, who decided it was time to drop his country-boy pose. "My guess," he said then, "is it ain't Crozat money."

"Private loan?" Cudlipp asked. He looked suddenly worried.

"Nothing that grand," Mike assured him. "The little runt who runs the place doles it out a dollar at a time. It's a shoestring operation."

"Silent partner," Cudlipp muttered.

"That," said Gough, "could be bad news." He poured himself a fresh rum, but sat without sipping it. "I guess it won't hurt none to tell 'em. We been working hard in Chicago. Equity Petroleum's a big customer of the bank up there that holds Crozat's note, the one he made a year ago. It's overdue and the bank was going to let him string along. Equity sort of convinced them to call it due right now, no extensions, no explanations, no leeway. Pay or take foreclosure."

Mike let out a thin whistle. "You gents don't fool around none, do you?"

"Try not to," Gough admitted with a sly smile.

"We have us a situation," Cudlipp boasted, "where the bank forecloses by the end of this week or we move a considerable corporate deposit to some other bank that understands how to treat a good customer."

"Nothing Crozat can do to save himself?" Mike asked.

"Pay up." Cudlipp laughed. "From what I hear, he hasn't got the cash to buy a ten-cent cheroot."

"No," Mike agreed. "But . . ."

The three men sat waiting. In the silence, Mike could almost feel the greedy tension in the room. These were real meat-eating gators, these Yankees. He almost felt sorry for Edmund Crozat. But not quite.

"You were saying . . ." Gough urged him.

"He ain't got the cash," Mike Leathers told them, "but his father-in-law does."

Cudlipp filled everyone's glass. "I think we're straining at gnats, gentlemen." He lifted his glass. "We have Great Southern by the oysters. There will be a lien and a sheriff's man on every piece of equipment they own. Crozat can have ten fathers-in-law, but I say: Great Southern is finished."

Solemnly the men clinked glasses. Tasting the strong sour-mash whiskey as it coursed down his throat, Mike Leathers looked at the other men around the table. Vultures, drinking a dead man's blood.

When Cudlipp grinned, Mike Leathers could see all his teeth. He felt surrounded by Yankee incisors. Until now, he'd suffered only at the hands of his own kind. Gazing at all those teeth, Mike wondered how long he'd last in his new line of work.

52

In the live oak at the far end of the garden, early sun spread a horizontal flare of pale orange that seemed to set the filmy mesh of Spanish moss on fire. Kate pushed aside the heavy draperies of her bedroom on the second floor of the new house. Placing her palms on the cool limestone windowsill, she leaned out into the morning freshness.

The moss flamed brilliantly. She inhaled and watched the sun's beams spread until the entire branch blazed. Between her and the tree stretched a long lawn, grass so new it glistened pale as chartreuse. Kate had planted the border of the lawn with flowers that were now pushing slender shoots upward through the dark soil. None would be in bloom for a week. But it didn't matter. Today would be cool and sunny and perfect.

Everything about the new house was perfect. And although some of her family and friends had seen it as it slowly rose from the ground, today would be the official housewarming. It was Saturday. Everyone was invited for early afternoon. Later, as night fell, there would be a barbecue; red snapper, guinea hens, a yearling shoat, and back ribs.

There would be lanterns and a small band Jed had booked for her. Later there might even be dancing, if people were of a mind. She took another deep breath. The air was clear and, for New Orleans, dry. Spring had been cool, and the early summer, not yet taken over by mosquitoes. Kate glanced at the borders of the lawn and saw that Henry had already installed citronella pots at the base of each lantern pole.

The perfect house rose two stories from its corner lot in the Garden District, a pale beige limestone set off by blinding white scrolls and curls.

Until the final iron- and woodwork—columns, window frames, door decorations, gates, and shutters—the house had looked a bit severe to Kate, hardly more than a breadbox whose flat roof was relieved only by chimneys at both ends. She had in the past called this to Edmund's attention and had been given unsatisfactory answers. Now she realized that the house had been sparsely planned as a background for the elaborate curves, reverses, ornaments, and finials that Edmund had commissioned from the city's blacksmith and carpenters.

Inside, Edmund had stepped aside to let her work with the architects. Breezeways bisected the two floors, setting up their own gentle currents of air and keeping rooms cool even in the heat of the day. Edmund had left the landscaping to her as well. She had brought in stately cypresses and stands of dogwood, magnolia trees, and a boxwood hedge along the front that had already produced enough leaves to get its first careful pruning.

In the distance, Kate heard the bells of St. Patrick's strike six times. She turned back and stood watching Edmund asleep in their bed, not the cramped one from the Pontalba apartment but a grand *letto matrimoniale* imported from Turin. Her husband's body lay kinked like a prawn's, his knees drawn up toward his chest. His face pressed heavily into the pillow.

Kate observed his fingers for a moment. They lay motionless. There had been no tremors for some time now, none of the night sweats that had worried her so.

In the nursery across the breezeway from their bedroom, she could hear the baby making his usual morning gurgles. If not fed soon, he would grow louder, though no more coherent, until he could be heard downstairs. Kate glanced down at her breasts. In a few weeks she would have to wean the baby. It would be hard for both of them to give it up, but it couldn't be postponed much longer. Young Edmund, five months old this month, was already at work on crusts of bread, trying to free his first teeth from the pink depths of his gums.

Moving silently, Kate left the bedroom and tiptoed past the nursery to the room at the back of the house that Edmund had fitted out as his office. The furnishings were sparse, since he seldom worked here. To be truthful, Kate told herself, Edmund seldom worked at all. He wandered about the house and grounds a lot on what he called supervisory jobs. But few of these remained. To his wife his wandering reminded her of a man groping in fog.

It suited Kate at the moment that Edmund not plunge back into work. But it was only a matter of time, she told herself, before he would recover enough to want to go upstate to inspect the ruins of Great Southern Number One. He would then learn of her little plot with Rynders to rebuild the drill site underground.

Kate sat down at Edmund's desk and picked up a quill pen lying in its ebony trough. The virgin nib had never touched ink.

Before Edmund could find out on his own what was happening upstate, she would have to tell him. There would be a scene, she had no doubt. It would be much more of a test of their marriage than the trouble between them when Edmund had been absent the night of his son's birth. This time, she would be judged at fault, guilty of bringing her father into the situation, of channeling cash from him to Rynders, guilty of doing it behind Edmund's back because, if presented to him beforehand, it surely would have been rejected.

Kate by now understood stubborn Creole pride, the kind that had caused his father to invalid himself, that purebred cut-off-the-nose-to-spite-the-face Creole arrogance that would have let Great Southern go bankrupt rather than take outside financing.

The kind of pride, Kate reminded herself as she played with the pen's feathery shaft, that finds it proper for a man to surrender to his own demoralization rather than give up control of what is his.

Edmund had rather wallowed in degradation of late. Kate smiled slightly as she thought of it. He rose these days well after ten in the morning and made a three-hour ritual of breakfast and bath. Such enterprise required a brief nap to fortify him for those afternoons when he felt energetic enough to sally uptown for a brief café conference with friends. Dinner at home and early to bed rounded out a full day for Edmund. The fancy men of the Tenderloin exerted themselves about as much as Edmund Crozat these days. Kate's smile grew broader.

Her father had warned her it might happen. He had made no objection to financing the rebuilding of Southern, on the sly, so to speak. "But you don't do a man like Edmund no favors paying his way," he cautioned Kate. "His kind go lazy without a challenge."

Kate drew a piece of unmarked paper to her and dipped the quill in the inkwell. "Dear Jed," she wrote, "since this is my first time on the boards in the role of Lady Bountiful, please let me know what must be available for the musicians with whom you have contracted. They can take their intermissions in the kitchen, so there is no danger of them starving, but a thirsty musician is a dangerous contradiction in terms. Please let me know what potables they are used to taking on the bandstand."

She stopped, frowning. "Ever, Kate," she scribbled quickly. Then, as a postscript: "Give your reply direct to Henry. He is instructed to buy whatever you tell him."

Waving the note to dry it, Kate moved quietly down the green carpeting that covered the broad curving stairway. On the main floor she moved along the breezeway to the kitchen at the rear.

Henry and his wife, Belle, had come highly recommended as a young couple with extensive domestic experience. Henry was, in fact, the oldest son of Neil Blood's cook, Julia. Tall and grave, he stood now at the big wood-burning range and carefully poured boiling water into the top of an enameled drip pot sitting in a hot-water bath.

He and Kate had known each other since childhood. Nevertheless, they bowed solemnly, as if meeting for the first time. "Five minutes mo', Miz Kate."

"Is Belle up?"

"No'm. She ain' no early riser like us'ns." He winked.

Both of them stood watching the thin trickle of steaming water drip down into the open top of the pot. It couldn't be poured too slowly or too fast. Kate found herself thinking that Henry's accent was pure New Orleans, as hers was not. An "early" riser was "aily." New Orleanians drank a whiskey called either "baibon" or "boibon." Kate herself still had too much of her father's way of talking to qualify as a true native speaker.

Once dripped, the coffee was poured in two enamel mugs and dosed with milk and sugar. Silently, standing almost side by side at the stove, Kate and Henry sipped the coffee quickly, before the handle of the mug got too hot to hold.

"Can you take this note to Mr. Benjamin before you start your errands?"

Henry accepted the note with the same grave expression he took most things. "He on Royal? That theatrical man?"

"The very same. Wait for an answer and buy what he tells you for the musicians. Probably a keg of beer, but they may drink lemonade."

The gravity of Henry's expression gave way to a solemn grin. "Musicians? Lemonade?"

Both of them chuckled.

Madame Fleurigant had spent the night in the little cottage on Rampart Street, fitfully sleeping in a chair drawn up to the bed in which her daughter slept. The pains had begun yesterday afternoon. Then they had mysteriously stopped. While this was not unusual in the midwife's experience, she knew Ynes would be grateful for company through the night. The girl had been mopey for weeks now, like a little bird covered with dust, wings drooping, head down.

Madame could hear the bells of St. Louis cathedral ring seven times. She stirred. Coffee would go fine right now. She opened her eyes.

Ynes was staring wildly at her, white all the way around her pupils. A mad stare. Mouth constricted in a grimace of silent pain.

"Chile!" Madame Fleurigant jumped to her feet. "What is it, chile?"

Ynes' head shook violently from side to side. She made a mewing sound somewhere at the back of her throat.

"Comment, bebe?" her mother urged. *"Dis-moi, p'tit chou."*

The young woman's head shook wildly, as if snapped by rods. Her mother took her chin to stop the motion, but the girl's neck muscles were too powerful. "Ynes!"

53

The two men guarding the entrance to the Provenzano warehouse on North Peters Street stepped in front of the doorway as Chief Hennessy approached. Patrick Blood walked out ahead of his chief.

"Gangway," he told the guards. "It's the chief himself."

They moved aside to let the men through. The stench of half-burned produce choked the air with acrid fumes. The two policemen surveyed the wreckage inside. In the night, wanting to cause smoke, not flames, someone had draped oily waste over every bin of vegetables and fruit, then set the rags afire.

"Wasn't there nobody working here last night?" Patrick asked.

Hennessy jerked his chin in the direction of a squat, burly man who was standing in a far corner conversing quietly with two others. His glance shot across the smoky warehouse to stare at Hennessy. "Massimo," the chief called. "What the hell?"

"Looka dis." Provenzano spread his hands out, palms up, to indicate something hidden in a corner.

Hennessy and Patrick walked over to the warehouse owner. There, covered with banana stalks, lay four men, each with his throat cut. They lay on their backs as if sleeping, hair matted in the communal pool of almost congealed blood.

"They didn't have to kill 'em," Hennessy muttered. "They could of coshed 'em."

Provenzano nodded dumbly, his eyes fixed on the blood. Hennessy saw that the toe of his boot was touching the pool. He took a step back-ward. In an undertone he addressed Patrick Blood. "It looks," he mur-mured, "like a certain message was never sent."

"Or nobody paid no attention to it," Patrick added.

His chief eyed him with distaste. "Either way . . ."

"I know."

"It's war," David Hennessy told him.

This was the third night in a row that Olivia Crozat had spent with Jed Benjamin. As far as her mother was concerned, she was sleeping at the new home of her brother and sister-in-law, helping Kate with final touches. Olivia had grown quite used to the routine. Since Jed's servants went home each evening, she could spend from dinner through break-fast with him, except on those nights when he had a concert or reci-tal.

Having grown accustomed to this, she hardly moved at the breakfast table when Kate's servant knocked at the front door. Instead of running upstairs to dress in hiding, Olivia sat calmly sipping her coffee as she finished the chapter of *Madame Bovary* she had been reading aloud to Jed.

"No, no," she heard Jed telling Henry. "A small keg of beer will do. But it must be chilled, you understand?"

A moment later he returned to the breakfast table and stood there with a peculiar look on his face. "Strange," he said at last.

"Not at all." Olivia looked up from the book. "What could be more natural for a woman like me to read?"

"Not the book. Henry."

"Yes?"

"This is the second time in three days Kate has sent him here with a message. It's almost . . ." He frowned down at her. "Just how intimate a pair of friends are you?"

Olivia finished a paragraph, closed the book, and set it aside. "Do you imagine I would even hint at our liaison to Kate?"

"Then why does she keep sending us early-morning messages?"

"You are imagining it."

"It's as plain as day." Jed began pacing, his heavy brocaded dressing gown flying out behind him. "She . . . It's her way of telling us she knows what we're up to."

"Utterly fantastic."

"You don't know Kate."

"But I do," Olivia insisted. "She has her hands full. She has a new home, decorating it, new servants, training them, a monstrous house-warming party today, with dozens of guests, a nursing infant, and a husband who stalks the house like a monk pacing his cloister. Please be good enough to sit down, Jed. You are making me dizzy."

He sat opposite her and ran his fingers through his thinning red hair. "Kate is used to handling that kind of chaos," he said in a quieter tone. "And having her little joke as well."

"There is no way she could have found out."

He decided to believe her. "If you say so, my dear. But the Irish are noted for a very fey sense of humor."

"What time will you make your appearance at the Palais Crozat?"

"Is that what they're calling it?"

"Just my Creole sense of humor, Jed. I shall be there most of the day helping Kate. How early can you come? Lunch?"

"No, no, no. Too obvious."

"I see. Tired of me already."

"My dearest Livy."

"It's been three consecutive nights. But you don't seem any the worse for wear," she observed, sighing contentedly. "It's all very Parisian, isn't it? Very French. Even to the novel from which I am now taking lessons."

"In my opinion Flaubert took lessons from you," Benjamin said dryly. "If I remember correctly, the lady came to a bad end."

"The worst. But what could she expect? She was, after all, a married adulteress."

An odd silence settled between them. Olivia had never raised the subject of marriage, ably reinforced by Jed, who would, perhaps, have liked to toy with the idea. Perhaps she was doing him an injustice, Olivia thought, smiling across the table at her lover. On the other hand, it may have occurred to him, as it already had to Olivia, that marriage would have ruined a perfectly satisfying relationship.

"Do come before dark, then," she told him. "I want to give you a tour of Château Crozat before the serious drinking begins."

The messenger from Postal Telegraph, in his heavy blue uniform, looked hot as he rang the front doorbell at nine o'clock. Belle answered the summons and brought the envelope to Kate. She stared at Edmund's name handwritten on the outside with his Carondolet office address below it. Someone had scratched it out and added, in pencil, "Try Livaudais and Washington." So the new address was already common knowledge, was it?

When she awakened him, his eyes opened wide and he stared for an instant before recognizing her. Then his glance shifted to the blue-bordered envelope. "Damn," he said.

"My sentiment, too."

He sat up, ripped the telegram open, and read the message. "Damn," he repeated, but the force was out of his voice.

Kate stared at the telegram:

OUR QUERIES IGNORED, WE ARE HEREWITH CALLING DUE NOTE OF DECEMBER 1888. PLEASE BE ADVISED YOU HAVE FIVE BUSINESS DAYS FROM RECEIPT OF . . .

She let the paper drop to her lap. "How overdue is it?"

"Six months." He lay back and turned away from her, as if trying to go back to sleep.

"Edmund."

"We'll talk about it later," he said, his mouth muffled by the pillow. "Or not at all."

"Edmund, what can they do?"

"Foreclose." He laughed abruptly, a sharp, harsh sound devoid of humor.

"On the drill site?" She took a sudden breath. "The house?"

"Anything they can lay their hands on."

Kate sat silently for a long moment. "Then perhaps you'd better not go back to sleep."

"I don't have a devil of a lot to stay awake for."

"But you do," she told him. "If they're going to take the house, we must have a huge, bang-up party today. In case it's our last."

Glancing out the hidden side door of his apartment, Jed Benjamin looked both ways, then ducked out of sight. Olivia Crozat came through the door and walked briskly to the Royal Street end of the passage. She turned right and continued a square to her parents' home, letting herself in by the front door.

She stopped in the foyer and took a long, steadying breath. One could become quite used to this adulterous life, Olivia realized, and more than that, quite eager for it to continue indefinitely. But her father's house still had its ancient power to reduce her to a frightened child.

The lemony smell of furniture, often oiled but rarely used of late, made Olivia's nostrils flare. She looked down at the pattern of sunlight on the Persian carpet which had lain in the foyer for as long as she could remember. In the distance, slight sounds came from the direction of the kitchen, beyond the central courtyard.

Moving slowly, trying to shake off the little-girl guilt, Olivia went to the kitchen.

Gri-Gri, their cook, was slowly stirring one lone pot on the stove. She glanced up. "Mornin', missy."

"Gumbo again?"

Gri-Gri glanced down at the pot. "S'onliest thing that po' man will take."

Olivia nodded. "And Maman?"

"Com'toujours," the cook replied.

Olivia mounted the back stairs to her father's room and gently eased the door open. Her mother sat in an easy chair by his bed. In her hands lay the morning newspaper. As always, she had been reading it aloud to her husband, but she seemed now to have fallen asleep, head tilted back, breathing slow and regular.

Olivia stood at the foot of her father's bed. He lay with his eyes closed, but she knew he might well be awake. He had always been a thin man. Now he was almost skeletal. The flesh had dropped away from his face and hands, leaving his bones covered by the thinnest of skin. As she watched, his eyes opened.

His right hand jerked slightly, as if he had wanted to raise it in greeting. The effort made the waxed gray tips of his mustache quiver. Olivia smiled. *"Bon jour, Papa. Tout va bien?"*

A rusty, grating sound came from between his teeth. Olivia nodded patiently. The man had not talked since his seizure. She started to turn away.

"Ça marche."

Olivia whirled back. "Papa!"

The old man seemed as surprised as she. His eyes, sunk in deep sockets, were wide with wonder. *"Ça marche."*

"Papa, you spoke!"

"Ça marche." It was a thin crow of triumph.

Trembling wildly, his right arm . . . moved. It made the distance from his chest to his head in agonizing slowness. Finally it reached his face, and his fingers, curled these many months in dead repose, suddenly straightened.

"Bon jour!" he cried, giving his daughter a salute.

54

At eleven, a *sous chef* from the Wicklowe arrived with meat and fowl. He supervised the setting up of an iron barbecue grill and *tournebroche* frame at the bottom of the garden under the live-oak tree. Kate had finally gotten Edmund through coffee and a bath, trying to hurry him along.

Her mind was a dark room filled with every kind of anxiety, old and new. To the usual worries of holding a social event as ambitious as this one, and so fraught with significance for their future in this lovely new house, were now added buzzing gnat-worries about Edmund's own future if the bank foreclosed. Was it the end of Great Southern? If so, it was the end of Edmund, the end of her as well. Yes, of course, she would survive with her beautiful little son, that was clear. Her father and family would see to that. But . . .

The anxieties traveled in chains, the tail of one in the mouth of the next, twisting in that dark room of her mind which she knew must not be entered. She must pass and repass that door all day without going in. Otherwise she would never get through the day.

The beautiful day. Sunlight streamed down on the fresh new lawn. Henry had returned from his first round of errands. He and Belle moved swiftly through their chores. Little Edmund had been put out in a blanket on the flagged patio that fronted the garden. He banged his toys and escaped again and again from the blanket to the grass, crawling rapidly.

Kate or Belle retrieved him a dozen times until Edmund emerged from his bath, dressed and available for light work. He placed a chair on the flagstones of the patio and read his newspaper. From time to time he headed off the more adventurous sorties of his son and heir.

Heir, Kate thought, watching the two of them from the parlor window. To what great estate? What fortune?

The inner courtyard of Alexander Badger's lovely old house on Dauphine Street received the sunlight directly. In the cool shadow next to a bright square of sun, the master of the house sat before hot coffee and powdery *beignets* and made hostlike noises and gestures.

His guest, a big blond man, nodded from time to time. "Badger," Neil Blood said at length, "are these *beignets* from the market?"

"My housekeeper makes them fresh."

"Mrs. Fenwick?" Blood's eyebrows went up.

"Not Mrs. Fenwick," Badger said. Then he stopped talking.

Ned Blood sipped his coffee. "But you don't eat, you skinny little half-portion."

"I have a different breakfast." Once again Badger seemed on the edge of saying more, but didn't. His glance shot sideways to the kitchen door. Someone was moving inside. Rich smells floated out into the open courtyard.

Neil Blood sniffed. "Kippers?"

Badger nodded. "My usual repast."

"And bacon?"

"And shirred eggs. And baps." His mouth snapped shut, but couldn't stay that way. "Hot. Wi' butter."

"Dear God, Badger, who is your housekeeper, man?"

The screen door to the kitchen swung open and a huge tray of food moved out into the sunlight. Carrying it was a tall dark woman. Neil Blood's eyebrows went as high as they could.

"Josefa!"

"Mornin', Mr. Blood." The woman moved with smooth grace across the courtyard and began transferring dishes from her tray to the table. "Poppa's kippers," she announced. "Poppa's eggs and bacon. And these here funny things."

Badger pounced on a bap and broke open the round bun. Delicious steam floated upward as he knifed a bit of butter into the hot center. "Try one?" he asked his guest.

Neil Blood had not taken his eyes off the mulatto housekeeper. "I will be a great horned toad," he stated.

"You gem'un 'joy y'breakfast," Josefa told them, retreating to the kitchen.

Neil sat back in his chair, which creaked dangerously. "Poor Mrs. Fenwick," he said then. "She never had a chance, eh, Badger?"

"Not much of a cook," the man from Fiddoch, Larned said. "No great shakes as a baker."

"And in the percale?"

Badger's face went crimson. "That was not a portion," he said stuffily, "of Mrs. Fenwick's competency."

Cornelius Blood stifled the urge to guffaw. Instead he finished off his *beignet* and dusted the powdered sugar from his fingers. "My daughter's expecting you at the housewarming," he said then.

"Ah, yes. A lovely house, from what I've heard." Badger wiped melted butter from his chin. "Will the rest of our group be there?"

"Our group?" Blood smiled grimly. "Did you read that article in the *Mascot*? A cabal, they call us. A conspiracy." He sighed. "Not all of us," he said in a suddenly somber voice. "Some changes are being made, as you know."

Badger nodded and began cutting at his kipper. "He hasn't taken kindly to it, so they tell me."

"Matranga? He's furious. But I sent him every last cent he ever put with me, Badger. Plus interest. He's got no complaint."

Badger munched industriously. After he swallowed and dabbed at his lips, he smiled brightly. "To whom could Tony Matranga complain?"

Blood nodded heavily. "That's the problem with being a law unto yourself. There ain't no place to appeal. Which is what bothers me. He's furious, but he's made no move."

Badger attacked his eggs and bacon, piling up bits on the downturned tines of his fork and transferring them rapidly to his mouth. "Do you think your decision was a wise one?" he asked at last.

Blood snorted. "Months ago I gave the man a message from Davy Hennessy. Now, Hennessy don't need me to carry messages. He was asking would I step in and be a peacemaker. Otherwise he could've sent a note by mail. Has there been any peace?"

"Very little."

"He won't let up on the Provenzanos, our former associate won't. He's telling the world he don't give a fig for Chief Hennessy. But it maybe looks like he also don't give a hoot in hell for Neil Blood, neither. You follow me?"

"Afraid I do."

"So, wise or not, the decision's made. I can't have a man in this town thumbing his nose at me and getting away with it. I may not be the choosiest when it comes to business partners. But there was always something about the bastard gave me a cold chill."

"Choosy." Badger laughed briefly. "One makes no money in New Orleans being choosy."

"Judging by how much you hauled home to Old Blighty, you ain't been the world's choosiest investor, neither."

Badger blinked. He had thought he had shipped the two chests of bullion to London unnoticed. "Foolish of me to think you wouldn't know," he murmured.

"Damned smart idea," his guest complimented him. "I'd've done the same if I could." He sighed again. "Ever since I first met him, there was an undertaker's look about Matranga. Like he was measuring me for a coffin. Now that I've eased him out, things will be different. For one thing, I had to let Luca, my crusher, go. He was a cousin of the Matrangas. I got a pure-blooded Fenian guarding the door now. And a few more guarding me."

Badger's mouth being full of bap, he had no reaction to this news but a wide-eyed look.

"Well may you goggle," Blood agreed. "That the day should come when Neil Blood freely can't walk the streets of his own city."

"Why, then, in God's name . . . ?" Badger demanded.

"Did I break with him? I have done business with pimps and perverts and murderers. With crazy men. With the slipperiest snakes in the swamp." He planted his thick hands palms down on the table with such violence that the cups and dishes rattled. "But never all of them in the shape of one man."

"Oh, come, now. He's just another crook."

"It's this organ-eye-zation of his that buffaloes me. We have our cabals, but what Matranga has is an army. And treaties with other armies in Mobile and Biloxi and Baton Rouge, all the way to Florida and Texas. Did I say an army? Call it a nation. A country of its own hidden away inside the borders of the U.S. of A."

"Oh, now, really."

"I notice the idea has enough power to stop you from eating Josefa's cooking."

The Englishman glanced down at his plate. "But the risk of offending him . . ." His voice died away.

"You might say taking risks is part of my particular business." Blood set his coffeecup down with a definitive click. "You might say I'm weeding our group a bit. Christy's the next to go."

"No."

"Some information came my way." Blood got to his feet. "The man's loyalty is . . . ah, under suspicion."

"But . . ."

His guest picked up a narrow-brimmed panama and carefully placed it on his head. "Thanks for the *beignets*, old friend. I can see why you switched housekeepers." He paused. "Badger," he said, "I'm not a great one for giving unasked-for advice." He paused again. "Josefa's one hell of a woman," he went on. "But you'll keep it all . . . ah, sort of casual?"

"Pardon me?"

"Casual. Nothing formal, in writing, so to speak." Neil Blood grinned at his host. "Otherwise, old friend, it's gonna get expensive as the devil. Those two chests in London." He laughed. "They won't last long."

Dr. Theobald was well past eighty years old. For anyone to have lived that long amid New Orleans' fevers and plagues was an encouraging sign in itself. Theobald came of a long line of freed blacks who had owned property in the city since the early years of the nineteenth century. Like his father and his grandfather, he was a general practitioner, but with some gifts as a surgeon.

"But I have not performed such a section in many years," he was telling Madame Fleurigant.

He stood by Ynes' bedside in the cottage on Rampart, his black top hat still on his head, his black leather case still clutched in his hand.

"But you have done so," Madame insisted. *"Ce n'est-ce pas un grand travail.* In the backwoods, I have heard, even a *papa-loi* can make such a cut."

The ancient doctor's head swung slowly left and right. "There is much risk. The dangers of the birth would have to be quite great for a surgeon to agree to a cesarean section."

"You can see for yourself, *maître.* The girl is too narrow. There is no room." The tiny birdlike woman swept back the covers from Ynes' body.

Dr. Theobald turned away quickly. "I have seen. Cover her, madame."

"Then you agree?"

"You are the *accoucheuse.* How great is the risk?"

"To the infant, perhaps fatal."

"And to the mother?"

Madame sighed unhappily. *"La même chose, cher maître.* If allowed to run its course, they both may die."

Theobald removed his hat and opened his bag. "Bring me water, then, and quickly."

The long floor-through office of the *Weekly Almanac* was deserted on Saturdays. Anticipating a late night collecting scandal in the Tenderloin, *Almanac* reporters rarely showed up at the office during the day.

Which was why Ned had chosen Saturday to work. He had prepared himself with four bound ledgers. Inside, on the lined spaces to the right of the vertical red line, he had begun what he envisioned as either a very long article or a book.

"I do not pretend," he began, writing slowly to preserve legibility, "to understand the secret workings of other great American cities. But when it comes to New Orleans, we have an example—often exciting, colorful, titillating—of a society based almost entirely upon the degradation of women and the use of their bodies as a commodity as common as potatoes and twice as cheap."

He sat back in his chair and read the paragraph several times, changing "potatoes" to "rice" and then changing it back to "potatoes."

He dipped his pen and continued. "We have seen vast dynasties founded on nothing more awesome than a beaver pelt in the case of the Astors or, in the case of the Carnegies, pig iron. Yet it is no exaggeration to state that where the considerable personal fortunes of New Orleans were once based on cotton, sugar, and the shipping or factoring of both, the very business structure of the city, the fund of capital upon which it depends, is nothing less than the brutal prostitution of young women, most of them from farms and rural communities in Louisiana, Texas, and Mississippi."

He made a face and began tinkering with the last sentence, trying to break it into two shorter ones, without much luck. Shaking his head, he began writing more rapidly.

"Yes, it may be possible for the corrupt ring of business and political leaders who rule New Orleans to point to legitimate sources for their wealth. But none indicate the mother lode from which these magnificoes mine the basic cash flow that enables them to venture into more acceptable investments.

"For the revolting fact is this: with few exceptions, most businessmen in New Orleans are heavily invested in the bordellos, cribs, barrel houses, theaters of pornography, flogging racks, and opium dens of the great Tenderloin district centering around, but certainly not confined to, the infamous Basin Street."

He sighed and put down the pen, realizing he was letting his writing get excited. He would have to go back and strike adjectives. Father Mouton, who had taught him composition, had warned him about modifiers. "Tell it with verbs," he would say, often stressing the idea by a thoughtful whack of a ruler on the student's upturned palm.

But, meanwhile: "To add up this profiteering would produce a dollar figure too vast for comprehension," he scribbled. "But to balance that total by the number of ruined lives, disease-eaten bodies, corpses in the river, parents searching in vain for lost daughters, to lay that heavy burden upon the opposite scale is to tip all into the gruesome meat grinder New Orleans has become, squeezing out of the bodies of young women a profit too filthy to conceive, too shameful to ignore.

"The time has come," he wrote, "for just such a grim reckoning. And it is my purpose to put all down on paper, names, places, dates, amounts, as well as I can determine and verify them. Here begins this accounting."

He pushed away from the table, got up, and paced the paper-littered floor of the *Almanac* office. Who would print this for him? *Harper's*, perhaps? Pulitzer's *World*? Hearst's *Journal*?

He glanced at the wall clock and saw that it was just past noon. He was due at the great housewarming around sundown, although Kate had asked him to come early. Any other time . . . But with luck he had six hours of solid writing time before he had to join the merrymakers, some of whose names would be prominently featured in what he was about to write.

"You have a knack for fatherhood," Kate told her husband. She had carried a tray out to the patio, to find Edmund sitting back in his chair reading a newspaper, with small Edmund face down on his lap, fast asleep.

Her husband nodded. "He sleeps through everything."

"Here," Kate said, placing sandwiches and lemonade on a bench. She poured Edmund a glass.

He sipped. "I had hoped to share my son's lunch," he said, eyeing her. "He seems to enjoy that beverage far more than lemonade."

Kate felt her cheeks heat up. "That beverage, dear Edmund, in your case must be reserved for dessert."

"What? Like ice cream?"

"Hardly iced." She looked flustered. It had been a long time since he'd made these kinds of jokes with her. She took the glass from his hand and gave him a ham sandwich in a napkin.

"But afterward, dessert?"

"The supply is not unlimited."

"And this imp gets it all." Edmund folded his newspaper over the baby so that only his head was showing. He took a bite of his sandwich.

Nervously Kate sipped his lemonade. "Is this," she began tentatively, "a bad time to talk about the telegram?"

"Is there a good time? The Chicago bankers have me, Kate. If I had been able to get the crude flowing . . . But that's ancient history."

"And if you could get it flowing?"

"If pigs had wings . . ." He continued eating his sandwich.

"It might not take as long as you think," she suggested.

"If I had the cash, yes."

"As a matter of fact . . ." She stopped.

"Yes?"

Surely, she thought, she had to be mad to broach this on the day of the housewarming. But the arrival of the telegram had upset her.

"As a matter of fact . . ." She stopped again.

"Kate, I have the most ominous feeling." His wide-set eyes moved back and forth, scanning her face.

"As a matter of fact, Rynders has been digging in new storage tanks at Great Southern Number One," the words tumbled out. "He has two already in place, and two more within a week. The derricks are up, and the—"

"What?"

She watched him start to his feet, then remember the child in his lap. He sat back, glaring at her. For the first time in quite a while, his eyes looked fierce. "Using what for money?"

"Mine."

In the abrupt silence, a mockingbird at the bottom of the garden began to sing a long, cheery trill.

"I was not aware you had your own money."

He sounded absolutely cold with fury. Kate moistened her lips. "It was a gift. To me. From Da."

"I . . . will . . . be . . . damned!" He lifted the boy off his lap and laid him face down on the grass like a log of wood. Striding back and forth across the flags, Edmund glared first at his wife, then the house, his son, and the noisy mockingbird.

"That meddling, sly, nasty old man," he sputtered. "Getting at me though my wife? More *his* daughter than *my* wife, wouldn't you say? Damn me, Kate, there *is* a matter of loyalty."

"Financing you rejected. This is a gift, Edmund. From a wife to a husband."

The bird stopped in mid-trill and began a series of clucking sounds. Small Edmund lifted his head and stared at the live-oak tree. He started crawling toward the mockingbird, which changed its song into a shrill, rattling whistle.

"A gift," Edmund repeated.

"A loving gift."

She let her son crawl halfway across the lawn and then went to pick him up. When she returned, Edmund had sat down again in the chair. He was sipping lemonade. "Kate," he said at last, "I don't understand you. I do not."

"It needed doing." She planted the baby in her lap. "I had hoped you would accept it in the spirit I gave it. Oh, I knew you would hate it. But I thought perhaps this would be more important than pride. Because there are much bigger things in the world, Edmund, than a man's pride."

He laughed unhappily and waved his hand at her in a silencing gesture. "We're back to that 'American' idea again, is that it? The marriage as a kind of partnership?"

"Which it is."

He exhaled violently. "To think I once admired you for your spunk. How little I guessed what it might lead to." He thought for a moment. "I'm overlooking for the time being that Rynders kept this secret from me. When did he say the crude would start flowing?"

"He's said nothing."

"And how much has this cost you?"

"A gift, Edmund. No price tag."

He banged his palms on his thighs with such force that his son blinked at the noise. "How often have you heard me say it, Kate? I must do things my own way."

"It's your drill site. It's your land. It's your company. Nothing is being done except your way."

"God, Kate, what the law lost when you decided to become a wife and mother." He stared at her, a look half-helpless and half-angry on his face. "What am I to do with you?"

"This once, Edmund, accept your wife's gift. It came from her heart."

"Rynders will give me an accounting of every penny."

"Edmund . . ."

"And you shall get every penny back."

"Please . . ."

He fell silent. Kate suddenly realized that in his own Edmund way, he had accepted the gift. For some reason, this gave her no joy.

Hennessy and Patrick Blood watched the horse-drawn ambulance leave with the bodies of the four murdered Provenzano men. The chief of police glanced down at the pavement outside the smoky warehouse and touched a blot of red the size of a silver dollar with the tip of his boot.

"It's still dripping out of 'em," he muttered. "The thing was done around sunup, wouldn't you say?"

Patrick shifted from one foot to the other. "Looks like."

His chief made a face. "As if we needed clues. The thing has Matranga's name all over it. Look, get back to headquarters as fast as you can and bring in a few of the men." He eyed Patrick closely. "The right men. Tiffany and Mulcay and Herbst and Balducci and Jimmy Mougin. Nobody else."

Hennessy had just reeled off the slim list of detectives who could be trusted. Patrick felt a surge of joy at being included. "I'll do that right now."

"I want them in my office at one o'clock, ready to do what I promised that Sicilian butcher I would do if he broke the peace."

"It's broken, all right."

"Get going."

The skeletonlike old man was seated in a rocking chair. Olivia and her mother and Dr. Amabile stood in a semicircle around him. "But your left arm . . ." the doctor began.

Crozat frowned with effort and slowly lifted it from his lap to his chest. He patted himself. *"Voilà."*

"A miracle."

Olivia watched the two old men congratulating each other. Not quite a miracle, she thought. Her father's words were slurred, and produced with great effort. He had yet to say more than a few syllables at a time. Gone were the great rolling periods of abuse and moralizing. Perhaps his mind would never again be able to send forth those rumbling trainloads of advice that had such power to hurt.

"We are tiring him," she said then.

Her mother carefully helped him to his feet. "You are hungry, perhaps?"

"Very."

Olivia turned away in sorrow. He couldn't—yet?—pronounce the *v.* He had said "bery."

As soon as her mother had settled him on the bed, he stood up again. *"Jamais."*

"Never the bed?" Amabile interpreted. "I can understand your feelings, old friend. Perhaps a—"

"A cane," Crozat interrupted.

"Ye-e-es," the doctor agreed uncertainly. He turned to Madame Crozat. "I have one of the traveling chairs. On wheels. I will have it delivered here."

"D'accord," the skinny old man agreed.

"He will soon be moving about like an army recruit," Amabile promised them. "There will be no stopping him."

55

At two o'clock Kate and small Edmund were closeted alone in the nursery, the only time on this particular day that either of them would be fully at rest. Downstairs the house had begun to hum at an increasing pace.

Edmund and Henry had been choosing beverages from the new cellar, fully stocked as Neil Blood's housewarming present with whiskey and other spirits, as well as some of his own supply of wine. In her preparation of food, Henry's wife, Belle, had the assistance of her mother-in-law, Julia, as well as the crew from the Wicklowe building a broad pit of glowing charcoal in the garden.

The only island of peace was the nursery. Down the street Kate could hear carriage wheels and hooves. A moment later the noise stopped in front of her house and escalated into bedlam. Her three nieces had arrived with their mother, Alderman Hinckley's proud wife, the former Mary Blood.

It seemed only a second or two later that the girls who walked (or, more normally, ran) had pounded up the stairs and into the nursery, followed by their mother, carrying her third daughter in her arms. "Still nursing?" Mary inquired.

Kate fended off small fingers plunged at Edmund's eyes. "And good afternoon to you, too, dear sister."

"They do say boys are backward a bit at this age . . . compared"— Mary seemed to preen herself slightly—"to girls, that is."

"Not entirely," Kate recalled. "You were terribly backward as a baby."

Mary's mouth closed down to a thin line. She sat on a chaise longue and put her youngest on the floor to crawl. Her two older girls were trying to snatch knit booties from their cousin Edmund's feet. They had managed to distract him from his feeding. Noting this, Kate tucked her breast back in its halter and buttoned over her frilly white blouse.

"I'm here to help," Mary announced. "It's always a busy day for me with this brood"—she somehow managed to repeat the preening gesture without so much as moving her hands—"but what good is a sister if she can't rally around in times of distress?"

"This is not such a time," Kate responded with total calm. "There are no cries of distress. All is under control."

"I mean," Mary continued, that grievance-seeking look appearing in her eyes, "what good is all my experience as a hostess if I can't help you get through your first social engagement?"

Batting away her nieces' clutching fingers, Kate set her son's face forward on her lap so that he could fend them off with his own hands and feet. "How is Abner?" she asked, hoping to distract Mary from her self-appointed role as social savior.

"Busy, busy, busy. This Story movement has him working night and day."

"The idea to herd all the girls into one district?" Kate sat back and watched Edmund defend himself rather expertly against darting fingers. He seemed to enjoy the encounter. "It'd be a blessing to Da, I think."

Mary frowned. "I don't think it's proper discussing such a topic in front of children."

"Nor would I if you hadn't brought it up."

"You were the one asked what Abner was up to."

"But I had no idea he spent all his time on the girls of Basin Street."

Mary's gasp closed the interchange and produced a long healing moment of silence. "There is one thing you can help with," Kate said. "Martoche delivers the flowers in a while. Belle will show you vases and such. You can make the floral arrangements."

Mary nodded and got to her feet. She seemed about to leave the nursery and, with it, her three daughters. "Go with Mum, girls," Kate urged her nieces. "Mum has pretty flowers to play with. Go on, now."

She shooed all but the crawling niece from the room. Thoughtfully she surveyed the remaining girl, who seemed docile enough, sitting on the floor and pushing one of Edmund's toys, a small wooden dog on red wheels. "You look harmless enough," she told the girl. "Are you Brigid?" The girl looked up at the name. "Play nicely with Edmund, now."

Kate went to the window overlooking the garden. The day was fair and warm, but not hot. Tiny puffs of clouds relieved the strong blue of the sky. At the bottom of the garden, instead of arranging flowers, Mary was telling the Wicklowe crew how to barbecue.

Kate turned back in time to see Brigid bring the wooden dog down on Edmund's head. The boy shifted sideways so quickly Kate's eyes couldn't follow the movement. The dog smashed harmlessly onto the floor. Apparently Edmund could do all right on his own.

Downstairs his father and Henry arranged bottles on a long refectory table set up in the breezeway. Crystal goblets and wineglasses glittered along the linen runner. Mary came in from the garden, two girls in tow. "Dear me," she said, "another tribute to the demon rum, is it?"

Edmund turned to her as Kate came down the stairs carrying both his son and Brigid. "Too early to offer you a drink, Mary?" he asked in a falsely bright manner.

"I haven't touched a drop since . . ." Mary stopped. Edmund had the ability to make her feel ill-at-ease, Kate knew. "You're joshing me again," Mary finished lamely.

"With so many fine children," Edmund persisted, "no mother could be blamed for a bit of a tipple now and then."

Pride surfaced through the confusion on Mary's face. "I don't find anything so debilitating in raising three girls that I have need of false stimulants." Her narrow glance swept sideways to her sister. "Boys are what give the trouble."

Edmund relieved Kate of her son. "This boy is trouble," he stated firmly. "This boy," he added, "takes after his mother." His eyes shifted to Kate. "Between the two of them, life has become quite diverting." His mouth twitched into an off-center smile.

Poised on the bottom stair, Kate watched him closely. "Diverting," she echoed. "How is one to take that?"

The smile broadened to a grin. "As a compliment," her husband told her. "Life would be quite dull without the two of you."

". . . $200,000 loan tendered by Senator Gravier's bank to the consortium headed by Judge Davenant and Colonel Page against a $50,000 cash deposit in Gravier's coffers. Such collateral," Ned Blood wrote, "is quite legitimate. The cash, unfortunately, had no such provenance. It represented the 'take' of one month's degradation of prostitutes in two houses owned by the consortium: the Climax on Franklin Street near St.

Louis Cemetery Number One, and Miss Harriet's on Rampart beside Congo Square."

He let the pen drop to his desk, sat back in the creaky chair the *Almanac* provided for him, and glanced around the long, narrow office. His eyes hurt. Very little light came in from either end of the place. His fingers hurt, too, but at least he had twenty pages of writing to show for the pain.

Facts. Names. Places. Amounts. For an investment of fifty thousand in cash, earned by the girls, their masters had financed control of about three hundred acres of right-of-way, to be sold eventually to the Illinois Central for nearly half a million dollars. The whole transaction had taken less than a year to produce a ten-times profit on the original cash.

"Thought I'd find you here."

Ned looked up. Mike Leathers stood in the doorway grinning at him. "Is it no rest for the weary or the wicked?"

"Take a look," Ned suggested. "I have finally started the magnum opus."

"The what?" Mike leafed slowly through the journal. "I understand," he said at last. "Well." He sat down opposite Ned and immediately put his feet up on the desk.

"New?" Ned indicated the dark leather boots.

"You are looking at a man of means, my boy," Mike said. "The Yankee dollar has begun to flood over me."

"Anything interesting?"

Mide nodded and hooked one arm on the chair back. "Not for you. For your brother-in-law."

"I'm seeing him . . ." Ned glanced at his watch. "Dear God. In an hour. The day has gone fast. What can I tell him?"

Mike hesitated. "It's a tad delicate for a man of honor like me. Knowing how much love I have for Edmund Crozat, you wouldn't blame me for saying nothing, now, would you?"

"Knowing how you love even more the Yankee oil interests," Ned countered, "I'd say your course is clear. Give."

"It's a death sentence." Leathers grinned happily. "My employers are a group called Equity Petroleum. They have Crozat in so tight a bind he'll choke by the end of the week."

"You came all the way downriver to tell me that?" Ned gave him a curious look. "Or is there more?"

"Just the how of it."

"I doubt a hanging man cares about the brand of rope."

Mike stirred restlessly. "You're a cool one."

"My mind's on other things."

Mike lifted the manuscript. "I did pick up a few bits about that shipping contract Congressman Flornoy wangled. He is an enterprising scoundrel."

Ned looked over his friend. "New suit, new boots," he commented. "New shirt and hat. Treachery agrees with you."

Mike brought his boots down to the floor with a double bang. "Unfair, Ned."

"You left town lean and hungry. You pop back swelled up like a frog, so full of yourself you don't even ask if I've located Luanne for you or how she is or what she's doing. You're so fat with scandal you drip." Ned took back his journal. "Far be it for me to turn my back on scandal. It's my bread and butter. But there's a question of style. One doesn't . . . gloat."

"Give me time," Mike said at last. "When I've had your years of experience with slime, I'll be as sleek and sassy as you."

"Touché," said Ned. "And what the hell are we two dueling for?"

"It's the work," Mike told him. "What do you hear of Luanne?"

Ned turned away. "Not a thing."

A week ago he had found Luanne in the charity ward of the Hôtel Dieu, incoherent although her wounds were healing. The sight of her pitiful body was what had spurred Ned to begin his exposé. There was no time to lose when people like Carolina Duffy could get away with murder.

They'd trussed Luanne, bloody and unconscious, in a burlap sack and dumped her into the Mississippi off Gretna. Without her hair she would be unidentifiable when found. An Italian drayman, fishing on his day off, had accidentally hooked the sack and rushed the dying girl to the hospital. To tell Mike all this now and send him to the bloated, bald creature at the Hôtel Dieu, was no favor. Such news would wait until Luanne rejoined the human race.

Ned tidied up his notes for a moment. "It's the work, all right. We both spend too much time with the great corrupters of the earth."

The lanky man nodded somberly. "It's a contradiction, an honest man making his living among thieves. And where you have a contradiction, a man can get pulled apart."

"Am I looking at such a man?" Ned demanded.

"Get off me, Ned," Mike growled. "I came down here to do a good turn."

"All right. I'll tell Ed . . . ." He stopped. "Better yet, tell him yourself. I'm due at a big housewarming. Nobody said I couldn't bring a guest."

"No, thanks."

"What're you afraid of? Edmund doesn't bite anymore."

"Tame as a house cat?" Mike murmured. "No, thanks."

"It'll be a big shindig. You'll enjoy it."

"That's my point," Mike Leathers confided in him. "I'm getting to enjoy it too much. Sitting at the table of the high and mighty is ruinous to a man's backbone."

"Nevertheless . . ."

Dr. Theobald stared across the bloody bed at the tiny face of Madame Fleurigant. No, she had not yet seen, he told himself. Absorbed in her work, she had patted the baby dry, spanked him into a long, mournful wail, and then tied off the cord.

"*Eh, bien,*" she said at last, closely bundling the baby in a small cotton blanket and placing him against Ynes' breast. "*Voilà, bèbè. Un grand garçon, très brave, très charmant. L'image de . . .*" She stopped.

The ancient doctor reached across the bed and picked up the infant. "*Madame, je regrette . . .*"

"Ynes!"

"*Courage, madame.*"

"Ynes!" she screamed.

In Dr. Theobald's arms, the newborn baby opened his mouth and wailed. Choking in a gigantic breath of air, he wailed again. And again.

Darkness filled the eastern sky. Overhead, the bright blue had turned to mauve. Only in the west did the day still glow orange as the sun began to sink below the horizon. Waiters borrowed from the Wicklowe moved swiftly through the garden and patio, lighting lanterns and citronella candles.

Near the barbecue pit four black musicians arranged their plain pine chairs in a half-circle. The players adjusted their instruments with small, finicky movements, one twisting the ebony tubes of his clarinet into a tighter fit, wetting and reclamping his reed, the other fingering the ivory-tipped valves of his silver cornet, blowing into the mouthpiece. The drummer had arranged his bass drum between his knees and set his snare in a small tripodlike stand. Only the sousaphone player sat immobile, eyes closed, the coils of his instrument surrounding him like a silver python that had dined too well to move.

In the breezeway, Henry stood over an oak tub and carefully chopped a hundred-pound cake of ice into shards. Some he placed in the punch bowl, nearly brimming with straw-colored liquid in which orange slices and bits of strawberries floated.

Across the hall, his wife, Belle, turned the handle of the ice-cream churn with a slow, deliberate motion. After a while she got more ice from the oak tub and resumed her churning.

Upstairs Kate and Edmund eyed each other for an instant from opposite sides of their bedroom. They stood in their underclothes at the doorway to their respective dressing rooms, Edmund holding the trousers to an ivory-white suit, Kate the glossy flow of her best green dress.

"So I'm diverting to you," she said in an undertone.

"Very."

"And without me life would be dull."

"Dreary."

"And that's the sum total of it."

He frowned at her. "Do not confuse what I say to that idiot sister of yours with how I really feel."

She put down the dress and padded over to him in her white-stockinged feet. "Only diverting?" she teased.

He made a more-or-less gesture with his hand. In the half-dark his eyes looked black. "Lately, diversion has been very welcome. Also surprise gifts."

She smiled up at him. "You accept?"

"With surly ill grace, yes."

She laughed and kissed his mouth. "Edmund, you're a great gambler, are you not? You gamble with your empire of oil. And with your wife's affection."

"But do I win?" he asked.

He took her in his arms and kissed her more thoroughly now. Kate pressed against him, feeling his ribs and the hard muscles across his belly. He had not held her like this in a long time. When they kissed, it suddenly had the old taut give and take, sharp, probing, urgent.

"Oh," she said, her voice husky, "with me, you cannot lose. I'm a fool to confess it, but you already know."

His hands were stroking her hips and flanks. "You're something of a gambler yourself," he said. "You knew I'd be angry over the business up at the drill site. But you took the chance."

"It seemed to me I had to."

His eyes flared with light. "Motherhood has made you even more daring." His hands covered her buttocks, and she felt herself being moved backward until the edge of the bed pressed against the back of her knees.

"Edmund. Guests will arrive at any moment."

In the kitchen, to the rear of the first floor below them, Julia opened oven doors, peered inside, shut them quickly to keep the kitchen cool. From time to time she left to supervise the children playing on the patio flagstones. The three Hinckley girls had cornered their baby cousin, who seemed pleased at all the attention. Under his aunt's eyes, he sparred with the girls, laughing and swinging his arms.

"A regular John L. Sullivan," his grandfather announced, striding out onto the patio from the breezeway. The tall blond man stooped to kiss his daughter Mary, then picked up each granddaughter for a quick peck before lifting his grandson over his head. "Look at them muscles," he crowed.

Behind him, stepping into the torchlit twilight, Alexander Badger smiled benignly at everyone and patted his little potbelly. "What a beautiful garden." He sniffed the air. "Is that a shoat they're barbecuing?"

In the doorway, Father James Aloysius Blood appeared in his black suit and reversed collar. "Good evening to all." He turned to see his sister-in-law behind him. "Nelly, where's Patrick? You came alone?"

"That I did. He'll be here soon's Hennessy lets him."

The priest glanced about him with the same complaint-gathering look of his sister Mary. "Don't tell me it's to be Bloods and only Bloods?"

" 'Family first' is no bad motto," his father told him. "And where's your ma?" he demanded of small Edmund, now perched on his shoulder and hanging on his thick neck with both arms.

All the Bloods looked upward at the inner limestone facade of the house to the second floor where the master bedroom lay. Pale white curtains fluttered out through the open windows.

"Dressing, I expect," Neil Blood said at last.

He placed his grandson in Badger's arms and left abruptly, moving back through the breezeway to the outer door. He peered outside. At the corner of Livaudais and Washington, two young bruisers in tight jackets and derby hats stood under a streetlamp. Blood jerked his thumb toward the river. Both men nodded and moved off. Blood looked the other way, where two more men stood in the distance. He made a spreading-out gesture to them, and they parted company to take up separate posts along the street.

A cab drew up to the curb, and his son Ned got out, followed by Mike Leathers. "Father."

"Evening, Ned." Neil stared coldly at Mike. "You never was too choosy about the company you keep," he told his son.

"Family failing," Ned responded.

Mike's sweeping glance took in the guards posted here and there along the street. "Expecting trouble?"

"Other than you?" Neil asked.

"Ease off, Da," Ned countered. "Mike came down to do a favor. That's why I invited him to the festivities."

"You inv . . ." Blood stopped in mid-word and his face went stony. "Very well," he said at last in a faintly strangled voice. "It's not my house or my party. If somebody kicks him the hell out, it won't be said he wasn't warned."

"Charming," Ned said. "Gracious. Come on, Mike."

His father watched the two young men enter the house. Through the open door he could see them pause at the punch bowl set up in the breezeway, then settle for straight whiskey poured by Henry. Neil Blood checked the position of his guards once again and returned inside the house.

He brought cups of punch to his daughter Mary and his daughter-in-law, Nelly. "Where's Paddy?" he asked her. "Still gumshoeing around?"

"Does he tell me annytin', Father Blood?" Nelly asked in a brogue far thicker than Neil's. "But sometin's stirrin', of that there is no doubt."

From the garden came the sound of music. The small band was playing a waltz in the French style, thick with clarinet arabesques and the almost military three-quarters beat of the snares. Neil Blood heard footsteps on the inner stairway. He looked up to see Kate, her red-blond hair flowing down to the pale green of her gown, descending the stairs on the arm of her husband in his ivory suit and vest. Edmund had tucked something green in his lapel, a sprig of boxtree leaves. They were laughing as they came down the long, curving stairway.

"Good luck to the new home," Neil Blood announced in a big, penetrating voice.

Everyone turned to him, and seeing Kate and Edmund on the steps, produced a series of echoes reinforcing Neil's toast. Glasses were lifted and touched. The ring of Waterford crystal reverberated through the breezeway and out into the patio. Two Hinckley girls began chasing each other between people's legs, shrieking with delight. The party had begun.

56

By seven, night had blanketed the garden. To Kate the torches gave the scene a faintly piratical look, as if these people—there were nearly sixty guests by now—in their colorful finery were disporting themselves aboard a ship. At the far end of the garden the barbecue pit smoked and the yearling shoat turned slowly over glowing coals, fat sizzling as it dripped, sending up puffs of aromatic smoke. Elsewhere the night lay thick around them, but in this long-shaped space, bounded by lanterns, guests looked like a riotous crew of buccaneers. In the distance, Kate heard the ambulance bell clanging. But here all were safe from the city and the night. Nothing would have the temerity to spoil this house-warming.

She watched Edmund and she watched her father. They seemed to circulate without once encountering each other. She did not pretend to understand how Edmund felt toward her father, but she knew that Cornelius Blood's only interest in Edmund was to make sure he did right by her and the boy. "No love lost" was the apt phrase, she thought.

Edmund was talking animatedly to Ned, and then, with sudden reserve, to the tall dark-haired man who came up to them. She could not remember ever seeing him before, but apparently he and Edmund were acquainted. Then, abruptly, they broke off talking and disappeared up the staircase to the second floor. A moment later she saw the light go on in Edmund's study.

At that moment she caught sight of her father staring up at the light.

334

He looked grim as he moved ponderously through the crowd and mounted the stairs.

"Quite true, dear lady," Alexander Badger was telling the wife of a senator. "I am reliably informed that she has lost each and every lock of her hair. What one sees at the opera as she sits in her box is sheer artifice."

". . . thirteen percent on the principal," a planter was complaining to a Cajun politician from the delta country, "and no more slack in the bank's line than a barge rope pulling upstream."

Kate knew that the true Creole contingent of guests would arrive late, as was their custom, but she had expected Olivia to appear long before this. And her brother Patrick, too.

". . . death of the whole sugar market," a state legislator was telling the Spanish consul, resplendent in a suit paler even than Edmund's. "Nosiree, I see no great need to liberate the Cubans."

". . . another waltz," Badger murmured in Kate's ear. "Dare I ask my goodly hostess for the honor?"

"Perhaps later," she said, "when the rest of the guests have arrived."

In Edmund's study, all three young men stood around the desk eyeing each other. Mike Leathers had just finished speaking and was rocking back and forth on his heels. He seemed to be enjoying the encounter.

Ned was the first to break the silence. "Who the hell is Equity Petroleum?"

Edmund gestured impatiently. "With that kind of money to spend," he said in a low, urgent voice, "they can only be a kind of corporate front for the Rockefeller interests. No other would have the capacity to exploit so much land." His eyes flashed angrily. "But two can play that game."

"You don't have many chips left," Ned told him.

"The game of camouflage," his brother-in-law snapped. "The note on the Chicago bank is signed by me and no other." He took a long breath. "I signed as an individual. Nowhere is there mention of Great Southern, nor of my status as an officer or chief shareholder. Do you follow me?"

"Nope."

"You're a lawyer," Edmund said, addressing Mike Leathers. "You understand the position?"

"Only too well," Mike drawled. "There is no way you can hide behind Great Southern. Them Yankees got you by your own tail, personal."

Edmund gave him a disdainful look. "You miss the point. Or rather, you don't follow it far enough. It makes no difference to me if the bankers try to get their money out of my hide. As long as they cannot touch Great Southern."

"But you *are* Gr—"

"Not after tonight," Edmund cut in brusquely. "Here. Sit down. Draft a gift deed. You know the form?"

Frowning, Mike Leathers sat at the desk. "But I sure as hell don't understand the content."

"I intend to make a gift of Great Southern, right now, tonight."

The study door opened so quietly that none of them saw it. Neil Blood's big body filled the doorway. "To whom?" Ned asked.

"To my son, in trust. With my wife as trustee."

Leathers stared up at him. "That's crazy."

"It's been done before," Edmund retorted.

"You mean . . ." Mike paused a moment. "When the banks go after Great Southern property on a foreclosure, it'll be off limits? They'll have to get it from you?"

"They can try," Edmund assured him. His face was suddenly split by a lopsided grin of pure malice. "Perhaps in the bankruptcy courts. The law gives me a dozen ways to evade them once the tie between me and Great Southern's property is severed."

"Then who," Neil Blood asked in a suddenly powerful voice, "is gonna run Great Southern?"

Edmund's grin disappeared. He turned slowly toward his father-in-law. "How many others are eavesdropping with you, sir?" he demanded.

"Don't mount that high Creole horse with me, son." Neil Blood stepped forward and clapped Edmund on both arms. "You have got an A-number-one brain. I always stood in awe of the Crozat way with business deals. Only, I never saw no signs it'd rubbed off on you. Now I see I was wrong. But I don't want Great Southern losing your valuable services, if you get my meaning."

Edmund's face had become a noncommittal mask. He looked neither angry now, nor interested, for that matter. When he spoke, it was with the cool politeness of a host with a casual guest. "Something can be arranged. In the East now there is a new class of entrepreneur, the professional manager. Great Southern can hire me at a salary, perhaps."

The Shadow Mayor of New Orleans focused an intimidating glare at Mike Leathers. "Okay, lawyer, start scribbling."

"Fine with me," Mike said in a huffy voice. "But how long d'y'think this dodge will work? In a few months they'll be circling around Great Southern all over again like a pack of wolves, but with some new way of gobbling it up."

"That's where you're wrong," Neil Blood said. "Because once ownership changes, I have a notion Great Southern's financial policy'll change, too." He stared at his son-in-law. "Am I right? Would the new ownership look down its nose at new money? I have been standing in the wings till the spots're damned near worn off the greenbacks. But there's plenty there, and they're ready to go."

Edmund smiled coldly. "You have the patience of a spider, sir. You are well aware that my position has been changed for me, behind my back. New money has already been accepted."

"Chickenfeed. I'm talking about an army of iron men, enough simoleons to buy you all the storage tanks and derricks and drills and pipelines and barges and—"

"I had no idea you were an oil man, Da," Ned interjected.

"I have never claimed to be anything but a money man," his father told him. "People think of me any way they have a mind to, whoremaster, tavernkeeper, fixer, bagman, the names don't mean a thing. No more than you could say, yes, he's an oil man, a railroader, a shipper, a real-estate fella, a broker, the names all come down to one thing . . . money. That's me."

"And power."

"Two sides of the same coin, Neddie."

Edmund laughed softly, once, and turned to Mike Leathers. He dipped a pen in ink and handed it to him. "Begin," he said.

By ten o'clock there were a hundred people, but no sign as yet of Olivia or Patrick. The band had been playing little two-steps, along with muzurkas and polkas. Most of the women had contented themselves with cups of punch, Kate saw, while the men had stuck closely to whiskey and rum. The noise level had risen accordingly.

The four children had been put to bed in the nursery, with Julia to watch over them, but Kate had no illusion that they might actually be asleep. In the garden, the shoat had melted away quickly, along with the red snapper and the guinea hens. There remained only the back ribs, glistening red with sauce as they sizzled on the barbecue.

Her husband, her father, Ned, and the other man had yet to return to the party. From time to time she could see one of them pace past the upstairs window. Ned had descended once, to find one of the judges and bring him up. Another time the tall dark man with the country look had come down and brought Alexander Badger back to the secret conclave.

A second hundred-pound cake of ice had been chopped up. The ice cream was ready, but held in reserve. Julia's seafood casserole had all been eaten, along with her biscuits and rolls. The punch bowl had been replenished five times. Everyone called the party a roaring success.

It was too bad none of the men upstairs were bothering to enjoy it. Whatever was happening—and Kate could only hazard a guess—her presence was not needed. Nor was it needed anymore at the party. The thing had its own life now. Kate could have deserted it long ago, and no one would have noticed. Neither her husband, nor her son, nor her father. Her work was done. She felt superfluous, a feeling she had experienced only once before, when her father had given her job to Billy O'Hare.

The band had stopped playing for a few minutes. The musicians clustered in a discreet circle around a small keg of beer nestled in chunks of ice. The sousaphone player, in his grave deliberate way, worked the wooden tap, filling each of their glasses and neatly blowing off the foam. In the sudden silence, people's voices grew quieter, as if they had been shouting indiscretions while the band music covered their voices, and now had to murmur softly.

". . . Knights of Labor'll never show their heads in this parish again, believe you me," a congressman was telling a navy commander in civilian clothes.

". . . can't hold a candle to you, missy," a man muttered hoarsely in a woman's ear. "You are so light and so soft and so sweet and so . . ."

From the direction of the breezeway there was an abrupt silence. Kate stood on tiptoes to see over the heads of her guests. What was happening? Who had arrived?

Olivia, on Jed Benjamin's arm, moved slowly out onto the flagstones. Behind her came her mother, Ana Almonaster-Nunes Crozat, walking slowly beside a . . . a wheelchair pushed by Henry.

People around Kate gasped. Huddled in the wicker chair as it rolled forward was a skeleton of a man, his hair too long, his eyes almost hidden in their deep sockets, his bony fingers clutching the arms of the chair, his mouth set in a rictus of social amiability, all teeth, like a mask of death, but lively, terribly lively.

Kate tried to push through the throng of onlookers, but the rush to surround this apparition was too great. She could see someone at the study window upstairs, a flash of a head; then the curtains fell back in place. Struggling now, Kate advanced slowly through the crowd until she was standing next to Olivia on the flagstone patio.

"Is he . . . ? Can he . . . ?"

Olivia turned away to murmur directly in her friend's ear, "He has the use of his body but not yet his mind."

In the rising tumult, the two young women looked at each other. Jed

Benjamin managed to clear a space in front of the rolling wicker chair. "M'sieur Crozat," he said, "may I present your hostess?"

Feebly Jean-Paul Crozat raised a skinny hand to take the one Kate proffered. He raised it to those papery lips, and Kate felt a faint brushing sensation. "*Enchanté, mamselle*," the old man said in a voice as dry as his lips.

"It is '*madame*,' Papa," Edmund said, appearing to one side of the chair. "This is my bride, Katharine."

"Ah, *oui*," his father agreed amiably, yellow teeth glistening, skull-like head bobbing up and down. "*Très belle*."

Across the space between them, Edmund looked at his wife for a long moment. "*Attendez, Papa*. I will bring you your grandson."

"*Bon*."

Ana Crozat moved in beside her daughter-in-law. "He remembers so little," she said in a soft voice. "He really has only a vague idea who any of us are, except that we take care of him. It is no miracle," she breathed in Kate's ear. "But it is certainly a blessing."

In the distance, the band swung into another of the fast two-step marches, looser now, closer to the kind of music the musicians normally played. They had been on good behavior long enough tonight.

Cornelius Blood, standing in the background and watching as his grandson was presented to the other grandfather, made a peculiar face, almost of pain. Out of the corner of her eye Kate caught the involuntary grimace and then saw her father pull out a bright red bandanna and blow his nose. The Shadow Mayor of New Orleans was enjoying a quiet cry.

Then something caught his attention beyond the border of light. Kate turned to see what had attracted his eye, but there was nothing there, and when she turned back, her father was gone.

Subtly the band was loosening its music still further, syncopating the melody line, moving farther from the original tune. If any of the guests had been paying close attention instead of crowding around the man in the wheelchair, they would have recognized jazz, by no means a novelty anymore, but rarely to be heard at galas of this stature.

57

At eleven o'clock Patrick Blood finally left police headquarters. Although he knew he was late for the party, he could find no cab. Walking along Tchoupitoulas in the direction of the Garden District, he thought at one point that he could see ahead of him the squat, powerful figure of his chief, who had left headquarters only a few minutes before Patrick for his own home in the District.

It had been a heavy, frustrating day. Among them the handful of trustworthy detectives had managed to pull in six Matranga uglies for sharp questioning before a spy in the police force got word to the Matranga laywers, who swarmed in with demands for instant immediate bail.

No sooner had the first contingent been released than the detectives had rounded up a second bunch, and on their release, a third. Chief Hennessy estimated the legal fees alone would put a deep crimp in Tony Matranga's budget.

Finally, an hour ago, Hennessy had sickened of the whole idea. "We're making the bail bondsmen and shysters rich," he complained. "Let's lock up for the night, and tomorrow we'll see if . . ." He broke off, aware he was operating among informers.

Later, in his office, with the door closed, the chief worked out with Patrick and three other men his plans for arresting Matranga and his brother tomorrow and questioning them at a substation in the north end of town for as long as they could.

Patrick tried to relax as he plodded along Tchoupitoulas. He had been tense all day, and an experienced copper had to learn how to save himself a bit in moments of high pressure. Otherwise he'd never make the long run, would he?

Shots.

Patrick sprinted forward. In the distance he saw men running.

More shots.

On the pavement ahead, a man lay holding his stomach. "Paddy!" groaned Chief Hennessy.

Patrick knelt down. Thin streams of blood pulsed up between Hennessy's fingers as they clutched at his belly. "Dear God!" Patrick gasped. A man was running toward him. "You there!" Patrick shouted. "Call an ambulance!"

Windows were slamming open along the street. "It's Chief Hennessy!" Patrick called. "Get an ambulance."

He pulled off his jacket, rolled it up, and shoved it under Hennessy's head. "Help's coming," he muttered. "Chief, who done it?"

The older man groaned softly in pain. "Who done it, chief?"

" 'Twas the dagos done it, Paddy."

"How many?"

"A whole slew of 'em. A dozen or . . ." Hennessy choked, coughed, stopped talking. A moment later he stopped breathing. Paddy felt for a pulse, but the heart had stopped beating.

In the distance an ambulance bell clanged. Patrick glanced around him; only a few people had come out of their houses, and of them, only a handful had come closer to him than a few yards. They were afraid. The men who had gunned down Chief Hennessy might be waiting to remove witnesses as well.

The ambulance bell grew louder.

Off the Crozats' kitchen a butler's pantry led to a side door meant for the servants. In the darkness of this hidden vestibule, the two figures contrasted ludicrously, the big heavyset blond man and the tiny birdlike woman.

"*Hungan,*" the woman said, "I had no choice."

Neil Blood nodded ponderously. "No choice," Madame Fleurigant repeated.

She unwrapped the coverlet so that a faint light from the window shone on the baby's tiny face. In the distance, the band was playing a joyous song called "Muskrat Ramble." The clarinet swept upward through the warm night in a series of joyous whoops.

Neil Blood stared down at the little face, with its wide-set eyes and small, careful mouth. The newborn boy's skin was pure white, but he knew that might change in the months ahead. What would never change was the Crozat look of his face.

"What can anyone do?" asked Blood.

"He must be fed, *hungan*. I must find a wet nurse, or he dies."

"Better that way."

"*Non, jamais!*"

Neil Blood covered the baby and returned him to his grandmother. "I know what you're feeling, *mama-loi*. I lost my own dear wife in childbirth. It's the worst of what God has in his bag of tricks, to take away someone you love and leave behind a stranger."

"A stranger who also will die, *hungan*."

"There is nothing I can do."

Madame Fleurigant opened and closed her mouth twice. Then, tensely: "Your daughter still has her milk."

Blood stepped back from her. "You can't be serious, woman."

"I will do anything I have to, *hungan*. I will call on any *loa*. This boy must live."

Neil Blood took a second step back. His acquaintance with voodoo was adequate for dealing with those of his people who believed in it. In the same way that he could bluster through the hated free-masonry rites if he (a devout Catholic!) had to, he could impress a voodoo adept as being at least his peer, if not his superior.

It had worked before with this little woman when the life of his own daughter and grandson were at stake. But Blood was well aware that, once they parted, Madame Fleurigant was no longer within his reach, in any sense of the word. What she might do, what spells she might work, what plots she might hatch, would not be foreseen or guarded against.

"There is little I can do," Neil Blood said. "But if you need money, I can help. As for the rest . . ."

"The brother of this boy sleeps in this house," she told him in a voice thin almost to cracking. "Here stands the *mambo* who saved the life of the brother. If not for me, the brother would be dead. He must share the breast of his mother with this *pauvre enfant*. It is not too much to ask, *hungan*."

"No," Kate said from the darkened vestibule. "It is not too much to ask."

"Jesus, Mary, and Joseph!" her father cried out. "Katie, you don't know what you're saying."

"He's Edmund's son, isn't he?"

"That's as may be." Her father reached into his pocket. "Madame, here is money, much money. Take it."

Kate stepped out of the shadows and took the baby from his grandmother. She peered down at the boy's face. "He's Edmund's." She stared into Madame Fleurigant's eyes. "Your daughter was very beautiful, madame."

Madame Fleurigant's great eyes filled with tears. Moaning, she stumbled forward and clutched at Kate, who put her free arm around her. "You saved me," Kate told the little woman, "but you couldn't save her."

"Kate," her father said, voice thick, "you mean, all along . . . you . . . ?"

Kate clung to the tiny mulatto woman. "I have always known about Ynes," she said.

Far away, the music moved into a slow, draggy blues. The cornet's pure tone came across what seemed to be miles of distance. Closer at hand, carriages were rolling up to the front door on Livaudais and people were shouting happy good-byes.

"Get back to your guests," Neil Blood demanded. "I'll handle this."

Kate turned to him, her arm draped around the tiny woman and baby. "Da," she said, "they belong here. They will stay here with me."

"Never."

"Yes, Da."

"Lass, I'm begging you."

She turned suddenly and led Madame Fleurigant and the baby back inside the house by the servants' door. Sitting in the darkness of the butler's pantry, the sounds of departing guests in her ears, Kate loosened the front of her gown. Softly she guided the newborn baby's lips to her nipple. For a moment the infant failed to react. She tickled his mouth. He gave a great sigh and began to suck.

Neil Blood stared down at the scene. "That I should live to see such a sight," he muttered. "That I should raise a lass so weak she—"

"Weak?"

Kate's voice rang through the pantry. "You call it weak?" Her green eyes seemed to burn as she stared at him. "It's a strength you'll never be asked for."

He started to reply, but something stopped him, the knowledge of what had gone on upstairs tonight as the entire corpus of Great Southern had been, in effect, transferred to this eldest daughter of his, on whom he was now pledged to shower millions. And there she sat, nursing a quadroon's bastard, the fruit of her own husband's shame. No, she was right. "Weak" wasn't the word for it.

"Katie," he said, hearing his voice shake. "Of 'em all, from Father Jim to little Ned, I have to say it. Lass, you've got the balls of a brass monkey. You're a chip off the old block."

By two in the morning the last of the barbecue coals had turned to pale gray ash. In the kitchen, Julia and Belle finished the dishes and pots. Henry moved about the garden and lower floor gathering glasses in a basket. Citronella pots smoked in the flickering light of dying lanterns.

A mute jammed in the bell of his cornet, one black musician played a small, slow melody that had no name. He stopped, finished his beer, wiped his lips, and played another chorus of it, almost to himself. Then he blew the horn clean and pulled a sack over it.

In the study upstairs, Kate stood at the desk and reread the papers Mike Leathers had prepared. They had been signed by Edmund, notarized by Judge Mornay, and witnessed by Leathers and Badger. Folding them, Kate locked the papers in a desk drawer and moved on tiptoe to the door of the nursery.

The newborn boy lay in small Edmund's old crib, while his half-brother slept in the new bed he had begun using. Madame Fleurigant sat in a rocker, fast asleep, her great eyes hooded, her aquiline beak of a nose tucked down.

Softly Kate closed the nursery door and moved silently across the breezeway to the master bedroom. A candle burned in the far corner.

Edmund had chilled a bottle of champagne. It lay in its ice bucket, uncorked. A bit of it was left at the bottom of one of the tall fluted glasses his mother had given them. He had planned to share a final good-night drink with her, but having sampled the champagne as he waited, had fallen asleep in his dressing gown. He lay on the bed, arms outstretched, blissfully asleep.

Kate pulled a sheet over him and undressed. No point waking him, she thought. All the shocks waiting to make themselves known to him could wait until tomorrow.

Tomorrow he could meet his other son. Tomorrow he would begin the long-delayed repair of his empire. Tonight, he slept.

Kate stood there watching his serene, untroubled face. A very lucky man, Edmund.

She took the other glass and half-filled it with wine. Raising it to her husband, she drank a silent toast.

Then she blew out the candle and slipped into bed.